Seat of Power

Seat of Power

A Novel

Gerald P. FitzGerald

VANTAGE PRESS
New York

FIRST EDITION

Published by Vantage Press, Inc.
419 Park Ave. South, New York, NY 10016

Manufactured in the United States of America
ISBN: 978-0-533-16039-6

Library of Congress Catalog Card No.: 2008903319

0 9 8 7 6 5 4 3 2 1

This novel is dedicated to my father . . .

Daniel L. FitzGerald . . .

Born April 1900 in Albany, New York of Irish immigrant parents . . .

Entered the seminary from the Albany Diocese in 1917 . . .

Was selected to continue his studies for the priesthood at the North American College in Rome in 1920 . . .

Resigned one year before ordination and returned to Albany . . .

Five years later married Marie M. McShane and moved to New York City to raise a family . . .

Died in Flushing, New York, May 1, 1972.

His was a life of humility and patience, kindness and compassion.

Contents

Acknowledgments

I would like to acknowledge those who contributed to the completion of *Seat of Power*.

To my family and friends who gave encouragement and advice after reading the first draft . . .

To those who offered their ideas and suggestions for change . . .

To my daughter, Eileen FitzGerald Veith, for her advice on the challenges of publishing . . .

Especially to Bob Furey of Flushing, New York, for his copyediting and work as research guide on multiple drafts . . .

To Tom Daley of Bronxville, New York, for the many dinners we shared, discussing story background and development . . .

For the many friends in the Aviation industry who supported the marketing efforts at airports . . .

Thank you all. There was great fun in the doing!

Seat of Power

One
Spring, 1980 Washington, D.C.

A soft rain caressed the windows of Dan Gerard's office blurring his night view of the Capitol dome. The weather did little to dampen the fever that had been raging the past few months with polls showing the vulnerability of a sitting President. The campaign rhetoric leading to the summer conventions was creating gridlock in congressional committees.

The *Washington Tribune* prided itself on its stable of scoop-hungry journalists. Making news was as important as reporting news and they had to be prepared to do just that. Dan Gerard, newly hired investigative reporter from a major New York paper, was enjoying his exposure to the bottlenecks of government and the speculations that echoed through the corridors of federal offices.

The note from Jack Roman, the paper's managing editor, had been staring up from his desk all day. Dan was to provide the main briefing for the weekly editorial staff session the next morning. Although he had participated in only a few of these meetings, it was clear the intent was a hard-nosed examination of subject matter for follow up. With assignments likely to come from the discussion, questions were thorough and probing.

Since his arrival, he was clearly being treated as "new kid" on the block. This request appeared to be the first opportunity where there might be real benefit from his presence.

Dan found confidence in the credentials he brought to the new assignment. It was not his first time in a new work environment. Promotions from three papers following prizewinning series on criminal and bureaucratic conspiracies gave him credibility. He could rely on confidential source relationships and an innate ability to sense the timing challenges important to investigations. However, hired by the publisher, over the objections of the managing editor, the ring of "what have you done for me lately" became grating.

1

The thought of leading a strategy discussion pleased him. The subject matter pushed him into a familiar corner bringing back feelings hard to describe.

Being asked to lead the weekly session with a description of the politics of a Vatican Conclave would not have been his choice of an introductory assignment. There was agreement that the Pope's illness had taken a turn for the worse. If the medical teams couldn't produce a miracle of their own, a successor would be needed. If major news developed, there needed to be an understanding of the Conclave process. Fate might well be arranging to have Pope and President gone by year's end.

With Dan's background as a seminarian studying in Rome and contributing to the work of an earlier Conclave, he was properly asked to lead the discussion, but there it was again, the same old bullet.

As often as Dan Gerard tried to bury that part of his life and forget the path he had been pushed onto, it seemed to come back at the most inopportune time. Why not a presentation on how he exposed illegal French payments to New York State and federal officials forcing the supersonic Concorde into JFK International Airport over the objections of the noise activists? Why not a presentation on how he dared to challenge organized crime's control of the paving contracts for the City of New York? Why must this presentation be about a time in his life when he made all the wrong choices and for all the wrong reasons?

The rumblings of those around him announced the close of another day. The dilemma of the requested presentation had been growing throughout the afternoon. The street light shadows that danced on his office wall offered some company but Gerard was alone with his thoughts.

Washington was the plateau he had been climbing toward during all those years on the city beat. He built his reputation with risk taking and carefully fashioned alliances resulting in the recognition he enjoyed so much. Just when his career goals were within reach, family tragedy delivered a blow to his concentration.

His legs were heavy as he lifted them from the file boxes that crowded his space. He wandered over to the coffee pot for one more swallow to soothe his pained throat. Looking at his desk, the clutter around the ashtray reminded him how badly he was failing in his promise to cut back on the habit. With the love of his life taken by cancer, the two kids needed him more than ever. He promised he would kick the habit.

A gust of wind-blown rain on the window drew his attention. His reflection in the glass reminded him he was young no more. Still, it was twenty years since high school graduation in Albany and even now he wore the same size clothes to cover his five foot ten inch frame. Only a few gray strands showed in the crop of brown hair hiding the turmoil that pounded inside his brain.

"Why must I be forced to look back when all I want to do is look forward," he asked himself.

Trees were bending under the weight of rainwater. He thought of the sudden storm in Lincoln Park in Albany, so many years ago. Two young wanderers, not yet burdened by the realities of life, delighting in their enjoyment of each other, were laughing at the futility of trying to stay dry in a spring rain.

Their together laughter opened the door to emotions both had sensed for months but could not express. Seeing each other that day in the park led to a first kiss. Raindrops had never been the same since. First love had been lost through thoughtlessness. It remained a painful memory.

Dan liked to think that a new person had emerged from his Albany experiences. The old self had fallen into a dark well. He really had not fallen. He had been pushed. It had come from a troubled family with proud plans for his future and friends whose own choices brought havoc to his life.

Presenting the basics of a Conclave the next day would be easy. It was the answers to the probing questions that he felt could present problems. How far should he go into raw Church politics? What obligations of confidentiality remain, he asked himself. Should he apply the same zeal he brought to his investigations of organized crime in New York to a discussion of institutional Church weaknesses or is religion entitled to a pass?

Dan was being forced to choose. He remembered the forced choices that had gouged his life. It made him wince.

Family and peer pressure arrived early for Dan. Thoughts on his future were secondary to conflict between Father and Mother. He had to choose between his mother's wish for him to

3

spend his life as a priest and his father's political plans that started with West Point, meanwhile ignoring the pleas of his own young love. He had to choose between concealing a friend's crime and personal ruin.

Pacing his Washington office, Dan again moved to the window and allowed the thoughts of his earliest friends to reenter consciousness.

Albany, New York, in the early sixties was a good place to be a teenager. Neighborhood, school ties and the nearby Adirondacks offered support and excitement that shaped relationships. There was Tom Feely, his good friend and protector on the back streets of Albany. Their night encounter in Lincoln Park brought together two very different personalities that came to rely on each other in difficult times. There was his first love, Margaret Mary Connelly, Meggie as her friends all called her. From the moment she entered the class in St. Michael's school, Meggie was different. He finally responded to her openness at a high school dance. They remained together until the choice had to be made. She was a soft and comforting soul mostly concerned about her family and helping those around her.

How did Tom Feely move from the backstreets of Albany to being General Feely and into the corridors of the White House? How did that wild ass, hot-tempered kid, make his way to the top? His mild-mannered smile and blond hair concealed the quick moves of a cobra ever conscious of the advantages of throwing the first punch. Their friendship had served them both well in those days but violence changed the relationship.

How did Dan's fellow Vatican seminarian, Lou Baracini, move so steadily from family ties in Chicago, to become Cardinal Baracini, in such short order? From his days at the North American College in Rome, Dan recalled time together with Lou in the Italian countryside. He learned his family was not the only one willing to press a career on an offspring. In Lou's case, however, he was burdened by the thought that "the family has decided." He made it sound as a way that when decided, "the family" never left your life.

The Baracini name was used to explain Lou's frequent invitations from the finest families in Rome and the relative freedom

4

he enjoyed compared with the other seminarians. It became obvious to Dan quite early that prayer was not Lou's first priority but that political alliances were. Lou's attention to these details proved their importance when he was assigned to key support roles during the early days of the Vatican Council and brought Dan along. Both, however, had been ill prepared to face the undisguised power mongering revealed to them in the halls of the Vatican.

Dan Gerard's experiences with friends had positive, and brutally negative moments. They gave direction to his life. He looked on Tom Feely and Lou Baracini as instruments of his own success but both had pushed him into darkness first.

"With a Presidential and a Papal election on my agenda, how can these people be coming together at the same time," Dan mused.

His Irish mother's words came to mind. "There are no coincidences in life," she would say. "There is merely an awareness of the Holy Spirit presenting you with your destiny."

The blinking red lights of vehicles crawling through the streets were giving him a signal to search his past for the benefit of the present. *Was it time to get on with work and organize his presentation or slip into remembrances of past events?* he asked himself.

Long-buried emotions overcame the desire to focus on work. He was thrust back to June 1965 and the sounds of the passengers waiting in the Alitalia lounge at JFK International Airport.

The smell of the European cigarettes was in the air. He could see flight departure monitors flashing gate assignments. His stomach was tightening as he thought about his return to Rome and what was before him.

Exploratory surgery in Albany's St. Peter's Hospital that summer had found the source of his months of misery. A partially ruptured appendix had been removed but recovery in the care of Meggie, produced a long delayed intimacy. Since Lou Baracini had provided tickets home to protect him from Italian doctors, Dan felt it was necessary to tell him personally why he was resigning from the seminary.

5

He remembered the walk to the coffee bar in the airline lounge and the wall-mounted TV. The news was startling. Pope John XXIII had died. The call was going out to Cardinals around the world to come to Rome to bury the Pope and participate in the Conclave. Dan's surrender to long denied feelings had blocked out all other concerns and left him vulnerable to the blow that came with the news. It was to be a signal moment in history and he could participate. More than that, he badly wanted to be part of history.

Two
The Politics of the Conclave

He recalled how he could not sleep on the long flight over the Atlantic. He began his journey back to Rome with a strong personal conviction. His four years of halfhearted commitment had to come to an end. With the news of the Pope's death he could feel himself wavering as he so often did when faced with conflicting emotions. How could he satisfy both desires? The months in Rome had been positive but the recent release from his illness convinced him it was time to leave. Why then was he thinking about helping Lou, about the many political nights at the villa and the dignitaries he had supported during the working sessions of the Vatican Council?

The dome of St. Peter's coming into view over the wing of the aircraft made him even more anxious to hear Lou's assessment of the coming struggle for power.

With excitement gripping Rome, his entrance into the lobby of the North American College was barely noticed. Dan was not sure how he would react the first time he saw Lou and if his absence had created long-term damage with his friend. They caught sight of each other across the open courtyard and exchanged warm smiles as they met face to face without saying a word.

Finally, Lou said how glad he was to see him and remarked how well he looked. The next sentence, however, said more. "Let's hope the twisted appendix was the source of all your problems. We have a great deal of work to do in the next few weeks."

Months of doing favors and positioning himself had paid dividends for Lou. As teams were being selected, it came as no surprise that his name was on everyone's list and his support needed.

Lou had offered a detailed plan for early interaction with Bishops he supported during the various Vatican Council meetings. The plan had been accepted by Monsignor Delgado, an inside and very conservative player in the Curia. He wanted Lou to begin arranging delegate contact meetings with specific agendas. Hotel bookings should be arranged to keep certain people together and others apart. Other discrete lobbying activities had begun to make use of the time before the Cardinals entered the Sistine Chapel to cast their votes.

A meeting was taking place that night at the Belardino Villa with key players of Opus Dei. Lou was hoping Dan would be up to joining him. Lou was not sure he could get him into the meeting but had to make sure he would come before asking for the favor.

Thanking Lou for keeping him a part of the in crowd, he said how anxious he was to attend. He agreed to meet him at the Villa limo pickup point in two hours. With international history unfolding all around, Dan was indeed pleased to be a part of the event and sensed Albany slipping into the background.

Back in his dorm room, Dan changed into seminarian garb and stopped at the residence post office to examine the mail that accumulated in his absence. After sorting through the usual junk, he was surprised to find several telegrams from committee members he had assisted during Vatican Council briefings. They urged his assistance with lobbying arrangements, contacting members of arriving delegations and retrieving papers from Council meetings. He brought the telegrams with him to share with Lou and headed for the pickup point.

The Meeting at the Villa

Approaching each other on that street corner in Rome, and exchanging greetings, Dan sensed he was still in good standing with Lou. After an embrace and a handshake, Lou gave Dan one of the heavy briefcases he was carrying as he opened the door to the waiting limo.

After they climbed into the back seat, the driver began a conversation with Lou in Italian. Dan realized his ear for the language had fallen off after his time in Albany. Lou was able

8

to convince the driver to go on, after explaining the extra passenger was a guest. Gaining entrance to the Villa was not as easy.

Lou asked Dan to wait on the side portico of the Villa while he received permission for him to enter. Meanwhile other limos were arriving and discharging passengers. Many of the faces were familiar to Dan from Vatican Council days. The large portico windows allowed Dan a clear view of the main greeting area of the Villa.

As the doors of the arriving limos opened at the bottom of the Villa steps, Don Bellardino, the head of the local family, greeted each guest personally. All gave a bow and kissed his hand. Dan had the thought that the Church practice of kissing a Bishop's ring must have originated in Italy.

He realized they were likely to be the only seminarians at the Villa as had been the case in the past. It was through the good fortune of room assignment on the boat from New York that Lou and Dan had become such good friends. It only took a few weeks for Dan to realize that through this friendship, he was benefiting from Lou's influence. They were being granted privileges unlike other students.

The College Rector was more than anxious to receive the thanks from the archbishop of Chicago for taking care of the Baracini family representative studying in Rome. The same eagerness to please was obvious in the committee assignments offered to Lou and Dan during the Vatican council. Resumes in the Vatican always included access to important relationships.

Walking to the rear of the portico, Dan observed Lou talking to a group of the guests in a corner of the hallway. Lou was visibly upset and turned to the Don himself, who after listening to Lou's plea, gave a nod of the head. Lou turned to go back outside. He found Dan and said the way had been cleared and he was to be a part of the meeting.

It was a night burned into memory. A plan to manipulate church factions brought lofty thoughts crashing down and did much to bolster Dan's decision to leave the path to the priesthood. There was a sharp contrast between the mourning for the dead Pope and the agenda of the meeting. The cry of the poor was a distant sound from the windows of the Villa that evening. The bitterness of his thoughts startled Dan.

9

He remembered how the questions that had raced through his mind ignited his feelings about investigative reporting. It was on that night, that Dan first experienced a desire to shed light on the plans of the few, who plot to take power from the many. A path opened with a motivation absent in past decision making.

In years to come, the plans proposed that night came to mind as Dan observed the workings of political campaigns. It was a well-organized, focused effort for a preferred candidate, with careful measures designed to disrupt the campaigns of opponents. In this case, the Holy Spirit was going to need some assistance with the inspiration to be provided during the Conclave in the Sistine Chapel.

After the customary glass of wine, everyone assembled in the basement of the Villa. It was Dan's first visit downstairs and it stood in stark contrast to the medieval décor of the first floor. There was a large meeting room with smaller rooms off the well carpeted main corridor. At the end of the hallway, there was a high tech room of some kind that revealed itself, as restricted members of the staff opened and closed the door.

Many members of the meeting had small wire ear plugs dangling from their left ear with grim expressions on their faces giving them a sinister look The leaders of the meeting were obvious in clerical black, with various levels of supporters gathered at a head table, flanked by the latest presentation equipment. The packed room grew silent as Lou's associate Monsignor Delgado, the Opus Dei course instructor from the College, approached the podium.

Delgado, as champion of Opus Dei, was a topic of heated conversation among seminarians. He had risen quickly from the University in Barcelona to be the Bishop's secretary, a short assignment in Mexico, and then on to Rome as assistant to the leaders of the Opus Dei movement. He appeared at most sessions with the Cardinal of Madrid and incredibly appeared in the background of many pictures published of the Pope. He seemed to be involved with every important committee meeting and Council compromises.

"Most of you have met before, so there is no need for introductions," he began. "When we first brought this group together, we had no idea that the opportunity we were planning for would be thrust upon us so quickly. The call to heaven came much earlier for good Pope John XXIII than we anticipated. It was surely the work of the Holy Spirit in preventing more damage to our Church than has already occurred.

"No one realized that the opening of the windows of our Church, brought about by the work of the Vatican Council, would invite so many errors," he continued. "Those of us in this room understand the damage that has been done by the changes the Council brought to our thousand-year-old teachings. There is urgent need to begin the repair and that is what our agenda tonight will cover.

"The plan is simple. If we can block the early selection of another liberal Pope, we have a chance of electing whom we want if the balloting goes to more than five rounds.

"During the debates of the Council," Monsignor Delgado emphasized, "it became obvious where the voices of change were coming from. It was also obvious, where the voices of the apostles were being heard as they fought for our long-standing traditions. These distinctions are now the basis of our call to action.

"We have prepared a list of the 'devil's change agents' to isolate them as much as possible in the days leading up to the Conclave. Our friends, on the other hand, will be brought together, as often as possible, to support the needed strategy.

"The first part of this plan has been put in place through the Vatican travel office, the coordinator of all local arrangements here in Rome." Monsignor Delgado then clicked the first slide onto the large screen dominating the front of the room. "Certain Cardinals, and their staff, will be spread over Rome in the most remote locations possible, assuring that they will face the greatest difficulty in attending meetings and socializing with fellow Cardinals.

"Seating arrangements at dinners and committee meeting have been similarly prepared to maximize the separation of key opponents."

The slides kept clicking.

"Daily schedules for some of the delegates will have more than the normal Italian errors to insure they miss key gatherings. The schedules shown here are the official times for all

11

meetings and you should take care to keep these documents confidential.

"We have already assigned homilists to all official ceremonies and key meetings of the delegations. Here is the list of these speakers." A new slide came on the huge screen. "You should support them with compliments after they speak. All other requests to address the Cardinals before the start of the Conclave must be approved by the Curia in advance. We have restricted the lists of those wishing to speak.

"Temporary committee chairs have been assigned, as shown on the next slide. We have delivered into their hands copies of Council papers that represent our position of returning the Church to where it belongs. A list of those papers can be found among the papers in your briefing books and are shown on this next slide as well.

"Nuncios from those countries with Cardinals pushing for the greatest change have delivered to us a collection of press releases from their newspapers criticizing local Church leadership for local ills and calling for resignations. You have copies of those press releases in your packets, which correspond to the countries shown on the next slide.

"Rejected Council papers from these same countries have been made available to our committee representatives to show the Church's rejection of their proposals for change. Copies of these Council papers are quite extensive and will be found on the rear table of this room. Please take a copy before you leave tonight and make sure they are seen by those who seem undecided.

"To make it clear exactly who these Cardinals are, we have prepared this list, shown on this next slide, along with the liberal positions these men have taken in recent months. These positions should be criticized as often as possible with the rejected Council papers as the basis."

Moving to a new slide with a tone of satisfaction in his voice, Monsignor Delgado called for careful attention.

"Our primary and secondary candidates have both given us assurances that one of the first things they will do, if elected, will be to double the number of participants on the Papal Birth Control Commission with our suggested Bishops to insure there will be no change in long-standing doctrinal position. They have also agreed to leave in place the majority of Curia positions that automatically vacate with the death of a Pope. If these changes can be stabilized and openings filled with our believers, issues like liberation theology, celibacy, a married clergy and the role of women can be marginalized."

Monsignor Delgado began a slide presentation with an organization chart of the Curia with all its components shown on the screen.

"The Roman Curia," he began, "usually means: the Secretariat of State, Nine Congregations, Three Tribunals, Eleven Councils and a complex of offices that administer Church affairs," he explained, as he pointed to the organizational chart on the huge screen

"Although all these areas theoretically report to the Pope on the same basis, some are more equal than others and most importantly, effective power is concentrated in a few offices. We need to give attention to influencing the power centers of the Curia."

The next slide explained the office of the Papal Secretary of State and the voting Cardinals from that office.

Monsignor Delgado reinforced the importance of controlling existing international relationships. "The Secretary of State position," he explained, "is more important because it oversees the work of Papal Nuncios in each country. All communication with the Vatican in each country must flow through the Nuncio. They become the best source of understanding the sense of the leadership in that country. As I mentioned to you earlier, we have been in contact with most Nuncios and will receive their cooperation, in exchange for their remaining in place after the election. Some of the Cardinals in this office are more liberal than they should be. Their names are shown on this next slide."

A following slide explained several Congregations of the Curia but focused on one. Monsignor Delgado was quite careful in his discussion of this office.

"There is one super Congregation that comes before the other eight," he emphasized. "This is the Congregation for the Doctrine of Faith. It has been called 'the supreme' congregation because it plays the gatekeeper role on doctrinal questions. The staff of this Congregation is listed on the next slide and should be noted by all for appropriate contacts whenever possible.

"The two Cardinals leading these offices, the Secretary of State and the Congregation for the Doctrine of Faith, are the two most important men in the power structure of the Church, after the Pope. We have one of these positions clearly in our camp," smiled the Monsignor. "The other needs to be isolated."

The next slide explained the Institute for Works of Religion. Its name was unfamiliar to Dan at the time. He later learned its more common name, the Vatican Bank.

"The next slide," Monsignor Delgado emphasized, "is a list of the principal depositors of the Vatican bank." Dan was surprised to see that every Catholic order and institution was included on the list along with important international conglomerates. Its twenty billion dollars in deposits were described in terms of the largest depositors and their concerns for future stability.

Monsignor Delgado called the attention of the room to the list of major depositors. "We should claim the support of these groups for our position. They have all expressed concern if the wrong person takes control of the finances of the Vatican which could affect their ability to continue work.

"These contacts have been the responsibility of Vincent Biscardi," Monsignor Delgado noted, as he turned to the only member of the head table not in clerical garb and surrendered the podium to him.

Biscardi described a series of meetings with a group of leading depositors. He detailed his efforts to assure them about the continuation of existing bank policy that would take place, if the right person emerged on the balcony overlooking St. Peter's square

"I have included a list of these depositors in your briefing packages," said Biscardi. "They will be making select calls to express concern over their financial future. A list of these contacts is contained in your briefing packets and you should feel free to make reference to them in your discussions with undecided delegates."

Monsignor Delgado returned to the podium and continued the briefing.

"The next series of slides," he said, "details our rating system and establishes target audiences for your contacts in the nest few days. I will explain the primary and secondary identifiers."

Three slides came up on the screen at the same time.

"The first slide describes those who are firm supporters of Opus Dei," Delgado pointed out, "and the second describes those Cardinals who are undecided. The third slide are those Cardinals who are clearly among the 'devils for change'."

Dan sat fascinated. Each of the undecided Cardinals was assigned personally to a group of the Villa's participants with scheduled meetings already established to influence their vote. It became clear from the chart that the Opus Dei Cardinals in slide one could easily block a vote in the stages but they lacked an overall majority to elect a new Pope. Monsignor Delgado addressed this point.

"I would like to emphasize," he continued, "that this early opportunity to return the church to its roots did not allow us to gain the kind of clear advantage that could show itself in the future. It is a beginning and will require years of dedication before we can be certain the chair of St. Peter is occupied by the appropriate person."

It was interesting to Dan that throughout the meeting, "the candidate" was not mentioned by name nor was the "secondary candidate" mentioned either. There were assumptions being made about the names and he was not at all clear about it.

The meeting also lacked the Bishops and direct staff of the Cardinals. If discovered, no leading candidate could be connected directly with the group.

The final part of the meeting summarized contact responsibilities, distributed schedules of key meetings and the plans to block primary opponents from attending these sessions.

When the meeting ended, Lou introduced Dan to their principal contact, Monsignor Flores from the Congregation of Divine Worship and a close confident of Monsignor Delgado.

Lou and Dan were given a variety of assignments. Lou was asked to reconnect with the delegation from Poland as he did during the Council with his fluency in the language acquired from his mother in Chicago. He was to determine where the

15

Cardinal and his young Bishop from Warsaw appear to be in the vote. They were considered as undecided on the first ballots but there was doubt about how far into the voting they could be relied upon.

Dan was asked to contact the American Bishops who were working at the Vatican as part of the Curia. They lived together in Villa Stritch, considered an incubator for serious cases of "scarlet fever," those planning on becoming Cardinals and eager to show their loyalty to the Curia. They knew where challenges to the power structure of the Curia would come from, often heard about strategies planned by others and understood all too well the thinking of the American Cardinals.

Dan detected a clear level of disdain in the comments of Monsignor Flores about the American church as he finished explaining his assignments.

Dan remembered the Flores speech given to him that night as much for the European tone as for the content.

Looking Dan straight in the eye, Flores began his diatribe. "Americans focus too much on youth, have too great a respect for power, measure success in terms of wealth and prefer a policy of political isolationism. They lean more toward Calvin and his emphasis on individual importance than on the good of society as a whole," Flores said. "They feel comfortable thinking their opinion is as good as any other, whether they have taken the time to be well informed or not. Economic and political liberalism seems to be the essence of American society, which stands in contrast to the rest of the world. You are not considered a super power in the theology world," shouted Flores, "as you are in the military one and you need to get used to that. You need to keep these issues in mind as you carry out your tasks," he concluded scowling.

Dan was caught off guard. "Don't tell me that Americans don't care about the world community," Dan replied. "If it wasn't for the American blood spilled throughout Europe to settle the battles created by independent states, you would all be speaking German today."

Lou quickly deflected the response from Flores and injected the importance of the telegrams Dan had received instead. He managed a delicate situation as he so often did. The exchange ended there.

The telegrams from Vatican Council delegates to Dan provided new information on the plans of those opposed to Opus Dei. Monsignor Flores left their table and brought back Monsignor Delgado. An intense analysis of the telegrams took place with some given to others for follow up. Dan was given a new assignment as a result of the discussion of his telegrams. In addition to tracking the American position, his relationship with the South American Cardinals would allow him to interact with those pushing Liberation Theology positions. Whatever information Dan could elicit would be important.

Lou was involved in discussions with Don Bellardino's staff and Dan was asked to wait outside. Once again, he sat on the side portico sipping wine and watching the last of the visitors say good night to Don Bellardino, with the same humility they demonstrated on their arrival.

The next weeks were filled with activity, intrigue and late night meetings at the Villa. Dan began distancing himself from Lou, scheduling meetings that kept him unavailable at just the time Lou wanted him. He also made an effort not to pass on to the Opus Dei forces any information he considered valuable. He understood their tactics to be the opposite of their public statements. This was something he would come to despise in all future political interactions.

The Victory Celebration

The election of a new Pope seemed to please the crowd at the Villa. There were several parties planned to thank the participants. Dan and Lou were invited to a function in downtown Rome for a select group of supporters. Dan noticed the party was different from those at the Villa. It was smaller than the others and the average age of the attendees was obviously below the normal crowd.

They were to dress casually and bring their singing voices with them. The party had a variety of young women in attendance leading the singing and dancing to the music. Two of the ladies found Lou and Dan attractive and would not leave them alone. They were petite, with dark hair and bright Italian eyes looking out from smooth dark cheeks. They were draped in soft colorful silk that did not conceal the energy within. After weeks of work, the drinks and the music, female attention was pleasing to the crowd.

After the party ended, the ladies asked for a ride home and convinced Dan to help them. Despite some resistance from Lou, Dan shepherded the group to their limo and they were soon in the streets of Rome.

Arriving at the ladies' residence, over a small restaurant, the young men were persuaded to join them for a good-night drink. Dan saw no harm in it and convinced Lou to dismiss the limo, have one last drink and grab a cab back to the College.

They sat at a small table in an alcove off the main entrance to the restaurant. The waiter seemed anxious to take their order and returned quickly. A warm breeze was moving the air across their table and bringing with it the aromas from the nearby kitchens. The evening seemed a very pleasant relaxing time in stark contrast to the past weeks. Dan remembered thinking it would be a perfect opportunity to tell Lou that he was leaving Rome.

Before Dan had half finished with his drink, he began to feel queasy. He suggested to Lou that it was getting time to leave. Lou insisted he wanted to finish his drink and then leave. That was the last thing Dan remembered.

With sunlight coming in the open windows, Dan realized it was early morning, he was in a strange bed and his clothes were gone. Raising his pounding head, he came face to face with a young lady beside him who was naked as well. He was sick to his stomach. His movements stirred the lady. She pushed him back down saying, "Stay a while longer, we had such a great night."

Dan sat up and saw Lou across the room in a similar bed and in similar circumstances. His head fell to the pillow, panic rushed into every bone in his body.

"Lou," he shouted, "we have to get out of here. Lou, wake up. Lou, Lou," Dan continued.

Dan finally dragged himself across a swirling room, pushed the other young woman off Lou's chest and made him sit up. With that motion, Lou's bed companion fell to the floor motionless.

"Maria, Maria," came the call from the other bed. "Make us some breakfast." There was no response.

"Maria, Maria, you know I don't cook. Get up," the lady in Dan's bed kept repeating.

Dan leaned over and tried to wake the motionless Maria. He suddenly understood that Maria wasn't going to be making anything, for anybody. Her eyes were wide open as was her mouth. She was not breathing.

Lou, now able to speak, was trying to remember what happened. "I remember taking you upstairs, Dan, when you didn't feel well at the table but after that I can't remember anything."

"Well, for a couple of guys who knew what they wanted, you seemed okay to us," offered Millie from the edge of Dan's bed.

Now, Millie was trying to wake her friend but without success. She put her hand over her mouth and began to cry. "I told her so many times, to stop the drugs, but she wouldn't listen to me. The last time this happened, I took her to the hospital but she came out of it okay. I told her it was time to stop the drugs. She said she would but I could tell she didn't."

Millie fell onto her friend and began sobbing. Lou looked at Dan and said, "What do we do?"

After several attempts at standing up, Dan walked to the kitchen, made coffee and tried to console Lou, who by this time, was back on the bed and sobbing. Dan forced some coffee into Lou's mouth. "Get some of this into you so we can figure things out."

The early morning sun filtered through the old curtains, covering the room in shadows that hid the naked body on the floor.

"Millie, where did Maria buy her drugs?" asked Dan as he jerked her close to him.

"I don't know," she said, "all around town. There was one place I used to meet her and she was with the strangest people. It was Bellini Square Park."

"I think I know the place," said Dan. "Lou, you and I were approached by some druggies when we sat on one of the benches during one of our walks. You commented that it was a major drug hangout."

Lou, still having trouble understanding the situation, made no reply. Tears started down his cheeks.

Dan walked to the back of the apartment and looked out the bathroom window onto a small tree lined patio. It reminded him of Lincoln Park in Albany.

"I don't fucking believe this," he said to himself. "Another fucking body! Well, if I did it before, I can damn well do it again."

He went back into the front room and announced, "Get dressed, right away; we're leaving. That means you too, Millie. We are taking Maria with us."

"Do you have a beach blanket?" Dan barked. "Yes," she answered.

"Well, get it and get Maria's clothes while you are at it."

The cab circled the park three times before stopping at a corner of Bellini Park in a deserted section of the soccer field. Three of them got out of the cab, with Dan holding Maria against his chest, as he moved from the cab into the tall grass at the park's edge. With the large beach blanket under her, and her eyes closed, Maria looked to be in a comfortable sleep as she lay among the tall grass. Leaving some empty drug packets on the blanket next to her, the three slowly walked out of the park.

Several days later, Dan scanned an account in the paper about a young woman dying from a drug overdose in Bellini Park. Checking the hospital, the police found she had been treated for overdoses several times before but failed to heed the warnings of the doctors. The police had interviewed a close friend, Millie, and were satisfied with their conclusion.

Lou, however, was anything but satisfied. He had almost come completely apart, missed all classes since that night and told Dan he was planning on resigning from the College. Only with Dan's support was he able to make it through the following weeks.

Finally there was a break in their schedule. Dan suggested a night out for dinner. It was the first occasion they had any time alone to go over that night in detail. Lou wanted to go to the authorities and confess involvement. He could not deal with the guilt any longer. Dan pointed out the time element as the obstacle to this approach.

It took most of the night for Dan to convince Lou that there was no guilt. They had too much to drink and a drug addict overdosed herself the way she often did. What was there to gain by saying more? On the other hand, there was everything to lose and for what good? After a long evening, Lou allowed himself to be convinced. On the dark streets of Rome that night, Dan felt he did a service for his Church by saving one of her priests.

Three days after their dinner Dan found a note in his mailbox. It said, "I need to tell you what happened that night. I have to leave Rome. Before going I must tell you how sorry I am. Meet me at La Scala restaurant Friday night at 9. Don't come to my apartment." It was signed, Millie.

Dan was at the restaurant at nine and waited until midnight. Millie never arrived. He waited to hear from her but she never called or left more notes.

Lou came into Dan's room two days later and read him an account in the paper about a young woman falling in front of a train at the Rome rail station while on her way back to her family in Milan. The police had interviewed her landlady and determined that she had recently moved out of her apartment and was on the way back home. They gave the address of the apartment. The landlady was quoted as saying that "Millie had always been a good tenant."

"That must be her," Lou said, "it must be her. Now no one knows what happened." Lou appeared relieved with the accident that removed the only witness to their indiscretion.

Dan agreed that their secret was locked up in a place where it would be kept forever. If Lou was relieved with Millie's death, Dan was not comfortable with it at all. This was God's providence?

He tried to convince himself it was a matter of circumstances. He could not be convinced. He tried to figure out if it was a setup. Is it possible that somebody was planning on finding us there but with the girl dead they didn't know what to do?

21

Maybe, we were supposed to call the Villa for help. It would have put us in debt to them, thought Dan as he continued to consider the possibilities. Maybe it was a way to embarrass Lou to get at his father in Chicago. Maybe we were not supposed to dismiss the limo driver as we did? The questions continued. No answer made sense.

With all his reasons for returning to Albany, Dan couldn't bring himself to leave Lou just yet. He returned with Lou to several classes and agreed to accompany him to his next meeting at the Villa.

That night was unusual for its lack of an agenda. It seemed to be a more social gathering for a select few. Dan's instincts were on alert. He could sense negative vibes floating in the air. Lou engaged in his usual banter with Monsignor Delgado and the rest of his friends.

Dan sat at a remote table and watched the interactions. Two members of the Villa staff tried to engage him in conversation but Dan remained quiet. Several other attempts were made to bring him into a group, Dan rejected the offers. A final approach was made by one of the Don's own associates.

He began by asking, "What do you think of the new Pope's changes so far?"

Dan jumped on the opening. "I don't know," Dan said. "I believe that things are never as they appear and that it takes time to understand what has happened."

A quick reply came from his questioner. "We are planning a weekend in Palermo for those friends who were so helpful during the Conclave. We were hoping you could join us." Dan's answer was given carefully. "I would like to take advantage of your offer but I have travel plans that must come first, unfortunately. Perhaps after a few weeks we could talk again." The silence that followed said much about the conversation.

Dan noticed his table companion move to Don Bellardino in the far corner of the room and begin talking. They both turned their eyes toward Dan and said nothing further.

An animal sense of physical danger ran through his body. Discomfort forced him outside and into the cool night air.

The next day Lou expressed satisfaction with the Villa meeting and began acting like his old self again. He suggested they accept the invitation to the Palermo gathering. Dan seized the opportunity to break the news to Lou about his leaving the priesthood.

It came off better than Dan imagined. Lou was happy to see Dan return from Albany and his medical problems. Once he left the College, Lou assumed Dan was gone for good. When he returned, Lou thought bringing him into the activities around the Conclave would recommit him to the Church. It didn't happen. Lou was understanding and wished him luck in trying to find himself.

Their last day together was an emotional one. Their friendship developed in a way that could not have been anticipated. Lou was indebted to Dan. Ashamed to say it, Lou was glad the two girls were dead. He felt guilty thinking such a thing but that was indeed how he felt.

Dan was drawn to Lou from the moment they met on the boat. Lou was what Dan could never be. He deeply appreciated Lou's including him in so much of what he did. He would be forever in his debt for that openness.

Dan made no comment about that awful night and its aftermath. He was not finished with his review of the circumstances but he had to get home to Meggie and that required him to leave.

They simply said good-bye. Lou wished Dan success in finding a new life. Dan left Lou standing in the courtyard in Rome with the hope that they would meet again—someday.

Dan remembered feeling a sense of purpose for the first time in his life.

From the simple paths of Lincoln Park, Dan found himself in one of the historic events of the century by being inside at the Vatican. However, being that close did not become the means of solidifying his commitment to the Church, it exposed the human weaknesses of the institution and confirmed his instincts to leave. In the process, he remembered thinking he might yet find a career worth pursuing, a career that might even promise a greater good for society than the priesthood.

With the past keeping him from working in the present, Dan finally left his office and returned home to relieve the baby sitter.

Three
The Staff Meeting

Dan fell into his swivel chair the next morning at 9 AM well after the majority of the staff were into their day. One of the conditions of accepting the new job was an understanding that early morning hours belonged to his family. The nights after his wife's funeral had rarely been consumed by sleep but found the two children huddling with him in all corners of the house. After many months, the morning ritual had become the essential part of the day for sharing, planning and resolving school and personal conflicts for the three of them. Dan had no intention of making changes.

Jack Roman's voice could be heard well into senior staff offices announcing it was time to begin the staff meeting and that asses should be in motion. With thoughts of the previous day fresh in his mind and with notes in his hand, Dan took his place at the head of the long conference table. Following the usual congestion at the coffee urn, the staff settled into their chairs and gave eyes and minds to the boss.

"If we are to remain the leading news force in this town," Roman began, "we must stay in front of the pack on the election coverage. We have a global reach and it must be leveraged against those who lack our resources.

"With religion continuing as a major element in politics, we will be expected to provide the background for the questioning in the candidate debates and then add our own perspective. Today's agenda begins with a discussion on the impact of the admission from the Vatican that the Pope's illness is more serious than previously disclosed."

Turning to Dan on his left, Jack continued, "I have asked Mr. New York here to lead the discussion since one of the mistakes of his youth involved study at the Vatican while he pondered the chances of becoming Pope himself. I expect to conclude with recommendations from each of you on how we develop this meeting into problems for the next President. OK, Dan, the floor is yours."

Dan rose and walked to the display board at the front of the room. He pinned several sheets of paper on the wall revealing a series of points outlining his presentation.

"I expect I will be able to cover these points in about fifteen minutes and provide a basis for developing potential story lines," he began.

"Upon the death of a Pope, a centuries old replacement process is followed to name a successor. The election takes place in a meeting called a Conclave. The term Conclave comes from two Latin words meaning, *with a key,* and describes putting the electors in a locked room and refusing to let them out until a successor is chosen. The modern process has evolved into something more than that.

"The electors today are the handful of men appointed Cardinals by the Pope as regional directors of the Church around the world. Technically, the Conclave begins when the Cardinals enter the Sistine Chapel and doesn't end until they have chosen a new leader. However, that is like saying the Democratic nominee for President is chosen at a national convention. As in any large human institution with a chosen leader, politics is part of everyday life and shows its ugly head when opposing forces clash over power."

Dan turned over one of his sheets and revealed the word, *Camerlengo.* This is the title of the person named in advance to act as the administrator of the church during the time between Popes. It becomes a powerful position in organizing the events that lead up to the election in the Sistine Chapel.

"Two other men will hold great political influence during this same time. One is the number two man in the Vatican, The Secretary of State and the other one is the person serving as the Dean of the College of Cardinals. If the position of Camerlengo is vacant at the time of the death of the Pope, the duties are carried out by the Dean of the College of Cardinals. As fate, or perhaps good planning, will have it," Dan added, "the position of Camerlengo is vacant as we speak, so those duties will indeed be combined with those of the Dean of the College of Cardinals.

25

That means Cardinal Delgado of Madrid. He is a colorful and interesting character and I will have more to say about him in a moment.

"The number two position, the Vatican Secretary of State, was filled a few months ago by a long-time Vatican insider, Cardinal Baracini, the only American in the Curia and one who has enjoyed a meteoric rise to prominence.

"Each country has a Papal Nuncio with the responsibility of reporting to Rome on local events. This flow of information goes directly to the Vatican's State Department.

"By the way, the word Curia refers to the group of men who oversee the affairs of the church from their offices in Rome," added Dan. "It includes several groups of administrators who are comparable to what we would call 'main office Vice Presidents'.

"The Curia is not unlike corporate America. There is a Chief Operating Officer, the Cardinal in charge of the Office of Doctrine, a Chief Financial Officer, the one in charge of the Institute for Works of Religion, better known as the Vatican bank and as mentioned, a Secretary of State.

"Just like a President's cabinet, when the Pope dies all the top Cardinals resign their positions. The office awaits reappointment by the new leader. As in American bureacracies, the number two man in each department takes over the administration until a new leader is elected. However, there is a big difference in the Vatican.

"Since all these 'out of office Cardinals' vote in the Conclave, any indication from one candidate or another that he will leave men in their jobs could well win their votes.

"There could be anywhere from fifteen to twenty days from the death of the Pope until the Conclave begins. In 1978 there were nineteen days between the death of the Pope and the time the electors entered the Sistine Chapel. During this time the Cardinals meet in a daily session called the General Congregation to discuss church issues. In 1978 there were fourteen such meetings. It is here that political pressure is felt the most. It is likely that there will be fifteen to twenty meetings of the General Congregation this time. We should plan to focus on these sessions."

Dan unfurled another of his outline papers and checked off the title "Political Parties."

"There are a variety of parties within the Church, groups of voters organized around a particular set of issues," he began. "These parties are already at work and they will make their move to win votes well before the Conclave gets underway. These issues are in two traditional areas, concerns about internal church workings and concerns about external relationships. Each of these has a left wing and a right wing explaining their position. The one to follow is the development of the internal struggle, with its focus centered on power vested in Rome vs. local churches. It is fight for institutional control and always about the exact authority of the Curia.

"External issues call for action in questions of social and economic justice and the root causes of poverty, hunger, illiteracy and war. The internal and external forces tend to seek coalitions with other movements in society that share similar objectives.

"The liberation theology of South America is often a discussion point. This is a group that will aggressively bring their issues to the world's attention and harp on the failure of the United States to exercise a leadership role. They will promote the issues of poverty and democracy which will find their way into many of the Presidential debates.

"Here is a good early warning indicator," Dan added while glancing at Jack Roman. "I would suggest we should be evaluating the press releases of the Papal Nuncio offices in major countries to determine the patterns of support that emerge before the Conclave."

Dan unveiled the final page of his presentation. "Like all large human institutions," he said, "the church is burdened by the schemes of those who seek to gain personal goals. When we discuss politics we have to include a consideration of the manipulations by those who function behind the scenes. Whether it is a president, a governor, a mayor, a chairman, an executive director or any other face of authority, visible leaders have risen to these positions with the support of 'behind the scene operators' who maintain great influence over what they do. The extent of this influence is difficult to determine in advance but they will be forced to show their hand when the seat of power opens for the taking."

Dan opened the last page on his chart. "It's here," he said, as he marked the words. "Follow the people as well as the money. Watergate confirmed the value of the money path as an indicator of activity but by following the travel and meeting patterns I think we will learn even more.

"From my own experience, I can vouch for just how successful this approach can be. By following the lobbyists meetings and the French consulting payments to New York State legislators, I found why the injunction against the Concorde landing at JFK airport was lifted. By following the trail of contract awards and the travel of certain city commissioners, I found the role of organized crime in influencing the paving of New York City streets and highways.

"The activities of the Vatican are ordinarily conducted in such secrecy that it is very difficult to trace money trails but meeting trackings are somewhat easier. The possibility of a Conclave presents an opportunity to look inside a global enterprise and see how the players are positioning themselves for the change in power."

Dan moved to the second item on his money chart. "The most important function in the Vatican is the most secretive. It is the Vatican Bank. We understand today how the Italian seeds of organized crime were planted in our own country. Should we accept the premise that in their home country the Italian Mafia declared the Vatican off limits? I don't think so.

"Should we accept the premise that a recent Pope died of natural causes after only a few weeks in office and that the bank official who hung himself at the same time was truly a suicide? I don't think so," Dan added with a move away from the conference table and over to the coffee urn, slowly refilling his cup.

"I could go on and on with other observations," Dan continued, "but I will give you just one more connection to make a point about international positioning.

"In 1938, Eugenio Cardinal Pacelli, the soon to be Pope Pius XII, traveled to New York and visited one of the most connected politicians of the time, Joe Kennedy. Pacelli was behaving as any candidate running for office would. He felt he was a man who could attract a sufficient number of crossover votes to win election. He was seeking the support of a known player in Italian politics.

"In the writings of John, Bobby and Ted Kennedy they all recall the visit of Pacelli to their home in Bronxville, New York, to meet with their father. A short time later Kennedy becomes Ambassador to London and Pacelli becomes Pope."

"Oh come on" came a voice from the back of the room. "Joe Kennedy could fix a Pope's election as well as his son's. Give us a break!"

"My thoughts exactly," exclaimed Roman! "Where are you going with all this? The coming Conclave has already been fixed?"

"No, not at all," replied Dan, pleased with the heightened attention.

"Politics is politics wherever it is played. The church is no exception. Pacelli knew he had to deal with Mafia influence inside Italy, whatever that might have been in those days. He had to create a feeling of comfort about his handling of local politics if elected. He was the Secretary of State for the Vatican at the time and had influence in the American State Department.

"Did his support of Kennedy play any part in Joe's appointment as ambassador? Did Joe Kennedy's support swing the vote to Pacelli? We'll never know but it illuminates my point about following meetings as well as money."

Moving back to the head of the table next to Jack Roman, Dan tried to set the stage for staff work in the coming weeks. "The necessity for wielding political influence at the time of a papal election will open up channels of Church communication not normally utilized. We should be prepared for those openings, track them and make the most of what we learn.

"I suggest an observer record the names of the Cardinals dining together in certain restaurants in Rome that are known to be the meeting places of various political factions. One such spot is L'Eau Vive, a French restaurant located behind the Pantheon in the historic center of Rome. Another is the Abruzzi, near the Gregorian University. One closer to the Vatican and a favorite of the conservatives is Roberto's on the Borgo Pio. The pattern of important people moving through these centers of political opinion will give signals about what is developing behind the closed doors and allow us to pose embarrassing questions to those in attendance.

"We should begin tracking the travel patterns of the known leaders of the conservative movement, Opus Dei, since they represent the forces trying to maintain centralized control. Conservatives can't stop everything but they will try to influence what they can."

"Hold on one more time, Dan," came the admonition from Roman as he sat up in his chair and pulled himself closer to the table. "I've heard of Opus Dei before but don't know much about them. Before you send us off on a wild goose chase, we deserve to know why you have selected them for special attention."

"Sorry, Jack," came the reply, "let me give you the short version of Opus Dei, which translated means Work of God.

"The age old political clash between conservative and liberal wings of the Catholic Church came to a head during the Second Vatican Council in the early 1960s. After months of debating and maneuvering, the liberal forces were the clear winners in bringing the institution into the modern world.

"The defeated conservatives regrouped around Opus Dei, a traditional priestly society founded in Spain in the 1930s and very much influenced by the Franco regime's doctrines of absolute authority and surrender of free choice. Suddenly, the society's position that Opus Dei was right and the world wrong, was no longer extremist but necessary in the fight against the changes of the Council.

"Using its bases in Spain and Mexico, the order has gained membership worldwide while gaining political and social influence inside the power circles of Rome. The upcoming Conclave will be an opportunity for Opus Dei to marshal their forces and push for their candidate to win the election.

"The Opus Dei secret rites of initiation, daily rituals and the surrender of free choice have encouraged their description as a dangerous religious cult. These practices and their behind the scenes financial transactions, led to their being called the new Knights Templar of the Catholic Church."

30

"When do we hear about King Arthur and Merlin the magician, Dan?" came a question from the earlier heckler.

"This is a little different," chimed Roman. "The Knights Templar, for those of you deprived of a liberal education, are no fairy tale. They became a financial and political force in the Middle Ages. Those of us who have benefitted from belonging to the fraternal order of Masons and who understood its leadership role in US and world affairs, appreciate the many contributions of the Knights Templar. Many of the founding fathers were members of the Masons, starting with Paul Revere, John Adams and George Washington."

"You've done well up to now, Dan; let's see you explain the Knights Templar."

"You are right on the money, Jack," continued Dan. "The Templar movement is worth mentioning.

"The Knights Templar were a force in the Middle Ages and a challenge to power structures across Europe. During the years that the Crusades fought to oust the Muslims from the Holy Land the Knights Templar were both an organized fighting army and a powerful economic influence. Based upon their exploits in the Middle East, they became a religious force moving on a much different path than most of Christianity at the time.

"Their saga began after the first Crusade in 1099 and the recovery of the Holy Land from Islamic control. Several leading families of Europe dispatched nine noblemen to Jerusalem to become protectors of the Temple of Solomon, thus the name Knights Templar. Their primary task was not just protection but excavation beneath the ruins of the Temple searching for treasure and religious artifacts. The site today is beneath the Dome of the Rock in Jerusalem.

"History has never been able to determine exactly what was found during the time the Knights controlled the area but there is no question that from this pious beginning the Knights Templar grew to become rich and powerful with thousands of members. The architectural skill acquired over the years was almost supernatural in its quality. The results of their work can be found across Europe. That skill was the foundation of the Masons which evolved into today's restricted fraternal order that

31

claimed members of our founding fathers as well as many of our presidents.

"The Knights' independence from both King and Church brought about their demise in 1307. King Philip of France and Pope Clement had two thousand knights arrested across Europe on Friday October 13, 1307 and their leaders burned at the stake for refusing to surrender their secrets and their treasure.

"The remaining members went into hiding, keeping the spirit of the Templars alive as a secret society. Their cult status was enhanced when both the King and the Pope fell victim to the curse of the last Templar Grand Master by dying within a year of ordering him burned at the stake. The vast wealth of the Knights was never recovered and has become the object of extensive treasure hunts down through the ages.

"Calling Opus Dei a cult group similar to the Knights Templar is accusing it of being in opposition to mainstream thought and heretical in their beliefs. It is a political tactic of the left trying to isolate the right, a not unfamiliar ground in any battle for power. When a group is a victim of an organized attack, it is a sign they are making progress against those in power. Opus Dei is the group to watch in the coming Conclave."

It was more than an hour later when Jack Roman finally spoke up and interrupted the steady flow of questions posed since Dan's remarks ended. "It seems to me," he said, "that we have opened up several new issues where the Conclave might take us and where its back wash is likely to spill out into the elections. Tim, I want you and Dan to divide these issue between you. Work up themes we can pursue and get back to me by day's end." With typical abruptness, he left the room.

No more than an hour later, the team had Roman's assignment broken into manageable pieces. It was agreed that Dan would probe the Executive Office building and other connections to the White House looking for pieces that might contribute to the theme development they were working on. Tim Scanlon, the Tribune's international specialist, was to contact their Rome bureau to begin the monitoring Dan suggested. Tim would prepare a summary paper for the boss.

Four
Camp David

With the groan of the Marine helicopter lifting off the Andrews pavement and the dome of the Capitol coming into view, General Tom Feely could not help but remember the many other helicopter rides he had endured during his career as an infantry officer. From the first training flight at Fort Benning, to the failed attempt to rescue POWs in North Vietnam, helicopter rides produced anxiety butterflies in his stomach. This ride was no exception.

Although he had met the President as military aide to the National Security Advisor, he had never been called to his sanctuary outside Washington for a personal briefing. The Camp David weekend had been planned as a review with the President's top election campaign advisors. That mornings CIA briefing to the Vice President added a Mid East incident to the agenda and a call for a briefing by Feely.

Just as he returned the salute of the Marine Guard at the base of the helicopter stairs at Camp David, the General caught sight of Paul Tozier, the Vice President's deputy chief of staff, walking to greet him. "Glad you could make it on short notice, Tom," Tozier began. "This morning's briefing caught us all off guard and the President wanted to hear your assessment on the incident."

"Paul, I appreciate your explaining the conflicting information the President was given," responded Feely. "I am better prepared as a result of your call. I owe you a dinner for this one."

Tozier parked the General in the ready room off the corridor of the main house. His reflection in the mirror hanging on the far wall of the room gave him the opportunity to check his appearance one more time before seeing the President.

Tom Feely's six-foot-one-inch frame and tight body, wrapped in the dress green uniform, gave him a picture-perfect image of the fighting man that he was. His Vietnam wounds of course were never visible and he had found ways to distract his mind from signals often sent to his brain by a pain-troubled body.

He was careful in the selection of decorations he wore to Washington meetings. In this case the airborne ranger and combat infantry badges were enough to show that his star rank was appropriately granted. Ever since his first haircut as a plebe, he felt most comfortable with the close cropped hair that set him apart from civilians.

The door to the room suddenly opened. "We are running late on the campaign financing session," said Paul, "but I don't expect it to last much longer. I'll be back to get you in a few minutes."

With the soft closing of the wood paneled door, Tom was again alone with the thoughts that had been dancing through his head since he left his Alexandria apartment that morning. For some reason, his mind would not let go of that small room in Lake George where he and his mother lived while she worked as a hotel chambermaid so many years ago. He was not unhappy with their life together in the heart of the Adirondacks and was worried when she said she had found a way back to Albany and a better life. He never liked Dennis Nolan, the rotund construction worker who became his stepfather. He didn't think he needed a more sophisticated school system than the one supported by the summer vacation colony but his mother wanted more for her only son.

Albany was where his father had died in an accident. He was never anxious to learn about the circumstances but he agreed with her plan to return if she thought it was right. In retrospect, without Albany there never would have been West Point and for that alone, Albany was a good moment in time. Without the decision to move, there would be no Camp David this morning but she had paid a terrible price for her sacrifice.

He regretted those teenage years when he withdrew into his hideout refuge in the woods of Lincoln Park because he couldn't handle the family tension that emerged from an alcoholic stepfather eager to show who was boss to his fragile wife. His early friendships had helped him navigate those troubled waters and emerge unscathed from some difficult circumstances.

34

General Thomas Feely turned from the window and tried to prepare himself to report to the President. He was only just back from Jordan and disappointed his weekend was interrupted again. He had so little time to spend with Meggie but she always seemed to understand the demands of an Army wife. When he left the last time, he promised he would spend more time at home but they had both heard those words before. He knew all too well that the demands of the Mid East problem in an election year would make the promise a hard one to keep.

The door swung open once again and Tozier hurried back into the room. "Let's go," he said, "the President asked the campaign staff to take a short break so he can hear your report."

Both men walked hurriedly down the long hallway and into the congested conference room.

Paul moved Tom along a row of chairs directly behind a document-strewn table, with the President at one end and the Vice President at the other. There were about ten additional people at the table with a tall slim gray haired presenter standing to the side explaining information appearing on a brightly lit screen behind him. "These numbers," he said, "are the goals we have established for the banking and investment community's support of the election campaign. We have doubled their contributions from the last election based upon our legislative success over the past four years. These totals are then distributed to those States where we expect the challenge to be the most critical. The distributions can only be made after we have received a request for assistance from an authorized independent group legally established in each state. The creation of these independent groups is substantially complete and some of the requests for financial assistance have already been answered."

When the briefing came to a close, Tom could not help but note the various charts hanging on the wall with red circles around cities and other overlapping colors emphasizing the importance of certain locations. He was reminded of the briefings he witnessed with General Westmoreland in Saigon and the similarities. Both presented campaign strategies followed by suggested tactics down to small unit engagements. Politics and war,

35

he thought, share common drivers with war, of course, an extension of politics for the soldier.

"Gentlemen," announced the President, "I would like to take a short recess in our campaign conversations and spend a few minutes with General Feely. I would ask all of those not part of the official White House staff, to wait across the hall until we are ready to resume the discussions."

With that request, more than half those in attendance left the table. Paul Tozier then motioned to Tom to stand at the table mid-point, in front of the screen that had just been used for the financial briefing.

Once the room had been cleared and the doors closed, the Vice President began the discussion. "At this morning's CIA briefing," he said, "we received the usual update on the whereabouts of the our most sought-after Mid East terrorist, Ali Abdullah Teekah, and his top lieutenants. Our inability to bring him to justice for his attacks on US interests is becoming more and more of a campaign issue ostensibly proving how weak we have been on global terrorism.

"We hoped the bounty put on Teekah's head by Iraq for his failed chemical sale would force him into our hands but this has not occurred. In fact, we have learned that just the opposite has happened.

"There has been a capture attempt made against Ali Teekah and his family on the West Bank by a Russian/Syrian commando force. The Russian-led team is one of the few with the capacity and experience to capture Teekah and return him to Iraq. General Feely was in Jerusalem at the time and will provide additional details on the failure of the attempt and how it impacted our plan to intervene."

Without a visible sign of the tenseness that gripped his body, Tom Feely began his presentation to the assembled White House staff of Presidential advisors.

"Our special operation forces were on alert following receipt of the information that an action was underway to capture Ali Teekah on the West Bank. After meeting in Jerusalem with my Israeli counterpart, I relocated to Jordan and monitored the communications from a double agent embedded with the Russian commando force. At that time all elements of our approved plan were intact and functioned as intended.

"Although details of the plan vary based on location, the underlying concept remained in place," he said. "US forces are not to be part of the primary contact elements in any capture attempt but will take Ali from the initial units after they have secured him and initiated the first move to a safe area. In this way, we meet the objective of not being responsible for Ali's death or injury during the assault. We will only activate our plan when he is removed from his own security force. These elements were in place and followed during this event.

"The elements of our plan were tested in this failed capture attempt. Ali Teekah's hiding place on the West Bank was wired against intruders in a manner even the local security force was not aware of, let alone the double agent who was a member of the commando unit. The home exploded with most of the commandos inside and with Ali and his family in a safe room in the basement."

Tom gave a signal to Paul Tozier, who flashed the first slide on the screen.

"Here is a satellite picture of the damaged residence we believe was Teekah's hiding place," commented Tom. "You will note the damage to the adjoining buildings that must have occurred when the internal explosives were detonated by the security system.

"This next slide shows fishing trawlers in the area that we believe were a backup escape plan if the submarines that delivered the commandos encountered difficulty.

"This morning's CIA briefing on the operation," continued Tom, "described the composition of the attack unit, its Russian and Syrian support forces and what led to its failure. The details have been verified by my sources in Jordan.

"We know the commando unit was assembled in Syria, moved through the countryside to Beirut, traveled to the Harri oil depot where they were assigned fuel trucks to drive to the seaside village of Lahoud and there board fishing vessels to take them out to waiting submarines.

"We know from communications from our double agent that both commando groups made it safely to the Teekah hiding place with the cooperation of local Palestinian forces," continued Tom over the silence that dominated the room. "We were poised to

37

intercept them on their return to the beach with the cooperation of the Israeli forces and the multi-national strike force we had assembled in the area. Unfortunately, the entire commando force was wiped out in the explosion or taken out by their escorts. The capture event was a failure."

While turning off the slide projector, Tom turned to face the President. "I would like to emphasize that none of our forces were detected and our evacuation plan, although not used, was in place and ready to go."

Tom moved slowly down the table next to the Vice President, folded his arms and looked at the President who had remained stoic during the presentation.

"Mr. President," Tom continued, "the reports that our limited involvement in the failed capture event was detected are not true. We have legitimate reasons to be many places and this will always be the case. The usual speculations surrounding these events should not be a reason to change plans. We have legitimate reasons for our presence in these areas and our strategy is built around explaining our role in these operations.

"Although the mission must be judged a failure since we did not capture the terrorist, it confirmed our ability to meet one of your most important directives, not to be discovered until the terrorist is in our hands. I believe we did that and the support of the plan should continue until we have Ali Teekah on trial in the United States."

The room was quiet and awaited the reaction from the head of the table. "I have approved your concept, General," responded the President, "but have grave concerns about the execution. Our involvement with the Israeli units could be as damaging as much as our being part of the strike force. There is absolutely no room for error. We cannot be seen as having our forces directly infringe upon the territory in the West Bank. Direct involvement in a failure would provide a campaign issue I want to avoid. If even our indirect participation is revealed, we will disclose our desire to go to great lengths to capture someone we have repeatedly declared is of little concern to us in the fight against terrorism. The coming election campaign is too sensitive at this point to give our opponents a gift of an international US embarrassment. We could be better off doing nothing.

"On the other hand," continued the President, "bringing a person to justice who is responsible for so many acts of terrorism could also swing the election very much in our favor. These are my concerns, gentlemen, and I would like your reactions."

Tom allowed a brief pause to occur as he moved back toward the center of the table and looked directly at the President.

"We are capable of executing the plan you approved and we remain confident it will meet your objectives," he replied. "I understand the political sensitivities of exposure but as a super power I have always felt it was our duty to take risks for the good it might produce. I think the consequences of doing nothing could be far greater than proceeding with our plan and having it somehow fail."

The urging of the General gave the Vice President his opening.

"Mr. President," the Vice President began, "we have discussed the do-nothing option in the past and all agree, it is not a satisfactory approach in these turbulent times. The proposed plan provides the necessary cover and offers a chance to bring home a major prize at an important point in the election campaign. The question before us is about continuing a plan that has shown itself to meet some of our objectives. Not being in the game at all, is the wrong choice."

"With all the other campaign details we discussed today being so positive," said the President, "I am reluctant to introduce the potential for a negative. However, under the circumstances, we should continue with our plan and attempt to capture Ali Teekah wherever we find him.

"You have my approval to move forward, General," said the President, "but you must remain in close contact with either myself or the Vice President as any situation develops."

The Vice President turned to Paul Tozier and directed him to bring the other group back into the conference room and let the campaign finance discussion continue.

Having the approval of the Commander is not always a good thing, Tom thought to himself, as he crossed the lawn to the waiting helicopter. He had been given similar approvals in the past and had difficulty delivering. In this case, the prize was well beyond just another medal for bravery. Success here could lead to the offices of the Joint Chiefs of Staff.

Five
Friendship Connected

The telephone message slip shouted to Dan from his desk of neatly piled papers and rows of action folders. The name General Feely was boldly printed across the top line indicating a return caller and finding itself on a special stack. After more than six weeks of calling, the return call was more sorrowful reminder than pleasant surprise.

After a chance meeting in Paris several months before, Tom Feely had appeared sincere in his assurances that he intended to break the pattern of the past and return telephone calls. Months was an improvement over years. Perhaps we can build on that, Dan thought to himself as he dialed the new number.

"Administration" came the voice at the other end of the wire. "I am trying to reach General Feely," Dan said inquisitively. "Who is calling?" came the reply.

"Dan Gerard is retuning his call," was the answer. "Just a moment please" seemed like a positive response, he thought.

"Dan, is this really you?"

"Tom, yes it is and I am glad to hear your voice again."

"Dan, let me apologize for the delay in returning your calls after I was so specific in Paris that you should call me once you relocated to Washington. I have been out of the country more than the usual amount of time and just haven't caught up with my contacts the way I would like. I intend to make amends for the delay by living up to my other promise and having dinner with you as soon as you are available."

Taken aback by the suddenness of it all, Dan was not sure how to reply. A blur of thoughts crossed his mind. Looking at his calendar for the evening he could skip the Press Club dinner and see Tom and capitalize on the babysitting arrangements in place for the children. His new assignment required more contact into the staff in the Executive Office building and Tom certainly fit that description. The tightness in his stomach was reminding him of the emotions that were left after the meeting in Paris.

"With an offer like that one, Tom," Dan replied, "I want to take it tonight, if that is OK with your schedule."

"I'll have to clean up a few things here first but I will make it tonight," Tom answered, "and with a suggestion that we avoid the usual D.C. gathering spots."

"Fine with me," said Dan. "Let's make it at a small Italian restaurant on K Street I just visited, called Pescatore, say around 7:00."

With arrangements in place, the two Albany men, now Washington insiders, agreed to meet for only the second time in fifteen years.

Dan was having difficulty concentrating on Tim Scanlon's briefing on the first reports from the London office on the status of the Pope's health. Tim sensed Dan's mental drift and he asked a probing question.

"Where are you, Dan?" he asked. "If you would prefer, we could continue this in the morning."

"I am sorry," came the answer. "I am in another world at the moment. There are a few personal issues coming to a head tonight. I would like to take you up on your offer and go over the items first thing tomorrow."

With that, Tim stood up and stopped at the office doorway. "I am glad you were honest with me," he said, "and didn't waste time having to go through all this again tomorrow."

Dan was reaching to close the office door before Tim finished his sentence. He was falling into another one of his introspective moods requiring quiet surroundings. The pull of Albany days and coming of age, were thoughts not easily resisted. Recalling his days as one of a local threesome, became a therapeutic diversion from the sorrow of rebuilding a family struggling with the loss of a mother. The past relieved pressures of the present, even accepting the fact that recollection embellishes the good times and minimizes the bad.

He was about to encounter his old friend and call up times past. Paris had been an ice breaker but tonight would be something different. His first encounter with Tom crept back into Dan's mind.

Young Tom Feely

It was a late night return from the Connellys' house that had nearly proved Dan's undoing. They had been watching television and Meggie had fallen asleep on his shoulder. She was warm and he felt comfortable on the old couch, he couldn't get up. Realizing it was near midnight, he knew it was well past his time to be home.

He woke her with a small kiss on her forehead and said goodnight.

Once outside and free of the old house, he began to run with a sense of urgency brought on by anticipation of the harsh words he was sure to hear when he entered his own kitchen so late. With any luck, his father would be out at one of his political meetings and he could escape a lecture.

Trying to save time, Dan considered a shortcut through the park. He never entered the park after dark, hearing stories of late night goings on. In some ways, he thought they were exaggerated.

Facing a difference of almost twenty minutes in the two routes and thinking of his father's face in the kitchen, Dan entered the park path and began to run toward the east end.

Within a hundred yards of the entrance, the lights from the neighborhoods faded and the well spaced walkway lamps were the only source of illumination. Dan remembered thinking that the shadows seemed to have eyes and that the trees were extending arms.

He continued to run, with head down and a concentration focused on keeping up his steady pace. He tried to ignore the feeling that someone was on the path behind him. He tried to tell himself he was just being nervous running from shadows.

As he turned to look behind him for the source of his concern, he ran into a live body that suddenly jumped from the darkness onto the path before him.

The impact of arms and legs brought them both to the pavement. In one motion, he was down and then back up and off the lighted path headed into the woods.

He could hear several voices yelling behind him as he crashed into a wall of branches and vines. His pace was slowed as he felt his legs strain with the demands of a steep hill. At the top of the incline, he rolled under a thicket and lay silent. The shoes and keys rushed by him.

After a few minutes of silence, he moved back down the hill hoping to find the walkway and the open path to the east end.

Within a few steps back on the cobblestone path, two arms wrapped themselves around his ankles and down he went for a second time into a pool of mud and slime. The arms moved to his body and held him tightly in their grasp.

"Got 'im," the voice yelled, "he's over here."

There were three of them, all looking as one might suspect nighttime prowlers to look. Strange clothes, long hair and gaunt faces with sarcastic smiles brought on by the capture of their vulnerable prey.

Jumbled conversations announced the presence of the group's leader and evidence of the gangs he heard about so often from others.

He was giving instructions to the other two. Taller, heavier and older than the others, he became the questioner, while fiddling with a key chain.

"What are you doing in my park?" he laughed. "Don't you know you are not allowed in here without my permission? I don't remember giving you my permission. In fact, I don't remember you even asking for my permission. Did you ask for my permission?" he snarled as he came nose to nose with Dan.

"Without permission, you have to pay a fine, if you want to get out of here. How much money do you have?"

"I don't have any money," Dan stuttered.

"Then how are you going to pay the fine?" the response came.

"I can give you my watch, it's a pretty good one. If you let go of my arms, I'll take it off and let you have it," answered Dan.

The two released his arms, after the signal from their captain.

As soon as he felt his arms go free, Dan made a quick move to his right and he was off and running again, this time staying on the path with firm room to run. He was increasing the distance between himself and his chasers, when once again, he was brought down by sudden arms wrapped around his legs.

This time the crash dragged his face along the cobblestone. He could feel blood rush into his eyes.

Before he could move, more arms were added to the pile. He was pulled to his feet just as his pursuers arrived.

He was held by three new figures with a much different look about them. A taunting dialogue began, between the nighttime forces seeking to claim their prize.

The most recent band's leader had the most to say. He was an impressive figure even in the darkness. He stood straight, his clothes were tight around his muscular body. In the dim light, his light hair partially covered a very slim tight face with a slightly protruding jaw. His mouth released his words without showing much of his teeth. His arms were folded across his chest with his hands under his biceps. His very stance seemed authoritative.

His voice was firm and dripped with sarcasm as he expressed disbelief in finding these same three in his park, after he told them before not to set foot in his territory again. He positioned himself just off the face of his nighttime counterpart and brought him down with a blow to the face.

With all the bodies now engaged with each other, Dan took off once again into the woods but this time avoided returning to the lighted path.

By the time he made it home, it was well beyond his time, but luck was with him. His father was out again at one of his meetings and his only greeting was the open arms of his mother. Although annoyed, she washed the cuts and bruises, brought him fresh clothes and warm milk. As usual, there were no questions.

He was in bed not more than ten minutes when his father entered the kitchen. The house was dark and the man followed his usual path to his bed. There was no conversation coming from his parents, so Dan was able to drift off to sleep.

In less than a week, Dan would meet the nocturnal commander of the territory he had trespassed.

The Basketball Encounter

Dan's basketball team was playing the Roosevelt High JV team at Christian Brothers Academy gym as part of their regular schedule.

44

Before the game started, the team captains met to shake hands in mid court. Looking at that face, there was no doubt about it. When the opposing captain gave his name, Tom Feely, Dan recognized the voice as the second leader from the park.

During the game, it was obvious Tom Feely was more interested in handing out punishment than playing ball. The fouls he gave were meant to deliver a message. He was in charge of the space and everyone should give him distance.

The game was close but a win for CBA. Roosevelt was well known as a poor loser. They often made an effort to leave their mark on a gym before leaving the building.

While members of both teams were scrambling in the hallway, young Tom Feely was caught in the locker room breaking into a candy machine. Three players were holding him down while another player ran to get the security guard.

Dan yelled out, "Stop, everybody stop." They did as the captain ordered.

"Let him up and let him go."

With a look of surprise in his eyes, Tom Feely rose to his feet.

Dan walked up to him, extended his hand and said, "Thanks."

"Thanks for what," grumbled Tom.

"Stay a few minutes and I'll tell you," replied Dan.

After a while, the post game mingling was completed and most of the Roosevelt team left the building. Dan picked up his bag and caught up with Tom as he was pushing open the double doors of the gym. The cool night air felt good as it removed the stale smell of sweat and school hot dogs from his senses.

Before Dan could say a word to Tom, he offered his own thanks.

"I did a stupid thing," Tom admitted. "I was mad and wanted to do something for spite. A little damage is one thing but stealing money from a candy machine can look pretty bad if someone wants to make trouble. I don't know who you are, but you saved my butt and I owe you."

"I guess we are both in the butt saving business," said Dan, "because you saved mine the other night in Lincoln Park when you dropped that guy with one punch."

45

"Was that you who took off?" chuckled Tom. "You were gone before we knew you were there."

With the laughter growing in intensity, the young men shook hands and walked off to the local corner store to hang out and get acquainted.

After several hours, Dan had to press Tom for the smallest bit of information about his personal life. It didn't happen that first night. It was weeks before the personal side of Tom Feely began to emerge. He would talk about many things but home life was always last on the list.

Tom's mother lost her husband in a trolley car accident on State Street in Albany. He fell into the path of an approaching streetcar and was killed before her eyes with young Tom in her arms. They were taken in by neighbors and lived with several different families for years. In an effort to strike out on her own after years of depression, they moved to Lake George Village where his mother found a job as a chambermaid in one of the hotels. They lived there for several years and moved back to Albany on the advice of the school principal who recognized Tom's potential and understood the shortcomings of the rural school system.

After facing the burdens of a single mother in Albany and concerned about the education of her son, Tom's mother accepted the proposal of marriage frequently offered by a local character, Dennis Nolan. Although he was a respected heavy equipment operator and apparently capable of supporting a family, Nolan was also well known as a heavy drinker and a barroom brawler eager to take on challengers for a small cash prize.

The stepfather arrangement never worked for Tom and he could not deal with what his mother had to do for his sake. He often begged her to leave but she refused. She had found them the financial support they needed but little else.

The end came for the marriage when Nolan refused to pay for a private high school for Tom as he said he would. When his mother then refused to deliver her side of the marriage, physical abuse began. Dennis Nolan enjoyed pushing and shoving his wife in front of her son. The times Tom attempted to interfere, the stepfather enjoyed teaching the boy about brawling.

46

Reacting to his home environment, Tom dug a small shelter out of a hillside at the swamp end of Lincoln Park. He created a refuge, a place where he could be in charge. He roamed the park at night and asserted his control over this portion of existence. He did find the time to read as well as roam. He knew success in school pleased his mother and he wanted her to see that the failure to send him to private school was no failure at all.

Tom Feely was a blend of rogue and scholar. His home in the park reminded Dan of Robin Hood and his merry men. His success in schoolwork was a priority he talked about every day but often was in contrast to the trouble he flirted with as he asserted control over those around him.

The Chance Meeting in Paris

Dan's mind changed gears again. From Albany, he moved to the chance meeting with his friend Tom Feely after almost twenty years. It was on the streets of Paris and his first business trip outside the US.

Dan found himself in Paris on business following the trail of consulting payments to New York State Legislators from Washington PR firms. The British and French were fighting the injunction obtained by the Port Authority denying landing rights to the Concorde at JFK. While people-watching from Dan's sidewalk chair at the Four Cats restaurant on the Champs-Elysees, who walked past his table but uniformed General Tom Feely with another officer.

Instant recognition produced smiles and embraces. There was genuine regret expressed by both men for the lack of contact and a willingness to reenergize friendship. Sensing a need for privacy, Tom's fellow officer left them to catch up on an interrupted past.

Dan's reporter's questioning led Tom through a time tunnel of events from multiple tours in Vietnam, early recognition as a battlefield commander and his Medal of Honor engagement.

Tom's military achievements were topped off by good luck in saving the life of one of the most respected and eventually most influential officers in Vietnam. The personal connections Tom made during the evacuation of Saigon added to the political weight he needed during later promotion board reviews. When the White House was looking for a hero to bring into public view during an election year, they made him one of the youngest generals in the army.

After several drinks and almost two hours in that Parisian café, the Tom Feely of Albany's Lincoln Park was gone and Dan was with General Thomas Feely, United States Army. His boyhood friend had made a transition to the polished corridors of power.

When Tom's questions turned to Dan, it provided an opportunity to sketch the battle from resigned seminarian and disgraced family member to award winning journalist. Dan's Albany abyss was skipped over and the climb from New York paper to New York paper was detailed along with brushes with organized crime. His Concorde story was the first involving global influencing at the highest level.

Dan remembered the sudden change he triggered when asking about Meggie. Tom replied that Dan could answer that question himself. She was with him and he would have her join them for dinner that very night. Dan's mind fogged over at the mention of her name.

Margaret Mary Connelly was in Paris? She was here to be seen and talked to? All of Dan's reasons for avoiding the dinner that night were brushed aside by Tom as only he could do. The evening was set for a reunion of the Lincoln Park threesome and that was that, Tom emphasized, as he walked back into the crowd.

Dan remembered sitting alone on that sidewalk in Paris and recalling his last good-bye to Meggie. After a long delayed physical surrender to each other, he was leaving for Rome to resign from the seminary and return home to marry her. Here it was fifteen years later and he would look into her eyes for the first time as the wife of his old friend. *How did all this happen*, he thought. How does anything happen?

The Dubliner Pub

Dan's concerns about the morning briefing to the paper's staff and the thoughts of the Pope's health were being pushed aside by pictures from his past. It was time to take a break, change surroundings and breathe some fresh air.

Dan left his office and headed for a new refuge, the Dubliner Pub by the Union Station. It was a noisy and comforting place at the same time. When feeling his moods coming on, Dan often sought out places like this as a distraction. He sat down in a corner table and people watched those at the bar. There was the usual combination of shirt and tie people along with the tradesmen crowd. What are their stories, he wondered, what choices did they make that brought them to this point in their lives?

The dinner with his old friend and partner in crime was an hour away. He hoped the night would be unlike their meeting in Paris where the most troublesome part of their relationship was never discussed. Dan was planning on bringing up a subject they had agreed never to talk about.

The Dubliner corner table reminded Dan of the table that had the place of honor in the dining room on the second floor of his family home on Summit Avenue in Albany. Of all the meals at that table and of all the pronouncements of his father, the defining moment for Dan was the night he was informed about the choice made about his future. The battle that ensued was bitter. It could not be avoided.

Dan consoled himself with the knowledge that he did not destroy the wife-husband relationship at home. It had dissolved many years before when his mother blamed his father for not being home when his twin sister died of the flu. The absence of warmth in the house was a product of unresolved blame.

A second drink at the corner table of the Dubliner Pub led Dan back to that family battle and its strange outcome.

Six

The Choice

The charade of filling out college applications came to a conclusion on a Sunday night when "the father" made the grand announcement that today's meal was to be a special event, one requiring the good dishes from the china closet and special wine. His older brother, Maurice, looked as puzzled as Dan and with a familiar roll of his eyes made it clear that he was not looking forward to another soliloquy by the head of the household.

Mary Kelly Gerard, usually not one to show emotional response to any statement made by her husband, brought out the best table cloth and the good dishes with a certain smile on her face. The smile reflected the opportunity to move her plates from their safe place and allow them to brighten the room. Among all her possessions, the china talked with whispers of home.

The usual silence was observed through most of the meal, when finally and grandly it was broken by the father's commands to listen to the news he had for his family.

"My good friend the governor called today," he began. "Their meeting last week with members of the New York State congressional delegation was more successful than even he had hoped. The governor wanted to express his thanks for all the hard work done together that led up to this very important meeting. The governor was particularly pleased to have the opportunity to deliver the good personal news he had received from Washington. The appointment to West Point, they all had been working on, had come through for Daniel. The news was greeted by warm applause from those at the meeting," declared the father, a smile of satisfaction on his face.

"On this most auspicious occasion," he continued, "it's fitting to be together at the family table to celebrate the good news. Our son, your brother Daniel, a first generation Irish-American, is about to follow in the footsteps of other great American leaders. He is about to embark on a journey to greatness. An opportunity offered to only a very few of the best and the brightest and a chance to distinguish themselves among the country's elite. West Point is a path others have taken to the White House. Perhaps some day my son will might confront a similar opportunity."

The father's comments and reflections on the importance of the occasion went on for some time without comment.

The speech was interrupted by a sudden move of Dan's mother reaching across the table to remove the father's plate, knocking over a glass of water in the process.

The water spilled into Maurice's lap and he jumped up to avoid the soaking of his pants.

Edmund Gerard's voice boomed across the room. "Sit down, sit down now! I'll say when it's time to leave this table. I'm not finished."

The room was now filling with a of cloud of anger, animosity and fear, always the case when the father imposed his will on those around him. This was not an opportunity for dialogue, if ever there was one, but a moment to listen and obey.

The uncomfortable silence at the table allowed the slow ticking of the grandfather clock to dominate the air.

With the members of his family now upright in their chairs and heads bowed in obedience, Edmund Gerard continued his grand announcement by detailing the schedule for the coming weeks and the arrangements that had to be made to arrive at the academy for the start of the new plebe class.

His father's announcement was more like something from the featured speaker's remarks at his political club than mere dinner table remarks. Dan's stomach and sweat glands told him it was now or never.

The night so far had not been a surprise for Dan. He understood it had to come, from the moment his mother won the high school battle four years before. That fight allowed him to attend CBA and remain in Albany rather than attend a prep school feeder to the Academy.

Most of all, he worried that she would not win the fight a second time. The last occasion had been a time of tears, shouting and threats. It ended with a concession from the father that it would be the last time he would consider any other alternative. Life's hard decisions required determination, the father had proclaimed. He knew a firm hand was essential in these family matters.

Listening to the summer schedule and picturing reporting to the academy as a Plebe, Dan could feel the tension growing inside like an anaconda wrapping itself around its prey. How could he escape? He wanted no part of anything military. He didn't know exactly what he wanted to do with his life, but killing people was not one of them.

His mother's push for the priesthood offered the exact opposite of the military and had its attractions. Dan never felt a deep sense of any lifelong commitment to church but it was an alternative.

Why must this most fundamental life decision be a choice between a father's plan and a mother's hopes? Should his decision be made not to hurt someone, or to do what he wanted?

Without moving his eyes from the flower on the carpet beneath his chair, Dan spoke up.

"I think it's my life and I should have something to say about it," he said.

His mother and brother shifted their eyes in his direction, looks of surprise on their faces.

"I love what my family has given me," Dan continued, "but a person reaches a point in life where he needs to separate himself from that family and make his own decisions. It's his life and he should be allowed to live it!"

The astonished look on his father's face told him he had an opening and should seize the moment.

"I agree that your life should have an element of service in it," Dan added, "but in my case the service will be for a more powerful force than the US government. It will be as a priest in the Catholic Church. I have discussed this at CBA with the brothers and they agree with my choice. That is what I intend to do."

As he finished, Dan looked into his mother's eyes. In that brief moment, he saw a reflection of the happiness that was so often missing.

His father's response was predictable. "You will do no such thing! You will follow the instructions of your father, as the commandments of your Lord tell you. Honor your father and your mother, is a directive from God! If you want to serve anyone, it should begin with those who raised and educated you. If you have any thoughts about the Church you should start with keeping the commandments.

"I've been able to bring you this far in life and I'll not let you throw away an opportunity like this one," shouted his father.

"You won't waste your talents, as some poor parish priest wiping the noses of first communion brats. You have the potential for greatness and you need a firm hand at this time in your life, as so many young people do. I see my responsibility as a father applying that firm hand for your benefit," he exclaimed hammering on the table.

"This appointment was won at great expense in political contributions and personal favors for many people. You can't disregard the cost here. I understand your reluctance but you will thank me someday for putting you on a path to a real meaning for your life.

"You will go to West Point and I don't want to hear any more talk about it. It is the best decision and gives you a chance few boys your age ever have. It's a decision for greatness aren't you allowed to refuse.

"If you think you are becoming a man, your first thoughts should be about meeting your obligations. This is your first test. The matter is over and done with. It's decided. You'll behave like a man."

"No, Dad, no. You and all your plans for the world and all your political friends can go to hell," Dan was yelling, pounding the table as his father so often did.

"Daniel, be still in the name of God!" his mother shouted, coming around to his side of the table and striking his face in desperation.

No one had seen her do this before.

For the second time at the meal, Edmund's eyes reflected disbelief, as he looked at the woman standing before him.

"It is not done and it is far from over!" she asserted. "You are going to listen to a lot more about it," she said, in a tone never heard before.

"The conversation is just beginning," declared the quiet woman who was visibly shaking and whose eyes were already tearing.

"You are not going to steal from God what is His," she said to her husband. "Thou shall not steal is on that list of commandments you so conveniently quote. This boy has belonged to God since the day his sister died.

"And let's not forget," she continued, "what the commandments really say, it's to honor both your Father and your Mother and not just your Father!"

She turned to the two boys and said, "Maurice and Danny, you are excused from the table. Get out!"

With this sudden release, both boys jumped up and burst from the house. Edmund moved from the head of the table and into the side porch without saying a word. He began his nightly routine of reading the paper in the big red leather chair. He was a fighter who had been knocked to one knee for the first time in his career.

Round one was over. There had been no knockout.

In reflection at the time, Dan knew he had no chance to win on his own. His other college options would have been wasted without the support of his mother and that was not what she wanted. Bringing her into the fray changed the dynamics. It was a lesson in confrontation he would long remember. One needs allies!

The days that followed were tense but moved toward compromise. Dan's promise to flunk out of the academy before summer was over was becoming a real threat the more he thought about his determination to avoid the military.

He tossed back the often used phrase of his father to demonstrate his point. "You can lead a horse to water but you can't make him drink." Dan never rode a horse, let alone led one to water but it was one of his father's expressions that suddenly meant something to him.

His mother had been energized in a way Dan had never seen before and in a way the father was having great difficulty comprehending. Together, mother and son and the forces of Church, were wearing down the thick Irishman.

Day after day, their bedroom door muffled their words but Dan could tell from the tone of the shouting and his father's storming out of the house, that the tide was turning in his direction.

Sensing victory, Dan wanted to make a gesture he thought would add something to the relationship of father to son and seal the compromise.

On a quiet evening, after his father had read his paper on the side porch, Dan began a review of the confrontation. He never had a conversation like this before but he never had much to say either.

"I want to be a priest," Dan began. He agreed with his mother that God had saved his life at the time his twin sister Margaret died of the flu. "There must be some purpose for my life and a military career is not it."

He believed he had a calling to serve in some way that would support goodness in the world. He didn't want to seem ungrateful for the effort made for the West Point appointment.

He had an idea how the effort could be made even more important and be a step in his path of helping others. If his father would consider his request, it would be an important step in his manhood.

Would his father change the name of the appointment to his friend Tom Feely? His father had met Tom often enough to know who he was and the family circumstances.

The response was as Dan expected, a firm no. However, the old man's pattern of behavior had become more obvious in recent months. The father said no to everything but thought about most things well beyond the initial reaction. Dan stalled in a subtle way, reminding him of the importance.

A week later, while Dan was sitting on the back steps watching the sun go down over the garage roof, his father sat down beside him. In as few words as he could use, he told Dan the appointment had been cleared for Tom Feely. After a warm thank you they sat there in silence. Turning to say a few more words, Dan found the step empty. The shadow of his father could be seen walking into the fields, hands in his pockets.

Having concluded he could not win the battle on his own, Dan Gerard joined forces with his mother and the Brothers of

55

CBA academy and thwarted the plans of his father. The victory was followed by an effort to repair the relationship. It was a significant learning experience. In the end, his goal was reached with a compromise but it was indeed reached. He thought about his friend in the process.

Seven
The Meeting

Aromas of Northern Italian cooking brought Dan's thoughts to the present while entering Pescatore and receiving the smile of the hostess. Tom had not arrived. He was able to select a rear table far from the K Street hustle outside. It was the site of his final interview before joining the Tribune and he welcomed the relaxed atmosphere. He expected the conversation might be anything but relaxed. The contrast would be helpful.

The sight of Tom walking toward the table in gray jacket and black turtleneck brought confirmation from stomach to brain that this would not be an easy night.

With drinks in hand and opening amenities exchanged, Tom repeated his apologies for his failure to respond to Dan's calls. It led to a discussion of business issues and the unyielding demands of a Washington schedule. With the professional landscape on the top of the agenda, Dan moved to international matters, Tom was happy to contribute.

For over an hour they exchanged experiences, laughing at some, becoming silent at others. With certain sensitive topics avoided during the Paris dinner as a reminder, Dan decided to probe the most notable of Tom's combat actions in Vietnam. This resulted in Tom's first cigarette of the night, combined with a lowering of his voice and a blank stare in his eyes. The more he went into the events around that rescue mission, the more detached he became. There was a dark side to the Medal of Honor acclaim.

Tom's comments seemed directed at someone in the distance but he appeared eager to give details. "With the early casualties among the senior officers on the mission," Tom's soft voice began, "I took the lead of battalion-size force and moved into the jungle. Several days later we had fought our way through to the objective and rescued the Special Forces group that had been trapped for days. Returning to the helicopter pickup point with the enemy on our heels was the problem. On my way in, I had observed a perfect site for an ambush. My idea was accepted and we sprung a trap on our pursuers.

"Like most helicopter landing zones in Viet Nam, we had an indescribable time fighting our way out. I barely survived.

"The commander of the Special Forces unit we brought out was a Colonel Mallory. He became a political and personal mentor for me. Mallory, a fellow Academy graduate, knew the right buttons to push at the crossroads in my career. It began with an assignment to Westmoreland's staff after my recovery. Then an appointment as Mallory's deputy on both a POW rescue mission and the evacuation of Saigon."

"You have a great deal to be proud of, old friend," said Dan in an effort to shift the mood.

"That's the problem," replied Tom. "There's a hell of a lot not to be proud of as well!

"The ambush I set up to cover our retreat was a killing field beyond anybody's imagination. Bodies piled up like bales of hay waiting for shipment. We had to finish them off to keep them from following us to the pickup zone, I never got over the sights and sounds of that night."

Turning his eyes and mind back to the table, Tom appeared anxious to move back to the present. "Let's turn the subject over to the award winning journalist," he said. "You gave us the details of your move from one paper to another but I was curious how you broke the story of the payoffs to public officials on the Concorde."

"Good journalists are good detectives," answered Dan. "Once you are onto a story that doesn't meet the smell test, instincts take over and initiate a determination not to give up until finding genuinely satisfying answers. After leaving you in Paris, I stumbled onto a party in my hotel for French travel agents given by the Orlando Airport Authority counseled by a Washington PR firm.

"When one of the airport executives discovered I was from Albany, he introduced me to the husband of the PR executive who was giving the presentation. The husband was from a law firm in Albany that lobbied state officials. I learned later that his brother-in-law was Chairman of the State Assembly Oversight Committee had pressured the Port Authority to change noise rules to allow the Concorde in to JFK. It appeared to be a perfect path for influence peddling and it was.

"It would not have been much of a story except that the Director of Aviation for the Authority was conveniently under committee-directed suspension for an expense irregularity when he was scheduled to testify in court against the Concorde. The events just matched so many other investigations that it was simple to keep digging. Some officials believe they are in the Seat of Power when most of the time real power is held by others off in the shadows.

"When I was able to trace the consulting payments to the right people it became front page news. But even when an exposé hits the press, the real power brokers are rarely flushed out into the public eye. I see that as my main challenge, to expose those who manipulate from the shadows."

With the delivery of dessert and the after dinner drinks, Dan thought it was time to leave career aside and discuss another agenda. He began a move into the past.

"I often remember those Albany days," Dan laughed, "we spent hours in your hideout and debated what the three of us would do and if there was any way out of the old city. Here we are years later and those days seem so far away."

Tom took the opening and moved into the very area Dan was probing.

"You know," he began, "I told you back then that there was no way I could ever repay you for convincing your father to use his influence to help me with an appointment to West Point. I still don't understand how it happened. It came from far out of the blue that it confused me completely. In all our plans we never discussed the possibility of the Military Academy. You sprang it on me so quickly. I barely had the grades but no one could outperform me on the physical side. The combination of the two is what kept me hanging in there all four years.

"So let me say again, thank you."

Dan felt the opportunity to ask one of two painful questions. He made the most of the chance.

"I was not aware that you and Meggie had developed a relationship that was serious enough for marriage," Dan asked.

Tom sat up, reached across the table for his drink and put both arms on the table. The discussion was moving where Dan wanted.

"Look, Dan," Tom began raising his eyes from his glass. "Meggie was your girl. We all knew that from the beginning. It was hard to understand why that was. I left it alone while you were there. When you decided to go into the seminary it seemed all bets were off.

"I bothered her as much as I could from West Point. It was close enough for me to see her from time to time and close enough for her to come up and stay at the Hotel Thayer for Academy socials.

"To answer your question, we began a relationship after you were gone. In all honesty, I was shocked when she accepted my proposal to marry after graduation that summer. I had hinted at the idea more than once. As close as we had become, she gave no indication she was ready.

"She was very upset by the death of her mother. I was able to be with her for the funeral and days after. She felt alone and the thought of staying to care for her father and brothers was depressing. All I know is, I asked her one more time and she said yes. Her only request was to marry immediately and leave Albany, which we did."

Dan's question had been answered. He hadn't known what he was expecting to hear. It was still painful. It added to the guilt he felt for not coming home as promised.

"Looking back on the decision," continued Tom, "I would conclude that it was made in haste. Neither of us understood what it meant to be an Army wife. Army officers feel married to the service because its needs always come first. It's a hard realization and it can be slow in coming. Hardship tours often break a relationship. Of my fifteen years of service, eleven have been considered hardship. My time away from home has been unusual but I wouldn't be one of the youngest generals in the Army if I chose not to make the sacrifice."

Dan's next question was even more sensitive. It too involved Albany days.

"Tom, I know we agreed never to talk about our incident but after all these years and many sleepless nights, I ask you to allow us to break that agreement and discuss what happened.

"We were too young and not prepared for what we had to face," Dan continued. "We did what we thought was right. The years have changed my perspective on life. I have a need to get it on the table."

There was the long silence. Tom's facial expression changed. Frown lines emerged across his forehead. He reached for another cigarette and lit it quickly. He called to the waiter and made a hand motion for a written check. He began to shift his body from one side of the chair to the other. Finally, he spoke.

"That morning we watched the sun come up over Lincoln Park. You were in tears and trembling. I told you then and I'll tell you now. Some things in life you have no control over. When they happen, if you can push them aside and get on with your life you should.

"We agreed at the time to do just that. You had your chance back then to do something different and you didn't. There is no purpose in digging up the past. I have greater nightmares than that incident. I am doing a fairly good job of coping with my actions. I do not intend to complicate my life by reliving an event from over fifteen years ago."

With that Tom grabbed the check from the waiter and stuffed some bills into the folder. He stood up and offered his hand across the table.

"I have no argument with you, Dan. We are old friends. I want to keep it that way. With both of us working in Washington there is a good chance we will see each other again. It should be on a positive basis."

Tom Feely walked slowly out of the restaurant.

Eight
The Incident

Dan stared at the empty ashtray and vacant chair, feeling empty beyond description. He had hoped for the therapy of talking through the incident, confirming recollections and sharing the guilt. Tom did not want to resurrect ghosts. It was not that easy for him.

Although the waiter cleared the table and dimmed the restaurant's lights, Dan was unable to move. Unable to talk about that night, he was about to relive it. The happy moments of graduation week came back. Anticipation of the future and the prospect of new surroundings brought a sense of real achievement to the graduates.

Their final days together were fun filled, from a graduation party at Nick's house on Manning Boulevard, to an all night party at Tom's Lincoln Park hideout. The final week gave ample time to let loose every high school complaint and relish the fun of starting college life. They were starting to feel like men in charge of their own destinies.

That Saturday started off with a graduation ceremony on the grounds of the Christian Brothers Academy (CBA) followed by an outdoor reception. The same afternoon was to be an important one for his older brother Maurice. He had the best pitching record of anyone in the high school league that year. He was starting in the finals of the league championship before the scout from the Philadelphia farm club. The team had expressed interest in the young lefthander and a contract was possible.

If the offer of a contract came, Maurice had every intention of leaving school for a baseball career. He and Patsy Reilly were close to being engaged anyway. She was eager to get married and leave Albany.

Maurice was pleased at the outcome of Dan's confrontation with their father. He felt more willing to face the consequences of leaving school and getting married having witnessed the resolution of the West Point debate.

The game was a thriller. St. Michael's won 2 to 0. Maurice pitched a one hitter. He was carried off the field by his teammates, past the scout and smiling eyes of Patsy Reilly.

The CBA boys joined the St. Michael's celebration well into the evening. Tom and Dan found themselves alone as darkness covered the closed Lincoln Park pool.

Dan remembered a fog of melancholy overtaking his mind that night during the walk home in the darkness. He felt a sense of brotherhood and excitement about what was ahead for both of them, along with a sense of loss in leaving familiar surroundings.

Tom asked Dan to stop off at his house on the way home so he could show him the latest material from West Point.

Climbing the old wooden stairs to the top floor, they heard a commotion coming from Tom's apartment. Tom ran the last few steps to the door and forced it open. Neither was prepared for the sight before them.

Tom's mother lay on the floor of the kitchen, in a fetal position, with an arm raised across her face in an effort to ward off the blows delivered by her crazed husband.

His belt wrapped around his big hand and a sick smile on his face, Denny Nolan was not distracted by the intruders.

Nolan was a hulk of a man who enjoyed using his size to humiliate others. He delighted in a good barroom brawl and had a body that soaked up punishment.

He was drunk, as he so often was, and his bare chest and bruised eyes gave evidence of a fight earlier that night.

Tom froze for a moment. He was again feeling frustrated with his inability to protect his mother as well as her refusal to leave Nolan. He had tried before to stop the beatings and had always been frustrated. He had to try one more time.

Tom jumped in front of his fallen mother and said nothing but looked straight into his stepfather's eyes.

"We've been through this before, Tom," slurred the drunken man. "I've shown you more than once who the man of the house is and I'll be happy to show you again, if that's what you want.

"Get out of my way and let me do what has to be done."

In true street fashion, Tom threw a desperate first punch squarely into the big Irish face, which took the big man by surprise.

Dan had seen this punch delivered before and witnessed its crippling effect. In this case, it did little damage.

"So, that is what you want, is it?" smiled Nolan. "Well that's what you'll get.

"I guess you forgot that last lesson I gave you," he said with a smirk. "Consider this lesson to be my going away gift you can think about when you are in that fancy school," he said with that lilt in his voice.

Fists and hands flew before Dan could think. His instinct, as always, was to run but he couldn't. He had to join in the battle, though it looked like a losing cause.

Tom tried to grab his stepfather's arm but was tossed aside and thrown into the pantry with a crash. Pots, pans, dishes, chairs and anything not tied down took flight as the two traded punches.

Although they were destroying the room, the boys were having little impact on the old barroom fighter. He was clearly enjoying himself and made a move to do damage to Tom. He brought him down with a sudden move, kept him pinned on the floor and began kicking him.

The groans of his friend threw Dan into a panic. He grabbed a pot of stew from the stove and with both hands threw pot and contents at the brawler. The burning liquid turned Nolan's attention away from Tom and toward the new pest. He picked Dan up with one hand and smashed his head into the wall while delivering a punch to his face. A sudden numbness joined the rush of blood from Dan's mouth and eye as he fell.

The momentary distraction allowed Tom to use the fallen ironing board to jam between the big man's legs and bring him crashing to the floor. Stunned, he was slow in getting to his feet. Tom seized an iron skillet from the stove and slammed a powerful blow to Nolan's left arm. The noise and accompanying scream said the arm was broken.

It was clear from the arm dangling at his side, that Denny was disabled. The contorted face was struggling to understand the pain. The smirk was gone. Uncontrolled rage was in his voice and a dark glare came from his eyes.

Nolan's good hand reached above the refrigerator and took down a knife. He turned back to Tom and slurred out his intentions.

"I will give you more than just punishment this night! I will leave you with no ability to be a man again," snarled the wounded fighter.

Much like a hungry cat, Nolan began a slow and determined move toward Tom. There were no flying chairs or quick moves, just the fixed gaze and the knife held low at his side. The other arm was dangling as if it was not connected to his body.

Tom had nothing more than an old soup ladle left to defend himself as he was being maneuvered into a corner of the kitchen by a determined hunter stalking his prey.

Regaining his breath and clearing the blood from his eyes, Dan was in shock from the damage done to his body. He was starting to grasp the scene unfolding before him and the threat from the wounded animal. He did not know what he could do.

He felt a towel on the floor next to him soaked with the stew he threw into the fight. He could see Tom's face over the shoulder of his stepfather.

In a single motion, Dan leaped on the back of the hunter, dropping the towel over his face and eyes and holding on for dear life.

Now blinded, and with only one arm to remove the nuisance, Nolan turned away from Tom to throw off the pest.

Street instincts tell you when an opening occurs, if only for a second. Tom understood the opportunity. He rushed the struggling pair and brought both down to the floor. All three slid across the slick kitchen floor, Dan on the bottom.

Dan's breath was gone. He could not move with all the weight on him. He could feel the fierce struggle over him. Then, he was slowly aware that the hulk was no longer moving. He carefully released his grip on the towel.

Moving out from under the pile, Dan felt warm liquid on his face and his side. He realized the blood was not his. He lay motionless for a few seconds. The quiet was interrupted by a scream from the woman in the corner.

Tom staggered to his feet and helped Dan squirm out from the bottom of the pile. It was then that he saw it. A sight he would remember all the days of his life. The handle of the old knife protruded from the man's bare chest surrounded by steady squirts of red liquid.

Dan didn't know if the fall did the damage or if was it Tom's action itself. It didn't make any difference; the deed was done! The battleground gave evidence of the fierce fight. The floor was littered with the ingredients of the family dinner, broken dishes and chairs and the blood of the combatants. Dan knew his life was now part of the mess.

The friends said nothing as they surveyed the results of their struggle. The silence was broken by a knock at the door and the sobbing of Tom's mother. Tom immediately responded. "Is that you, Mrs. Monahan?"

"Yes, it is, Is everything all right in there?" she shouted.

"Yes, Mrs. Monahan, as I have told you many times before, we are alright in here and this time is no different than the others. But thank you for asking and a good night to you."

With the footsteps fading down the hall, came the realization of what they were dealing with. *Now, dear God, what can we do?* Dan thought. The debate began.

A call to the police would mean the end of all the plans for the life they had been celebrating the past few weeks. How the act would be seen by the authorities, was any body's guess. Twenty years for murder or a suspended sentence? Both young men had the same vision, their lives were ruined.

How quickly life can remove what it so generously gave a short time ago, Dan thought. Tom expressed what he saw as the best gamble. Hide the act! It was worth the effort and it was the only chance to save their lives. All other options destroyed the future.

Dan didn't like the gamble. He was ready to postpone his life and salvage it later, in order to avoid certain prison time for hiding the body. He thought the path that beckoned was the one offering the best chance to avoid jail.

Tom wouldn't consider any option but an attempt to escape responsibility. If Dan didn't want to help, he would do it alone.

Understanding his part in the act, Dan saw no sense in leaving. His thoughts turned to moving the body.

One of his afternoon chores involved delivering fish for the Moran fish market. He drove a van for the deliveries and had a set of keys. The van had a set of hand trucks and dollies for heavy deliveries. The back of the van was often stained with fish blood and would be a good cover.

Dan left the apartment and found the delivery van right where he had left it for the weekend. The drive back to Tom's apartment reminded him how powerful the smell of fish could be.

By the time the partners in crime were ready to move the body, it was 3:00 in the morning. Although there were noises from other apartments, no one met them on the stairs or in the alleyway of the building. They decided the Hudson River offered the best chance of losing the body. They were able to weigh down their bundle and slip it into the river before sunrise.

After returning the van, the two made their way to Tom's lair in the park where their soul searching began. The debate went on all day. It ended with Tom coming nose to nose with Dan for only the second time in their friendship.

"What's done is done," shouted Tom. "We will deal with what happened when we have to and not before. You need to stop the sniffling and crying. We didn't start anything. We responded to a bad situation. Now let's agree never, never to talk about this again, with anybody, period! Agreed?"

"Agreed."

Dan reluctantly agreed and they left the park, hoping their remaining days in Albany would go calmly but not enjoying a full night's sleep for some time.

Tom continued with his arrangements to move his mother to Glens Falls. Dan finalized his plans to enter the seminary. Their friends commented on how serious the boys had become as their days in Albany came to an end.

The incident played out with one twist neither had anticipated.

The big brawling Irishman was not missed for some time. He had been known to go off on drunks and return weeks later. When his body finally floated to the top of the river and it was learned he was stabbed, most people thought it was the result of one of his barroom encounters. Not much else was said. It was just another one of those Irish from the south side.

Later, Tom learned that his mother had taken out a life insurance policy on his stepfather without his knowledge. She was preparing for the time when one of his fights would indeed be his last. She had purchased one of those policies where an agent came to the house every month and collected the premium. Tom had found the agent in the house from time to time and thought nothing of it. However, in looking back, Tom realized his mother had little money of her own and would have had difficulty paying for such a policy. It was a situation never discussed with Tom. Dan felt he knew the answer. It complicated the events of that night.

Suddenly Dan was aware his drifting made him the last one in the restaurant. He apologized to the waiter and walked into the night air of K Street. Once again he had relived his loss of innocence.

Nine
Santiago Compostella

Santiago Compostella, on a far western edge of Europe, might easily have been a place visited only by shipwrecked survivors lucky enough to have been washed up on its Spanish shore. History spun a different tale.

Modern excavations support the local belief that religious ceremonies were held here at a time as far back as Stonehenge. Sites of prehistoric sun worshipers were found beneath the Roman ruins that formed the foundations of Christian churches. The later Islamic occupation added to the mix of religious uses that characterized early city life. The recognition of its spiritual significance after centuries of pilgrimages confirmed Compostella as a place with special significance to the gods.

Monsignor Roberto Flores had visited the ancient city many times before but never on such a mission as this one. He was pleased to receive a call from the Cardinal's office in Madrid to meet him in Rome. It had been some time since they had seen each other and he was anxious to repair personal tensions that had developed between him and the Cardinal. He didn't really understand the reasons for Mid East negotiations being handled in this way but following instructions had always been his strong point.

The final leg of his journey to Compostella and the privacy of the hired car allowed him to refresh his memory on the history of the city as a unique destination.

The legend of local involvement by one of the twelve apostles, St. James, was the cornerstone of Compostella's status. Following his conversion of the locals, St. James was martyred on his arrival back in Jerusalem. His disciples recovered the body and returned to Spain. Its hiding place was lost for centuries until a vision revealed the location. The ghost of St. James led the natives in a successful revolt against the Islamic occupiers

69

only a short time after Muhammad himself had come to visit the mystical place.

Christian churches emerged thereafter and the faith of the people grew until it was time to erect a Cathedral to St. James. The cathedral became one of the great shrines of Europe with a sufficient number of miracles and visions to establish Compostella as a site worthy of being the single most important visit in a pilgrim's life. The spiritual eminence of the cathedral made it the focal point of the great Plaza del Obradoiro in the heart of the city.

Long after it was constructed, the Cathedral of St. James was discovered to be one of seven great churches of Europe that shared essential structural features. All were constructed along identical astrological and planetary lines although they were hundred of miles apart and built at different times. How did the builders determine the exact measurements of latitude and longitude that linked the structures, years before such concepts were understood? How does one account for the fact that the seven churches were found to relate to the seven planetary sites selected by Druid oracles centuries before Christianity? After the medieval Order of the Knights Templar mandated a pilgrimage to Compostella as a required stop on the initiation "Path to Enlightenment," its place in history became truly mysterious. These things Flores had heard many times before but few reasonable answers had ever been provided.

He was enjoying his walk to the meeting place. It traversed the ancient city, its side streets filled with porticos and small shops, tourists, pilgrims and locals, living life in the midst of visiting crowds. After twenty-five years as a cleric, his legs were feeling the strain of carrying his short circular body though narrow cobblestone streets laid down by the Romans in their attempt to civilize.

He reached the plaza at noon and sat down at the main fountain, waiting for the contact. After two hours in the sun he was growing impatient with the noise of the tour busses depositing their catches of visitors amid the clamor of vendors hawking relics and souvenirs. As Flores was raising his sweat soaked body from the edge of the stone wall and glancing up at the statue of St. James perched above the doors of the Cathedral, an elderly nun was suddenly in his face.

"Good day, Monsignor," she began, her black and white habit covered with the dust swirling around the plaza. "So glad to see you praying here in this sacred place," she continued. "It was the result of prayers like yours to St. James that the people of Compostella were able to defy the Islamic invaders so many years ago."

The next sentence caught him by surprise.

"I've noticed you like to read the psalms," she said. "Do you have a favorite?"

He was quick to give the required reply.

"Yes I do," he said. "My favorite is the 25ᵗʰ psalm and the part that is most important to me is the line that goes, 'For your namesake, Oh Lord, you will pardon my guilt, great as it is'."

Then he asked her the required question. "Which one of the psalms is your favorite?"

"Oh," she said, "my favorite is the 27ᵗʰ; do you know how it begins?"

"Of course," he said, "it begins, 'The lord is my light and my salvation, whom shall I fear?' Do you have a favorite part?" he said, looking into her eyes.

With her eyes now peering directly into his and with her apparent frailness having faded, she answered, "Give me not up to the wishes of my foes, for false witnesses have risen up against me," she replied.

There it was, the question and the responses. Flores's heart raced as he awaited the next words.

Suddenly, she knelt and thrust a package into his hand. She told him to go to the restaurant at the Hostal de los Reyes Catolicos just off the plaza that night at 8 o'clock. He was to sit in the basement section in the rear booth under the crossed swords reading the books in the package just given to him.

Realizing her task was accomplished, a smile crossed her face. She joined her hands before her, turned her back and slipped into the crowds leaving Flores perspiring in the Galician sun.

He drew a deep breath, mopped his forehead and examined the package in his left hand. A sense of exhilaration came over him; at the same time he knew much more was to come.

The church bells clanged him back to reality. He was still in the midst of a busy crowd and being gently borne toward the church doors and the next service. It was easier to drift with the people than attempt to struggle from the plaza. He found himself again before the apocalyptic figures in the magnificent Portico de la Gloria inside the cathedral. He recognized the similarities between these symbols and identical figures in the cathedral at Chartres. The message of the figures continued to elude him as they had others for centuries.

Those around him began to push closer to the center of the church to witness the event of the day. Eight priests were about to swing the 120-pound ancient incense burner over the heads of the assembled congregation, as had long been the custom. With pilgrims having walked from all across Europe and indifferent to the modern concern for cleanliness, the use of incense in the past was essential to cope with the smells of the congregation. It had little do with worship.

Once free of the crowds, Flores's thoughts turned to the failures that had damaged a once-promising career. He was holding in his hands the wherewithal to return to a position of importance.

Entering his hotel room, Flores noticed that the papers on his desk had been moved from the three neat piles he had arranged before he left for the plaza. His nerves began to tingle to the intrusion before he determined that nothing was missing. After several walks around the room and back into the narrow corridor, he found no reason to be alarmed. He moved to a chair by the small window and unwrapped the package given to him in the plaza.

There were three old and tattered books, one in Spanish, *The History of the Islamic Occupation of Spain,* another, in French, *The Merovingian Kings and the Stenay Monastery,* the last, in Latin, concerned *The Troyes Fraternity.* With his background in languages and spiritual studies, Flores found the topics irresistible and began devouring their contents.

He began with the *Islamic Occupation of Spain* and found markers inserted in several sections. The sections discussed the history of a little known School of Spanish Mystics during the

Moorish occupation. It mentioned the school's collection of remarkable spiritual happenings in Spain hundreds of years before the influence of Christianity. The school reportedly claimed Christian, Jewish and Islamic scholars worked together translating major texts and using each other to reach common understandings. It made reference to a band of Jewish astrologers working under Arab rule in Toledo with information on the signs of the zodiac from the Temple of Solomon. The book claimed that it was this joint discovery and interpretation that attracted the attention of religious scholars from the Mid East and inspired the visit of Muhammad himself to Spain.

The second book traced the history of abbeys across Europe to the Stenay Monastery in the Ardennes. The account claimed Stenay had been the successor to the Citeaux Monastery, a depository of spiritual studies from 600 years earlier and a special concern of the leading families in Europe. Markers were placed at the visitations between the School of Spanish Mystics mentioned in the first book and Stenay. It described the famous Rabbi Rashi Kabbalistic Spiritual Academy at Troyes and how he was instrumental in facilitating the meeting with the Spanish scholars.

The third book was the most worn and its Latin the most difficult to read. It asserted that the most influential families of Europe had formed the Troyes Fraternity as their center of consolidated power. Spiritual and temporal powers were inexorably linked in the days of Constantine and continued as the basis of nobility's control over the masses.

They centralized their search for mystical secrets in Stenay and eventually moved the center to the Chartres Mystery School in Clairvaux. Family members were often appointed as bishops and abbots and through this influence summoned the Church Council of 1127 at Troyes. It was at this very meeting, the book claimed, that agreement was reached to launch a Second Crusade and begin a search for the treasure of Solomon.

To increase the group's influence, to provide the means for protection and expansion, it was further agreed that they would form the Order of the Knights Templar. A highlighted section presented a summary of the activities of the Knights. It covered most of the history known to Flores, the Knights as members of influential families, warriors assembled to protect the Holy Land and the accumulation of a substantial amount of wealth.

To Flores's amazement, however, an assertion found in the Troyes writings claimed that the primary intention in forming the Order of the Knights Templar was to search for secrets throughout the Middle East including the Zodiac scrolls from the Temple of Solomon perhaps buried in Jerusalem. There were extensive references to Templar centers in Syria, as well as relationships with Muslim scholars that seemed to support their search for esoteric knowledge. The Stenay documents were entrusted to the Knights and they in turn added materials captured during the Crusades.

Engrossed in the old texts, Flores had little time to spare before keeping his 8 o'clock appointment at the Hostal de los Reyes Catolicos, a converted fifteenth-century hospital and one of the city's main attractions. It had been established to care for the many sick pilgrims seeking miraculous cures and only recently converted to a restaurant and hotel.

Perhaps, I will find a cure for my sick career this evening as well, Flores reflected as he entered the courtyard of the hotel. He had made his share of blunders and realized he was now a "throw away" for men above him. No one could instruct the Curia when it came to using people and, if necessary, denying them in case of scandal.

The interior gardens of the restaurant were covered with ivy and hanging plants, colorful floral arrangements were spread about the tables, murmur of quiet conversation echoed from the stone walls. Moving down wooden stairs to the basement room, he was disappointed to find all the booths occupied, including the booth beneath the wall-mounted swords. The cooking aromas that drifted about the air were almost overcome by the dampness that one would expect from a basement room with low ceilings.

It was several minutes before eight. He was fortunate to find a chair well positioned to observe the table he needed. Flores ordered wine and cheese and opened the book on the Troyes Fraternity.

At eight o'clock, the waiter moved to the rear booth and hustled a young couple on their way. The table was left to him. He brought his glass of wine with him and continued reading.

Within a short time, Flores noticed the waiter talking with a dark-skinned man with a mustache, dressed in a white jacket, white hat and dark slacks. As their conversation ended and the man approached his table, Flores sensed his mission was about to enter the next stage.

The stranger approached with a smile, as a good friend might and greeted him by name. "Monsignor Flores, how nice to see you," he began in a raspy voice. The handshake was firm. The hands were rough and bruised compared with those hands of the middle-aged priest. A quick embrace allowed a body check and a positioning of the stranger on an outside chair.

"I am Anwar Saeed," he said, "the one who made the contact with Cardinal Delgado in Madrid. I impressed upon him the importance of our meeting here tonight. I am looking forward to our evening together."

Saeed motioned to the waiter, removed his hat and rested both his arms on the table.

With every word from the stranger, Flores became more uncomfortable. The contrast in appearance and mannerisms were memorable. His weather-beaten skin against the white jacket, the forced smile that accompanied the raspy voice and the deliberate moves, spoke to his control of the meeting. His deep-set eyes had a darkness that discouraged friendly responses.

With a large plate of tapas between them and soft red wine filling their glasses, the men began the meeting in a dimly lit corner of a very ancient place that had seen many such discussions over the centuries.

It was several hours later before Flores could find sanctuary in his hotel room and set about organizing his thoughts. He began writing an outline of what he had heard before attempting to confide the details to his recorder.

The rays of the sun crawled across the walls of his room in the former monastery as he raised the microphone to his lips and pressed the record button. His mouth was dry. He felt a tremble in his hands as he glanced at pages of notes scattered about the floor.

"A recording at Santiago de Compostella by Monsignor Roberto Flores" were the first words out of his mouth. He carefully noted date, time and location.

"The details of the meeting requested by Anwar Saeed are as follows," he continued.

"Contact was made in accordance with instructions. It was as intended, with Anwar Saeed himself, the associate of the Palestinian terrorist Ali Abdullah Teekah.

"Anwar Saeed claimed the choice of Compostella as meeting place was to be the reopening of ancient lines of communication between Islam and the Vatican and that similar meetings had indeed taken place here by men interested in greater cooperation between people of faith.

"Saeed provided Vatican library references to verify the dialogues carried on with Islamic scholars in this city. It had been selected in the past as a place holding common religious themes and with a recognized site of spiritual enlightenment. It was chosen for the same reasons today.

"The long ago lines of communication between the Vatican and Islam were closed for centuries until the late Pope John XXIII initiated contact. It occurred before he was elected Pope during his appointment as the Vatican Ambassador to Turkey. He was seeking an innovative dialogue between Christianity and Islam. In the second year of his Papacy, he looked to contacts in the past at Palermo and Madrid to expand the dialogue. They never developed as he hoped.

"Although Saeed does not claim to represent the Islamic groups who sought such meetings in the past, he is trying to follow the suggestions of Pope John to reach out to Rome. He proposes a plan of substantial benefit to his leader Ali Teekah as well as to benefit spiritual values held dear by the Vatican.

"Ali Teekah requires protection from certain elements in the global community seeking to capture him and his family. They are seeking him in exchange for oil leases promised by Iraq. Ali claims that the allegedly poor quality of goods delivered to Iraq was not his fault but was orchestrated by his enemies. He needs time to defend himself before those seeking his capture are successful. Time is critical to him.

"It is because of his desperation that he has been forced to advance a proposal he feels would help him and at the same time protect the Church. The values of the Church would be protected in exchange for a short-term sanctuary of Teekah and his family.

"Saeed explained his proposal is meant to prevent important relics and related documents from falling into the hands of Church detractors and to protect the Vatican from the scandal. It was described by him as an offer of mutual benefit.

"Although the subject of the meeting concerns the protection of long held Vatican secrets, Saeed claimed that it only would have been a matter of time before others gained similar knowledge and the negative consequences would be even greater. Therefore, to bargain now seems to his side to be in the best interest of the Vatican.

"The focus of this offer is the findings of the Vatican Mystical Study Group, a collection of scholars Saeed claims was organized by Pope John XXIII to critically examine the long held secrets of the Vatican. There was a concern that if its findings were not managed properly, it would wreak havoc among the faithful everywhere and particularly on the credibility of the Church's leaders.

"Saeed claimed that the study group's preliminary findings documented a deception carried out by Church leaders in the Middle Ages that continues to this day. Explaining this deception was one of the reasons Pope John called for the Vatican Council. The work was suppressed after the Pope's death.

"Certain books were given to me today in the plaza. They were quite enlightening," emphasized Flores to the shaking microphone. "They were chosen by Saeed to demonstrate knowledge and access to the study group's work. The first was a Spanish book on religious cooperation among various well-known scholars, the second a French work on the collection of mystical knowledge held in abbeys across Europe and the third in Latin and most difficult to decipher but addressed the role of the Knights Templar in adding to the knowledge assembled at Chartres. I will keep the three volumes in my possession for discussion later.

"To further demonstrate his knowledge of the study, Saeed described the report's conclusion that the Vatican had an excellent understanding of the value of other faiths' mystical experiences but refused to acknowledge their worth. The most important element in understanding these experiences was the Holy Grail, the cup Christ used at the Last Supper. Saeed claims the Vatican has had the Grail in its possession since the Middle Ages."

With a hesitation in his voice and after taking time for deep breaths, Flores continued.

"Anwar Saeed claims that his associates have removed the Grail and related documents from the Vatican hiding place. More importantly, Ali claims the documents with the Grail include the Vatican's confiscation of the works of the Chartres Mystery School and spiritual secrets of religious experiences collected from around the world.

"The Grail and the related documents will be returned to Church representatives upon the granting of Ali's request for sanctuary. If the request is denied, Ali will turn these items over to other groups in the Mid East who have their own thoughts on their disposal.

"Anwar Saeed is requesting a meeting in the Cathedral at Chartres with Cardinal Delgado within five days. At that time, he is prepared to demonstrate further knowledge of these issues and arrange the return of the Grail and documents in exchange for sanctuary. Confirmation of the meeting is to be made through the channel in Palermo and Madrid.

"End of recording."

Flores slumped into the arms of the chair as the microphone fell to the floor. *How much of this was the fabrication of desperate men and how much of it is factual, was anyone's guess*, he reflected. He heard the Vatican whisperings for years about Chartres and the finding of the Grail but it seemed so much chatter that he never considered it real.

There were some most unusual assertions made during the meeting. It will be up to the Cardinal to fashion a response. Is this where two thousand years of belief have taken us? he wondered. *Must men have signs and wonders before they believe?*

Feeling the bitterness of exhaustion washing over him, Flores began throwing clothes and papers into his bag. He must return to Rome and deliver the message personally as directed. He hoped his driver remained nearby as he had said he would.

Ten

The Meeting at Chartres

"Monsignor Flores," snapped the Cardinal, a sting in his voice that recalled his time as a Vatican instructor. "Must you always find it necessary to disrupt the pleasure of silence with meaningless chatter."

The two had been mixing with the crowd in the cathedral for over an hour with no signs of their contact. Both were feeling the tension.

The Cardinal's fingers moved nervously around his neck trying to find the absent roman collar. Civilian attire made him uncomfortable and his mood reflected his displeasure with the day.

Flores decided to skip attempts at small talk and turned his attention to the handheld radio describing the artifacts of Chartres. He juggled the handset a few times but he could not get it to function. He turned to an elderly couple a few feet away and asked the woman if she could help him with the same kind of set she was holding to her ear.

She looked startled for a moment, then took the small radio and held it to her ear. She pressed some buttons and returned the device to Flores. "I think it is working now," she said and hurried to catch up with her companion who had moved along with the crowd.

Watching her walk away, he had a recollection of seeing her and her companion before but could not place them. She had that mark on her cheek that his mother had. He had never seen anyone else with it before.

He continued listening to the recorded history of the Chartres Cathedral and followed the Cardinal on his stroll behind the main altar.

The name Chartres came from a Late Iron Age Celtic tribe called Carnutes, the recorder commentator remarked. It was a main center for the Druids, priests of the Gallic region. Caesar captured the city after the revolt of 52 BC. Roman temples were built upon local religious sites after the Roman custom. Several cathedrals have occupied the site since but fell victim to the curse of most wooden structures in European towns, periodic uncontrolled fire.

The foundations for the present cathedral were begun in 1134 and survived later fires to allow the eventual construction of the present structure.

Flores led the Cardinal into the main nave of the church to the point where they would both be standing on the famous Chartres labyrinth, constructed in 1200.

It was made up of black and white flagstone circular designs occuping half of the floor space and challenging the traveler to find his way as a form of a spiritual journey.

Flores noted that the radio briefing made no mention of the building's unique astrological relationship to Stonehenge or the Temple of Luxor in Egypt or other sites in Europe. What was mentioned were the remnants of stone temples that had been on the site of the cathedral long before the Christian era and the cultures that found spiritual significance in the area.

Flores was anxious to hear the tourist version of the founding of the Mystery School. It agreed with basic history, first covering the decision by a local nobleman, Bernard de Fontaine, to enter the Cistercian branch of the Benedictine order of the Catholic Church, along with a group of thirty nobles from the best families in Europe. A short time later this newly ordained group of priests established the Abbey at Clairvaux. With scant explanation, the recording mentioned Bernard's rise to the position of abbot and his call for a Second Crusade on Easter Sunday in 1126. There was brief mention of local fascination with the School of Mystics located in the abbey and Bernard was described as the father of all clairvoyants.

Bells striking the hour, reminded the clerics that they must be at the specified meeting location, the famous Royal Portal. They made their way to the portal and began to wait the prescribed fifteen minutes.

With light from the great stained glass windows bathing the crowds, Flores's device described their importance.

80

Dating from the early thirteenth century, the glass escaped harm during France's religious wars and today constitutes one of the most complete collections of medieval stained glass in the world. The chemical composition of the blue glass has never been duplicated and remains one of the mysteries of the cathedral.

The north rose window holds another mystery. Its placement creates a special effect of the sun shinning through during the summer solstice. A thin ray of light passes through a small clear panel in one of the stained glass sections, which precisely illuminates a single flagstone on the cathedral floor. This lone panel was found to hold other astrological clues hidden by the builders connecting the structure to the Templars, whose influence has been found throughout the structure.

The lighting of the floor panel was a unique feature of the windows which in addition to the lives of the saints and the miracles of the gospels, depicted the twelve Signs of the Zodiac.

The radio commentator mentioned three other examples: a window depicting the Nativity sharing images of Aries and Taurus, the window showing the Veil of Solomon's Temple in Jerusalem and the Last Judgment with similar references. No other church in Europe so openly mixed astrology with the gospels and yet escaped retribution from Rome. Chartres Cathedral was the lone exception.

At last, a face familiar to Flores emerged from a tour group passing the portal. Although he did not wear a Compostella white suit this time, the weathered and mustached face was the same as the one that delivered the news that the Grail treasure had been moved. With one hand in his pants pocket and the other grasping a camera strap, Anwar Saeed gave all the appearances of a thoughtful tourist.

"We meet again, my friend," the face began. Saeed extended his hand to Monsignor Flores. "I am glad you were able to convince your associate to join us. I am pleased to see you both. Our meeting can take place, as we suggested. If you will follow me to my car, we will be able to relax and discuss our mutual concerns over dinner."

The trio mingled with the crowds as they worked their way to the huge doors leading out onto the crowded plaza. Monsignor Flores had to stop for a moment to return his radio to the desk clerk at the side altar by the gift shop. As he did, he saw the woman who helped him with her companion. The man's face was not familiar but this second look at the woman convinced him he had seen her before, but where?

The view from the rear seat was pleasant enough for Monsignor Flores but it prevented his participation in the exchange taking place in the front of the car. Finally, a small vineyard came into view with an outdoor restaurant visible at the end of a long stone driveway. The men left the car and approached the door of the inn walking under a long trellis holding grape vines with young plants just coming into bloom.

After a few words with the elderly greeter, they were led to an outside table shaded by the same vineyard plants. The wooden tables were surrounded by small but comfortable armchairs and colorful tapestries hung from support poles separating the aisles. An outside speaker played soft music that fought with the slight wind stirring the flowers on the corner of the table.

The waiter brought a small tray of assorted cheeses, a carafe of red wine and several menus. He quietly returned to the kitchen leaving the men to their own thoughts.

"Shall we look at our choices before we begin our discussion?" Anwar Saeed suggested as he opened the menu. Monsignor Flores reached for one of the menus just as Cardinal Delgado's hand came down on the table. "I don't think so," said the Cardinal. "We are anxious to conclude our business and be on our way and have little time for pleasantries."

"That is really too bad," came the reply. "I rarely discuss business on an empty stomach. You'll have to wait for me to finish eating before we can discuss the position in which your Church finds herself. It's entirely up to you if you prefer to wait," concluded Anwar Saeed, as he opened the large menu that covered half his face.

Cardinal Delgado's hand left the menu pile and brought one of the copies to his plate. Without saying a word he began reading the offerings.

More than an hour had passed before dinner was completed. There were few words exchanged among the three men. Finally, the movement of his chair and his body language gave the signal that Saeed was ready to present his case.

He motioned to the waiter for more wine and then reached into his jacket pocket for several folded papers. With red wine in one hand and pages of notes in another, Anwar Saeed began his important conversation.

"I offer our appreciation for the talks held in recent weeks concerning the case of my good friend and associate, Ali Teekah. We extend our apologies for removing your sacred items from their age-old hiding place but without that removal we might have failed to gain your attention.

"Now that I am assured your thoughts are well focused, I want to present of our request in a manner not possible in other surroundings, surroundings that offer too many possibilities for unintended listeners.

"Our plight," Anwar continued, "is the product of a Mid East conspiracy to discredit the path of Palestinian Statehood advocated by Ali Teekah by corrupting his business dealings with Iraq. The fact that there is an oil bounty on Ali's capture shows how successful that plot has been. Time is required to reveal evidence of the efforts to destroy him and his movement. We believe this time can be purchased with the provision of the ancient privilege of church sanctuary. Not just any sanctuary, however, but recognized global protection of the highest order, inside Vatican City. We need a safe haven for a time, to allow us to explain our position and make preparations for a permanent safe location.

"Under normal circumstances, your Church would not consider any request for sanctuary involving the politics of the Mid East but the circumstances surrounding our request are anything but ordinary. I will describe some of these and by so doing, describe the mutual interests that will be served by Vatican sanctuary.

"The death of Vatican Scholar Marcel Villieu in Rome some time ago brought to light his assignment by Pope John XXIII to chair the Pope's Official Mystical Study Group. Father Villieu presided over the commission conducting the study. His preliminary presentations convinced Pope John that calling for a Vatican Council was essential. Unfortunately, the Pope died before

83

the Council could address the findings. Villieu's death revealed some of the papers he had collected for the study. These papers have come into our possession.

"The Pope's Study Group completed the most extensive review of man's mystical experiences ever collected and revealed a long-standing conspiracy by Church Father's to keep hidden essential elements of Christian beliefs. The findings seemed to threaten the formal institution of your Church.

"To convince you we appreciate the value of what we have, I will connect some events described in the Villieu papers."

Anwar Saeed turned to Monsignor Flores and directed his comments to him.

"The selection of Compostella and Chartres as meeting places are based upon the work of the Study Group. Both locations are described as having significant spiritual meaning for centuries for Islamic scholars no less than Christian and Jews. Chartres holds the key to the issues we want to discuss. This is why we find ourselves in this place.

"The volumes delivered to you at Compostella were taken from Villieu's library. They trace the European collection of spiritual studies over hundreds of years and included Islamic contributions that found their way into the Chartres Mystery School. It was the additions to the school sent by the Knights Templar from Jerusalem that filled in missing pieces of the ancient puzzle, keeping with the intentions of the organizers of the Crusades. The spiritual understanding of the monks in the Chartres Abbey eventually led later to finding the Grail and the entire treasure of the Knights Templar."

Turning to Cardinal Delgado, Saeed came to his next point. "Villieu's documents had much more to say, so let me continue.

"There are two issues that we see as the basis for our negotiation," began Anwar Saaed. "First, the conspiracy by your Church to hide a well-developed understanding of the spirit world and second, the concealment of the Grail for fear of the paths it might open.

"We apologize for disturbing your Grail but having it in our possession gives us the ability to make the conspiracy of the Vatican public. We believe we have identified significant global

84

issues that can form the basis for an agreement," said Saeed with a tone of reassurance.

"We are discussing Vatican held documents and what they say about the past," he continued.

"The findings comment on man's attempts to comprehend the spirit world in a special way. The megalithic ceremonial sites, at Stonehenge, Compostella in Spain and the area of Rennes-le-Chateau in France are shown by these sources to have significance when linked to each other. There are references to Islamic experiences and cooperation that describe a time when men were at peace with each other. There have been times when elements of Christianity and Islam were at peace with one another but leaders on both sides were consumed with ambitions much the same way as they are today.

"The meaning of these past relationships was revealed in the spiritual study centers located in the monasteries at Citeaux, at Stenay and eventually at Clairvaux. Their work reflects a thousand years of study as well as support from the ruling families of Europe. These families controlled the Church and organized the Second Crusade to possess the lost secrets in Jerusalem. The nine knights sent to protect the Holy Land were in truth sent to plunder it. They were successful in the completion of their task and much to the dismay of those who sent them, refused to turn over what they had found.

"According to Villieu records, sometime in the early thirteenth century the Grail comes into the hands of the Knights Templar with the fall of Constantinople. One of the Grand Knights of the Templars, Geoffrey de Charney, takes the relics to France to use in his negotiations to save the Templar movement with King Philip IV and Pope Innocent II. Charney knew full well that the secrets in his possession were the motive for the Crusades.

"In 1314, both Grand Masters of the Templars, Geoffrey de Charney and Jacques de Molay, are burned at the stake by King Philip IV, but not before they had completed plans to have their treasures hidden from the people who sent them on their search.

"From Islamic records in Jerusalem," continued Saeed, "we have evidence that the Templars sent documents and other material from their journeys in the Mid East back to Clairvaux from the moment they entered Jerusalem. There was a sudden and continuing need at the monastery for Arabic translators while the Templars were busy with their tunneling.

"The Villieu records contain much insight into the great cathedral at Chartres. They identify the many messages contained in the design as well as the construction techniques that were so remarkable for the time. They point to the north door on the cathedral holding a carving, which alludes to the Templar excavations beneath the temple of Solomon and a related discovery.

"The nativity window is mentioned for the important role astrology played in leading the wise men from the east to be present at the dawn of the Christian era. Our very heavens are credited with bringing together the same cultures that today remain at odds with each other.

"The church's stained glass blue windows baffled alchemists at the time and continue to do so. The records raise many more questions, which I am sure you have considered.

"Almost two hundred years would pass before the Church found the path back to the Grail. It would come through the Vatican's investigation of spiritual experiences reported in a fifteenth-century manuscript *The Cloud of the Unknowing*. When the Vatican sent the manuscript to Chartres for study, the resulting analysis astounded Church leaders, providing a further review of the Abbey and its possessions.

"It was soon realized that the monks of the Abbey had been translating and studying the documents in their possession for some time and grasped the importance of their secrets. What had not been understood before then was the extent of the collection in the abbey. It included studies from Stonehenge, the Temple of Solomon, Egyptian and Babylonian mythology, the Sufi Mystery Schools of Spain, the Orleans Spirit School and the Buddhist Black Tantric Sect. Father Villieu's comments in his diary speak of his amazement.

"With assistance provided by the monks at the abbey at the time, the Grail and its documents were found a short time later. It was located on an island in the Baltic called Bornholm, a place found to have an astrological link to the pyramids on the Giza Plateau in Egypt and Chartres. The island was twenty miles long by ten miles wide and yet had hundreds of standing prehistoric stones and fifteen churches.

"With the Chartres secrets, the Grail and the treasure of the Templars in its possession, the Church moved to conceal the findings by closing the abbey and scattering the monks across Europe. Anyone searching for spiritual experiences outside the Church was thereafter branded a heretic and burned at the stake. Protection of Church authority is the goal in keeping the findings secret.

"I have finished my discussion of the two great issues and the current willingness of Church leaders to continue the conspiracy," said Anwar Saeed as he emptied his glass.

He moved his chair close to the table and looking into the bewildered face of Delgado, asked, "Are there any mutual interests to be served by further discussion?"

For the first time that evening the Cardinal responded to Saeed's narrative.

"I object to your one-sided and self-serving view of history," he began. "Referring to ancient manuscripts and scholars without the context of society at the time, twists the facts. The church's responsibility was to protect the faith from distortions coming from all sides of an uneducated society. Some of the methods of the past have in fact been condemned but who knows what the outcome might have been if every thought uttered was granted validity."

In the middle of the Cardinal's reply to the Islamic view of the Middle Ages, Saeed called over the roaming guitarist playing in the vineyard and asked him to play "Granada" for the tourists from Spain. The Cardinal's face reddened with frustrations, as conversation was halted by the sounds of the guitar.

With the players drifting to another table, the Cardinal continued his rebuttal only to be interrupted by Saeed placing a finger across his lips and asking for a pause.

"I am not here to engage in a debate. I was merely trying to demonstrate our understanding of the Vatican's benefits in the proposal we are making," he said in a more deliberate tone than before.

"If I have made a convincing argument for our mutual benefit," offered Saeed, "we can move on to the next steps, or we can conclude our meal and I will drive you back to Chartres. How do you propose we continue?" he asked as he looked into the eyes of a man unaccustomed to ultimatums.

"Monsignor Flores," began the Cardinal, "I would ask you to leave us for a few minutes. We will meet you at the car for our trip back."

With a look of surprise and disappointment on his face, Flores rose, responded with a curt, "As you wish," and walked out of the vineyard.

As he leaned against the car in the small side parking area, Flores reached down to the pebbled driveway and came up with a handful of small missiles he tossed into the roses at the end of the walkway.

There are relationships and there are relationships, he complained to himself. He had never been sure about the one between him and Delgado. Tonight's event confused him even more than before, he thought.

It was almost a half hour later when the other men appeared at the doorway of the inn and approached the car. They were walking in silence. Neither had an expression of satisfaction on his face.

When the car arrived back at the side of the Cathedral, Anwar Saeed finally broke the silence that had dominated the drive. "We will await your contact and receipt of the signals that indicate you have begun your side of the arrangement. When this occurs we will complete our side of the bargain and the first step will have been completed. Time is truly of the essence. There can be no delay. You must respond promptly."

Before leaving the car the Cardinal leaned back at Saeed and left him with a final message. "Our contact will come when you have given signs that we can rely on your completing your task." The door was slammed to give emphasis to his point.

With the car speeding off, the Cardinal turned to Flores and offered his apologies for excluding him from the end of the meeting. "We are involved in extremely delicate matters and the fewer numbers of people who know the details, the more likely it is we will be able to avoid confusion. I must go to Rome; I want you to come with me. We leave tonight."

The two men hurried down the narrow streets back to their hotel. One was feeling much better about his relationships than a short time before. The other was burdened with knowledge of the truly global confrontation he had just put in motion.

Eleven
The Hotel Meeting

The morning provided more than the usual family time with his children. Dan found himself in the kitchen with Kathleen assembling the ingredients for the cake Kevin was expected to bring to his schoolmates to celebrate his birthday. They laughed and complained about school events, car pooling with cousins and difficulties taking part in after school activities. They rode in the car together to school and delivered the paper goods to the classroom before the teacher arrived. Their liveliness told Dan they were emerging from the loss of their mother. If only he could find the strength to emerge from that darkness as well, Dan thought as he turned from the school parking lot.

His schedule usually cooperated with the activity. Today was no exception. It called for him to appear as a speaker at the Willard Hotel in Washington, the annual meeting of The Society of Professional Journalists to describe his techniques for investigative reporting. The hotel was one of the regular haunts for Washington insiders and provided good opportunity to engage in his hobby of people watching. From his lounge chair vantage point, Dan could observe the parade of strangers marching through the lobby on their way to meet the world. When he caught sight of her walking toward him he felt his stomach tighten and his eyes launch a disbelieving stare. There she was, Margaret Mary Connelly.

He followed her down the corridor to a meeting room displaying the United Way of America sign and watched her respond to the greetings of those already at the tables. The printed agenda next to the coffee urn gave the answer, Human Services Committee monthly meeting, Mrs. Thomas Feely, Vice Chair. The allotted time was shown, 9:30-11:30.

He watched her in the middle of the room offering her soft smile to those around her. The brown hair rested gently on the blue blouse emerging from a tan suit jacket and revealing small gold earrings. Her face shoved his insides into a long forgotten corner.

Dan's panel commitment was one hour of the morning seminar. He knew he could be in the hall to see her when her session ended. It reminded him of the accidental meetings he used to arrange to meet her in their school days.

Dan found his place in the front row of speakers but was having difficulty concentrating on his remarks. The sights and sounds of the seminar were drowned by a flood of old images and failed conversations. The thought of being with her alone was making it difficult to focus. Tom Feeley's hastily arranged Paris dinner brought them face to face for the first time in more than fifteen years but Tom was a presence the entire time. His presence kept the conversation outwardly cordial but their eyes spoke volumes. Important words never came. Perhaps today would be different. Perhaps there was much to be said.

Against his will, Dan was reliving days he had tried to long forget. Without his lost partner keeping him focused on the present, he was being dragged along by emotions long supressed. He remembered flying back to Albany after resigning from the North American College.

He was in the air again over the Atlantic, planning life with a person who loved him. He realized the few weeks he promised had turned into much more but still that new life was about to be born.

He imagined the smile on her face and the feel of her arms around his neck. No more separations, no more being apart, no more decisions. Life was about to burst all around them. They would find their way together.

He worried about his own family situation especially his mother. He was comfortable with the prospect of giving to one woman while receiving strength from another.

With the skyline of New York visible at 2:00, Dan hoped he could make it to Meggie's house that night before having to open the door to his own kitchen. He could be on the 4:30 train to Albany, arrive by 7:30 and be at Meggie's by 8:00. His stomach churned with the thought of holding her once again.

For most of the ride along the Hudson, he entertained visions of their last time together, his hands on her shoulders, the kiss in the park, the "Theme From a Summer Place" in the background and the togetherness they shared.

Dan worried that the sound of a taxi across from her house would give him away before he could spring his surprise. He draped his coat over his arm, picked up his bag and walked across a street crossed many times before. The familiar old stairs seemed so easy to climb. The doorbell had kept its groan.

The door swung open and in the light from the living room, stood Billy, the younger brother. "Well look who we have here," said Billy, "if it's not the good Monsignor.

"How are you, Dan? I didn't expect to see you standing here; I thought you were tied up in Rome with the Pope thing. It's a shame you couldn't have been here last week. You would have enjoyed the party."

"It's good to see you, Billy, but I'm really looking for your sister," asked Dan as he leaned inside the apartment.

"Meggie," answered Billy, with a frown coming on his face. "You haven't heard the news."

"What news?" Dan stammered.

"That's the party I was talking about," said Billy, "and I guess it was more than a party, it was a wedding."

"Meggie and Tom Feely were married last weekend," he said. "It came as a surprise to us. We knew she had gone to West Point dances and other events but we had no idea it was this close. It was a swell day, lots of food and plenty to drink. The party went on into the morning before the happy couple took off for their honeymoon."

The news staggered Dan. He felt the blood rush to his feet and his knees melt. His bag slipped to the floor and it pushed the door open even wider. He could see presents and flowers on the dining room server against the far wall.

His mouth dropped. No words could come out. His mind slammed into a total whiteout. He stood in the doorway frozen, as Billy's words fell on ears closing from the inside out.

Finally, Billy realized that Dan did not hear much of what he was saying and asked if he wanted to sit down. Dan was able to stutter, "No, thanks, I have to be getting home. Give my regards to your mother and father and your brothers when you have a chance." He weakly picked up his bag and started to walk away.

"Oh," Billy yelled as Dan turned away, "I guess you didn't hear but my mother died a month ago. We never thought it would happen, she had been sick for so long. Meggie took it the hardest and couldn't snap out of it until Tom showed up. She seemed much happier with him around. She should be doing better now, Tom's first assignment is in Hawaii. That won't be too hard to take."

The walk down the stairs took forever. When Dan finally reached the air he was sick to his stomach right at the curb in front of the building. He wanted to be sick, he wanted the pain and the smell. He deserved it.

Jumbled thoughts were banging through his head asking questions without answers. Could he have been that wrong? Why had he not pay attention to the only thing in life that mattered? How could he have been so insensitive as not to reach out to her in all this time? Why was history so much more important than his own life? Why, why, why?

What is happening to me? Dan asked himself. *Can't I get anything straight in my own life?* The questions spun his mind like a roulette wheel. He wanted badly to drop to one knee.

He boarded the Western Avenue bus and rode it to the end of the line. He crossed the street, boarded another and stayed on it until it reached the Hudson River overlook. He wandered for several blocks and found himself at the abandoned ice factory. The grounds recalled the time when river ice would be cut and stored for sale in the summer. It was a familiar place that also had no future. For both of them tomorrow had been cancelled. He sat by the river all night. The first rays of the sun reflecting off the water below summoned him from numbness.

The inside of him had simply collapsed. Internal debate was replaced by silence. The voice that had kept him going the past few years had nothing to say. He was facing the truth about himself. It hit like a bat across the stomach.

Faced with a choice at home, he chose his mother's plans rather than his own with the realization that it would be a slap at a father who had emotionally drained the family. In the final

93

analysis, he had cheated only himself. Game, set and match for the old man!

He chose his friends because they were not like him. Tom Feely had that rogue quality. He had an aggressiveness that brings down an opponent with the first punch and a need to skirt the edges of the rules. Something that Dan could never have.

The Lou Baracini friendship had similar traits. From their first exchange on the steamship, Dan realized Lou had an intellect and a way with people he could never hope to match. It was a friendship that took Dan to places and people he could never have seen on his own and which allowed him to participate in Roman politics in a unique way.

Meggie's loss drove home how much he needed her. Meggie was now his greatest mistake, his greatest loss. His choice about her was the choice of a lifetime. The others were choices for the moment. Why hadn't he been able to see the difference?

He thought of Tom Feely's eyes taking in her beauty. He thought of Meggie surrendering to his and giving herself to him. It was painful to imagine.

He then understood why they called it a "broken heart." The pain in his chest felt as if his heart wanted to leap out of his body and stretch its shattered pieces across the sidewalk.

He held the collar of his coat with both hands, leaned his head back on his neck and looking up at a cloudless sky, yelled as loud as he could for as long as he could. The sound reflected the feelings of someone dying under torture.

It had been a night of torment. Now he must go home and face a day of torment.

His clothes were wrinkled and soiled from sitting on the edge of the river. His eyes were swollen from jet lag and the unfamiliar tears that had fallen onto his shirt. He was unshaven. His face reflected an utter anguish. This was the sight his mother and father had thrown on them, as he pushed open the kitchen door and found them both at the table.

His mother jumped up and embraced him. His father sat in silence as was so often his reaction to sudden news.

"It's over," Dan said, in a low and matter of fact way. "I've resigned from the North American College." He took his mother's arms from around his neck, picked up his bag and went into his room. He collapsed on the bed.

Exhaustion was kind to him. He slept dreamlessly for fourteen hours before awakening to reality. As his eyes opened, pain came back into his stomach. As often as he tossed, sleep would not return. The familiar tick of the grandfather clock outside his room was telling him that time had run out.

Next morning, he knew he could not remain in the house and was out the door before his mother could engage him in conversation.

Dan remembered the walk that day as "the Meggie walk." First it was to St. Patrick's schoolyard where he first told her he wanted to be with her. It was a walk down the familiar streets to her house. It was back to the scene of the church dances where he could not take his eyes off her and of course, it was back to Lincoln Park.

He could recall the first kiss in the boathouse. He sat in the tall grass where they held each other and on the bench where they drifted together with the tones of "Summer Place."

It was then a required walk back to her house and a stare at the curtains that had watched them in their first intimate moments. The window was open. Warm air was washing the shadows from the walls.

Looking at the two-family house at the end of Summit Avenue, he knew what awaited him. He didn't care. The walk had depressed him so much nothing else seemed to matter. Opening the kitchen door he found the family at the table, Maurice included.

All conversation stopped as he entered the room. His father told him to sit down in his chair. He obeyed the command. The father, known for being a man of few words, lost no time in getting to the point.

"Look at you, a person who listened to the sounds of his mother's apron strings rather than the voice of his father, someone who deals in the cruelties of the world.

"Look at you, Mr. know-it-all, worrying about saving the poor souls of the world but giving no thought to saving himself.

"Look at you. You just wasted the most important years of a man's life and for what? You could have a degree from a prestigious college and more directly from West Point as I offered you, but you knew better.

"Look at you, the result of saying no to the opportunities I gave you. The appointment to West Point, and you say no. Then, I have you sent off to Rome, and you say no again. Can't you say yes to anyone who wants to help you?

"Look at you, alone in your mother's kitchen when you should be that young lieutenant that married your friend and on your way to Hawaii.

"Look at you, a waste of talent, after years of study with no degree, no place to go and nothing to do.

"Do you have any idea of the seriousness of what you have done and the prospects for the next forty years of your life? You have succeeded in ruining yourself in just a few short years and wasting whatever chance that ever existed for making something with that warped sense of self-worth you have. It makes me sick to look at the mess you have made of your life."

With that, the father rose and after throwing his napkin on his plate turned his attention to the quiet woman at the other end of the table.

"In some ways its not all his fault. He was a young boy eager to do what was right. If it's anyone's fault, it falls in the lap of you, his mother," he said as he moved closer to her.

With an angry finger waving in her face, the father continued.

"You never tried to do what was best for him. Your goal was always to hurt me. Whatever I wanted for him, you would see to it that it didn't happen. Admit it!

"Well, you got your wish. Look at him sitting there with no education and no future all because of what you wanted. If you had listened to me, without bitterness in your heart, your son would not be a broken and lost person today. If anyone at this table is to blame for what slumps before our eyes, it's you, his mother."

Silence gripped the room as the angry man pulled the coat rack to the floor as he reached for his jacket.

"I hope you are pleased with what you achieved! You have destroyed your son!" The door slammed behind him before anyone could say a word.

The only sound came from the sobbing woman at the end of the table. She ran to her room and slammed the door.

In spite of Dan's pleading, she would not open the door or say a word. Dan left the house and headed for Tom Feely's old hideout in the park.

The hill hut was still there but covered with vines and weeds from years of remaining hidden from the world. Hidden was where Dan wanted to be. He crawled in and huddled in a familiar corner. If he had to be in the pits, this was as good a place as any.

After several hours of sleep, the internal debate raged again. He tried to be blunt with himself in assessing where he really was.

He had to admit, his father was not off the mark. He didn't think his mother was to blame. It was his own fault and a result of his own choices and his unwillingness to face confrontation. He had hurt his mother by leaving the priesthood but that path had been a shaky one from the beginning.

The events of the past four years started to add up as more than just negatives. Yes, the end result was not what he had wanted but he had been involved in great things.

From captain of a small town high school basketball team and editor of its newspaper, he found himself a player in the politics of the Church in Rome. He handled the break with home and survived the seminary years, learning a lot about himself in the process. He had formed an important friendship in Rome, mastered a new language, made himself valuable at the Vatican Council. He had learned a great deal about men who crave power.

For someone who couldn't handle confrontation, he had survived several murders and maintained his composure well enough to save his best friends. If he thought life was a problem now, what would it be if any of those incidents involved the authorities? There are times when even the best kept secrets are discovered. *What are the consequences of past events intruding on the present*? he wondered.

He had made good decisions about his health. During the return to Albany he finally acted on his emotions with Meggie. His biggest failing was with her and his attempts to keep these emotions in check. He would never let that happen again, he promised himself.

As the sun peaked through the trees into the Lincoln Park hideout, Dan felt a sense of confidence he had not had when he entered. He remembered the words of the old priest at Niagara Seminary. "Until you fully experience the darkest part of night, you will never appreciate a sunrise."

He entered the hideout in a state of depression about his failings in the eyes of others. He was leaving with a sense that all was not lost, his experiences were worth something and that it was up to him to take charge of his mistakes and make a life. He was still young and needed a new path. Somewhere, there is a place where he could find himself.

Dan remembered the next days were spent comforting his mother and convincing her it was his own choice, not hers that sent him to the seminary. He recounted for her the interactions at the Vatican Council and her spirits rose when she understood where he had been and what he had done.

The calling of his name by the panel moderator over the hotel speaker system cut short Dan's return to Albany.

Twelve
Opening the Door

Dan's presentation was delivered with his usual ease, though his mind was far from the subject of investigative reporting. The seminar participants were bursting with questions for him. They were interested in how he was able to skirt the wrath of the New York crime families during his years of exposing their corruption of city officials. His brief but pointed answers revealed a need to return to his seat. Once seated, Dan's loss of focus brought his mind running back to her.

The Albany abyss was a thing of the past, forgotten until that meeting with her and Tom in Paris. His conversation with Tom on the Champs-Elysees had been pleasant enough but the insistence on a three-way dinner was a jolt. Dan's walk back to his hotel that night shut out the sights and sounds of a city that had engaged him completely earlier in the day. Anticipating seeing her for dinner after all those years, he simply lost the ability to keep the past from ravaging his mind. He saw again the park sunlight dancing from her hair and the joy in her eyes when she saw him smile.

Glancing into that French restaurant, he tried to catch a glimpse of the two of them but came face to face with Tom and Meggie on the crowded pavement. He turned so abruptly he bumped right into them. He remembered being close enough to Meggie to see the streetlights reflecting in her eyes.

The clever things he had been planning to say fled. He looked at her unable to speak. She responded in the same way but managed a subdued hello. The two stood frozen, looking into the other's eyes.

Dan remembered how she sparkled after all those years. Her five foot two frame carried the same weight as the last time he saw her. Her eyes twinkled as they always did. Her auburn hair framed her face in small waves that caressed her chin. Her skin had the same soft glow that needed nothing more than lipstick to color her smile. Yet, she was not the same. Just lovelier than he remembered.

Tom interrupted their gazing with a push of the door. He walked over to the maitre d', requesting a table against the wall where he and Meggie could sit side by side and face Dan.

There they were, seated without a warm greeting or the words of friends coming together after a very long time. It was in stark contrast to the meeting Tom and Dan shared a few hours earlier. *It was probably a good thing*, Dan thought, *sometimes words don't adequately fill a silence.*

Tom prodded Meggie to say the first words. "So what do you think of our long lost friend?" he asked.

Meggie raised her head and for a moment looked into Dan's eyes without saying a word. Dan could feel knives.

She looked back at Tom and answered his question. "He looks like he always did," she said, turning her face to him. "Like a little boy!"

It was a hard look, one Dan had never seen. It delivered the blow he knew he deserved. It said, why, why did you do this to us? Why did you abandon me just when you said I mattered? She turned her eyes back to Tom.

Dan understood the cut. She was across a table linked to her husband and groping for some way to strike out. He didn't blame her. He never had. With a reporter's skill he turned the comment back to her.

"In some ways, Meggie," Dan began, "we will always be as we were during those Albany days no matter how hard we try to shake them. The raw material of who we were has been hung out for the world to see. It was shaped into something the world decided we are. Underneath it all, we haven't changed."

"Let's not talk philosophy or politics," Tom interrupted as he called the waiter over for the drink order. "Let's talk where we have been and what we have done. Dan, you go first. Bring Meggie up to date the way you did this afternoon."

At the moment Dan began, the piano in the rear of the restaurant broke its silence. It evoked a warmth that put him at ease.

Drinks in hand, the conversation moved along the lines Tom had suggested. Dan moved directly to his New York experiences, the moves from one organization to another, his awards for reporting.

Wine and music softened Meggie's demeanor. The tightness around her mouth was replaced by a smile. Dan moved to his family situation and Meggie's body language changed again. His discussion of his marriage and his two children coincided with a glaze that came over Meggie's eyes. During the description of his wife's final months, he sensed another change. Her arms unfolded; her head was raised from the back of the booth. Her lips opened and her eyes were suddenly flooded with pain.

Dan ended his talk about family when he realized he had depressed the tone of the conversation down to his grief. He concluded on an upbeat note describing his assignment in Paris.

Turning the conversation away from himself, Dan asked for a description of the new Washington assignment Tom had mentioned earlier. It had the effect he wanted it to have. Tom started off, the way only he could, bringing Meggie along with him, careful to give her most of the credit for their successful social life in the capital.

The evening moved through dinner and into a second bottle of wine before an awkward moment came. Until this point the music had been a mere backdrop to their conversation. It slowly claimed a place of its own as the melody from "A Summer Place" drifted across the room.

Dan was listening intently to Meggie's tales of the Hawaiian Islands when she stopped in mid sentence. The music had gotten to her. It was Lincoln Park. She stopped talking. Tom asked if something was wrong? She said she was just tired of talking and that it was time for someone else to carry the conversation.

With that opening Tom jumped in and began an account of his first meeting with the President and other tales of Washington politics. Not much was being heard by the two people examining the empty dishes on the table.

When Tom realized they were the last ones in the place, he stood up and announced that the evening was over. He walked over to Dan, gave him a hug and turned to the waiter to settle the bill.

Dan turned to slip his chair under the table. He came face to face with Meggie. She stood silently, saying nothing. He returned her stare. Words were a struggle but they finally came.

"I am glad to see you happy and so well cared for," he said. "I enjoyed the evening more than I can say. You and Tom will do well in Washington."

Meggie looked back at him. "I hope you find the love and companionship you deserve." She extended her hand. He took it, slowly joined both of his hands in hers and thanked her for her thoughts.

Dan remembered watching the cab carry them into the Parisian darkness and possibly out of his life forever. He didn't notice the light rain falling until after several blocks, the water began dripping from his hair onto his forehead. Wiping away the raindrops stirred memories of a long-ago Lincoln Park rainstorm.

The movement of the seminar crowd into the hallway for a coffee break snapped him back from the past. He realized his daydreaming might have caused him to miss the end of the United Way meeting. He hurried into the lobby and down the crowded corridor.

The conference room was emptying but Meggie had remained at the front of the room chatting with several people. She walked toward the door catching sight of Dan in the hallway. She turned away and glanced at the floor. His greeting was barely acknowledged as she tried to slip past him.

"I noticed you this morning," Dan began. "Since we were both in the same building, I wanted to at least say hello."

"Hello," she replied and continued walking.

After additional attempts at small talk, Dan posed the question that Meggie didn't want to hear. "Could we have just a few moments to talk?"

She gave no answer. She stared into his eyes.

"Please" was Dan's next word.

"Alright," she responded, "I have another appointment I can't miss so we need to make it short."

The crowd pushed them along the hallway into the lobby. Dan led her past the line at the registration desk to the lounge. They heard the news that there were no tables at the moment.

He caught a glimpse of two empty chairs at the end of the bar and asked if she would object to sitting on a stool. She said she had so little time she couldn't wait for a table. The bar would be fine.

Small talk threatened to kill any chance of a real conversation. He remained quiet for a moment. Then turned to look into her eyes. She accepted Dan's stare and remained quiet as well.

He knew what her eyes were asking. "Where the hell were you when I needed you? How could you have done that to me after our last time together? Why didn't you keep your promise to come back to me?"

The stare continued. Finally, Dan spoke.

"I am sorry I hurt you. I could have been more thoughtful and I wasn't. Not calling, not coming back was simply my fault." If it was a sin, I was given a penance I could never have guessed existed.

He watched her eyes. The clear blue began to water. A drop slowly traced her cheek. She made no move to catch it. It found a path to the edge of her lips. She stood up.

"I mustn't miss my appointment," she said almost inaudibly.

With those words and no good-byes, she left the room leaving Dan among the noontime bar crowd, oblivious to the emotions that had just spilled out before them.

Thirteen
Sanctuary

Dan's morning routine with the family melted away with Tim Scanlon's 4:00 AM call to get to the office as soon as he was able. "There is a breaking news story that won't wait for sunrise" came the telephone voice. Eileen, the college kid next door once again accommodated Dan's work demands and arrived to oversee the children's pre-school arrangements.

The offices of the *Tribune* had a midday feel. Tim motioned to Dan to join the parade headed for the conference room. Flip chart pages were pasted around the walls tracing some kind of time line of events. Tim asked for silence and began the briefing.

"I will give you the same news I gave Jack Roman earlier. He is on his way from New York and should be here in about two hours. By the time he arrives we need a plan in place on how to develop our slant on this story. Here are the details we know now.

"The terrorist Ali Abdullah Teekah and his family have been granted sanctuary in Vatican City. Our contacts in the French and Italian press reported a rumor of the move several hours ago. We received confirmation of the arrival from our sources at Langley. The party entered the country at the Bari airport in southern Italy. They were transported to Rome in a caravan of heavily guarded tour busses. Nothing goes on in Southern Italy without approval of the crime families. We have friends asking questions on that score.

"There must have been communications with the Vatican well before the transfer but we have yet to determine where and when they took place," said Tim. Turning to Dan he launched a logical challenge. "This is your ground, Dan. It's up to you to find an opening we can build on."

"I'll be back to you as soon as I can," responded Dan heading for his office.

Roman's arrival brought a gust of activity. He started with his stock reminder about creative work and not living off crumbs left by competitors. Tim followed immediately with the latest news from Italy. Before Tim could finish his briefing he was interrupted by an announcement at the door that a Vatican press release was coming over the wires.

Vatican City—Louis Cardinal Baracini, the Vatican Secretary of State, announced the arrival of the Ali Teekah and his family inside Vatican City under the age-old privilege of "Church Sanctuary." Although the Pope is seriously ill, his action is intended to demonstrate to the world his long commitment of contributing to the Mid East peace process. "The independence and neutrality of the Vatican City State offers a perfect venue for the next round of Mid East negotiations," Cardinal Baracini said.

The White House has responded that the President's policy on capturing Teekah remains unchanged. "In managing the challenges facing the United States," said Press Secretary Jeffrey Allen, "the capture of a single individual is far down on our list of priorities. Responding to the threat of terrorism requires implementation of a much broader strategy."

The managing editor, as usual, was the first to express his opinion. "I don't buy that bullshit for a minute," he began. "The Pope has been sick for months, the guys in the head shed in Rome are planning for a changing of the guard and they suddenly decide to jump onto the world stage and get mixed up with the Mid East peace process? No way! Who is this Cardinal Baracini who issued the press release? What do we know about him?

"Where the hell is Mr. New York?" yelled Roman, the sounds echoing off the walls of his office. "Get him in here. I don't want to keep getting my Vatican information from the AP with a priest on staff!"

Dan was prepared for his summons. He had been on the phone with John Casey, Bishop of Baltimore and a fellow Albany seminarian from the North American College reviewing the Vatican situation. Considerable discussions had to take place before a decision on sanctuary was made; could the Bishop use his sources once again to give Dan some insight into what had just happened? With past favors running deep on both sides of their friendship, Bishop Casey provided clues to the events unfolding in Rome. Dan was eager to share them with his new colleagues.

"There is an indication," he began, "that the leaders of Opus Dei in Rome called a special meeting of key leaders from around the world within the past week. This group considers itself the ultimate insiders. They influence much of what the Vatican considers. Most travel is arranged by the Vatican travel office. I have confirmation of the trips authorized."

"No more Opus Dei mumbo jumbo, Dan. Give it to me straight; what's going on over there?" growled Roman.

"I would guess that the decision to provide sanctuary came from the latest senior staff meeting. No other leaders were called to Rome but the Opus Dei crowd. The pressure for the meeting had to be based on a problem the Vatican was trying to manage and had to call a face-to-face secure meeting to discuss. What that problem is we don't know but you can bet it is truly god awful. With the Pope seriously ill, he was in no position to decide anything. Those in control must have been upset with some kind of situation that might upset the politicking planned for the upcoming Conclave."

"Is this the same wild speculation I have been hearing for the past hour or is this something that is verifiable?" demanded the boss.

"I know your policy on sources," responded Dan, his annoyance showing. "I feel confident on offering this information based on a long-time and highly reliable resource."

"You've heard my theory on the Dead Sea Scrolls, Dan," Scanlon interjected, "could they be the basis for some kind of blackmail?"

"With the blackmail coming from a Palestinian," responded Dan, "one might be inclined to buy your idea, Tim. However, ever since the discovery of the Scrolls in Qumran in 1947 nothing contradictory to Christian or Jewish tradition has come from the manuscripts.

"On the other hand," he continued, "the lesser known discovery of manuscripts in a cave in Upper Egypt in 1945 has been a lot more troubling for the Vatican. Among these documents was the lost gospel of Thomas setting out a different approach

106

to salvation. These relics, called the Agnostic Gospels, were the only ones ever found of banned religious literature from the second century. The texts supported the idea of self-knowledge as the path to salvation not the reliance on an organized clergy. Church leaders in the second century condemned it as intellectual imperialism. My sources tell me there has been much going on in this area for the past few years. It could well be the basis for blackmail."

"What else does your reliable source tell you about Vatican secrets, Dan?" scowled the editorial chief.

Dan's reply came from years of responding to the same question from journalistic supervisors. "Whether you are inside or outside the Vatican, one has to wonder about the collective knowledge of a powerful institution with two-thousand-year history. Little is ever said about the holdings in the Vatican archives. The silence supports the suspicions that much is hidden. From the work of scholars over the years, it is clear the Vatican has simply refused to share significant knowledge from the past.

"During my time as a student in Rome, little was ever officially discussed about such secrets. On the other hand, some historical issues were continually debated, including the Pope's condemnation of the Knights Templar, the reasons for the Inquisition and the long-term negative impact of the Crusades on East/West relations, to name a few.

"The only class given on secrets of the spirit world covered the rite of exorcism, which involves recognition that evil exists as an autonomous entity and can be driven out of a person possessed by a prescribed ceremony."

"When you get that process down, Dan," interrupted Jack Roman, "I'll send you over to the White House and you can drive out the demons in the Oval Office. In the meantime, I want to know what is going on in Rome about the harboring of a killer of American troops and how this plays out in the election.

"I don't want to receive any more breaking news from any source other than my own staff," barked Roman as he stood to face the room. "Get on with it and find some basis for a unique lead story here."

"An urgent call for you, Dan," came a voice from the office doorway.

"Take a message."

"They said it was real important and you would want to talk to them."

Showing his annoyance, Dan shouted back, "Tell them I said to take a message!"

A few moments later the interruption occurred once again. "The caller said to tell you it is General Thomas Feely and he needs to speak with you right now."

The editor's eyes lit up with the name Feely echoing around the room. He turned to Dan and with an extra dose of sarcasm asked, "Why didn't you tell us you had established your own private line to the White House?"

"You never asked me did you, Jack?" snapped Dan as he hurried from the room leaving Roman fuming.

"Sorry for the delay," Dan began. He was immediately cut off by the standard Feely approach of getting straight to the point.

"I am calling you as a friend, Dan. I need a personal favor. There isn't anybody else who could possibly help me but you. Meggie's brother, Billy, was in an automobile accident outside Albany. He is at St. Peter's Hospital and in very critical condition. Meggie called me and begged me to come home to help her. I am in the Middle East on a Presidential assignment and I just can't let personal matters get in the way. Would you go up to Albany and just be there for the mess she might be facing? You know the family and the area. Perhaps get a handle on what needs to be done. I know you remember how close she was to Billy. I've got a feeling he's not going to make it."

An Albany Crisis

With no response from the several calls to the Feelys' private home number, Dan decided to begin the long drive from Washington to Albany before the evening rush hour jammed the Beltway. Air service to Albany was notoriously poor. Driving was usually his first choice if it could be justified.

No sooner had the road become the Maryland Turnpike than Dan's thoughts turned from what he was leaving to where he

108

was going. As much as he considered himself a New York City person, going to Albany was going "up home." The hum of the tires on the pavement lulled him into relaxation both physically and mentally.

He drifted back to the sixties when friendships and hopes were being cemented. The City of Albany was a fixture of Dan's past, with Mayor Corning serving in office longer than Richard Daley in Chicago. Change was a dangerous word in those days and was spoken softly. The idea that the Kennedy torch was being passed to a new generation thrilled only those not yet burdened with adult responsibilities.

Although Albany was the capital city of the Empire State, its elected officials had little to do with what came out of the legislature, most results being determined by the machine. Dan's father's dreams about becoming part of a Dewey White House died a slow and torturous death. The political disappointment did little to dampen the spirits of the people coming of age. Rather it encouraged them to look beyond the local landscape for their futures.

In this very typical Middle American city, three friends found each other and found lives that somehow came back together, thought Dan, picturing this return to his city on the Hudson. Thoughts of home quickly turned to his first love.

Margaret Mary Connelly, or Meggie as is all her friends used to call her, was a flower among Albany's shrubs. Perhaps it was the time of life or the simplicity of the surroundings that made such a lasting impression but it was there nevertheless. Those days came back to him as the signs of the New Jersey Turnpike whizzed past the car window.

The morning Meggie joined his eighth-grade classroom and stood in front of the nun's desk. He remembered his stomach trying to communicate with him.

When she first walked down the narrow aisle, he caught a clear view that remained in his mind for the rest of the year. Her dark hair hung softly around her shoulders framing a face quite pleased to have those blue eyes as windows to the world. When those lips parted and released the soft smile, happiness jumped out at you.

109

The day they met after school was well-planned, accident creating an opportunity to talk without the presence of her friends.

They talked about their families and their hopes for the future. She grew quiet when describing her place as the oldest of four children, with three brothers. They had moved from Buffalo to Albany to be near a doctor recommended for her mother's chronic breathing problems. Her father was a night watchman. Taking care of the family often fell on her shoulders.

By the time they reached her house, he remembered feeling as comfortable with her as with his best friends. It remained a moment for Dan that stirred emotions.

The meeting opened the door to a friendship that found them together in the school yard and having time together during the events leading up to graduation. He was to follow his brother to the Christian Brothers Academy. She was to attend St. Agnes, a situation that closed the door on schooltime meetings.

The summer months found him working as a grounds attendant at the Lincoln Park swimming pool seven days a week but he had every intention of keeping the friendship alive. The summer plans never materialized. It was almost two years before they met again.

The players from the CBA basketball team convinced their captain to join them at a church dance on Swan Street. Dan reluctantly agreed, even though nights at dances seemed like a waste of time. At the front door of the hall he found himself looking into the eyes he had thought of so often. "Why hello, Danny Gerard," came the greeting from the ticket taker. "I thought maybe you had moved away," she said, touching his hand with the other half of the ticket stub.

"Hi, Meggie," he replied, rather sheepishly. The evening ended with him walking her home. From that moment on, they were together as often as life would permit.

Both were working that summer but found ways to have time together. One late August weekend the Lincoln Park Pool was closed for emergency repairs on the filtration system. Dan was released early and Meggie agreed to join him for a walk in the park. While they were on the dirt path just past the pool, the clouds opened up and they were caught in a downpour. He grabbed her hand and they ran to the boathouse for cover. By the time they reached the wooden steps they were both beyond wet but laughing at the uselessness of trying to outrun the sudden shower.

The water coursed through her hair, onto her shoulders and down the collar of her badly soaked blouse revealing the outline of her young body. Their laughter subsided as both became aware of the rain's unexpected unveiling of her womanhood.

Their eyes spoke sentences.

Dan gently moved his handkerchief across her face, blotting the moisture and hair from her forehead. She slowly raised her head and stared into his eyes. Her lips moved from easy smile to invitational parting.

With her eyes closing gently, she moved her head back against her shoulders waiting for their first kiss. She was not disappointed. He could feel her warmth through the wet clothes as their lips met. He rested his head on her hair sensing her body leaning on him unashamedly.

The rain sealed kiss ignited a feeling neither had experienced before and would never forget. Words were not spoken. They were not necessary.

Rain was never the same again. Neither was the park!

After that afternoon, their time together was relaxed and fun filled from the back streets of Albany, to the hills and valleys of Adirondack Park. Teenage memories grow fonder as time subtly rewrites old lines.

The New York State Thruway ticket machine jerked Dan back from memory lane. Life had a way of turning simple beginnings into puzzles with many missing pieces. He reminded himself that dreams of the past are only dreams. His business was to find comforting words for a difficult moment.

The Thruway signs to Western Avenue signaled he was home. Turning onto Manning Boulevard, he remembered the night he and Tom raced through backyards to avoid capture by the police for breaking a window in the McDermott house. The turn onto New Scotland Avenue was the same turn he had made the day of his surgery. There was a friendly greeting coming from the streets. At least it seemed that way.

St. Peter's emergency room was like other big city facilities, crowded with people waiting their turns. He was directed to the intensive care unit. Meggie was sitting alone in the hallway. Her expression was one of utter puzzlement. "Why have you found me at a time like this?" she said, disgust in her trembling voice.

Dan explained Tom's call and his anguish for not being there himself.

"I am not surprised," she observed. "Why should this time be unlike all the others. I have become accustomed to the role of second wife. The army is number one always."

Dan recognized a familiar face coming toward them. It was Father Costello, the hospital chaplain. They had met the summer he had his surgery. Without much said they went into the intensive care unit to pray in silence over a figure encased with the tubes and wires. In a few minutes they were back in the hallway, sitting in silence.

Along with the first rays of sunshine came a figure from the intensive care unit. The words were as expected. "I am very sorry."

Meggie thanked doctor and priest and asked to make one more visit back to Billy's room. Back in the hallway, she asked Dan to take her somewhere to eat.

The Broadway Diner was a block away as it had been for thirty years serving hospital staff and visitors. They sat in a booth and began low-key and deliberate conversation about the suddenness of death and the regrets of life. For Meggie it had become a jumble of personal problems and much regret about having no family of her own. Billy's death drove home a sense of loneliness as nothing else could have.

Tears finally arrived and flowed freely. It was time to find fresh air. Dan helped her up from the booth and out into the night.

Dan held her shoulders and pressed his head to the back of hers as they paused at the door of the car. Meggie turned and faced him. Her face had a glow illuminated from the light coming through the diner windows. Her reddened eyes looked at him.

He moved his hand to her face, brushed her hair from her face as he did that day in the rain. Her hands slipped into his. They stood there in silence.

"I am sorry," she said opening the door. They drove in silence back to her hotel.

Her two brothers and their families arrived the next day. Dan was never alone with her again. His good-bye was offered after the mass at St. Agnes Cemetery. Meggie thanked him for being with her at such a difficult time. She wished him and his children well in their new life in Washington.

Before leaving the cemetery, Dan made a visit to his family's plot. Seeing his mother's and father's names on the grave set off a flood of thoughts about home. It was a good place to grow up but difficult. He was sorry about the conflict but it could not be helped. "That's what makes tragedies tragic," he reflected. "It's the inevitability."

Looking at his mother's name on cold stone spoke of the coldness she had faced at home. He saw her once again, at the bus station the warm afternoon he had left for the seminary. The noise of the crowd around them was a stark contrast with her silence. The station's drabness seemed out of place with the eagerness of the passengers. Her eyes told him she was again thinking of her lost daughter as she stood poised to lose a son as well.

Dan remembered waving through the window with forced gaiety only to witness his mother's grief spilling out on the platform. Thinking that no one could see her, with her face pressed against a gray column, her shoulders jerked in short spasms. She was letting go all she had been holding in that morning.

His mother had died of heart failure if you chose to believe her doctor. It was actually heartbreak, a simple absence of understanding.

The name and date of his twin sister's death on the tombstone brought an old thought to mind. How would life have been different if she had survived the flu epidemic? Would the troubled emotions of the parents been calmed? Would she and Dan have been close? What would it have been like to have a sister as a friend?

113

Seeing Maurice's name on the stone without a final date reminded him how bitter his brother had become as he retreated into loneliness in recent years. Maurice had cancelled his engagement to Patsy Riley because of his plans for a baseball career. She died quite unexpectedly the following winter from pneumonia. He never married.

It was time to go and look forward and not back. He would do battle with inevitability and pretend he might yet prevail.

Fourteen
The United Way Gala

Dan would remember the drive back to Washington for its torment. No matter how loud the radio blared or how often he changed stations, his mind would not let go of her. He had been able to remove her from his life once before. Was it possible a second time? He sensed the path he was on could lead to self-destruction. He wanted to be there anyway.

The Baltimore Harbor Tunnel meant a closeness to home. He thought about being more deliberate with the priorities of life. He would devote more time and attention to the children, as well as the demands of his new work environment. He concluded that he would not be distracted by her at such a time in his life.

As he pulled into the driveway of the townhouse, his headlights caught the smiles of his family running toward the car, happy anticipation on their faces. "Daddy, Daddy, wait until you hear what happened today," chirped the voices. The sounds and sights created by lost love had blocked out the thoughts of what might be.

His determination lasted less than a week. It was an article in the *Washington Post* that caught his attention. "The Annual Evening Gala of The United Way of America" jumped off the page at him.

One of the biggest fundraisers of the year for the beltway elite was scheduled for the following week. All the usual names were found on the list of Directors, including that of the newest member, General Thomas Feely.

A social event of this order was a good opportunity to network with those locals who considered themselves insiders even if they were not.

With the military advisor to the President in attendance, it would be the right circumstances to build a more meaningful

115

relationship, he could tell Roman. Attending capitol social events was something expected of any good investigative reporter, wasn't it?

More importantly, it would be an occasion for Tom Feely to thank him personally for the favor Dan had delivered.

After allowing his mind to give him all the reasons for scrapping his resolve, he was exhilarated at the thought of seeing Meggie in a gown.

Impressions of the guests thronging the lobby of the hotel were familiar from other gatherings he had been forced to cover. The room was filled with plastic smiles and look-at-me gowns of most beltway parties. The pre-dinner cocktail party was like the others, with a thousand of your closest friends in a room certified to hold five hundred. With little room to move and less chance to talk, Dan decided to return to the hallway where he could observe the entrance.

After forty-five minutes of rubbing arms and stomachs with denizons of D.C., a gong sounded calling the guests to the main ballroom for dinner. With a hungry crowd carrying him along a narrow corridor toward the main ballroom, he saw her smile over the shoulder of a rather large foreign officer. He watched as she moved to her table. She was stunning, with one shoulder covered by her black dress and the other presenting her body for the world to see. Her hair was loosely tied along the sides of her head with strands draped from behind her ears. The sweptback hairstyle gave full display to the gold necklace around her throat. She seemed at ease with the greetings and handshakes of those around her.

Taking her seat, Tom was not to be seen. There were two couples on either side of her but she was clearly alone. Tom must have returned to Jordan. What a pity.

Dan could not see her from his table but found a clear view from a mobile bar at the back of the ballroom. He noticed a young officer was spending a great deal of time at the table. From her pained expression, the attention was not welcomed.

Dan positioned himself in the ballroom just as he had positioned himself in the corridor of the Willard. Once again they would bump into each other.

116

It was not until the official comments of the evening began that she made her first move from the table for an obligatory visit to the ladies room. Returning to her table she would be forced to see him. What would she do?

Meggie saw him in the aisle just before her table. He appeared in animated conversation with an elderly gentlemen standing in her way.

From the corner of his eye, he could see that she had recognized him. Her mouth fell open as she stopped her stroll. Her hand went to her lips. After another pause, she moved quickly to her left and away from the table. Dan was disappointed but not surprised.

In his mind, she would approach him and initiate conversation with, oh, how nice it was to see him again. Unfortunately, that wasn't happening. She was moving away from her table and him. Perhaps the game had never really begun, except in his own mind. It wouldn't be the first time he had done this to himself.

With the speeches of the fundraisers completed, the band started up and the party portion of the evening began. Well, will you look at that, Dan mused to himself. There was that same officer with Meggie on the dance floor. They continued for several dances before she was back at her table.

The officer had taken the seat next to her and had his hands on her shoulder. Her expression made it clear these were unwanted advances. *An unescorted female at a Washington party was like a baby chipmunk at a falcon party*, he reflected.

Dan now had a reason to scrap his plan and make contact himself. She needed someone to rescue her and keep the evening from being ruined. So he thought. When he stopped at the table she appeared glad to see him. She introduced him as a longtime pal of Tom's. The officer was a friend of Tom's from the Pentagon. They had served overseas together and went back a long way.

With the sounds of a manageable tune drifting across the floor, Dan asked Meggie to dance. She accepted, leaving the admirer on his own. On the floor, she thanked him for saving her from what Army wives call, "the comforter." They are only too anxious to comfort women pining away over the absence of their husbands. She had seen this all before, she said, and appreciated the distraction.

The incident broke the ice and created some humor. They were able to dance for a while. Dan asked Meggie if she wanted to return to the table but the comforter was still there waiting so they moved to the back of the ballroom and shared a glass of wine. The conversation was calm and natural and it was her idea to return to the floor as the band left its disco beat for softer tones.

The ballroom lights dimmed. The air was filled with the tones of "Chances Are." Their conversation stopped. Dan's arm moved down to the small of her back and pulled her close to him. She did not resist. He moved their other hands from their dance clasp to a spot over his heart. He hoped she could feel it pounding.

They moved silently until she pressed her head to his. Their faces touched. At the same moment, he pulled the small of her back tightly toward him. They danced without saying a word.

When the music stopped, they separated. He was about to try some small talk but he was momentarily stunned. There were tears on her face. She made no attempt to hide them. They stood looking at each other.

A smile eventually crossed her face. She came back into his embrace and put her head on his chest. He held her for a moment, then led her from the floor back to her table. She held his hand and didn't let go even when she sat down.

Within a few minutes the "comforter" was back with an offer to take Meggie home. "It won't be necessary," she said. "Dan has agreed to take me home." His smile was in sharp contrast to the disappointment on the officer's face.

They engaged in the predictable small talk all the way to her door. Meggie thanked him again for saving her from the ugliness that would have surely come from her uninvited guest. Dan then heard the words he was hoping to hear since he left the hotel.

"Would you have time for a nightcap before heading home?" she asked.

"Yes," he said, without cracking his voice. "That's very kind of you."

The condo was early beltway basic, fully attached, three small bedrooms, two baths, and a one-car garage. Opening the door Dan was taken off guard by what greeted him.

She had the interior exquisitely done in a softness and an air of class that spoke of her travels around the world. The paintings and wall décor reflected an appreciation for Asian cultures. The lighting was arranged to illuminate the various wall themes throughout the house.

He was moved by the harmony of the themes. Not that he was expecting early Albany, but he didn't anticipate reflections of cultures artfully combined with comfortable living.

She fixed him a drink and gave him a tour of the collections that filled the house. She mentioned where she had found a painting, how she negotiated in a street market or tribal village for a vase or piece of pottery.

There were pictures of her receiving awards for humanitarian efforts during Tom's different tours of duty. She was obviously pleased to have had a chance to help good causes during her life. Then she brought up a subject he had long wondered about.

"I have all these pictures of me helping various children's foundations because we have no children of our own. We both wanted kids. They weren't in our cards.

"Tell me about your life, Dan," she asked. "Tell me about your wife and children."

After a time talking about his New York City experiences, his professional success and his marriage, he became quiet in describing the battle they had fought to save his wife from cancer.

Feeling he had put too much focus on himself, Dan turned the conversation back to his moment of regret. He fought to say what he had been thinking all night.

"I have lived to know pure mortification for letting you down," he said in words that slipped painfully from his mouth. "I will regret my selfishness until the day I die. Staying in Rome and not letting you know why, was one of those decisions that come from not understanding about the care and feeding of relationships."

Rome was a waste of very precious time and hard to forget. Dan's apology hanging in the air, Meggie added one of her own.

"My decision was even stranger," she began. "It was not from lack of thought. It was done to hurt you because you had hurt me. My mother's death made me very emotional. The expectations of my father and brothers left no room for my own life. When Tom came on the scene, I saw a way out and a way to get back at you at the same time. I have moments I now regret.

"Tom had proposed to me earlier at Academy functions," she continued. "The last time was somehow different. Military life has its pleasures. I have come to accept Tom's first love is the service and we make time together when we can."

They sat, on the edge of the sofa, hands clasped around a drink, staring at the floor, embarrassed to look each other in the eye.

She suddenly jumped up with an exclamation about not ruining a pleasant evening by crying over spilled milk. "What's done is done and we both have created lives and obligations for ourselves that require full attention. Let's focus on that," she said as she moved from the couch and walked toward the bamboo bar.

While mixing drinks Meggie turned on the stereo system and flooded the room with music. "Let's have some dance music and liven up the room," she said as she poured them another round. Having cried a little, they laughed a little and let the beat of the music move them around the room in true dance hall fashion.

"Finally," Meggie said, "I guess we should start to dial the party down and look to the end of the evening."

She walked over to the stereo and with the twist of a button brought softer music into the room. Before she had a chance to turn around, he took her into his arms and began a familiar turn. They moved around the room slowly. He brought her closer to him. She held his hand and in a few moments brought her head to his shoulder. Just as Dan was enjoying the moment, Meggie broke away from him and moved to change the tape. She returned to his arms with violins announcing the "Theme From a Summer Place."

The softness of the violins brushed across his body. He felt a shortness of breath as he reached for her hand and gently pulled her to his side. She came without resisting. He put his arms around her waist and she clasped her hands around his neck. He looked into her eyes for a brief moment only to see a reflection of what he was feeling. It led to a kiss, and an embrace, that left him weak from the experience they were both having. A second kiss followed the first and her arms were holding him closely.

When he touched the strap of her gown, she instinctively resisted. She looked into his eyes and offered a soft "no" and broke away.

He followed her and took her in his arms again.

"There is a something between us that won't go away," he said. "You have been in my thoughts like nothing else in my life. I respect your desire to have time to think this over but it can't end there. You should know I plan to do all I can to make sure you don't slip out of my life again.

"I want to spend a day with you, when you can. An afternoon where we can be ourselves. See if you can free up some time a week from next Saturday," he asked as he pulled her to him once again. He brought their lips together and Meggie did not resist.

She watched him walk slowly down the driveway. He did not look back. The slam of the car door brought her back to reality. She glimpsed at the picture of her and Tom with the President. "Dear God!" she asked herself. "Can you really mean for the three of us to confront such pain? What have we done to deserve this?"

the past to contact him but never had any success. I hope this time will be different."

"If you can pull that one off," exclaimed Jack Roman, "your byline will be page one, column one."

After further review of draft headlines, the boss left the staff to the work of preparing the first of the series for the Sunday edition. Dan's break from the work was to make an important phone call.

The call was more positive than he anticipated. Meggie agreed to a day together the following weekend and didn't seem bothered about his trip to Jerusalem. He failed to mention his plan to return to Rome to avoid a reminder of the past. The pending arrangements for Kathleen and Kevin to join their cousins at Disney would be finalized and take that worry off his mind while he was away.

With the plan approved by his boss and personal commitments in place, Dan had time to address the lingering doubts that hovered over all investigative assignments. Hard work and attention to detail was not always the key to success. Often it was a slip lip by a reluctant participant or a chance encounter with someone related to a major player. His good luck in Paris came to mind.

Investigative reporting in Paris consumed three fruitless days questioning a long list of Air France contacts without tangible results. Most of the people he had talked with spent more time correcting his French than answering his questions. In the end, a chance encounter in the hotel bar gave him the lead he needed.

The gift of critical information dropped into Dan's lap by accident. There was an Air France reception for travel agents in his hotel announcing direct service to Orlando. A bar conversation with a US travel agent led to an invitation to join the group as a fellow American.

In mingling with the crowd, Dan had a conversation with a lawyer from a lobbying group in Albany who was married to a woman in the PR firm holding the reception. The Albany lawyer's brother-in-law was chairman of the Legislative Committee providing oversight of Public Authorities in New York State. It was this committee that brought indirect pressure on the Port

Authority over the Concorde landing rights at JFK. It was eventually found to be the source of questionable campaign contributions at election time.

Would fate help him once again? Dan asked himself. Would he make that chance encounter or ask the simple question that unlocked the mystery behind the sanctuary being granted to a terrorist? His schedule of interviews would be difficult to complete in the little time allowed but the key was reaching his old friend Lou Barracini. He had failed in many attempts in the past. He hoped this time would be different.

Sixteen
The Bishop of Baltimore

Waiting in the comfortable offices of the Bishop of Baltimore, the Most Reverend John Casey, Dan could not help but think of a visit to the then Father John at a country rectory in Gloversville, New York, many years before. That afternoon together allowed him to share details of his resignation in Rome and ask for some thoughts on starting life over. John gave him the push he needed to climb out of his abyss.

The rural surroundings were a far cry from the halls of the North American College. The contrast between Rome and Gloversville was unsparingly sharp. It confirmed Dan's decision to leave the seminary.

Sitting in another church office, contrasts were everywhere. The formal setting had walls and furnishings that reflected power, even privilege. The wait gave Dan time to reflect on the uniqueness of his friendship with the Casey family.

It began with an introduction to John Casey at the North American College in Rome. John was from Albany but several years ahead of Dan. Their casual friendship expanded after Casey reached out to help when help was much needed.

John's introduction to his brother, Father Bill Casey in Brooklyn, was the key to Dan's getting his life back on track. Bill Casey had contacts at Fordham University and had managed a way for most of Dan's seminary courses to receive credit toward a degree in journalism. Bill also found the basketball coaching slot and that led to meeting the woman who became Dan's wife. Bill was there throughout her illness. The Caseys remained important friends.

"Sorry to keep you waiting, Dan," said the Bishop as he entered, extending a warm hand to his visitor. "My day is one long series of meetings without any time of my own.

"How is the family? How are they handling the move from New York? And how are you finding your new work?"

The rapid fire questions came as the two friends sat down in large upholstered armchairs in the bishop's office. Dan was pleased that their friendship seemed as strong as ever.

"The family has done very well, much better than I expected," he responded. "Leaving the old Queens surroundings helped relieve some painful memories. With relatives so near in D.C., my concern about the kids has been reduced but I worry about their development. The work situation, as I described to you during our phone conversations, is going pretty well. You have been unbelievably helpful in providing 'background', as the word is used in the newspaper business. Thank you again for your willingness to speak so candidly with me."

"Dan," said John Casey, "I was very appreciative of your working so closely with Bill when he found himself in trouble in Brooklyn. You broke the stalemate with that assignment as pastor in New Jersey. Those were difficult moments."

"You know, John," Dan added, "Bill's troubles started when some social workers for the Brooklyn Diocese became alarmed at his use of strong-arm tactics on boys in St. Vincent's home. Although Bill's tough love worked well for many years, the times were changing. Bill didn't have a degree in social work but learned from the school of hard knocks. It was a clash of cultures and no one should suffer in those circumstances," he said. "I was glad to help arrange a transition to a new assignment that seems to have worked out well."

"I couldn't agree more, Dan," said the Bishop, "but you were the only one who could appeal directly to the Archbishop of New York and ask him to personally intervene. It changed the dynamics of the discussion."

"The Cardinal and I go back to Vatican Council days. I helped him then, so he was ready to return the favor. It was that simple."

"Whatever the reason, Dan, I will never forget what you did. If I can help you in any way, I am happy to do so," Casey concluded.

"On that note, John, how did you make out with your search of Vatican travel records?"

"I have them here," said the Bishop, reaching for his briefcase. "I am not sure they will be helpful. You can have these with the understanding that they are for your eyes only."

127

As Dan glanced over the records his eyes caught the name of Monsignor Roberto Flores. "I am surprised Flores is still a Monsignor. He seemed to be in the middle of the power structure when we tangled during my days in Rome."

"He has trouble controlling his temper," observed Bishop Casey. He has often said a few wrong things to the wrong people. He can only blame himself."

Other familiar names sprang from the pages. Well look at Delgado floating around Europe too.

"Wait a minute," exclaimed Dan. "Flores made a trip with Cardinal Delgado to Chartres. That is odd. He was in Compostella only a few days before that with stops in Madrid both before and after. Why all the recent trips? They were friends during the Council. I guess that continued."

The following page held more interesting details.

"These records indicate that Flores and Delgado went to Rome after Chartres and remained there during the time the leaders of Opus Dei came to the special meeting you mentioned. I am surprised at some of the names of the leaders of Opus Dei. I remember some of them from Council meetings. They didn't seem like conservatives to me. In fact, they were excited about the changes the Council was pushing. Time changes many things. John, can you tell me what Opus Dei is actually doing in Rome these days?"

"Again, Dan," said the Bishop, "what I have to say remains between us. A carefully picked group of leaders manages Opus Dei's interests in Rome. They are known as the Group of Twelve. They claim the mantle of the Twelve Apostles. They are committed to regaining the conservative power lost during the Vatican Council and driving out the liberal philosophies they feel corrupted church teachings.

"I am sure you remember how Pope John determined to break the conservative grip on teachings by actions of the Council. Unfortunately, Opus Dei increased its influence since the Council and particularly inside the Vatican bank. That really complicates matters in today's environment.

"They have targeted those liberals who allow cafeteria Catholics to have any influence in Rome. They are at war with the tolerance of secularism and relativism in today's societies."

"Before you have to run off to your next meeting, Bishop, explain how Lou Baracini came to win his red hat so quickly and how he came to sign the Vatican press release on sanctuary for the terrorist?"

Settling back into the armchair and crossing his legs, John Casey began his description of their friend's rise to power.

"All the seminarians studying in Rome at the time of the Council have done extremely well. Just look at me sitting in front of you as an example. I am way ahead of the usual time for a Bishop. Lou is way ahead of me. But Lou was different from the day he arrived.

"He came with more than just the support of the Cardinal Archbishop of Chicago. The Baracini family made it clear from the day Lou announced his intention to enter the priesthood, that their son would have access to their own power centers of Washington and Rome. At first we thought you were part of Lou's entourage, coming from New York as you did. When the facts about your meeting on the boat to Rome and how you came to room together surfaced, we understood the relationship. He was the main man.

"Lou enjoyed more freedom and received more privileges from the Rector than any seminarian before or since. Unlike other first year students, Lou was able to accept social invitations from the best families in Rome and put aside the restrictions of the College almost at will. He was sought after for support work on the major committees of the Council and certainly was not shy in taking the role of manipulator in all he was asked to do.

"Lou actaully delivered key delegate votes during the Council confirming his influence, making him an important player from the beginning. Not your average seminarian!

"Council meetings provided face to face contact so important in any organization. The issues debated by the Council forced everyone to take a stand on one side of the aisle or other. Everyone was pushed into one brand of theology or another.

"Leadership qualities came out quickly in those days. Certain individuals became recognized as leaders and assignments for those men were very carefully chosen. Lou was recognized as a leader in his own right. It was no surprise that his name was at the top of everyone's list for partnering.

"What surprised me was the relationship Lou forged with Delgado after the Conclave. You had returned to Albany by then. Delgado's managing the details of committees when the Council reconvened, combined with Lou's ability to draw support from important places, made them a power to be dealt with.

"Not that they lacked principles that genuinely motivated them," Casey added. "Delgado was an archconservative longing for the old traditions. Lou was an idealist, convinced he could influence the distribution of wealth for the benefit of the world's poor. Both were politicians first and idealists second. It amazed me that Lou would join forces with Delgado after the Conclave. It was inconsistent with the independence he had shown before then.

"Their working together proved to be an effective partnership. If you look at what has happened to both of them. Delgado is now the Cardinal Dean of the College of Cardinals and Lou the Secretary of State. It just struck me at the time as out of character for Lou, but their alliance has proven itself.

"After ordination, Lou was kept in Rome to continue his studies. He worked with the Office of the Vatican Secretary of State with a focus on US affairs. He did very well there and had himself appointed to the Nuncio's office in Washington as Vatican contact.

"While he was there he did fund raising across the U.S. He delivered substantial contributions to the Holy See through his family's connections in Chicago. He returned a short time later to Rome as a Bishop and as you know he was in the last group of scarlet hats presented by the Pope. He is brilliant; no doubt about it. He has that Chicago politics in his blood. With that combination, the Vatican is the best place for him.

"However, Dan," added the bishop, "it is clear to me, he himself did not make the decision to provide sanctuary. That was made by the inside members of the Curia and most likely, Cardinal Delgado and his Group of Twelve were the driving force. You and I both have recollections of how Delgado and his clique made a major effort to pull strings during the Conclave. They were opposed by Bishops and Cardinals who wanted the changes in the Church to remain. That struggle continues to this day. Both groups want the hearts and minds of the Church to be with them."

The Bishop's story was rudely interrupted by Dan's exclamation of, "Holy shit. Pardon my French, John," said Dan, "but here is a travel record for Flores going to Palermo and back to Rome during the same time as the Opus Dei meeting was taking place. I'd love to know about the trip to Palermo? You have any comments on the Palermo influence?"

"Not really, Dan," answered the Bishop. "The only thought that comes to mind about Palermo is a weekend trip I missed out on when the Bellardino family arranged an outing for some seminarians and I had a sprained ankle and couldn't go. They were a very friendly group of people, as I recall, and regularly opened their homes to seminarians. Lou was a frequent visitor to all the Bellardino residences. It was also a favorite summer retreat of the leaders of the Curia. An invitation to join them was an honor. Delgado was quite a frequent visitor to Palermo as I remember it."

"I remember the Bellardino family quite well," Dan mused. "It was at one of their gatherings outside Rome where I had my run in with Flores.

"One final question for you, not as Bishop, but as the historian I know you are. We agreed the move of a terrorist inside the Vatican could only be done on the basis of some kind of threat. There are not many issues the Vatican would consider serious enough to constitute such a threat. What could it have been?"

"That is a very tough question, Dan," replied the Bishop. "You know from past conversations that I have given considerable time to the study of how the influence of the Middle Ages impacted Church teaching. It was a time of extraordinary cooperation among scholars and religious thinkers. It also led to an organized persecution of those very people.

"I am sure you heard all the whispers about hidden Church secrets when you were studying in Rome, as I did. My experience has taught me that when there is that much chatter there is probably a good reason for it. The focus of external guesses about

131

Church secrets always goes back to Jerusalem. I disagree with that. My feeling is that all roads do indeed lead to Rome!

"There is one issue that troubles me," continued the Bishop. "I was friends with the anthropologist, Joseph Campbell. I learned a great deal from his work on common religious messages in cultures around the world. He told me he was invited to a private Vatican seminar to discuss medieval religious themes. He claimed the sponsor was some kind of task force created by Pope John.

"Campbell was very impressed with what was shared with him by Vatican Library scholars. He was disappointed they were reassigned shortly after the seminar but it was one of the factors that led him back to the Church. He would not discuss what he has learned. Following the conference, he made reference to closely held Church secrets that could severely shake religious thought. Frankly, I was disturbed that an outsider like Campbell would be invited into discussions with Vatican Scholars while the rest of us were left out. Maybe it was injured pride but there was something I didn't like.

"Another comment Campbell made," said the bishop, a hint of annoyance in his voice, "was reference to another outsider who was there with him, a professor from the University of Virginia, an expert in parapsychology and director of the university's program examining near death experiences. It just seemed out of character for the Vatican to offer a dialogue opportunity to someone remote from scriptural research. It continues to trouble me."

"If I was to look in Jerusalem for answers, where would I start?"

"Not in any of the usual places," replied the Bishop. "If I were to go looking, I would start with friends of the Coptic Christians who have lived and worshipped in the Holy Land for centuries and who figured out how to remain at peace with their Jewish and Islamic neighbors. If you want to take the time for a visit, I can give you a contact who helped me with my masters thesis on visions in the Middle Ages and who is a close associate of one of the Coptic groups."

Dan jumped at the offer. "Yes, Bishop, I would very much like to meet that the contact. How can I get the information?"

132

After a light knock at the office door, a young woman entered with a reminder that the Bishop was several minutes late for his next meeting. Dan rose to his feet, embraced his old friend and thanked him for all his help. "I would like two contacts," Dan said, "the one in Jerusalem and then a big one in Rome.

"I plan to be in Rome next week, John. If you could get me in to see Cardinal Baracini it would be very important." Dan reached from his chair and grasped the hand of the friend who had reached out to him in the past and was helping him once again.

"I'll see what I can do," said the Bishop, "but that is a tall order even for me. Access to Lou is to be blocked from many different directions. I'll have my secretary call you with the contact in Jerusalem. His name is Ephram Segal. If he likes you he will be both cooperative and provocative. I'll try to add another name if I can."

"Thanks again," said Dan, through another warm handshake. He watched his friend disappear down the hallway and wondered why he had been so lucky with so many good friendships.

Seventeen

Pontes

The hard to hear public announcement brought groans from those waiting in the Eastern Air Lines shuttle area. A mechanical problem would delay departure to New York for at least an hour. The delay gave Dan Gerard time to consider his first trip back since relocating to Washington. He was counting on the words of the song to be true. "If you can make it there, you can make it anywhere, New York, New York!"

He had made it once but it was a long hard road. The first break came from a summer job with a travel magazine. A staff writer quit and Dan was assigned the task of covering the opening of the Port Authority's new passenger ship terminal. He learned of the Authority's difficulty in working with the city repaving the streets leading to the terminal.

After months of digging and fighting with a new employer, he broke a story on how the Department of Highways had justified closing city-owned asphalt plants in favor of outside contracts only to rig the bidding for the benefit of organized crime families. The commissioners who served jail time had imagined they were in the seat of power. The real power, as always, remained in the darkness.

Riker's Island prison came into view as the shuttle flight touched down on the LaGuardia runway with the predictable bump and the whoosh of engines reversing power.

The short flight did not give him much time to digest the information delivered by the Bishop in the Vatican travel documents. The more Dan studied the printouts the more he found clues about what might be going on within the walls of the holy city. He had to laugh to himself at the list of four-star hotels and first-class tickets that marked the travels of the servants of God.

The wait on the cab line outside the terminal gave him time to prepare for the dinner he had arranged with his friend Dominic Bagilio. Their relationship had been difficult at first, as might be expected with a reporter trying to question a crime family insider. However, a personal friendship began after Dan arranged a private audience with the Pope for Dominic's dying mother. It was her last wish and the favor earned him Dominic's lasting gratitude. Tonight would be another of those meetings at Dominic's favorite restaurant, Pontes.

The cab inched its way down the West Side Highway past the entrance to the Holland Tunnel, bringing into view the Twin Towers of the World Trade Center and their majestic reach into the nighttime sky. The Center's office lights gave evidence of hordes of office cleaners beginning their ritual of removing the remains of the day's activities.

A quick turn down a side street left Dan in front of the restaurant. The climb up the narrow stairs to the second floor brought back the sights and sounds of the restaurant killing in Rome that Lou and Dan had experienced after one of their church walks. Lou had just indicated a preference for a table at the rear of the place when two men entered the front door, shot three people at a front table and sprayed the room with machine gun fire. Lou pulled Dan under the table before the gunfire erupted. Bullets flew around them and their waiter fell alongside them. Lou later admitted his family's preference for rear tables facing the front door and his sense of what was about to happen.

Dominic's table selection in Pontes met Lou's requirements. The restaurant was on the second floor with only one entrance. The table was in a far corner of the room with Dominic's seat against the wall. His driver was stationed downstairs and his constant companion, Mario, upstairs. The layout and the superb Northern Italian food made it one of the preferred family meeting places in the city.

Dan remembered the many Pontes lunches he had shared with Dominic and his friends as he tried to unravel the web of relationships between the Highway Department and the bevy of paving companies who allegedly competed for the millions in annual city contracts.

Dan's request for seating at Mr. Bagilio's table was greeted with a smile by the attractive young lady at the door. She led Dan past Mario to the table with another associate of Dominic's seated at his side. Both men stood as he approached.

"Danny boy," came the exclamation from the stocky, balding, middle-aged man who opened his arms for a hugged greeting. "You don't look so good since you left New York," he said. "It must be that politician food they serve in your stone city. We can take care of that tonight by reminding you what food is all about, eh?

"Dan, say hello to Rick, he will be with us for a while tonight and then take you where ever you want to go. When we are finished, he'll help you locate whatever you need while you are here in the city," said Dominic, as he gave a wink of his eye.

Rick's handshake with Dan was more a test of pain management than a greeting, a challenge Dan lost even in the best of circumstances.

"Thanks for picking dinner for a change," Dominic said. "we can sit at my window table. The FBI only takes pictures of it from the roof across the street during lunch."

Having learned long before about Dominic's desire to get business over with first, Dan explained the reason for his quick trip to the City.

"Unlike my questions in the past, tonight's subject is not about New York," he began. "You must have heard about the Vatican providing sanctuary to a Mid East terrorist, Ali Teekah. Remembering your words about the control of the country by friends of the family, I wanted to hear your take about this move."

"Danny boy," Dominic began, "you know I owe you a lot but the same rules apply now as in the past. Whether it is in this country or some other, I will tell you what I think is enough but I have to protect you in the process. If you know too much it could be dangerous to your health. You know it's for your own protection. So, with that as the first pitch, let's see what I can tell you."

Before Dan could start with his questions, Dominic motioned to his bodyguard, Rick, and told him to go downstairs and have a smoke. The big man left the table without a sound and

136

positioned himself at the top of the stairs by the doorway at the far end of the restaurant.

"O.K., let's have it, Dan."

Dan's question was short and to the point. "If someone was coming into the Bari region of Southern Italy and needed protection, which of the families would be talked to about the movement?"

"Let me give you a little bit of history, Dan," said Dominic. "Southern Italy starts and ends with two families, the Rossellos on the West and the Bellardinos on the East. Bari being on the East, it falls under the Bellardinos. They have been the family with the responsibility to defend the boot from invasions from the eastern Mediterranean for a long, long time. They were united with the Rossello family in Sicily, from Palermo. This alliance had the East and West sides of the country supposedly covered from any invasion by sea. That relationship continues to this day, so remember that. If you are telling me the Bari airport was the transfer point, then the Bellardino family provided the security but it was with the knowledge of the Rossellos. They act as one."

"Thanks," said Dan, "we are off to a good start. Who can tell me the name of the person in the Vatican who made the arrangement?"

"It doesn't take you long to put your fuck 'n nose into places where it shouldn't be," sighed Dominick. "I've told you before, background information is one thing and names are something else entirely. I know what you are after. You should think twice about looking for that information."

"Look, Dominic," Dan said as he pulled his chair closer to the table and leaned across the glass of red wine sitting before him. "This is the most important thing I have ever done. You know I keep my sources confidential. I would like you to help me get closer to the Church's involvement. I am not after family connections. Those are none of my business."

"I don't mind helping you," replied Dominic, "I just don't want to push you off a cliff at the same time. I'd like to see you again. The boys in Italy play a different game than we do here in the States. You can't go rushing in without considering the toes you might be stepping on. That is my first caution. It always has been. Slow down and walk for awhile.

"You know most of my connections," continued Dominic, "come from the North around Milan. When you start asking about the south, particularly Palermo and its US connections, you need to go to Chicago where the families from Southern Italy have ties. The names that count in that city are Bellardino and Baracini. When you talk to one you talk to the other. They have been tight for more years than I can remember. The two families maintain a very low profile with a very slick operation that never gets any press. The Baracinis have done in Chicago what the Bellardinos have done in Rome, control from behind the scenes. I have to give them both credit for keeping out of the headlines all these years.

"I'll get you a friendly Rome contact for the Bellardinos' through Chicago but it might take a couple of days. Be careful what you ask for when you are in Rome. They might not like your questions."

Dan sat in silence for a few minutes. He always had known there was a connection between Chicago and Italy, and more directly with Lou Baracini, but he had never wanted to know the details. Having his suspicions confirmed didn't make things easier.

His thoughts went back to times with Lou and the parties with the families he knew in Rome. They had seemed innocent enough but looking back with experienced eyes it was a false atmosphere. *How could a vegetable business in Chicago provide so many contacts in Rome?* he often wondered.

"I understand the difficulties with the Rome situation," said Dan. "I lived there. I know how to be careful. But don't forget I am still a reporter for the *Washington Tribune* and that must count for something."

"Dan," replied Dominic, laughing, "if they whacked a Pope because he stuck his nose in the wrong place, what chance do you think you would have with the same people? Your paper doesn't mean a goddamn thing to them. Italian police chiefs and prosecutors have all thought they were important too and they suffered the same fate."

Although startled by the confirmation he had just heard, Dan's reporter instincts fought to keep the conversation alive.

"We knew they got to the Pope," admitted Dan, "and didn't give a damn about the consequences. How the hell did they manage to get control of the household staff in a place like the Vatican?"

Dominic smiled again as he looked up at Dan. "When it comes to getting control of people, they use every trick in the book. They wrote the book, okay? Breaking Vatican security was a piece of cake. There is a screening process where they get involved with all new hires including the Swiss Guards. It's simple. Power rests with people and you have to know your people."

Dan kept pushing.

"I always thought the priests in the Vatican were real priests. Maybe they aren't?"

"Don't get me wrong," answered Dominic, "the religious side of things are on the up and up. That is why your favor to me was important. I couldn't get on the Pope's schedule. On the other hand, it's the finance and administration issues that are controlled by outsiders. The priests and nuns are encouraged to pray and consider important questions like who are the saints. The unimportant things like the Vatican bank and all its depositors are handled by our professionals."

One more push, Dan thought.

"So, who made the decision to give Teekah sanctuary?"

"OK, Danny Boy," came the reply. "Don't go there. The conversation is over. You have more than you need to impress your new boss in Washington. Play with that for awhile and if you are still alive, come back and maybe we will continue our conversation."

"Alright, Dominic," said Dan, "you have given me enough to work on for now. I would appreciate the contact in Rome you said you could give me. Would it be a problem for me to go to Palermo and hang out there for a while or should I leave that alone?"

The reply was more helpful than Dominic realized. "Staying in Rome is a good idea. I wouldn't go to Palermo," he said with some determination in his voice. "They will only meet with people who already have special relationships with them and they feel they can trust. All other visitors are watched very closely and kept isolated."

"Hello, Monsignor Flores," Dan smiled to himself. "I think we know your game."

"It will take me a day or so to get you a name in Rome," concluded Dominic, "but I am sure I can do it. Is that all?"

"Yes, my friend," sighed Dan, "that's it for now. When you have the name, call me with it as soon as you can. Now let's have that special mixed plate of hot appetizers they make just for you and enjoy the rest of the evening."

While Dan was trying to mentally catalogue the new information, Mario brought two young ladies to the table. The introductions and friendly anticipation brought a new air to the conversation. The wine, the food and the company quickly eliminated any thoughts of continuing a business discussion. *Some people do know how to mix pleasure with business*, Dan thought, as he glanced across the table now filled with an assortment of appetizers. He again delighted in his friend enjoying the ingredients of a complete evening.

Eighteen
Jerusalem

The announcement "to bring your seat backs and tray tables to the upright position" woke him from the semi-sleep he had been in for several hours. The morning sun had broken over Israel and Dan had his first glimpse of the Holy Land. Cars moving along the highway were taking people to work the way they did in the U.S. The lights flickering in houses were telling the inhabitants to begin their day just as others were also doing around the globe.

The walk down the air stairs and onto a waiting bus was unlike the US loading bridge airline exit.He was at passport control in a short time. He had only carry-on luggage so once examined, he was eager to find a taxi to take him to the Hilton. The ride to the old city from the airport was pleasant enough but jet lag was kept him from being as observant as was his habit.

The hotel room was small but inviting. The view from his window looked onto the walls of old Jerusalem. He could imagine centuries of history returning his curiosity. Thousands of eyes of invaders had once gazed upon these same walls with mayhem on their minds.

The street fair where he was to meet his contact would not get underway for another three hours. The softness of the bed called out his name.

Sleep was delayed by the thoughts of Meggie and the emotional mess he had created for both of them. It only came after repeating of his mantra from *Gone With the Wind,* I'll worry about that tomorrow.

Hours later, the sunshine greeted him as he walked through the double doors of the hotel and onto the cobblestone walkway. The crowds of people strolling past sidewalk tables and across intersections gave no indication of concern for safety. Although attracted by the open gates of the old walled city, he had been told to wait for a guide before attempting its narrow streets alive with vendors. Dan hoped for a tour the following day if his contact could recommend a guide.

The Hasidic influence of the people walking through the lanes of the street fair made Dan self-conscious. But again, he was in Jerusalem after all he mused. After a pleasant fifteen minutes down the narrow lanes of the market, he found the table that identified his contact. It contained old coins as well as old books, with a blue and white awning providing needed shade from the afternoon sun.

Dan approached a gray-haired man in animated conversation with a woman over a book she was holding in her hand. Dan could not understand what she was saying but her body language was universal. She was leaving and she was not happy with the outcome.

Dan approached the elderly man now relieved to change his focus. "I am Dan Gerard; I believe we have a mutual friend in Bishop John Casey of Baltimore," he said. "He told me he would call you and let you know that I would very much like to visit with you."

The man behind the table did not react but simply stared at Dan with questioning eyes. After a few moments rearranging books and gazing at the passing crowd, he spoke.

"Who exactly are you looking for?" he asked.

"I'm sorry," said Dan, "I am looking for Efram Segal, I thought you were he."

"Efram is my brother. He told me there might be a caller from the US looking for him today, so you must be the one. He has not been feeling well these past few weeks and stays at home most of the time. He seldom goes to his office at the university. Occasionally he prefers being here at the fair among his books. They are his children and he wants them all to find new homes before he leaves them. He told me to bring you to him when you arrived. If you follow me, we will be on our way."

The canopy over the tables was brought down quickly. The trunk holding the books and coins was on wheels, making a move to the car quite manageable. After a short drive with many turns down smaller and smaller streets, they pulled up to a concrete row house with an alley barely large enough to accommodate the car.

Inside, Dan found the elderly Ephram Segal sitting in a rocking chair listening to classical music, a small fan providing modest relief from the heat. The introductions were cordial. Dan's instincts guided the discussion.

He was eager to learn how the connections were made between Baltimore and Jerusalem. Bishop Casey and Ephram had studied together first in Jerusalem and then later in Rome. Friendship grew from common interest in history and a shared belief in the power of the universe. It was through Casey that the Jewish professor had been granted unusual access to the Vatican library and there discovered rare documents critical to his research. He was more than willing to return a favor to such a friend, especially considering his own life was ebbing away.

Dan was careful to focus the conversation on the university work of his host, his standing as a respected professor and the nature of work yet to be done. With the Bishop's friendship the key to the conversation, a warm and friendly atmosphere emerged, allowing a frank exchange to develop on Dan's topics.

Ephram was willing to express his researched opinion on questions about Christianity and more directly, on Dan's interest in hidden Church secrets.

With Ephram's stories of his research successes and failures, many unidentified doors of history opened for Dan and brought him down rarely traveled highways. Ephram's voice had the tone of a teacher and very sensitive man. It was a tone Dan had never encountered among the rich and powerful he sought to expose. He was impressed and increasingly apprehensive, things that did not go unnoticed by his guide.

The conversation drifted from Dan's questions to subjects of Epham's choosing, beginning with the Crusades. He saw those battles as a desecration of Jerusalem by Christianity's rush to create shrines to its own belief. "It was an unnatural interruption of the history that had preceded it," he said with some bitterness.

Ephram carefully identified a number of sites revered as Christian Holy places but which he felt had little historical justification for their selection. "These choices were made by the Emperor Constantine's mother," he said, "on the basis of oral tradition alone and then embraced for political motives. There were enormous volumes of ancient texts that offered a sound basis for establishing locations of past events in Jerusalem. In the case of Christianity, they have been largely ignored," he sighed with unmistakable disappointment in his voice.

"The Christian leaders had short-term agendas. They were not going to be deterred by scholarly considerations. They were working for ambitious monarchs anxious to expand their influence and acquiring the wealth of others using religion as an excuse. Constantine was a king and a politician and then a person of religious sensibilities. He was one of many who grasped that it is easier to control men by threatening their souls than by threatening their lives. And yet, your church survived the dictator, or did it?" he asked in the mischievous look in the glance he threw at Dan.

"Although the Crusaders resembled the occupiers before them," continued Ephram, "they had a purpose in their madness. Once inside Jerusalem, they turned over the most important site to the Knights Templar, who then controlled what had been the location of Solomon's temple. Within a year, the Chartres Mystery School was working with Islamic translators on new Templar discovered documents from Jerusalem.

"I have personally found Islamic texts that make reference to the documents the translators used. When Jerusalem fell once again, tunnels were discovered under the temple. No one really knows what the Templars found or sent back to Europe in those early years but there is evidence that it was important."

Turning his comments back to the time of the crucifixion, Ephram offered his thoughts on the culture of the people of Jerusalem. "The ancient history of Jerusalem was well known by all its inhabitants," he said. "The early followers of Christ were aware of the potential for future conflict and the associated looting that would be carried out by the victors. They knew that important relics left by their leader had to be moved to a place of utmost safety. History proved them right. By AD 73 the Romans had virtually leveled the city. Similar upheavals would occur before the Crusaders appeared before its walls."

Ephram moved to address Dan's questions concerning the Grail. "After years of research and more importantly, reflection,

I have my own opinion on the plight of your Holy Grail. I have seen enough evidence to conclude that Joseph of Arimathea took the cup of the Christ with him when he went to Asia Minor a short time after the crucifixion.

"Joseph was a well-established merchant and aware of the dangers Jerusalem would face in the future. He would be careful not to leave anything of religious value behind. At the time, such artifacts had value only to him and it was wise to move them to a new location.

"There is considerable evidence that Joseph also took a cloth with the image of Christ on it. Early oral tradition confirmed the existence of such an image and my manuscript research supports that assumption. The cloth image and the cup are the artifacts actually mentioned by name in a variety of ancient manuscripts and confirm their existence beyond oral tradition," added Ephram.

"A village in modern Turkey was selected by Joseph as the place of safety for the items he considered sacred. It was called Edessa but also referred to as Breton and for this reason many thought it was a reference to France or later England. That was never the case. When I searched early Islamic texts, there were several clear references to the village of Edessa and its unusual holdings," said Ephram, a slight smile crossing his face.

"Some sources traced the original image cloth of Joseph to the tomb of Christ, others had it from women along the way to the crucifixion. Wherever it came from, there are more than enough ancient sources to establish the existence of a sacred cloth picture, as far as I am concerned. The cup of Christ, remarkably, doesn't receive full mention until some time after the image. Whether the image is your Shroud of Turin, I do not know, but an image on cloth is a fact.

"The Grail's importance," continued Ephram, "begins when strange events are reported in and around its hiding place. Local priests are said to have unusual powers over the people. These so-called powers are described in terms of near death experiences and visions of the spirit world and correspond with descriptions in Islamic manuscripts.

"I made other vision comparisons myself," Ephram said in a tone of authority, "and there are strange similarities that make one wonder why the Almighty doesn't speak more clearly. From what I have observed, I often find more relevance in my thoughts when I go outside my own Jewish tradition. Perhaps the more men speak with each other the more they hear what God has to say.

"Research has shown me that history is written by men, human beings' with personal agendas. They elected what to record and what to ignore. In some cases, the recordings of true historians are beneficial.

"In his work *War of the Jews,* the Romanized Jewish historian, Flavius Josephus, describes Solomon's Temple and its innermost sanctuary, The Holy of Holies. It was draped in a Babylonian curtain embroidered with bright colors and the figures of the Zodiac. There were candlesticks representing seven planets, a table of twelve loaves representing the Zodiac, an altar with thirteen spices for incense but no mention of the Ark of the Covenant."

Dan was taken by the details of Ephram's research and his use of Islamic texts for cross referencing. It was curious to Dan that manuscripts first concentrated on the image on the cloth and only later turned to the more famous Holy Grail.

Recalling his studies in Rome, Dan never heard of the reports concerning the group of local priests in Asia Minor who held unusual power over the people linked to the Grail. *Ephram's connection to other mystical events takes the story to a new level,* Dan thought.

After standing during his discourse, Ephram had to return to the comfort of the rocking chair by the small window. He was weary from the long conversation.

"All the local references to the image on the cloth," Ephram continued, "and the Grail itself, ended when the Crusaders sacked Constantinople. The reports of mystic experiences in Turkey also end around this same time.

"The removal of many treasures by the Crusaders is an historic fact. What constituted the treasure is another question but all the looted items were taken back to Europe. I think it is safe to assume that what they found went with them if it hadn't been sent back earlier.

146

"I have concluded," Ephram said with a new tone in his voice, "that the Crusaders involved with the sack of Constantinople took possession of both the Image and the Grail, not those who sacked Jerusalem. This means, the Grand Knight of the Templars himself, was the one most likely to have had control of the items when they returned to Europe."

Ephram walked across the room to a standing dust-covered cabinet where he removed an old map of the world heavily covered with pencil drawings over the ink outlines. He opened it up on a small table in the center of the room and continued his explanation.

"I have been asked on many occasions to express an opinion on where the treasure accumulated by the Crusaders was hidden once relocated to Europe. This map shows the location of the areas most often mentioned by serious researchers. Rosslyn Castle in Scotland, as the home of the Knights Templar, has always been a focal point with the hidden caves on Oak Island in Nova Scotia a possible spot for treasure seekers. This map shows these locations with notations from various documents describing the transfer. It all fits together too well. Any secret with this many clues was never intended to be kept for long. I have concluded, these locations should be considered with great skepticism.

"In my research," continued Ephram, "it is the unintended clues that are the real ones. Clues neatly assembled are inevitably false and intended only to distract.

"I have discounted the North American sites for this reason. My research shows Yugoslavia as the most probable location, as noted here on the map. My research, although unorthodox, shows that the Knights Templar separated the relics from their accumulated treasure and deliberately kept the two apart. They put little trust in Kings and even less in Popes.

"The Knights were the tool of powerful aristocratic families across Europe who already had in their possession a collection of religious artifacts from around the world. The Crusades were started to add to these collections. The Grail and the cloth image, of course met these objectives.

"It is difficult for men of the twentieth century to comprehend the sense of power that possession of relics gave to the

147

possessors. We have no comparable source of visual omnipotence. Wielding relics as weapons raised men to an almost divine status. This was blasphemy of the highest conceivable order. Today nuclear weapons are little more than a means to induce suicide.

"The Knights Templar were shrewd enough to keep the relics from power brokers. They were ahead of their time as politicians and businessmen. They understood the value of what they had and tried to use it to their advantage.

"Although the Templars had succeeded in acquiring the treasure their backers wanted, they lost their support when they refused to turn over their find and eventually fell prey to the king of France and the Pope. At this point the trail becomes difficult to follow."

Moving to the chair next to Dan, Ephram sat down and removed his glasses, pressing his thumb and forefinger into the depressions made in his nose by the well-worn frames. "I have to provide you with some very painful personal insights into the frailties of your institutional church," he said.

"The power to control hearts and minds through promises about the afterlife is an attractive feature of your church. We Jews have never been used that way. We have been abused many times but never used by those in power to control the minds of others.

"Your concern is where you should look next to answer your questions about the secrets of the Vatican," offered Ephram. "Look to Chartres Cathedral and the ancient work of its Mystery School. My research has found evidence that there were secret societies in existence at the time of the Crusades that included many of the families of Europe interested in power and wealth. They held collections of religious secrets from cultures around the world including practices described in Egyptian temples. They were fascinated with the heavenly linkages between Stonehenge, the Pyramids and the signs of the zodiac on the veil of Solomon's Temple. The Chartres history provides clues to all of these.

"The Mystery School established at Chartres was organized by one of these groups to consolidate its holdings and continue its efforts to expand their knowledge. It was this school that was used to support the Knights Templar and urge religious leaders to demand the Crusades.

"St. Bernard of Clairvaux, the leader of the Abbey at Chartres and a great mystic in his own right, was a pawn of these groups, in much the same way the Knights Templar were a front for them.

"I made these conclusions," said Ephram, "only after years of effort and in many cases I don't have the depth of proof that researchers demand to see. I do have enough evidence though to be comfortable myself in these views."

Dan rose from his chair and walked across the room to an old organ obviously not in good repair. Turning to Ephram, he asked, "How do you separate the good intentions of so many religious leaders from the desires of those manipulating them for dubious purposes?"

"Not an easy question," responded Ephram. "Unaccountable human institutions controlled by a few should always raise such questions but never do. Questioners are more interested in their skins than the truth.

"They should question the powerful about motives and intentions that disrupt the lives of so many others. Universities fall into this category and unless they are modernized they will not survive the scrutiny of new generations of scholars. Your Church, my friend, is the best example of an unaccountable large institution that rarely conducts an investigation of its actions. It urges the examination of consciences but fails to examine its own. What do they say about pearl merchants? They sell but don't wear? Indeed!

"This lack of accountability became even more obvious to me when I was visited by a Vatican study team that came to Jerusalem some years ago. They were working with the Pontifical Biblical Institute, a group I had collaborated with locally on a variety of issues. Their research was focused on a collection of manuscripts held in the Vatican library for hundreds of years.

They asked many questions but were most interested in my research connected with the Chartres Mystery School," continued Ephram. "They came to me based upon the work I had done in the Vatican through Bishop Casey. Their time with me was presented in a way to let me know that the church had something special in its possession. They were serious men seeking to understand about a long held deception.

"I had a very interesting exchange of ideas that few historians ever have," added Ephram in a satisfied tone. "I was pleased to be included in their work but was never told if my contribution was of help. They never followed up the visit in the way they promised. Perhaps they were prevented by higher authority."

Dan pressed Ephram to summarize his recollections of the visit. "What was the most unusual issue they discussed during their stay?"

"One of our most interesting conversations," answered Ephram, "was about their records of joint religious studies in the Middle Ages and how so much of that work had been suppressed. The Vatican does not have much of a reputation for coordinated research with other denominations so their interest was truly noteworthy."

Ephram again removed his glasses, and gazing out his small window, gave his sense of Dan's probing. "The conversations with my scholarly visitors gave me a feeling that they were trying to comprehend the significance of a large amount of newly discovered material and it was related to the Grail and the Knights' treasure. I learned long ago that my feelings are often more reliable than my research."

At this point Dan felt compelled to interrupt the discourse the elderly man was so intent on delivering. "You have no proof, but instinct tells you that the Grail, or something as significant, has been in Church hands for years?" asked Dan.

"As a researcher," responded Ephram, "perhaps it is something to be rejected. As a man of history, I see signs that say it's probable!"

The discourse was interrupted by Ephram's brother delivering two glasses of wine and a small plate of cheese and fruit to men deeply engrossed in historic mysteries. As the two paused to take advantage of the break encouraged by the brother, Ephram's mood and tone changed.

"The conclusion of all this, my friend," Ephram said, "is that even today, your Church is in the hands of men seeking power and influence through the ability of its leadership to control the hearts and minds of the people. If you are seeking the source of the blackmail that would result in the church granting sanctuary, look to the secrets of the Vatican and their connection to the Grail. Then look closely at those who control the Vatican money. History has shown those two matters have the greatest potential of corrupting the hearts and souls of even the best men.

"I can tell you where not to look," Ephram grunted. "Don't follow the path of the frequently mentioned Jerusalem Scrolls or the more popular theory about the bloodline of Christ. The press delights in these stories but there is little historical support in either case. The bloodline theory suddenly appears on the scene all at once, with so-called documentation, neatly assembled to prove its point. History never reveals itself in this fashion. Never!

"Giving the nobility of Europe a blood connection to the divinity of Christ is so typical of the praising of the royal families in the Middle Ages as to be a reason to dismiss it altogether. Now we see it for what is was at the time. A political ploy designed to flatter the class in power to gain favor. Just look at the name "Holy Roman Empire" and you start to understand the nature of politics. Even if it had been Roman and an empire, it most assuredly never was "holy" by any stretch of the imagination.

"The bloodline Grail story is consistent with a similar ploy of the Church itself around the same time. It is now referred to as the declaration of the Divine Right of Kings. A proclamation that since nobility came down from generation to generation, it was God's plan that they should be the ones chosen to rule the people. God's will must therefore be obeyed or else. To think ruling one's self would be sinful. How convenient."

Along with the setting sun, Ephram's eyes had difficulty remaining open and his voice became softer and softer. Dan thanked him for his willingness to share so many of his views and after giving the old man an embrace, climbed back into the car and began his journey back to the hotel. The city was in early darkness and the array of lights and noise from adjacent residences provided the defining character of the evening.

As Dan got out of the car at his hotel, Ephram's brother gave him the name of Ephram's choice of guide for his tour the next day.

Before entering the hotel lobby, Dan's eyes caught a glimpse of colored lights flashing along the walls of the old city. As he walked closer to investigate, he learned it was a "festival of lights" presentation. The event was staged to be an evening of music, light displays and commentary on the history of the walls themselves. Dan purchased a ticket and found himself a stone bench seat directly beneath the window of his hotel room. He watched the colored lights dance like lost spirits across the walls of the old city as the comments of the old scholar coursed through his mind.

His tour began the next day with a visit inside old Jerusalem, walking the streets that great men before him had chosen and visiting sites he had been told the night before were not completely authentic. After the city, the guide's car drove well into the countryside to visit Masada, King Herod's mountaintop fortress. Masada had been the refuge of the Jewish survivors of the sack of Jerusalem in AD 73. They were able to hold off a Roman army for months from the fortification before all committed suicide rather than become the slaves of the Romans. Seeing the remains of the Roman campsites still visible from the walls of Masada, brought home to Dan the reality of the conflict people have endured across the ages. When might Jew and Arab bid their neighbor's "Peace"!

The day ended with dinner at a small restaurant following a walking tour of the more modern portions of the city. Although the significance of the many points of interest could not be ignored, Dan was struck by the all too visible presence of armed soldiers on almost every street. The sight of their guns reminded him that thousands of years of conflict were not yet over for Jerusalem's inhabitants. They remain in the path of conflict.

The next morning's security check at the airport was the most thorough Dan had ever experienced. He was pleased to cooperate.

The Alitalia flight was loaded and airborne in short order. As much as Dan wanted to continue completing his notes on the visit with Ephram, his mind kept jumping ahead to Rome. His last time in the city he had left a disappointed Lou standing in the driveway of the North American College. Almost simultaneously he was painting a mental picture of Meggie waiting for him in Albany. *I turned my back on her. Lou turned his back on me. How the world had turned,* he thought! There are indeed painful symmetries!

Nineteen
Return to Rome

Instructions to fasten seat belts and return tray tables to their upright position awoke Dan from the nap he had fallen into toward the end of the flight from Israel. He was disappointed to find a cloud cover blocking his view of the Eternal City as the plane descended into its approach pattern. The cab ride to the hotel was more exciting than the plane ride, the cab fare more like ransom than payment for service.

The staff at the Villa Medici Hotel by the Spanish Steps offered a warm welcome to the jetlagged visitor. Dan's first item of business was to call Monsignor Cartwright in the States to learn if he had received his message. Luck was with him and Cartwright answered the call himself.

"It is good to hear from you again," he began. "The last time we talked you were still in New York and engaged in your usual digging for a story. I was surprised to hear your message about a return to Rome and the need for contacts, especially with Lou. I thought your past relationship with Lou would have made a direct contact easy for you. In any event, I've made some calls on your behalf to the Cardinal's staff and they said they would be expecting you. I have a personal contact in the history department at the Gregorian University and he has agreed to meet with you. I've sent a fax to your hotel so you should be able to have all the names and numbers almost immediately."

"Allan," responded Dan, "thanks for acting so quickly on my message and helping me out the way you have done so often in the past. I can't begin to tell you how much I appreciate our friendship. You might find it hard to believe but I haven't talked to Lou since I left the North American College all those many years ago. I would like very much to see him on my first trip back to Rome.

"In saying the words Rome to you," Dan laughed, "it seems strange to talk with you back in the States and my body over

154

here. I remember finding you such an interesting person with your stories about growing up in Oklahoma and riding the open range. The kid from the Northeast thought riding horses was just in the movies."

"Dan, I never forgot your kindness to me in those days," answered Cartwright. "Especially the time I had to cope with a broken leg and hobble around Rome to make classes. You were one of the few who made sure I had help and gave me the benefit of much of your own lecture notes. With the passing of time, those acts of kindness become more and more important."

"If I can't find your fax in the next few minutes," concluded Dan, "I will call you right back. I hope you can stay at this number for awhile."

With the contact information from Cartwright's fax, the numbers left by Dominic and Bishop Casey, Dan knew his time in Rome was going to be productive. His schedule now had the names and places spelled out.

The first contact was a breakfast meeting with Dominic's contact with the Rossello family, one Victoria Tomaselli. His recommendations in the past had been a great help and he was praying this time would not be an exception. The second contact was a lunch with Monsignor Tom Carterelli, a friend of Bishop Casey's now working at the Vatican Bank. The third meeting was to be with the history professor from the Gregorian University. Dan was saving the most important for the end of the day, his face to face with Louis Cardinal Baracini.

The breakfast meeting at the Gusto Restaurant was a short walk from his hotel. The sights and sounds of an awakening Rome were making the visit a comfortable one. The day became even more comfortable when a stunning woman sat down across from him and introduced herself as Dominic's friend Victoria. It was to be her responsibility to create a memorable experience while he was in Rome. Dan found her embarrassingly beautiful but probably unlikely to contribute significant background for the crisis at hand.

"Mr. Gerard, I hope you have found your stay in Rome pleasant so far and will let me arrange a schedule for you," she said using her right hand to brush away the soft blonde hair covering

155

her dark eyes. "If there is anything I can do for you, all you have to do is ask and it will happen," added Victoria as she crossed her legs against the table.

"Thank you, Victoria," Dan replied. "I have never had a more generous offer. I am sorry to say that I am scheduled to return to the US late tomorrow and haven't much time but there is one detail in my schedule you might be able to help correct. I am looking for someone who has been schooled in Italian history and could school me in the Sicilian influence across Southern Italy. If they had that background I would want to ask how that influence has shown itself in biblical studies at the Vatican." Dan explained his long held interest in Church history and his personal investigation of medieval secrets that were the basis for the article he was preparing for his paper back in Washington.

"Do you know anyone," Dan asked, "who might have university connections or working experience with biblical records in the Vatican library?"

He let the question slowly roll across the table so he could watch her eyes for a reaction.

"Well," Victoria said, taking her hands from her lap and grasping the water glass for a distraction. "I really don't know much about history. I spend my time reflecting on the benefits of the present."

"I didn't think you would have the details," said Dan, "but I was hoping you would know someone who would. Would you know anyone who has a reputation as an archaeologist?"

The stiff body language continued, as Victoria struggled for words.

"I am sure we can find someone to help you," she said. "How much longer will you be in Rome?"

"Unfortunately," said Dan, "as I mentioned, I am returning home tomorrow but would very much like a contact who might be able to give me the details I need for my research, and perhaps be willing to stay in touch with me as I develop my story."

If there was any benefit to keeping track of Dan's story, here was a chance to make that linkage. *Would she think maintaining contact was important?* he wondered.

"Where are you staying while you are here?" Victoria asked.

"At the Villa Medici Hotel by the Spanish Steps," Dan replied. "Here is the telephone number. If anyone could call me by the end of the day, I would appreciate it."

"Let me make a few phone calls for you, Dan," said Victoria, "and perhaps we can arrange a meeting for you early in the morning." With that, she left the table and disappeared into the rear of the restaurant.

In minutes Victoria returned to the table. "I am sure we will have a meaningful historical person able to join you for breakfast in the morning," she said while gently grasping his right hand.

"I don't know how to thank you for your help," said Dan.

"If you can't think of a new way," replied Victoria, "I am sure I can come up with a few suggestions, the next time you are in Rome."

The two parted in front of the restaurant and Dan had a difficult time turning away from her graceful strut into the crowd. He felt he had salvaged a meeting that looked like it would not help much with supplying information. He headed back to the hotel to reconnect with Washington.

Tim Scanlon detailed the unusual amount of information coming in from their sources around the world. Jack Roman wanted Dan back in DC at the first possible moment to review the information pouring in and brief the staff on the findings from his trip. Dan explained his schedule for the next twenty-four hours and hoped to be back in the office late the next night.

With the tedious call to the office ended, Dan made the scheduled call to his niece and the children on their tour of Disney in Orlando. Their voices were filled with excitement, detailing the shared experiences with their cousins and with sincere expressions about missing him. It stood in contrast to the school problems both Kathleen and Kevin had so painfully described to him during their last nighttime session.

He very poignantly missed a partner at home holding down the fort while he was away. Once again, Dan had to face the implications of forced choices about where he should spend his precious time. He was thankful this was to be his last day away from home. He wanted badly to return to the family.

The restaurant meeting place specified for the mid day appointment was not familiar to the hotel concierge but the cab driver seemed to know the area. It was in the residential section of Testaccio, one of the working class neighborhoods of Rome cluttered with apartment houses and little sign of tourist establishments. The cab driver left Dan off at the given address but it was only after approaching the building from the sidewalk that he was then able to find stairs down to the entrance to the restaurant.

The basement door opened into a cavern-like corridor which in turn led into a catacomb-shaped room with low ceiling panels hanging over groups of tables, creating a sense of closeness and warmth. The staff was very friendly but did not appear to speak English. This was clearly a local favorite not found in the guidebooks.

When Dan mentioned Monsignor Carterelli's name, he was led to an unoccupied corner rear table. Within moments, a tall lean man with a receding blond hairline, came in the door, dressed in clerical black and the standard white collar. He embraced the staff, offering smiles and banters in Italian. He made his way to the rear table and introduced himself as Monsignor Tom Carterelli, a friend of Bishop Casey's and host of the lunch. Dan responded with the usual small talk. Both men seated themselves against the wall looking out across a busy lunchtime crowd.

Before the introductions were concluded, a waiter arrived with an unusually tall frosted glass placing it carefully before Carterelli filling it to the top with a martini and dropping in several olives. After appreciative comments in Italian, Monsignor Carterelli turned to Dan with an explanation of the ritual.

"I come here quite often," he said. "I have an apartment several blocks away and they have come to know my likes and dislikes. They take good care of me. Will you join me in a drink?"

"I'll just have a glass of wine," responded Dan.

Once learning of Dan's time at the North American College, Monsignor Carterelli wanted to discuss the days in Rome they had both experienced as seminarians. They had many of the same memories even though Carterelli was guided through the various universities by the Italian equivalent of the North American College at a time several years after Dan's.

It wasn't long before Tom asked Dan about his decision to give up his studies for the priesthood. "Tell me," asked Carterelli, "how were you able to disconnect from the grip of Holy Mother Church when still so young and foolish?"

By the time Dan finished his well-rehearsed story of why he left, a second martini was being delivered in a new frosted glass to the smiling face across the small table.

"Tom," said Dan, "where exactly are you in the Vatican, what do you do and how did you come to know Bishop Casey?"

"Not many people ask me questions about myself these days," Carterelli began, "I will be glad to give you the long version. More than that, I feel we have climbed some common mountains that make us seem like brothers. For once I can be frank.

"Like many fine young Italian boys," laughed Carterelli at the end of his second frosted glass, "I was sure I had a vocation to work in God's vineyard and help the less fortunate of our world. I was the second son in a well-to-do Italian family and of course, the second son is an expendable item. Giving a family member to Mother Church is considered an Italian obligation and a good thing, so off I went at an early age.

"By the time I found myself in Rome finishing my studies, I was hooked. There was no way I could walk away and disgrace the family no matter how many doubts I had in my mind. That is why I want to hear more of how you came to break away from the force that held me so tightly. I find your will power admirable," he sighed. "I just didn't have it in me and I have lived to regret the outcome, some times more than others."

What is it about family placement? Dan thought. *Lou was the second son in an Italian family and he was the second son in an Irish family. What does it mean anyway?*

Dan signaled the waiter they were ready to order as Carterelli continued.

"I was quite happy at first with the way life was coming together after ordination. It was when I asked about continuing my education that reality struck me. Rather than allow me to study for a degree in social work, as I requested, Mother Church sent me to earn a degree in finance at Columbia.

"I was given John Casey's name from a friend here in Rome since I was to be staying in New York and he was from Albany. He invited me up to his family's summer home on Lake George and we have remained close friends ever since. Any friend of John Casey is immediately a personal friend of mine," smiled Carterelli, his eyes seeming to drift off to a different time and place.

"After New York," he continued, "I was sent on to London for more studies in international financial transactions before arriving back here in Rome at the Institute for the Works of Religion, or the IOR, as it is known in Italian. For us workers in the vineyard, it's the Vatican B.

"I accepted the business assignment for awhile, considering that I might help the needs of the poor and the Church in struggling countries."

"Let's order," interrupted Dan as a third frosted glass showed up. "I'm getting hungry."

"I'll have the usual pasta," said Carterelli, as he offered Dan the carafe of red wine the waiter placed on the table.

"So," Dan continued, "what do you do on a day-in-and-day-out basis?"

The answer came from a smiling but obviously troubled man, as he moved from the frosted glass to the carafe of wine. "I do whatever a good laundry employee is expected to do," he replied with a chuckle.

"You seem to be someone who might understand my being trapped inside a corporate prison with no way out," came the response to Dan's pointed question. "Since you know a little of how I arrived here, you might recognize growing frustration when you see it.

"Let's see now, what do I do? What an unusual question," Carterelli said, staring into his wine glass. "I take in people's money, I clean it up for them and then I give most of it back. In other cases, after I clean it, we send it off to people who prefer having their money come from the Institute for Good Works than other places. They are quite happy with the process. In the end,

160

considering the size of our fee, we are happy too. What a deal. We create happiness for God's children!

"Are you sure you don't want some of this wine? I don't want to hog it all to myself," said Carterelli.

"No, I'm just fine for the moment," answered Dan, sensing the opportunity to cast a line.

"Who are the customers at your laundry, if you don't mind my asking," came the request from Dan, as he sat back in his chair and swallowed the last of the wine in his own glass.

With their meal about done, it was obvious to Dan that the vineyard worker from the Institute for the Works of Religion was no longer aware of all he was saying. He wanted to continue his story but was drifting from one thought to another.

Before all sensibilities were lost, Dan launched a final question.

"Let me ask my question in a different way, Tom. Which of your customers has the dirtiest laundry?"

"Oh, that's an easy one, Dan," came the fast reply. "You will have to come up with harder questions than that one to impress me. Your very own CIA has the dirtiest laundry of all. Are you surprised? They use a wide range of our services and happily pay well for the privilege. But in all fairness, it's not all for them. Most of it is a favor to their friends but their laundry is the biggest as well as the dirtiest. Most recently they have been cleaning laundry for the Chaldean Catholic Church in Baghdad, I am sure a worthy cause to help the poor in that country. We seem to support many of their remote employees involved in God's work around the world," chuckled Carterelli.

As the waiter cleared the table, he brought two glasses of grappa.

Carterelli emptied his glass at the same pace as the rest. It too was refilled just as quickly,

"For all the authority of those of us working in the office," stammered Tom, "the name Vatican Bank should be changed to a subsidiary of Palermo. Those are the people who really run the office and put me in my own little corner every time I ask an indelicate question."

Before Dan could ask another question, Monsignor Thomas Carterelli was dozing in front of him.

The waiter motioned that he had called a cab and that it was waiting outside. He gave Dan the address and in a few minutes they stopped in front of an apartment building. Tom was half awake and half asleep but Dan was able to get him up to his apartment and into bed.

Dan glanced at the sleeping heap on top of the covers and realized it could easily have been him. Life offered painful choices and once made, one lived with the consequences.

When Dan arrived back at his hotel, he was startled to be greeted by a rotund gentleman with a large black mustache and walking cane. He greeted Dan at the desk, as he asked for his key and messages.

"Mr. Gerard?" the stranger inquired.

"Yes," Dan replied.

"I am Professor Eugenio Odani, chairman of the Medieval History department at the Gregorian University here in Rome and a friend of Allan Cartwright. I was hoping to meet you here in the lobby since I am somewhat early for our appointment."

"Oh yes," replied Dan. "Thank you so much for taking the time to see me on such short notice. Just give me a few minutes to clean up and I will join you back here at the bar."

"That is why I am here," came the reply.

Dan spent a moment in his room jotting down some notes from his very long lunch and wishing he had more time to absorb all he had heard. He was about to start his third meal. It was barely lunchtime back in DC.

The two men strolled outside the hotel and walked to a restaurant suggested by the professor as one of his favorites, Nino's, on Via Borgognona. "If we are going to talk business," he said to Dan, "we should enjoy ourselves in the process." The waiter brought them a large colorful menu signaling yet another meal.

"If you are interested in European history you are seated with one of the remaining members of the old school," began the professor. "When given the chance, I like to flatter myself since there are so few opportunities. However, I do think I am more knowledgeable than most in Rome on the subject of Church history.

"My research techniques run counter to the new computerized approach which often removes all sensibilities from the exercise and produces a product that assumes all thoughts are the

162

same. It's a pity what we have to put up with these days but that is the price we pay for progress. It is technological barbarism in my estimation."

"Well," Dan began, "my research is quite specific. It involves the search for the Holy Grail, the cup used by Jesus at the Last Supper. I was told that you might be able to confirm some of my findings and save me time from attempting to cross reference facts that seem clear to me."

"It sounds like this will be an enjoyable meal," responded the professor. "I have a singular opinion on the subject of the Grail and I am sure that is why Allan Cartwright sent you to me."

Dan carefully laid out a series of questions that he hoped would pull together what he had learned in Jerusalem.

"Would you agree," Dan offered, "with the premise that the Holy Grail, as a physical object, was brought into Europe by the Knights Templar sometime around the thirteenth century?"

"Yes, I would. My own investigations have shown that to be a logical and historically defensible assumption," replied the professor.

"If that is the case," continued Dan, "where and when does the transition begin that describes the Grail as the bloodline of Christ and not a physical object?"

"A very good question," responded the professor. "There is a media fixation on the bloodline theory that is certainly not shared by the academic community. The bloodline theory has been chatted about for some time. It appeared about three hundred years after the demise of the Templar leadership. The Templars were the ones who supported the Grail as a physical object with mystic powers of it own.

"In conducting research, timing is a basic underpinning of all assumptions," emphasized Odani. "It is interesting to note just when the bloodline theory emerges. Is it just a coincidence that it begins at the height of the Grail frenzy that gripped Europe? I abhor reliance on coincidence as historical explanation."

"No, it was not a coincidence."

"Coincidences must always be challenged. The theory clearly introduces a transition from searching for an object, to recognizing the importance of princely families. What is the political background at the time?

"At this very moment, the Vatican was struggling to maintain its power and land holdings against the kings of Europe. Why not flatter them with the notion that one of their own is literally divine? Is it also a coincidence that church leadership was creating the theological argument for the Divine Right of Kings to justify the nobility's claim on the people?

"Again I hardly think so. The Church was seeking political gain by justifying the continuation of royalty over the notion of self-government. I don't claim credit for this observation. It has been around the research community for some time but does not support the media's lust for sensationalism.

"In my view," continued Odani, "the church at least had knowledge of the Grail and wanted to discourage all searches for the object. It was successful but in certain ways something backfired. Organized searches for the Grail ended but doubts about church reliability were created. Allan has heard this theory from me before, now you have heard it as well."

"What other verifications do you have for the Grail as a physical object?" interrupted Dan.

"From a scholarly perspective I have several," was the the response. "In addition there was a political verification that influenced me a great deal. In the early 1940s, the Nazis began an all out search for mystical secrets including the Grail. This began in earnest after they discovered certain significant information while occupying France.

"It seems the Nazis discovered a collection Napoleon had gathered during his conquests. Napoleon, too, had a great interest in mystical powers and had a remarkable collection of artifacts taken back to France from his victories in Egypt and his capture of Rome, including the sack of the Vatican Library. The intensity of the Nazi effort was unusual. It added considerable weight to my own convictions.

"I find it curious that official records of World War II reveal that Roosevelt and Churchill discussed the German collection of religious secrets during the war. They concluded that the Germans had in fact found something but couldn't understand exactly what they had. It was Churchill who prevented any reference to this topic during all the war crime hearings. Churchill and most of his cabinet were members of the fraternity so to speak, and influenced by the Knights Templar accomplishments.

"In my view," continued Odani, "all the evidence supports the conclusion that the Knights Templar brought the Grail back from the Crusades. The Knights had a close relationship with the leaders of the Chartres Mystery School in the Abbey at Clairvaux. The school was involved during the conflict of the Pope and the King of France over the treasure of the Templars. The Abbey somehow got involved. Not much attention was given the Abbey until very recently and there is a surprising twist. Of all the sources to start speculation, I was surprised that it came from the Vatican itself.

"The discussion began with some of my colleagues at the university who had associates at the Vatican Library. Some years ago Pope John formed a small study group to investigate the history of the Chartres Mystery School and manuscripts from the Middle Ages. From all we could determine, the Church had found lost records relating to the acceptance by Bernard of Clairvaux of gifts from the Knights Templar. The real intention of the study group was never clear. We know they met with the Pontifical Biblical Institute in Jerusalem. Our own research has taken us to this same scholarly source and its work with the Dead Sea Scrolls. Although the group said they would meet with us and review their findings this never happened. The group was disbanded and their work buried in the Vatican as so many studies before them.

"The recent Vatican interest in the Grail gives weight to our original theory. We remain convinced the Grail exists as a physical object. The bloodline theory was created as a diversion and as a flattering of an opposing power structure," concluded Odani.

By this time, Dan was staring down at another full dinner plate and from the enthusiastic response to the food delivery by his guest, all discussion would be delayed until the meal was finished.

The sunshine, the strolling smiles passing their table and the body language of the professor, communicated the message of the culture. Don't let business interfere with the essentials of life! *Could this possibly work on the streets of Washington or New York?* Dan wondered. The thought brought a smile to the face of a reporter who had worked the tables of both cities!

After what seemed like an eternity, Dan tried to restart the conversation.

"What about the treasure then, Professor?" began Dan.

The question sparked a predictable response from the old man sitting across the small table on a sidewalk in Rome.

"You Americans have no balance in your life!" sighed the professor. "It is such a shame that you insist on leaving an appreciation of the finer things in life until the end of business. Sometimes there is no end to business and you miss the point of life altogether. Let's finish this fine meal, smell the wine and watch the people."

It was not until dessert that the conversation could continue. "So," the professor continued, "you want to find the treasure of the Templars. Let me give you my own view which I have shared with others who have asked the same question.

"If you are interested in understanding the clues to the treasure, you should examine the Templar messages embedded in the walls of Rosslyn Castle in Scotland. It was an early home of the Knights. There are many features of the St. Claire's Castle that relate to the Templar work at Chartres Cathedral. As a young man, Franklin Roosevelt's study of Rosslyn convinced him the treasure was buried on Oak Island in Nova Scotia. He led month-long expeditions exploring the series of ancient tunnels on the island but without much success.

"Many Templar clues point to North America and, like the Grail, the obvious clues are not the ones to follow. The Knights Templar outsmarted the king of France, the Pope. Once you understand how they did that the real clues will be found.

"If you want the Grail," said Odani looking across the table at Dan, "you should be looking for reports of unexplained mystical experiences. The Knights didn't understand what they had, just like the Germans didn't understand. It was there all along but couldn't be seen. My research says the greatest clue to the whereabouts of the Grail is in understanding the mystical experiences that surround it."

"From these clues," asked Dan, "where should one be looking?"

"I have always been fascinated by the popularity of Santiago de Compostella in Spain," replied Odani. "It was a site that had reported mystical occurrences for a consistent period of time no matter who was in control of the area. These experiences might provide clues to the Grail's whereabouts.

"I have one more theory," added the professor, "and this one too is known by Cartwright. To express it is to attract the wrath of Catholics from all quarters and risk being burned at the stake in St. Peter's Square as the Christians once were. But since you asked me, I'll tell you my own theory," smiled Odani.

"The visions of the Portugese children at the small village of Fatima were so close to the Compostella area that I have always believed that they were somehow related. The so-called secrets of the Fatima visions remain obscure. I don't know how or why but the Grail's mystical qualities and reported visions are connected through Compostella. The city has been on everyone's important spiritual sites for thousands of years.

"Is it possible," added Odani, looking up through his cigar smoke, "that the creator deliberately has given only a small part of His message to all the mix of the many religions man has used to try to find Him? Maybe it will take these groups talking to each other for a change before the path to God is really understood.

"Historically, the evidence left by the creator seems to be there but no one has been able to connect the dots," smiled the professor as he continued to taste the pastries left on the table.

"If you believe the Grail exists as a physical object and have some ideas on a general area," said Dan, "why haven't you done more to retrieve it, Professor?"

"Better men than I have tried and failed," came the instant reply. "Besides, I am too fat. If I am going to chase after something at my age, it won't be the Grail."

"You mentioned the study by the Vatican on the Chartres Mystery School and the work of St. Bernard of Clairvaux. What do you think about the significance of the abbey?" asked Dan.

"Chartres is a fascinating place in history and the cathedral having been constructed on a well-known pagan worship site is curious," came the reply. "However, the location is significant in the way it relates to the other great cathedrals across Europe. How can it be that they were all constructed on the same astrological lines as Chartres?" asked the professor.

"It confirms a point I made in the beginning of our conversation. Timing is so essential in studying the significance of historical events. The Chartres Cathedral is constructed after the Knights Templar work in their tunnel under the Temple of Solomon in Jerusalem. The Church is constructed with the famous Nativity stained glass window linking astrology with the Birth of Christ. It was done to perhaps make us consider a significant contradiction. Can the Old Testament prophets predict the coming of the Messiah but not the men from the east through the stars? What are we to make of the Bible specifically mentioning the wise men coming from the east? Why are they there? Is it of significance that east joins west at this time? I think that is the message and part of the contradictions.

"Why are the signs of the Zodiac on the veil of the Temple of Solomon? Have we missed something else? Is there meaning in the stars that mortals have yet to figure out? Looking back in time, we see seven great cathedrals of Europe constructed around the same period, linked to each other by seven planetary sites of the Druids. What was going on in the minds of these men involved in these events?"

"I appreciate your openness and candor, Professor," Dan added, as he called for the check. "It has been very helpful to the research I am conducting. I hate to end this conversation but I have one more appointment this evening that can't wait. Thank you for sharing your views with me. I would like very much to have your phone number and your address, so we can continue our discussion before my next trip to Rome."

"If you found any of my comments helpful," added the professor, "I would like very much to receive a copy of your papers when they would be available."

"If my research proves successful," answered Dan, "you will be among my very first readers."

Twenty
Past Meets Present

Dan's day had been partially consumed by a long telephone call from Tim Scanlon. Their mole at Langley provided new information on the sanctuary process provided to Ali Teekah and his party. The boss was expecting much from Dan upon his return. They were hoping he would be able to piece together the information arriving from all sources.

Dan was not pleased with his efforts to reach Lou. The Cardinal's staff had not been helpful and time was running out. He would make the early breakfast scheduled by Victoria's contact and then spend the rest of his time trying to get to Lou.

From the moment the man walked into the lobby of his hotel Dan felt uncomfortable. There was a stiff and deliberate walk that was in stark contrast to the casual gait so visible on the streets of Rome. His eyes were more tentacles than observatories. The lips were tightly closed with almost no room for talking or eating.

Without saying a word, the stranger approached Dan and finally spoke his name. "You must be Mr. Gerard," the man stated.

"And you must be Mr. De Felice," answered Dan. The usual small talk ensued, allowing both men to evaluate the body language of the other and move into the hotel breakfast area with its array of buffet items. Once seated with their selections, Dan decided to move right to the point.

"I would like to thank you for meeting me on such short notice," he began. "Victoria was not able to answer some of my research questions and I assume she explained the topic for our discussion. Is that correct?"

"Yes," came the reply.

"Good," responded Dan. "I would like to better understand the history of Southern Italy, and its influence on Vatican studies," continued Dan. "I realize that Sicily played an important role in the defense of the tip of the boot and was wondering how that relationship continues into the present. My research shows a profound respect for the affairs of the Vatican and was wondering how you might describe it today?"

"Is there anything else?" came the immediate answer.

"Of course," answered Dan. "As a writer, I am searching for the proper perspective to describe the relationship."

"Are your concerns about ancient history or current history?" came a question back to Dan.

"Both," he said.

"How does your paper plan to use the information?" was the next question.

Dan realized the exchange was moving into sensitive areas so he attempted to move in a different direction.

"My paper is trying to prepare for reporting on the coming Conclave with as much background as possible," explained Dan, "I would like to include comments from those who have respect for the process."

"I would suggest to you, Mr. Gerard," DeFelice said as he moved his hands off his coffee cup and closed them in front of his plate, "that you confine your questions to Rome and leave Sicily out of it. If our mutual friend, Dominic, didn't explain the benefits of this advice, it would be the first time he failed to mention such a point to one of his referrals. I assume you have taken it upon yourself to disregard his suggestions?"

With the words still echoing in his ears, Dan watched the quiet man leave the table and slowly walk out of the restaurant.

The meeting could be catalogued among the many similar confrontations Dan had back in New York during the city contracts investigation. It did have its own unique flavor and added a new level of discomfort. Rather than worry about the lost opportunity, Dan began to develop a strategy for reaching Lou.

He had the Cardinal's office address and decided to try a face to face approach. It failed the same way the telephone calls had. The staff was courteous but deliberate in their refusal to offer any chance of reaching Lou.

The more Dan walked through the streets of Rome, the more he remembered various select residences that housed dignitaries during the time of the Vatican Council. He decided to find as many of those old out of the way places as he could and see what might develop.

His first stop was Bishop's Row along the Via Della Conciliazione. It was here where he first remembered hearing the term, "scarlet fever" used to describe those Bishops maneuvering to become Cardinals. The next block had the small doorway that led to the original North American College, the Casa Santa Maria. It had one of the finest interior courtyards in Rome and through a family donation was converted to house US seminarians up until the 1950s when the new residence was constructed.

Admiring the ancient doorway from a distance, it opened and a familiar figure with two other clerics emerged. They were preoccupied in conversation and did not notice him staring at them from across the narrow cobblestone street. They jumped into a waiting car and sped away.

My, my, hello, old friend Roberto Flores, said Dan to himself, *we meet again after all these years. Now where is your good buddy, Delgado, these days?*

Dan watched the car and a new thought struck him. He hurried back to his hotel and asked the concierge to help him locate some special villas that might still be owned by leading families of Rome.

After Dan's description the concierge pulled out a picture of the Bellardino Villa just as Dan remembered it. It had been sold some years back to a movie star and was very restricted as far as the visiting public went.

Dan then asked for a hired car for the rest of the day to take him around Rome. One was available and made its way to the hotel in less than an hour. He asked the driver to position himself outside the old college building, the Casa Santa Maria, so they could see anyone entering or leaving. Several minutes later, two men dressed in black cassocks opened the door as a limo stopped in front of the residence. "OK, driver," said Dan, "let's see where they take us. Just follow them wherever they go."

Within a few minutes they were in the Aventino residential section on the outskirts of Rome in the Piazza Dei Cavalieria, named after the founders of the Order of the Knights of Malta.

171

A prestigious religious group created by the Vatican and restricted to those who could afford the price of admission. The car ahead of them suddenly turned into one of the driveways and the gate closed behind them. Dan and his driver positioned themselves down the street with a clear view of the gated driveway.

For the next hour cars came and went. *The activity around the residence is clearly more than social,* thought Dan. At that moment, another black limo came out of the driveway and passed slowly in front of Dan's car. Dan couldn't be sure, but it could have been Lou. "Let's follow that one," shouted Dan, "and see where it goes."

Almost a half hour later the car pulled into a small driveway on a quiet residential street in the Monteverde Vecchio section. *Interesting but not surprising,* thought Dan. *Nothing like living in the very best sections of town surrounded by the fountains, lakes and gardens of the Villa Pamphili Park.* The lone occupant climbed the stone steps to the front door and used a key to gain immediate entry.

Dan asked the driver to stay where he was and not leave for any reason until he got back. He climbed from the car, approached the house with a deliberate walk, and climbed the stone steps and rang the bell.

An elderly gentleman opened the door ever very slowly and asked, "May I help you?"

"Yes," said Dan, "I have a message from Cardinal Delgado for Cardinal Baracini."

"I'll be happy to deliver it for you," said the doorkeeper.

"No," answered Dan, "I've been instructed to give it to him personally."

"Just a moment please," was the reply, as the door was closed in Dan's face.

Moments later, the door opened again; Dan was invited in and asked to wait in a small sitting room.

Within a few moments, the door to the room opened and there, in the flesh, stood Cardinal Louis Baracini, an expression on his face that was anything but welcoming. It began to change as he realized that the past was meeting present.

"My God," exclaimed Lou. "What in heaven's name are you doing here?"

"I happened to be in your neighborhood," said Dan, "and thought I would stop in and see my old friend Lou."

There was silence as both men absorbed the reality of a face to face meeting with a long lost friend.

The silence was broken by the Cardinal's voice. He was saying Dan's name over and over in rapid fashion as he approached him. "It's been so long and I've thought of you so often," Lou said, as he extended first his hand and then both arms.

It was a strong but silent embrace as two minds recalled days and nights together from a different time.

It was Dan's turn to speak. "I am really sorry for barging in on you like this, but I have been trying for years to get in touch with you. No matter how hard I tried or who said they could help me, it never worked. So here I am in person.

"If you want me to leave, with no questions asked, I will," said Dan, "but, before going I hope you would give me an appointment to see you again and soon."

"That might become an impossible task," responded Lou, "no time these days is a good time. I am to be here for the next hour or so to have a quiet dinner. If you can, why don't you join me and let's see how much we can accomplish before I have to run off again on official business."

With that, Lou led Dan down a long carpeted hallway, its walls clothed by a collection of Renaissance paintings. They entered a large formal dining room with two large candlesticks spreading a soft light on a mahogany table with a single place setting at the far end. The elderly housekeeper from the front door added a place for Dan.

Conversation was slow and easy at the start, as each man described his struggles on the path he had chosen. There was little mention of their time together in Rome and no reference to that terrible night. Lou claimed he never knew Dan had ever made efforts to contact him. If he had, Lou said he would have been eager to meet.

After much discussion and too much wine, Lou suggested they move into the sitting room by the window overlooking the garden.

Sitting in a high backed red chair by a floor to ceiling window and flanked by paintings of Saints Peter and Paul, Lou turned to Dan and said, "Life has taken us on different paths and shown us many things. At the end of the journey, hopefully, we can look beyond our mistakes.

"If one feels he is making a difference in the world, perhaps life is worthwhile. I feel I am making a difference in the work of the Church, more than I ever anticipated when I entered the priesthood. That feeling has kept me going all these years.

"I know you remember that it was my family that directed me into this career. Once we heard the words 'the family has decided' discussion was over. They assured me it was the best path for me as it was the best for the family. The Church has benefited from my involvement in ways no one can ever understand." Dan wondered if Lou caught the rather naïve arrogance implicit in this remark.

To this point Dan was content with the details of how life had unfolded for the two friends. Now, he moved to the purpose of his visit.

"Lou, I hear what you are saying and I am trying to understand how you are dealing with your situation," Dan began, "but there comes a time when events overtake the best of plans. I believe you find yourself in this kind of a situation.

"The Vatican has chosen to influence politics and must face the consequences of that decision. You know that the attention you have attracted will change rules of behavior that comforted the church for centuries. You can't treat the world community as you did the flock of adoring faithful.

"With your decisions impacting all of us directly, we need to know what is being done and why. A handful of people can't choose for the world, nor can facts be manipulated by those in power to gain certain objectives, however exalted though they may be."

A black velvet curtain of silence dropped on the room.

It was broken by the reporter's question. "Why, in the midst of all your troubles, did you give sanctuary to a terrorist?"

Lou was on his feet as soon as he heard the question. By his movements, he signaled the end of the conversation. "I really

174

have to get back to my meetings," came the reply. "I am sure we can continue this conversation when there is more time."

Dan jumped to his feet and kept pushing.

I might as well cast out my fishhook and see if I catch anything, Dan said to himself as he had done so many times in the past in similar situations.

"Why wouldn't the disclosure of long kept secrets be a good thing for the Church in this day and age? Why would you give in to the blackmail of a terrorist?" Dan asked. "Why would you doubt the ability of people to handle truth? I don't get it."

Lou turned and looking Dan in the face, virtually shouted his reply.

"Because it is not easy to correct the mistakes of centuries. Past decisions were made with the best of intentions. A debate over philosophy and theology before an uneducated flock would only have led to confusion. Certain information was held by Church leaders to give them more time to understand what they possessed.

"The more time passed the more difficult it became to discuss openly. The delay created an atmosphere of secrecy which cannot be denied. The result today is an embarrassment over church secrets we need time to manage. We have decided to manage one crisis at a time. The first problem is the change in leadership.

"More importantly," Lou continued, "we have only touched a portion of the puzzle and the enormity of the task is difficult to explain. You, of all people, should know the pressures that others can create during crisis situations and we are in a crisis situation.

"To complicate matters further," said Lou, "our good Pope took a turn for the worse today and is not expected to live much longer. We are preparing for a Conclave on top of everything else and I know you remember what that entails."

Dan launched his boat on another fishing expedition.

"If your friends are not happy with the next Conclave, will they poison the new Pope as they did a previous one?" asked Dan.

"That is not a fair statement," shouted Lou. "With all you know it seems unlike you to say something like that. There is a very large core of good people here trying to do what is right. We tried to prevent that last attempt from succeeding. We just failed by underestimating certain people. I think we understand the risks better now and we can see our mistakes are not repeated."

A good catch, thought Dan. *Let's try one more.*

"Wasn't it a dangerous decision to create the bloodline theory around the Grail to hide the fact that it had been found?"

"We did not make that decision but we are living with its consequences."

Lou's face dropped with the realization of what he had blurted out in the heat of conversation.

"I am afraid our time together is ended," exclaimed Lou, moving out into the hallway.

"I'll let you go to your meeting, Lou," said Dan, "but I would like an agreement that we can meet here again in another week or so. You know I would be willing to work with you as I did many times in the past. You need a friend capable of giving advice on managing the media frenzy about to crash over you."

"I'd like very much to promise that, Dan," offered Lou, "but it might not be possible if a Conclave is in progress. I will simply offer that I will do my best to meet if you call."

"Your word has always been, Lou," sighed Dan, "I'll hold you to that promise."

The two walked in silence through a corridor of past images. Lou turned at the door with one last statement. "If I only had more time, I would enjoy spending a few days with you and repair our old friendship. It didn't end on the best of notes."

Dan looked at Lou and replied, "Do we ever know how much time we have left? Do we?"

Dan's silent walk down the stone steps was interrupted by the sound of the door closing behind him. He hoped that the door would not be closed forever.

Twenty-one
The Eastern Shore

No sooner had he exited customs at Dulles than Dan was on the phone to Tim Scanlon to compare notes and schedule a meeting with Roman.

Tim was glad to hear that Dan was back in the country. They needed time together to sort out the conflicting information pouring into the office. Roman was away with the President on a portion of the Far East visit planned as an election primer and not due back until late Monday. Tim had a problem with family commitments for the weekend and asked if they could meet first thing Monday morning.

Dan was delighted with the schedule. It gave him the time he wanted with Meggie on Saturday. His family would not return from their Disney trip until Sunday night.

Dan's next call was to Meggie. She was ready when he was. Her bags were packed and standing by the door.

Dan's shower at home felt like a spring rain, refreshing and full of new life. It helped put his business and family issues on the back burner and turn his mind to personal concerns. Sunday night would be enough time with the children to work out a week's vacation for the three of them to talk about where their new life was taking them.

The sound of the car's engine turned his thoughts to the time he and Meggie were about to share together. No chance meeting, no final good-byes, just an interlude to enjoy each other and think about options for the future, if there were any.

She was down the steps and in the car before he had a chance to bring it to a full stop. The back door was opened and her things thrown in before he could turn to look at her. When he did, he caught a glow that had been missing from her face. There was an abandon in her smile, an anticipation in her greeting, that made his stomach churn.

"Where are we headed?" she said, as she slammed the door behind her and slid close to him on the front seat. Dan fed gas into the engine, holding her hand in his.

"I thought we would spend a day on the Maryland Eastern Shore. I have the perfect place for the kind of time we need," said Dan as he turned out of her development. "The Refuge Inn on the edge of the wildlife preserve in Chincoteague is quiet and comfortable. It offers the comfort of a seaside inn along the paths of a wildlife refuge. I was there one time for a conference. I enjoyed jogging through the nature trails running through the refuge and onto the beach. It should give us surroundings that allow us to relax."

"Sounds comforting," she said, "and I think I need comforting."

As the inn came into view surrounded by tall pines, Meggie released one long slow breath. "It looks so cozy," she said. "The day is off to a great start."

Dan's thoughts went back to times in Lincoln Park and how her closeness was having the same effect it did back then. When she was with him, everything around him became so alive.

Following lunch on a patio overlooking the water, they rented bicycles and began their exploration of the wildlife refuge. A welcoming assortment of wild flowers greeted them at every turn in the slow winding path and with deer and pheasants running from the intruders. The sun peeked through trees filled with chattering birds commenting on the two cyclists enjoying each other's presence.

As birds flew out from their wheels and deer scrambled into the brush, an ocean breeze whispered through the trees. Their laughter hid the turmoil inside.

Dan stopped as they came to an opening in the path that led onto the beach. With the bikes left behind, they removed their shoes, walking hand in hand along the water's edge, letting the waves wash their toes in the sea water.

They stopped at a rock jetty along the beach and paused to look into each other's eyes. A seagull broke the silence with his welcoming song for the two people having their toes caressed by an incoming tide.

178

"Why did we have to wait so long for this moment?" she asked. "For the first time in a very long while, I am at ease with myself. I am not doing what is expected. I am doing what my heart tells me is right.

"My heart tells me I have no right to this moment. I belong to someone else by my own choice. It might have been an emotional choice but it was mine. I don't know why I have to dampen the moment but I feel as I feel. I am sorry," she said stepping into the surf swirling around their bare feet.

Dan reached out, pulling her back to him and gently touched her chin. He turned her face so he could look directly into her eyes. They were releasing their own moisture. The mist was walking down her cheeks.

"Don't be upset with my tears," she added. "I am feeling complete happiness for a change and I don't know how to behave."

"I don't know where all this will take us," Dan said, as he pulled her head against his chest. "I know I have been looking forward to a day like this for a long time. I plan to push out any thought ruining a time we both deserve. Let's just have fun, enjoy where we are, enjoy each moment and talk about tomorrow, tomorrow."

A smile started to break through her tears. Dan kissed her ever so gently. She came into his arms in the same way as in that boathouse kiss so many years ago. Her wet hair reminded him of the park summer rain.

She suddenly broke away, ran a few steps along the sand, threw off her clothes and soaked her blue bathing suit in the incoming surf. Dan followed her. They romped in the easy waves throwing off concerns about the future. They rode the waves in to shore bouncing in the sand filled water. Joining hands, they raced back in to the water to catch the next ride.

Meggie pulled a comb through her wet hair sitting on the beach towel. Dan could see her once again in her apartment in Albany brushing her hair after that rainstorm in the park.

With a sudden gust of wind and sand blowing across the deserted beach, Meggie pulled herself into his arms, wrapping them both in the towel murmuring softly, "Thank you for not giving up on me."

179

After a kiss, Dan rose and pulled her to her feet. "Let's go back," he said, "and change out of these wet clothes."

With the glow of the gas fire reflecting in her eyes, Dan brought her to him, his hands releasing the bathrobe belt and letting it drop to the floor. She was as he rememberd.

The last rays of the sun were barely visible through the shaded inn window as the two bodies tried to unwind themselves from the tangle of sheets and pillows in the king-sized bed.

It was an afternoon dancing with Albany memories. After his stay in the hospital and her nursing him back to health, he surrendered to the moment. That first time never left him, no matter how often he tried to block it out. He didn't want to remember with all the recriminations that accompanied those thoughts. But, this afternoon, those moments could be recalled with gladness.

A closeness, warmth, joy, a feeling of well being, washed over him as he felt her breath on his neck.

"Don't you think its time we looked for dinner," he said, as he raised his head above her chest, prying open her eyes with his finger tips.

"Only if you promise me we will come back here and tangle ourselves up in the sheets the same way," she replied.

The restaurant had an outside table overlooking a wooden deck with a stream that led back out to the bay. Two candles fluttered in the moonlight, giving a soft glow to both faces staring at each other.

"We had a great day," she began, "but like always, I feel burdened with guilt over being so selfish. I've made mistakes as we all have. I have difficulty living with them. What I did was not Tom's fault. He has been honest and decent in our relationship. As hard as I tried, our marriage never gave me what I had hoped for. Believe me, I tried," she said, watching the last rays of moonlight kiss the water.

"Over the years it became obvious to me. Tom's real wife was the Army. He loves her in a way he can never love me. I am offered the time left over, after she has taken all she wants. If there is ever a time for choice, I know where I stand," said Meggie with a regretful sigh.

"Once we found out we could not have children, physical contact lost its meaning. Not that Tom has been around much anyway, but when he was, we were out going places with other people, not taking the time to be alone with each other.

"The marriage became a friendship. We are good friends," Meggie said as she sipped the last drops of wine from the large glass that reflected the candles' glow.

"Just because it didn't work out the way I wanted," she continued, "doesn't give me an open door. Am I making sense in all this, Dan, or is it a jumble?"

"Our missed opportunity," Dan offered through his own heavy sigh, "was the result of my thoughtless acts and not yours. If I had returned as I promised we would not be here today. Let's not talk about past failures. Let's talk about today's feelings. Right and wrong involve judgments. Let's pass on that for awhile."

"Based on my feelings, I can't say I was terribly unhappy," continued Meggie, "I had my nursing career. The specialty in pediatrics helped for a while making up for no family. After a few years, I had to switch to geriatrics because the realization of no family became too great a problem around children. I mixed community service work with my nursing and the travel. It was a good life, that is, until I saw you in Paris.

"After Paris, sparks began to glow. They burned through life's façade. They left me no choice but to think about us."

Dan began an account of the meltdown in Albany when he realized he had lost her to Tom. He recounted a journey through the streets of New York, his marriage to a woman who made him a better person, two children and the good fortune of his investigative reporting bitterly negated by the death of his partner.

"After Paris, I felt a slow end of coldness," said Dan. "It was warmth returning to my life. Feelings that had been numbed came throbbing back. Every time I saw you, I couldn't deny or escape the force that pulled me towards you," Dan concluded. He reached across the table and held a hand that trembled ever so slightly.

Dinner came to a close with Dan offering the details of the crisis he was now following. He knew Tom was involved. Conceivably they might be forced to clash at some point.

181

Meggie interrupted, with the observation that Tom shared little with her about his work. She really couldn't help. Dan made it clear he wasn't asking for her help, just letting her know what he was doing and the need for him to be away.

They talked at length about the many tasks of reporting. How he was better able than most to uncover things about important people. "One of my insights has been to follow people in their travels. You learn as much as following money."

The ride back to town late that evening was a quiet time for Dan and Meggie. The silence was symbolic. If thought had a voice, it would have been unbearable.

The car pulling into her driveway forced Meggie to speak. "We had a wonderful time, Dan," she began. "We didn't find a path for the future. I am not sure there is one.

"Our closeness is very special. I need more than a few days together to know how to live my life. I want you to know that I hope this time will not be like the last time we feel this way. I need to talk to you and most of all, you need to talk to me. If I am alone again, it will have the same result, don't do that to me."

With that she opened the door, leaned back in and kissed him. She was up the stairs before he could find words to answer her.

During a slow drive home to a family that demanded his attention, Dan was determined not to let outside events control his life again.

Twenty-two
The Palermo Documents

The children returned from their Disney adventure exhausted from possibly too much fun with their cousins. The next early morning was filled with descriptions of the sights and sounds of Orlando. Each day's schedule was repeated for Dan's benefit including the time waiting for the special rides and the friends met at the hotel where they stayed. The emotions pounding inside Dan caused little interruption in the narrative the kids were reporting with obvious relish.

Dan's usual appearance at the *Tribune* brought a tired and exhausted Tim Scanlon to his feet. "Where the hell have you been all morning?" pleaded Tim, with a look of disgust uncharacteristic of the behavior Dan had come to admire. "I said we should meet in here as close to 6 AM as we could. Here you stroll in at this late hour and grace us with your presence. Are we supposed to thank you for giving us your attention after we have been working round the clock while you were skipping across the globe? What is going on with you?"

"Sorry, Tim," was Dan's apologetic reply, "I thought I made it clear about my schedule. There are some things I can't hurry. I have much to contribute this morning. Once you hear it, we will be able to focus on what needs to be done."

"Well," responded Tim. "My frustration level has been reduced with a call from Roman that his flight from LA has been delayed. By leaving the Presidential trip the way he did, he was left on his own for the flights out of Japan. He won't be back in the office until later today, so we will have time to get our act together."

"Sorry to interrupt the shouting match, guys, but there is an emergency phone call for Dan on line one," said the young lady at the door to the conference room. "Do you want to take it now or after your bout is over?"

183

"Very funny," smiled Dan, "I'll take it now."

Dan recognized Meggie's voice immediately. There was something different in her tone.

"Dan, can you talk now, or should I call you back?" she whispered.

"Now is fine," he said, "what is going on?"

"A few minutes ago, one of the couriers Tom uses came to the house with one of those locked pouches that get dropped off. The man made a comment to me it might be a nice gift this time because Tom was in Italy for a change and not the Middle East. He heard that Palermo was a great place and he always wanted to go there himself. He left with a smile and an 'enjoy your gift' response.

"We have two safes at home," Meggie continued. "One is Tom's and one is ours. When these pouches are dropped off, I am to keep it in our safe until Tom can transfer it to his when he returns. He told me he has some items that he cannot keep at the office and that is why he has a secure location at home. With your involvement in Italy and this package arriving, I thought you might want to take a look before I lock it up?"

"Thanks for thinking about me and trying to help," responded Dan. "I would like very much to do that but you need to think through what you've just offered."

After a pause, Meggie spoke very deliberately. "Yes, I do," she said, "and it didn't take me long to make a decision. I want to be with you on a road out of where I am. Our weekend was one step and this is another. I know where I am going. The question is, do you?"

"All I know is, I want what you want, and I am grateful for your thinking of me in this way," answered Dan. "I will get back to you as soon as I can."

Dan was out of his office in an instant and asked for Tim's patience one more time. He had to make an important stop before he could sit down and go over all their notes. The announcement sent Tim off on another tirade.

"Look, Tim," Dan shouted, "You will just have to trust me for a few more hours. If I fail you, then you can take as big a piece of me as you want but in the meantime just hold on. I need our photo guy to accompany me to make copies of documents.

Call down to research and see if there is someone reliable available. I have to be out of here in five minutes. We can continue our debate later."

With the photographer in tow and before his car exited the parking garage, Dan called Meggie. He asked her to meet him with the pouch at the House of Pancakes restaurant just off the beltway exit leading to her complex. He told her to come wearing a white scarf and remain sitting in her car until he approached her. He would take the material into the restaurant, have a look and then return it to her. He would park far enough away so the one person with him would not see her or her license plate. She agreed but was feeling more uncomfortable with every passing moment.

His first view of the House of Pancakes included a lone car at the far end of the lot with a single passenger in the front seat. Dan pulled his car into the opposite end of the lot and walked with his companion into the restaurant. He exited a rear door and walked slowly to her car. She handed him an envelope from the driver's window. "I am doing this for us," she said. "What will you do for us?"

"Trust me," came his answer.

From the time they made copies of the documents in the men's room of the restaurant, until they appeared on the wall of the screening room, Dan could not contain himself with the thoughts of what he might have. When the images came before him it was not what he expected. The pictures and documents from Palermo tore open a new chapter in the practice of deceptions created by those in power and determined to remain in power.

"What do you want me to do with these, Dan?" said his associate, who had no idea of what he had just witnessed.

"Make a full set of slides of all the documents. We will use them this afternoon at the Roman briefing, give the originals and all copies to me and that's it. Thanks."

Back in his office, Dan was preparing flip charts for coordination with Tim and the staff for the afternoon briefing, when he was told about another call waiting.

"There is a Bishop Casey on the phone for you, Dan, and he said it's important," came the message.

"Dan, Bishop Casey here, I have some news that I thought you should hear right away. The POPE IS DEAD! They are trying to keep it secret for as long as they can for obvious reasons. He died in the papal apartments last night. Rome will become the center of attention for the next few weeks so if you want to get over there you better be quick about it."

"Bless you, John," came the reply, "I can't thank you enough for the head start. I hope I can call you on your private line as this event develops."

"Knowing what I know, I will be heading to Rome myself," said the bishop. "I want to be part of the process that will have everything to do with influencing the Conclave voting. Most of the decisions will take place before the Cardinals enter the Sistine Chapel anyway and during those meetings I want to influence the right people."

"Again, thanks for the call," added Dan. "Once you're in Rome let me know how to contact you. I will be there!"

Tim and Dan worked feverishly to consolidate their information onto the required summary boards and present a strategy recommendation to the boss.

Later that afternoon when Jack Roman entered, all chatter stopped and the usual silence covered the room. Tim and Dan took a collective deep breath while those standing in the rear found seats out of the line of fire.

"Sorry I got hung up on my plane ride," offered the boss as he took his place at the head of the table. "If I thought the situation was important enough to leave the President's tour of Japan you better not disappoint me on the work you have done on the sanctuary story. Let's have it, down and dirty!"

Tim went first, as he and Dan had agreed. "I will summarize the key information from all our sources around the world, our media partners working the Rome situation directly and most importantly, our friend in Langley."

Tim began his review through five timeline charts pasted across the back of the conference room.

"We have been able to confirm our assumptions about the international efforts to capture Ali Teekah and qualify for the reward offered by Iraq for his capture. The failed poison gas sale was the basis for the offer of oil leases and it produced a great

186

number of interested parties. The parties have formed international teams to pool their resources and focus their efforts on bringing Ali and his family back to Baghdad to win the contracts. Among the most serious and well supplied are the Russians partnering with the Syrians, the French with the Iranians, the Germans with the Liberians and the CIA trying to play all ends against the middle.

"One of these groups penetrated Palestinian security and made an attempt to take the family captive. Our CIA source reports that the house had a basement safe room and the first floor was wired against intruders. All the assault personnel on the first floor were killed by wall-mounted plastic explosives. The ones lucky enough to escape the blast were shot by local security. Much of that security force was ordered shot by Ali when it was realized they had provided the access to the restricted areas. It has been assumed that parachutes were the likely vehicles for the attackers but our mole can't verify that.

"Within two weeks of the attempt, Ali and his family arrived in Italy at a small airport near Bari and were transported to the Vatican where they remain under Church protection.

"The public reason given for the sanctuary provided by the Church was its effort to resolve the Mid East crisis between the Palestinians and Israel. Dan will speak to this issue and the information he gathered in Jerusalem and Rome.

"The CIA has organized its own effort to capture Ali. The objective is to bring him to the U.S. for trial before the fall elections. It seems logical that the White House must know about the plans.

"The Andrews Air Force base departure logs show considerable movement by CIA and White House personnel around the time the capture attempt was made. It appears that General Feely himself was in command of the Special Forces team since he flew to Israel at the time.

"Our latest information has the General in Italy. The same assault units that accompanied him to Israel at the time of the failed assault have been put on alert and are preparing for a move to an unknown location.

"Considerable CIA funds have been transferred overseas in the past week beyond the routine payment traffic generally coming from Langley.

"Here are highlights of our latest combined information gathering with emphasis on inside contacts at both US and French intelligence agencies."

Tim turned to Dan and invited him to continue. Dan rose to his feet, moved to the charts on the wall and began.

- Vatican travel records show a series of meetings among high level Church officials, members of Opus Dei, and representatives of Ali Teekah in the days before and just after the attempted capture.
- I have found evidence of the blackmail issue we suspected was at the center of the request for sanctuary.
- "My investigation indicates that the Vatican located the so-called Holy Grail, the cup of Christ from the Last Supper, sometime in the Middle Ages and kept it secret to continue the faithful people's reliance on an organized clergy. For you who are not connoisseurs of religion, that is the equivalent of an atomic bomb.
- The Grail was taken from the Mid East by the Knights Templar in the 1300s. Their refusal to give up the Grail and their independent religious ways were the reasons for their execution and the liquidation of their movement.
- The Grail was found more than a hundred years later in its Templar hiding place. The discovery came about by accident during an investigation of spiritual claims from the far east. Abbots at a Spiritual School in Clairvaux led to its discovery.
- The blackmail trail includes references to a study ordered by Pope John XXIII when he learned of the secret. The study was undertaken by a team of Vatican scholars whose preliminary findings sparked the Vatican Council called by Pope John. His death prevented its release.
- The study centered on undisclosed documents held by the Vatican over the centuries. It brought to light the possible existence of the Holy Grail and its possession by the Vatican.

"Hold it right there" came the booming voice from the other end of the table. "We are not a tabloid and will not be taking our readers on a tour of heaven any time soon. We are not going to claim the Knights Templar as our source for this story. You better have some solid verifiable information for me before you end or this is going to be a painful meeting."

Dan moved closer to Jack Roman, rested both his hands on the back of a conference chair and lowered his voice. "I am confident that I can provide you with the comfort you need to move forward on the basis of our presentation," Dan offered. "Let me finish all the points and then you can judge if our suggestions are solid."

Dan moved to the center of the room and directed Jack's attention to the next point.

- I was able to verify the existence of a significant body of scholarly knowledge about the existence of the Grail as a physical object. More than that, both my sources, one in Jerusalem and one in Rome, had direct contact with a recent Vatican study group revisiting the efforts made by John XXIII. If some sources in Jerusalem had this knowledge, it seems likely that others had it as well. Here is the likely source of the leak about the Vatican's hiding place to Teekah and his followers.
- The bloodline theory of the Grail the media likes so much appears to have been part of a Vatican deception to discourage organized searches for the Grail once Vatican leaders had it in their possession.
- The Grail appears to be only a part of the story. Something else is being hidden but is not entirely clear. If we locate the Grail, we will find the rest of the puzzle.
- The bottom line? There is enough of a verifiable story to take the plunge on the existence of Church secrets as the motivation for the blackmail. We can leave the Grail out of it if you want but we have enough to start the story.
- The story is one of deception by a global institution and the deception angle goes much deeper. It could be more dangerous.
- I have two sources in Rome that clearly indicate that the Vatican Bank is under considerable influence by Italian organized crime if not effectively run by it.

- There are strong indications the Mafia was involved in the transfer of Teekah into Vatican City.
- In speaking with one of the administrators of the bank, it appears to be a main source of laundering money for a network of clients outside usual depositors.
- The CIA uses the services of the bank to funnel payments. It also appears it was the money laundering activity of the bank that led to the poisoning of a Pope some years ago.
- Certain documents came into our possession this morning that seem to confirm the fact that organized crime poisoned the previous Pope and has been using blackmail for years to control the Curia. Documents also show that they have well placed agents inside the Vatican at all levels and are prepared to do whatever is in their best interests.

"Ok, Ok," spouted the impatient managing editor. "Enough of your trip into fantasyland, Dan. Tim was at least more down to earth with his report. It seems we all need to be on a spiritual voyage if we hope to understand where you are.

"You know my ground rules. I want not only sources but verification. I don't intend to be caught publishing Hitler's diaries. Give me verification, some reason why I should accept what you have said about deception as the core of our story and the influence of organized crime in Vatican City."

"It's a fair question, Jack," answered Dan. "Here are the reasons and sources that respond to your concerns.

"We all have heard those basic assumptions about the influence of the Mafia throughout most Italian government activities. We have read stories about local prosecutors, judges and even prime ministers taken from their homes and shot for a public stand against the Mafia. Why would we think a global institution based in Italy would be free from this influence?

"The Vatican travel records referred to earlier came from a very reliable high-level church official. They were cross checked with airline and credit card companies. They agree. We have proof of senior level meetings in Rome by a small group of Opus

Dei members following face-to-face meetings with Ali's negotiators and crime figures in Palermo.

"This same source led to a most reliable contact in Jerusalem with connections to the Pontifical Biblical Institute based in Israel that revealed the workings of the Papal Study group. Finally and most importantly, the study as the basis for the blackmail was confirmed to me by the cardinal who signed the press release on the Teekah sanctuary decision. Jack, I think I have met your cross-check and verification requirements.

"The influence of the Mafia on the internal workings of the Vatican is an issue beyond sanctuary. I have two sources for the poisoning of the previous Pope by the Mafia, one in New York and the other in Rome. Today's documents will confirm the information provided by these two contacts."

"You have my attention now, Dan," said Roman. "Let's see the document file."

Dan began his explanation of the file he described as "the Palermo Documents." He began an explanation of his preliminary look at the contents recognizing the need for further analysis.

"We have first a series of ledgers of Vatican Bank records," said Dan, pointing to one of the charts at the rear of the room. "I believe we will be able to verify that they show payments to banks around the world to mostly charitable institutions but many are of a questionable nature involving rogue forces in dictatorial countries. They show payments to a variety of Swiss bank accounts, and directly to well-known double agents and killers for hire.

"Picture files describing Swiss Guards and members of the Pope's household are included. There are instructions about how to contact these individuals for special assignments. A large portion of the file contains pictures of sexual activities of both men and women going back many years. They were most probably used to keep influential people in line. These are some of the early conclusions. I am sure more will come after the documents have been examined," concluded Dan.

"Where did you get the documents and how can you verify their authenticity?" asked Jack.

"They came from the highest levels of our own government," replied Dan.

"Who?" shouted back Jack.

"I can't reveal that," came Dan's answer.

"Are you, and your source, willing to go to jail for a very long time to protect each other?" shouted Roman.

"Yes," was the one word reply.

"Well you better get ready," added Roman, "because if only some of what you claim is true, you will be seeing a special prosecutor on a regular basis.

"Let's assume your source for these documents is credible, how can you cross verify the information?"

After moving around the room and stopping to stare in silence from the window, Dan finally turned and faced the group.

"I will personally verify the authenticity of the documents."

Dan moved the slides on the screen back to the pictures depicting sexual activity.

"If you look closely at the next pictures, you will recognize me in my youth. The young woman shown with me was named Millie. She had the misfortune of falling in front of a train some weeks after these pictures were taken.

"In my defense, I would point out the condition of my eyes in these pictures. Perhaps an expert would be able to verify that I was in a drugged condition at the time. Although it sounds like a lame excuse, it's all I remember. The next pictures of me with the young men, I have no recollection of at all. Again, it's easy for me to say but I will stand on the contention that I was drugged and these pictures were staged as part of a blackmail plot.

"The next pictures are of my companion that night, one Lou Baracini, now Cardinal Baracini. You will see he is with another girl, Maria, whose death from a drug overdose can be verified in newspapers at the time. His eyes are even worse than mine in that they are closed completely in most of the pictures.

"These following pictures are of some of the seminarians and Church officials, I can identify who were at the same party Lou and I attended the night we met the girls and offered to drive them home after the party. The men and women in the

192

pictures with Lou and me are in some of the other photos in the file.

"I can only identify a handful of the men shown in the remaining pictures. The ones I know are in key positions in the Curia today. I will leave further identification of the pictures to our experts. With these documents we expose a scheme to control the people who control the Church. How much of it is to protect the affairs of the Vatican Bank and how much is to control the official church would be speculation.

"Controlling those who sit in the seat of power is the obvious intention. How far it goes and who has knowledge is what we must find out.

"We will hear shortly that the Pope is dead," Dan added, "and a Conclave will be called to elect his successor. Whatever confusion exists inside the Vatican over the sanctuary issue will be compounded by this change. The opportunity for the transfer of power should bring out all the politicians eager to use whatever they can, including blackmail, to maintain their positions of influence. We can be on the front lines of history if we pursue this story in the way we will recommend. The story isn't about terrorists, Holy Grails or dead Popes. It's about the most brazen subversion of a global institution anyone could conceive and for the most self serving reasons. Do you want the story or do we let the *Times* and the *Post* do it?"

Now it was Jack Roman's time to pace and ponder the consequences of what he had just listened to.

"This is either going to be the biggest story in the history of the *Tribune*," he growled, "or we will go bankrupt and probably all be dead. The second part is the most likely.

"I don't know why I am doing this, especially when I think a good portion of it is open to interpretation, but I want you guys to go for it and go for it hard." He slammed the conference table perhaps looking for the courage he was not certain he possessed.

"Before you run off, you need to listen one more time to one of my basic assumptions about the dangers of investigative reporting. Deception is the common infiltrator of all power structures. Abuse of power is concealed to keep people from understanding the workings of large groups, whether they are governmental or private.

193

"The greatest example of the victory of truth over governmental deception and the victory of an individual over a prejudiced society, is the Dreyfus Affair of 1894.

"The journalist, Emile Zola, proved that the power of the press could prevail against the greatest French republic on an issue that was not a popular one. After public condemnation by the establishment and a court ordered jail term for libel, he was forced to flee the country.

"As we know, truth set Dreyfus free. In our pursuit of the truth, we should not be deterred by the actions of establishments, by governments, by organized crime or any other force.

"I hope I have addressed your concerns," Roman concluded, "about how I feel and about the dangers ahead. Get to work!"

In the next hour the team agreed on a strategy for running series on the coming Conclave, apparent blackmail as the basis for church-provided sanctuary and organized crime's ability to influence governments. The daily stories were to be prepared by Tim and the staff and given to the boss early each day with Dan heading the effort in Rome covering the Conclave. Tim and Dan briefed the boss on their day's work.

"Be on the way to Rome tonight," Jack directed. "We know the politics and the partisan pressure that will take place before the Cardinals even enter the Sistine Chapel. I want to know who will be running the show with the Pope dead, Dan."

Dan began the explanation of a process he had once observed at close range.

"One of the senior members of the Curia is appointed as Camerlengo. He declares the Pope dead, smashes his ring of office, the pescatorio, to make sure no one issues any order over the dead Pope's signature. The residence and office of the Pope are closed and sealed; only the successor can throw them open to the world again.

"The real power is held by the Dean of the College of Cardinals, who arranges and presides over official meetings. As of now, it is Cardinal Delgado, of Madrid, the major force behind the conservative group, Opus Dei. As discussed before, they have mobilized the forces of uncompromising orthodoxy and will make every effort to regain control.

"The Cardinals are likely to meet more than a dozen times before the actual voting takes place. Each of these sessions will be presided over by Cardinal Delgado. He was elected to this position a short time ago but he will have everything to say about who speaks and who does not speak at these meetings. These sessions are often described as long-winded to prevent any real interaction from taking place.

"During the time of these so-called General Congregation meetings, the real work is being done in sessions organized around the edges, in discreet locations with those who share the same sense of direction as others. One good indicator of what to look for," observed Dan, "will be those gatherings that take place by language group and if they are visited by someone trying to play kingmaker. If we can identify these camps early we will have a handle on the outcome."

"Do what you think is necessary, Dan," said Roman, "just get your ass on an airplane as fast as you can to Rome. Let's get into high gear and snare the headlines like no other paper has ever done before."

Dan and Tim worked well into the night hammering out headlines for the story about to unfold. Dan was on the phone with his niece Terri making schedule changes for the children. The backup plan they discussed was well thought out but disappointing nevertheless. He knew he had to call Meggie. The thought of telling he was going to Rome was painful. His call switched over to her answer machine. He left a message to call him as soon as possible.

When she returned the call she was the first to speak

"I heard the news flash," said Meggie. "The details were on the radio. The Pope is dead! The news reached inside me and hit some very sore nerves. I couldn't help but remember how I lost you once before to the workings of a Conclave. I'm afraid it is going to happen again."

No matter how hard he tried, Dan could not find words to relieve her fears. He begged her to give him a chance to show that this was different. She remained unconvinced.

"Dan," she said, "there are choices we all have to make. I made one this morning. It's your turn now. Do you want me or do you want Rome? I'll wait for your reply." The only sound Dan heard after that was the dial tone.

Twenty-three
The White House Briefing

The black limousine passed the guard booth under the nighttime lights at the Langley entrance carrying Brigadier General Tom Feely and his Deputy, Marine Colonel Pat Garvey to their meeting with the Deputy Director of the CIA, former Air Force General Ed Anderson. They were escorted to the third floor through the usual checkpoints before arriving at the corner briefing room of the Deputy Director of the CIA. There were three other CIA staff members present to assist with the presentation, two men and a woman.

Anderson rose from the conference table and greeted the officers as they entered. "Good evening, Tom, nice to see you back in town. How was your return trip from Palermo?" he asked.

"Uneventful," came the terse reply.

"Colonel Garvey, nice to see you again too," offered Anderson.

"Ed, your people have been a great help to us at the White House these past weeks," replied Garvey. "We hope we can count on the same level of support as we plan our next move."

"That's what tonight is all about, Pat," Anderson replied.

Tom Feely took a seat at the head of the table, the lights in the room dimmed and the young woman seated in the corner stood up and addressed the group.

"This will be a summary of the continuing analysis we have been providing the White House on the Teekah search," she said, "and is documented in the folders before each of you. The death of the Pope, as recently reported, changes the options we outlined some weeks ago when we confirmed the family presence in the Vatican. We have narrowed the options down in the new location to two and if they are acceptable, we will have much work to complete in the next few days.

"Let's begin our briefing here," the young woman continued, as a picture of a bombed out one-story stone house came on the screen.

"This is what was left of the Teekah family compound on the West Bank after the capture attempt failed. Most of the commandos were killed inside the residence when the wall-encased explosives were detonated. The bodies of three of the others were found a short distance away, each shot behind the head indicating that their escorts took them out. Our operative inside the assault team, Colonel Kashani, was killed with the others. We still do not have confirmation of the circumstances of his death.

"The entire Teekah household security force was liquidated during the hours after the blast to make sure all of the unreliables were eliminated. A member of the team was absent at the time and killed a day later in Remallah.

"On the evening of the assault, we detected two submarines off the coast of Israel and later concluded they delivered the commandos. The Russians are the only ones with the capability and the experience for such an attempt, so we assume it was the Russian/Syrian team at work. They have been the most active of the groups searching for Teekah. The French and Iranians are next, with the Germans and the Libyans close behind. Several loosely formed mercenary groups are in the hunt but have yet to make any serious international contacts that would give their plans any chance of success.

"When Colonel Kashani briefed us about the planned capture of Teekah he was not clear which of the groups had hired him. We now believe it was the Russians, which complicates our plans under the next option.

"Under the plan developed with Kashani, the joint U.S-Israeli force was positioned to take Teekah and his family from the commandos after they were removed from the compound. This approach had always been our preference; namely allow some other team to make the seizure and then take Teekah from that group as they attempted to move him.

"We knew the compound had an unusual security system but could never confirm exactly what it was. Now we know. The wisdom of our preferred option was proven in this case.

197

"We are sorry, General, that you and our assault force had to waste time in Israel but if the plan had worked, Teekah would have been in our hands and on his way to our rendezvous point the day of the capture.

"We don't know how the family left the West Bank but we confirmed their arrival at Bari, in Southern Italy through our Rossello family contacts in Palermo. The party that was escorted to the Vatican included, Teekah, his wife and the three children and a security party of eight. All remain inside the Vatican."

With those remarks the young woman sat down and was replaced at the screen by one of her associates. He was a young man with the fresh scrubbed look of a military officer and the presentation skills of a Harvard professor.

"Our Mid East network detected the movement of Teekah's operatives from the West Bank into Spain. We located them in Compostella a short time before they met with a Vatican representative sent to begin negotiations.

"Four Palestinians left for Compostella some days earlier. They were spotted in Seville. After a few days, they regrouped in Compostella and met with a Monsignor Flores in the Plaza del Obradoiro in the heart of the city. After that meeting, we wired the Flores hotel room as a precaution and learned the details of the meeting and the basis of the negotiation for sanctuary.

"We have a printed record of the hotel listening devices in your folders. You are about to hear the recording Flores made in his room for his boss, a Cardinal Delgado."

The room grew silent as the voice of Monsignor Flores could be heard. "A recording at Santiago de Compostella by Monsignor Roberto Flores," the recording began.. "The details of the requested meeting are as follows."

With the end of the recording, the briefing continued. "Our agents observed the next meeting at the Cathedral at Chartres. Anwar Saeed was the principal negotiator as he was at Compostela and Cardinal Delgado joined Flores. They were both in civilian dress. Anwar's security team was in the cathedral at the first meeting and at the restaurant during the second. We followed them to the outdoor restaurant. Our listening devices were unable to pick up the details of their conversation. However, within a few days of the Chartres meeting Ali made his way to the Vatican.

"We have been tracking all known Palestinian groups in Europe and the movements of the Rossello and Bellardino families in Italy. We have been unable to locate the Grail package referred to in the Compostella recordings. When located, our agreed-upon plan is to take the Grail and all associated documents to Malta for transfer to U.S. control. Based upon information from a small religious sect in Jerusalem, we believe we are close to making this happen."

The third member of the briefing team and the most senior now took his place at the screen. He was unlike the first two, with gray hair and a slightly bulging middle, signifying many years of service at an analyst's desk.

"Through feedback from routine tracking of certain journalists here in Washington, we have discovered some interesting additional information," he added, looking toward General Feely at the end of the table.

"Dan Gerard, one of the new guys in town for the *Tribune*, has been a very busy person. He has a reputation for exposing dirty secrets through prolonged investigative reporting. He initiated meetings with Bishop John Casey of Baltimore. He flew to New York the same day and had a dinner meeting in Pontes restaurant with one Dominic Bagilio, a local Mafia insider. The restaurant's scrambling devices made it impossible for us to pick up conversation during dinner.

"From New York, Gerard went to Jerusalem for a meeting with a history professor and then to Rome for several more meetings. We lost him in the Rome traffic but picked him up again when he met with an operative from the Rossello family.

"After spending time with her, she apparently set him up with a contact from the Vatican Bank and then one of their strong arm men the next morning.

"His activities suggest he is interested in blackmail of the Vatican and perhaps knows about the Grail itself. He has been talking to a Vatican Bank administrator and attracted the attention of Rossello and Bellardino family capos as a result. Any serious questions about Vatican bank activities will create a dangerous situation for Gerard.

"When our agents lost Gerard in the city traffic, he was following a car from one of the Vatican residences toward the outskirts of Rome.

"The Vatican Bank activities Gerard has been asking about are those managed by the Rossello family and are particularly sensitive. A previous Pope ignored warnings about these matters and paid for his curiosity. Following policy, our payments to CIA operatives are never sent directly to the bank but pass through Bellardino offices in Palermo before moving to Rome.

"Although we have always been concerned about our dealings with the families in Palermo, they have been consistent on all transactions. Considering the frequency of those transactions, we have every reason to believe we can continue to depend on them.

"It is through the Rossello contact in the Vatican, Angelo DiNome, that we will be alerted to any attempt by any team to move against Teekah. We should rely on him for the best times for the U.S./mercenary assault team to make its move.

"With the recent death of the Pope and the number of journalists covering the story in Rome," continued the analyst, "we have to make a decision on the reporters we will be tracking during the Conclave. We don't have enough local agents to track them all. Should we have Gerard on our priority list with the other major reporters that will be in Rome or keep him on the secondary list where he is at the moment?

"With the alert of the Vatican Bank officials to Gerard's questions, we recommend his placement on the priority list and that he be assigned one of our people."

Ed Anderson rose from his chair at the other end of the table from Tom Feely and replaced the last analyst. He began the discussion of the objectives of the plan to capture Ali Teekah and relocate him to the U.S. for trial. The deputy director's demeanor and assurance gave a proper balance to the briefing as it moved toward its conclusion.

"There are two objectives in our plan," began Anderson as the next slide appeared on the screen. "First and foremost is the capture of Ali Teekah and his family. The Justice Department is prepared for his confinement and trial.

"The second and newer one, one which should not be underestimated in importance, is the capture of the Grail and its associated documents. Others have placed a value on its possession. We need to be in the hunt to have this negotiating chip on our side.

"We have intensified our efforts to locate and capture the Grail," said Anderson, "We think there is a high probability that this will be accomplished in the next few days. Our operatives across Europe have been picking up signals on special religious movements for weeks. They feel they are extremely close to reaching this objective. We will be paying a very high price for the ones who succeed. Once found, the Grail will be taken to Malta and flown to the Lodges in the Azores. From there it will be transferred to a U.S. military aircraft and taken to Andrews.

"Now for the plan to capture Teekah and the members of his family. Following White House directives, there will be no direct assault by our forces in the first stage wherever it occurs. If it appears successful, we intervene with the joint U.S./mercenary team and take possession of the prize. If anything goes wrong in the first stage, we can deny involvement as we did in Israel.

"If the primary assault by others fails, we activate option two, the actual use of U.S. forces combined with the Jordanians. It is clearly secondary but can be used if necessary by the order of the President. He has to give us the green light, however, before we go."

Feely interrupted. "For the record, option two has been discussed with the President. I understand the rules of engagement."

Anderson moved to the screen and began a briefing on Option Two, the U.S.-led Vatican assault plan. "The tunnel network of the Vatican shown here on the next slide," he said, "will take assault forces directly to the Vatican Library safe room where Teekah is located. Our inside security forces will assure Teekah is in the room at the time the assault is begun. The chemical fog we have used successfully in the past will be used here to incapacitate the targets before the move is made to capture. The timing is essential. We have arranged for the Bellardino contact on the Swiss Guard to notify us if it is safe for our plan to begin. To repeart: if option Two must be activated, it requires the approval of the President.

"We agree with your proposal, Tom," Anderson said as he turned to General Feely. "We have provided for a command center in the basement of our consulate in Milan for your control of the assault and the subsequent seizure of Teekah.

"If the assault by others fails and the President approves our own involvement, you will proceed as local commander to take Teekah. If we have the Grail before the assault, we suggest we contact Cardinal Delgado to enlist his support for the final move against the library. That will be up to you, Tom, and your evaluation of the circumstances at the time.

"I would like to pause to answer any questions you may have at this point," offered Anderson.

The room remained silent, except for the hum of the projector and the flickering images on the screen.

"Hearing no comments, I will continue my discussion of the details of the plan.

"We have completed the team formation arrangements you suggested, General, and concluded an agreement with a previously used professional force that has the capability and experience to lead the team into the Vatican tunnels and find Teekah's group. This element, combined with our special forces team and its Jordanian counterparts, provides the resources necessary to make this successful.

"The Rossello and Bellardino families have given us their contacts on the Swiss Guard and the Papal household staff. We will have this information in the hands of the team within a few days. Our own operatives on the Vatican security force have given us the maps of the tunnels beneath Vatican City shown to you earlier. The assault team will use this network for their primary entry and exit paths. Secondary paths include mixing with contactor workforces and several religious groups hired to support the ceremonies of the Conclave. These arrangements have been discussed with the groups inside the Vatican and await your approval, General.

"Command and control will be coordinated from Milan by you, General Feely, with secure lines to the White House.

"The pouch delivered to your home a few days ago, General," said Anderson, "has been analyzed and provided exceptional information on the various outside forces trying to influence the Vatican. We have assembled some of this information in a format the team will find useful. We thank you for obtaining the documents during your meetings in Palermo. They have already proven to be of substantial benefit to the intelligence community at large. Just one good example of what you brought to us, General," Anderson said as he moved the next slide onto the screen. "We have confirmed the identification of an important individual from one of the pictures in the central file. It was no less than Jack Ruby in some very compromising activities. We are not sure why he was in the file. We are going through the rest of the pictures to see what other linkages can be made to well-known individuals.

"During the next few days, our team members will be arriving in Rome with religious groups from Brazil dressed as nuns and priests. A Mafia-controlled contingent has been hired by several Italian contractors to provide catering services during the Conclave. They will monitor security checkpoints and be available for operational support if needed.

"The details of phase one are under way. Alerts are out to those involved. When we confirm the identity of any team making an attempt to enter the Vatican, it will be your call, General, on how to respond.

"We have learned there is thought being given to moving Teekah's wife and children to a location outside the Vatican to increase their safety. We believe this is an attempt to bring pressure on the Vatican by Ali from within. Such a move probably would not be made. We have a contingency plan to seize the family if an effort is made to relocate them outside Vatican City. The only way out is through the tunnel network and we believe we have that fully secured.

"The details of the weapons, the communications, the transport to Malta and the conditions on the final payments to the team are included in your folders. They are consistent with our previous discussions," concluded Anderson as he returned to his place at the other end of the table. He looked across the table at Tom Feely and asked, "Your reactions please."

After a long pause, and after moving from the back of his chair to the edge of the conference table, Tom looked directly at Anderson and said, "It has the right balance of primary and secondary measures. However, I am concerned about the consolidation and use of intelligence as events unfold inside the Vatican."

Now standing in front of the team, Tom Feely continued. "I will be at the consulate facilities in Milan with direct connections to three mobile commando groups outside Rome, to your center here in Langley and to the White House. Only one of the commando teams is US staffed and equipped and their use is a last resource only if Ali seems ready to elude us. I recognize it violates the plan concept of US forces remaining one step away, but I want confirmation of my ability to receive the latest information from your operatives and move the commando forces on a moment's notice if White House approval is given."

Anderson responded directly to the question. "Tom, you are the field commander in this operation and, as far as I know, the White House has given you complete discretion on how you deploy forces. You will have all our direct communication links with the various units working this plan."

"I need those assurances," answered Tom, "if we are to have the ability to respond to the events as they unfold.

"With that said, you are authorized to proceed with the full plan as discussed," said General Feely as he rose from his chair. "I will make the final contacts with our friends in Jordan and alert the State Department that Rome and the Conclave will become a hot zone for the next week or so.

"Any inquiries from State, FBI or any other agency should be directed to me at the White House," added General Feely as he rose to his feet. "Routine contacts should come through Colonel Garvey. He will know how to reach me in the event of an emergency. He will be the main point of contact throughout the effort and will be with me in the consulate in Milan."

With those remarks, General Feely moved around the conference table and thanked the participants. Ed Anderson asked

204

if he could have a private conversation with the General before he left. Tom agreed and stepped into Anderson's office.

"I don't know how to say this delicately, Tom, so I am just going to give you the facts as I know them. In our surveillance of Dan Gerard as a Washington reporter, we found some unusual contacts you should know about from a personal perspective.

"Gerard has been visiting with your wife on more than one occasion. He stayed late at your house after a United Way Gala. Last weekend, they were together at the Eastern Shore at the Wildlife Refuge Inn. I kept these facts out of the official report so they are not general knowledge but under the circumstances, I thought it was important that you know."

With an expression much different than the one he had been projecting during the meeting, Tom responded with an appreciative, "Thanks for the consideration. I will see to it that it does not interfere with what we are doing," he added.

"Under the circumstances, Tom," continued Ed Anderson, "I think we should do a complete background check on Gerard from the day he was born to see what we are dealing with and if there are any secrets he would prefer not to be made known."

"Don't waste your time, Ed," said Tom. "I have already done that. He's clean. Let's just keep an eye on him and his contacts in Rome in the next few weeks."

With that closing comment, Feely and Garvey made their way back to their car and left Langley in the midnight darkness. Tom's directed Garvey to prepare to implement option two as the preferred option. He had no intention of letting Ali slip through his fingers again. Besides, the next location might offer the ease of movement provided in Italy.

"Pat, you need to rely as much on our own sources of intelligence as these guys. We both know Air Force guys don't know much outside the cockpit." The marine nodded and smiled.

"Aye, aye, sir," he replied.

After the conference room was empty, Anderson moved quickly back to his office. He was on the phone watching the black limo exit the Langley compound. His call was answered routinely.

"Rich, this is Ed. I want you to do me a special favor and keep it off the record. I want a full background investigation of

Dan Gerard, the reporter for the *Washington Tribune*. You know the one I want, full details from the day he was conceived until now. It's urgent. Get someone on it first thing in the morning. Let me know anything that comes up as soon as you find it."

Anderson walked to the sink in his private facilities and stared at his reflection in the mirror. As often as he carried out his job of recommending movement of the chess pieces on the board, Ed Anderson longed to become a player himself. Perhaps, he thought, he might have found a way to play his own game.

Twenty-four
The Vatican Meeting of Opus Dei

As the elderly nun pushed her food cart past the doors to the Papal apartment, she turned her head ever so slightly to look at the red seals across the handles signifying the rooms were closed until the next successor to Saint Peter was announced to the crowds in the square. During all the times she brought the late pope his tea he was always so kind in his words and his actions toward her, she thought with sadness. He was different than those she was about to serve.

With the arrival of the afternoon teacart, conversation in the great room stopped and unusual silence came over its occupants. No one spoke to the nun and by their occasional piqued glances, she felt the need to hurry with her task and be on her way.

"Thank you, Sister," came the only sound from the leader of the Group of Twelve sitting around the large oak table that reflected the light coming through the three large curtained windows at the end of the room.

Once the doors closed behind her, all eyes returned to Cardinal Delgado as he resumed his plan for the meetings scheduled before the Conclave began.

"We have isolated those groups who have disclosed their intention of opposing our candidate once inside the Sistine Chapel," the Cardinal began. "None of them have been granted any time to address their fellow Cardinals, none will preside over any of the ceremonies scheduled for the next few days. We have taken care to see that they will be housed miles apart from each other and with groups who do not speak their language.

"For those Cardinals most often mentioned as candidates, we have released copies of critical local press reports from each of their countries to papers here in Rome and have been given assurances that they will receive ample coverage. These tactics have proven successful in the past and we expect the same results," concluded Delgado as he rose from his chair and approached a large tally board mounted on the wall in the corner of the room.

"Years of planning have brought us to this point. We need to remain calm and focus on our objective," he said as he looked into the faces of the cardinals seated around the table. "We do not have enough votes to elect on the first ballot but more than enough to block anyone else. Our task is to mingle with those who remain undecided and persuade them of the wisdom of our choice before we enter the Sistine Chapel."

Moving to a chart at the end of the table, Delgado turned several pages and called the room's attention to a list of appointments. "There are two remaining speaker assignments that have not been given out as yet. They will be assigned to the newest Cardinals who may be looking for national exposure while they are at the Conclave in exchange for their votes later. The names shown here are the those to be approached. If you have success, please inform me personally.

"The order of all formal processions must be adhered to by all the delegations," he continued. "We have our candidate surrounded by the elderly and the ill to make his appearance more acceptable to the TV viewers as he is identified as one of the leading candidates.

"From the presentation you just have heard by Kevin Collins, the head of Vatican Security, I am sure you will agree that the situation with Teekah and his family is under control and will remain that way until the conclusion of the Conclave. Negotiations for the resolution of the Teekah problem are continuing. The plan remains unchanged and is to provide sanctuary until we have the control we need. At that time, Teekah will be transferred to another location through the cooperation of our many friends. During that transfer, he will be captured by one of the group we have been negotiating with and taken out of our hands. If all goes well, our new Pope will be recognized as a leader cooperating with the world community in the search for peace and justice. It will be a very good beginning for our new leader.

"I am pleased to inform you," announced Delgado, "that the Grail and its documents have been returned to us according to the conditions for the sanctuary. A new secure location has been selected for safekeeping. It should arrive there within a few days. Many of the source documents used to prepare the Mystic Study Report have been removed from the Vatican Library and secured with the Grail. We have not used the services of the Jerusalem Marionites in the selection of the new hiding place as a result of the disturbances created in areas they suggested in the past.

"We have found the source of the disclosures from the Vatican Library that allowed the Grail to be taken from us by Avi Teekah. They have been dealt with. I have been assured that it will never be repeated.

"One final comment on our need for security," added Delgado. "Our security forces have been doubled for the next few weeks and the latest technology will be employed to detect listening devices during our meetings. All credentials will be double checked each day, so I urge you to guard your personal passes very carefully if you wish to have access to Vatican facilities. Now, my friends, your questions, please?

"Cardinal Baracini, you seem to have a question."

"Yes, thank you, I do," came the reply. "Through the papal nuncios from various countries, I have received many written requests from those wishing to speak on behalf of other candidates. I cannot continue to postpone as I have for the past few days. I have been told the delay we are creating will be reported to the press if it doesn't stop soon. We need to have new options to offer or the situation is likely to get away from us. Those asking are the same ones who have been blocked before. They are shrewd enough to know the importance of time."

"I am surprised they waited this long before delivering the threat," said Cardinal Delgado. "We have two possible openings in the schedule that I mentioned earlier. They could be offered to provide the appearance of a compromise. Both of the openings are the last session of the day when most people will be tired of the boredom of the proceedings. Both can be double scheduled with a conflicting dinner party at the last moment. Based upon how we are forced to use them, we will schedule a conflicting social event to keep attendance down."

The questions of the group turned to the planned reappointments within the Curia after the new Pope was elected, the reassignments of those who had not been cooperative and the schedule of the new Pope's reorganization of the National Councils of Bishops in those countries in need of new leadership.

At this point, Darci DiNome, the Rossello family advisor and one of the vice-chairmen of the board of the Vatican Bank, raised a question for Cardinal Delgado. Is Monsignor Tribel from Vienna on the new list of bishops we are circulating to the full delegations in Rome for the Conclave attendees?"

"Yes, he is," came the reply. "We need to go over that list one more time before you leave the meeting, Darci. I would ask you to remain for a few minutes when our other business is done."

Before adjourning the group, Cardinal Delgado praised them for their efforts over so many years. "Opus Dei has been on the front lines of taking back our Church over the years since Vatican II," he began. "We formed this Group of Twelve to symbolize our relationship with the first twelve apostles. Some of you joined after the death of our original members but have carried on in their tradition. I want to thank you for your loyalty and devotion. We stand poised to expel Satan from our midst.

"Please hold the individual Opus Dei meetings we suggested with each of the country delegations as soon as they are in Rome," he added. "Reemphasize to them the importance of their doing our work behind the scenes to forestall charges of lobbying.

"Let us remain focused on our primary task," he concluded. "Good day, my friends, and may God be with you."

A few minutes later Cardinal Delgado and Darci DiNome were alone in the meeting room. Delgado began with the tone of voice he so often used to demonstrate his lack of patience. "Haven't I asked you on many occasions before not to mention the elevation of any member of the clergy during the course of our meetings? Why do you find it necessary to raise the topic when you know how sensitive it is to me?"

Darcy DiNome moved across the room and glanced out the window onto St. Peter's Square and then turned to answer the question.

"Sometimes, you fail to respond to my suggestions as quickly as I would like. You benefit from the kind of reminder you just heard. "Sometimes, Cardinal," DiNome said, "your lack of response gives me problems. Then I feel you need to be given a problem of your own, to remind you how important my requests really are."

DiNome moved away from the window and next to the seated Cardinal. "Monsignor Treibel has been asking sensitive questions about the actions of the Vatican Bank in Vienna. Members of the board are concerned. His potential move to the new Congregation for Liturgical Worship here in Rome should get his attention and move him out of Vienna. It is an urgent request and not one that can await your Spanish schedule for timely action. He must hear the news while he is in Rome and understand what is at stake if he continues his questions." DiNome's words were on the verge of being hissed.

"You know I handle your requests as soon as I can," responded the Cardinal. "You know there are certain matters you must leave to me."

"How true! But enough! You answered my question," said DiNome. "There is no need to prolong this conversation. I have other meetings that require my undivided attention. I will see you tonight at our dinner at Le Tramerici." With that, DiNome strode from the room leaving Delgado to chew on his frustrations.

As DiNome entered the small café hidden in the warren of streets east of the Vatican three men interrupted their conversation as they saw him approach their table in a corner of the basement room.

"I cannot remain long," DiNome began. "We have much to do. The first order of business is to deal with the reporter for the Washington paper who has such a profound interest in the Vatican Bank. Contact our friend Rosa who has served us so well in these matters and pay her for the reporter assignment. Let her arrange a suitable exit for Mr. Gerard. I have been pleased with her work to date. This task requires her utmost care.

"Have you repaired that leaking vessel from the bank office?" DiNome inquired.

211

"Yes," came the laconic reply from across the table. "His reward awaits him in heaven."

"Good," replied DiNome.

"Make sure you follow Monsignor Treible while he is in Rome. See if you can detect any little weaknesses he might prefer to keep to himself. I have enlisted some of our friends to congratulate him on his pending assignment to Rome as bishop in charge of liturgical changes. It should be the first time he hears the news and feed his ambition at exactly the right moment."

After briefly discussing additional work assignments for the group, Darcy DiNome left the café to attend to other Conclave tasks.

Twenty-five
Dan's Arrival Back in Rome

Dan's inability to sleep during the flight to Rome stemmed from a clash of emotions on leaving Washington more than the concern about the unknown in Vatican City. The children's voices of gloom were only outdone by Meggie's silence listening to his apologetic tone explaining his departure. *Was it so wrong to want it all?* Dan asked himself. *The challenges of a career, the satisfaction of a family, the pleasures of a love, are these so incompatible that one must roll off the table?*

The jolt of landing gear hitting pavement snapped him back to the present. It was the start of a most important day and an opportunity to be part of an historic event. The schedule was ambitious but time was fast becoming his enemy. He wondered if time ever stalked Delgado or Roman as it did him?

The most important meeting before him was the one previously agreed to by Lou at his residence but linking up with Victoria to understand the Palermo connection was also urgent. Monsignor Carterelli had yet to return his calls. Bishop Casey assured him that this was often the case.

The thought of meeting Lou face to face cleared the emotional conflicts from Dan's mind. His anxiety increased every time he thought of the long ago pictures of Lou and the girls in that apartment. How could he have been so goddamn stupid and allow himself to be duped the way he was? *It is amazing what a few glasses of wine can do to one's ability to think,* he bitterly reflected. Heartfelt anger's first victim is always oneself, he remembered a coach assuring him.

He had mentally reviewed his confrontation with Lou over and over. It seemed to make good sense to him but only if Lou had been aware of the pictures. If the pictures had never been used to influence Lou in any way, raising the subject could be seen as an underhanded attempt to influence the current situation and backfire. Dan felt it was important to go ahead with his plan as soon as he could.

The first call from his hotel was to Victoria Tomaselli asking her to meet him later in the day to discuss her ability to help him access Vatican City. Professor Odani was engaged in pre-Conclave meetings and not available for dinner. The last calls were to the office and painfully time consuming. Dan had to fit in a coordinating session with Washington media types scheduled for the afternoon to review the coverage of the first meeting of the General Congregation.

As the cab dropped him in front of Baracini's residence, Dan's stomach started to get the better of him. The house had an ominous look to it that seemed to defy entry. Climbing the stairs, his feet did not seem to touch the old stone steps but lifted him softly to the top landing where the face on the bell was staring at him with puzzling eyes. For a moment, his "run" instinct tried to take control but he pressed the bell anyway. The same elderly gentlemen who challenged him the last time opened the door and led him to the same sitting area. Lou appeared almost immediately, catching him off guard.

"Dan," he said, "I hope this is as serious as you said it was because I have made quite a few important people change their schedules because of this meeting. Let's not waste time with small talk and get right to your point so I can get out of here."

"You won't be in such a hurry," said Dan, "when you take a look at what I've brought you.

"You and I never spoke much after our night of celebrating at the Bellardino party after the Pope's election. I want to talk about it now. We should both understand what happened and why!"

"Are you crazy?" shouted Lou, vitually distraught. "You made me change my schedule because you haven't been able to handle guilt over an indiscretion so many years ago? What is the matter with you? Have your lost all sense of proportion of priority?

"Do you know what is going on in this city?" continued Lou seething impatience in his voice. "I am astounded to be standing here having this conversation with you at this time. You, of all people, know what hangs in the balance during the next few days, to say nothing of the state of world peace that may be impacted as well.

"I don't have time for the resolution of your past personal problems," Lou said, as he sprang to his feet, turned his back and walked toward the door.

"I thought I might interest you in a review of certain photographs," said Dan. His voice was low and he spoke slowly, with a hint of menace.

That statement stopped Lou's movement. His head hunched over and leaning on the door he murmured, "I was praying to God you weren't going to say that."

Dan put his hand gently on his friend at the door. "Sit back down and hear me out," said Dan.

"I have often thought of our last night together and it always troubles me. It happened too quickly. The poor girl who overdosed on drugs was one thing but what happened later was something much different. I never told you about the details of what developed. You should hear them now.

"The girl Millie who helped us deliver the body of her friend Maria to that drug hangout in the park, called me and warned me to be careful. She said she was sorry for what took place and that she was leaving Rome for her own good. That call made me uneasy about the whole business but before I could think it through she was dead," said Dan, rising from his seat at the table to face Lou.

"The papers reported she fell in front of a train, I never believed it. When you saw her picture in the paper you were more relieved than sorrowful. You felt comforted that no one now knew what we had done. I was uncomfortable with the warning and the coincidence of her death. I was so mixed up in my own life at the time, Lou, I didn't have the chance to pursue the feelings that were churning my guts.

"A few days ago I had the answer given to me quite by surprise," said Dan reaching inside his briefcase.

He opened the large manila envelope and lay a series of pictures on the table, pictures of Lou, the two girls in all their nakedness on top of the pile. After glancing at them Lou stood up, turned his back to Dan and stared out the window.

215

"Whatever you think about your own failures," said Dan, "this was no personal failure. This was a plan involving a lot of people from the outset."

Lou turned toward Dan, a stream of tears running down his cheeks and asked, "What do you mean many people?"

"Just that," said Dan, "look at the other pictures in this pile and you will see friends and fellow seminarians who seemed to have exactly the same misfortune you did and coincidently, with the very same cast.

"One more thing about that night. We might have been pleased with the attention the young ladies paid us, but there were never any young men involved. Trust me, when I tell you, I couldn't ever have enough to drink to get me into that kind of mess. We are the only ones not smiling in the pictures and have our eyes closed. Knowing you as I do, I would guess you never studied the pictures the way I did. Now is the time for a really close look, so why not take it," said Dan as he slid the top pictures across the table.

Lou went through the pictures. With each new photo a look of deepening agony crossed his face.

"Thoughts of women were always close in my mind," said Lou, "I believed I would really go ahead and do the things in these pictures, if given a chance. Once you enter the pits, I thought that anything was possible even though I had absolutely no recollection of everything these pictures show in such detail."

After a few minutes of silence Lou turned from his fixed stare out the window and made a request. "Dan, I must borrow these pictures. I will give them back to you tonight but I must have them now. They will be used for a good purpose, I promise you that but I need to have them for awhile."

"They are yours, Lou, but I want to know what you plan to do with them," came the reply.

"Meet me back here tonight at eight and I will tell you what I have done with them and more. I will tell you more than you ever wanted to know about the Conclave and the sanctuary issue," Lou promised.

"That's a deal," said Dan. The friends embraced the way they did long ago.

Dan wondered if Lou could really handle the situation he was about to confront. On the other hand, his rise could not have been done without confronting power and its uses. He would be okay, Dan concluded, as he closed the door of the cab and gave the driver instructions to go back to his hotel. He had another appointment he could keep while waiting for Lou's response.

Not having heard from Monsignor Carterelli confirming their appointment, Dan decided to go to his apartment and see if he could contact him directly. It was lunchtime. Perhaps he was near his midday retreat looking for another liquid lunch.

Dan could not find the name on the apartment directory but remembered its location. He heard the door chain being removed after his knock but was surprised to see the face of an old man at the door.

"I am looking for Monsignor Carterelli," offered Dan. "Is he in?"

"No one here by that name," came the reply. "You have the wrong building."

"Are you sure?" asked Dan.

"Yes, I am sure," the old man said. "I have lived here for years. I really don't know who you are talking about." With that he slammed the door and firmly reconnected the chain.

Dan thought about calling Carterelli's office from a pay phone but he had such little success in the past with Italian operators, he decided to walk the few blocks to the restaurant itself.

He stepped carefully down the steep stairs and cautiously entered the basement restaurant. At first glance, he saw the same waiter who helped him out the door with Carterelli days earlier. Suddenly, the waiter lost his ability to understand or speak English. He was no help at all and sorry there were no tables available.

Once back in his hotel room, Dan called Carterelli's office but got no answer on the old number. It gave him the uneasy feeling that something was not right but what?

The conference call with Tim Scanlon and the rest of his support staff back in Washington made Dan realize the information on Teekah was becoming more complicated with every Conclave event. Speculation was fueling the rumor mill and making

217

it virtually impossible to verify any reliable facts about what was gong on inside Vatican City. The boss was looking to Dan to be the lead on the ground and clarify the Teekah situation. Tim passed along the priorities for the next front page story. Jack wanted focus on the terrorist not the Conclave!

Feeling the pressure building on the story and with most of the day gone and no word from Lou, Dan left the hotel to meet Victoria as planned. There were still a few hours until Lou's eight o'clock deadline. He was hoping Victoria could provide insight on the Teekah situation and more importantly, provide credentials to get him inside the walls of Vatican City.

It was a different restaurant than last time but equally charming. Victoria brought a companion with her to the table. "Dan, I would like you to meet Rosa, a friend of mine and a par excellence Roman guide who will make sure you don't miss anything during your stay in Rome," said Victoria.

Rosa was a young Italian beauty, with clothes and a figure that made her a companion for Victoria. The drinks and food brought a calm that had been missing throughout the day. Dan suddenly saw Lou's picture flash across the TV screen at the far end of the room.

"What are they saying?" shouted Dan, running toward the screen. Rosa followed him from the table.

"It seems that Cardinal Baracini has suffered a heart attack," exclaimed Rosa. "He has been taken to DaVinci hospital. He is in the intensive care unit in very serious condition. The prayers of the world have been asked for his speedy recovery at this very difficult time."

"I am sorry to leave you ladies before the night has begun," said Dan, "I'm going to the hospital to see what I can find out." Dan grabbed his jacket from the back of his chair and rushed into the Rome darkness not knowing what he would find.

"Wait," shouted Victoria, "take Rosa with you. She will translate for you at the hospital."

"Good idea," yelled Dan, as he yanked Rosa's arm and he hurried out of the restaurant and into a taxi.

Twenty-six
Call for Help

Dan's schedule was disintegrating. Odani was in Rome but had not returned his calls. Other contacts were becoming impossible and his faith in Lou's ability to handle confrontation had been destroyed. Remembering words that "timing is everything," he knew Baracini's trip to the hospital was no illness.

Helping Lou became Dan's first order of business. The options for access to hospital information were limited. Penetration of hospital security required understanding the medical environment. Dan had little. The disappearance of Monsignor Carterelli was equally troubling and surely related to the warning from Victoria's friend, probably closing the door on that relationship.

His only idea was a desperate one but at least it was an idea. Father Bill Casey, the Bishop's younger brother, had served as a part-time chaplain at DaVinci during one of his stints in Rome. He knew some parts of the building. He agreed to come and was willing to help in any way he could.

One person alone was not enough to break the hospital web but there was another idea that had seized Dan's wits. Could he convince Meggie to come to Rome? With her background and Bill's presence the combination might work. His first call went into her machine. He could not leave a message. Some time had to pass before he could make the next call. At least he was making contact and not leaving her in silence.

The call to Tim was long and complicated but the boss was happy at the furor caused by the front page. The pressure to create was off for another day. Calls to the family were difficult. Kathleen was suffering from more of the mean girls syndrome at school and Kevin was just keeping silent, never a good sign. Being away seemed to magnify problems not make them smaller.

The walk around the streets by his hotel was not helping clear his mind or deal with the pull between family and personal choices. It was time to try to call Meggie once more. Meggie's voice on the other end of the phone brought relief of a crazy sort.

"Is that you, Dan?" came the familiar voice.

"Yes it is," was the response. He tried, untidily, to quickly sum up details of the conclave and the search for Teekah. An emotional mess came at the end. "It's hard to explain how I feel," he added. "I just want to run to you and yet I know that doesn't work. If you could join me it would be important in so many ways. Let me give you time to think about that. Is Tom going to be at home or is he away for a while?" Dan felt he knew the answer to this question.

"As usual," came the reply, "he's away. I'm not sure when he is coming back."

"OK," Dan replied, "I want you to hear the circumstances prompting my question before you answer.

"The situation in Rome is getting more and more complicated every hour and in ways no one could have ever anticipated. I don't want to make the mistake I made when we were so close to having a life together.

"It is more than just being here with me," Dan added. "That is the practical part of my request. You can help unravel a hospital problem that has just been created. I had to call you. Give me a few more moments to explain."

"Go ahead, I'm listening," said Meggie.

"Have you seen the news about the Cardinal Baracini heart attack?" asked Dan.

"I have," came the reply. "It seemed odd. I guess those things happen."

"Heart attacks in the middle of a crisis," said Dan, "need to be looked at very closely. It might be the result of stress but it could be a cover to take him out of the Conclave altogether. With a recent Pope dying of a heart attack after he announced plans to change the Vatican Bank, Vatican heart attacks need to be verified.

"I met with Lou," he continued, "and I presented him with some of the information I discovered about the Conclave. He became very determined to present those facts to the Opus Dei leadership. He left me with a promise to return and review the documents further. He was in excellent health when he left for the meeting.

"I have been trying for hours to get into the hospital and find out what is going on but I've been turned away everywhere I go. I have an idea of how to get into the hospital. I need your professional help.

"Can you come to Rome in the morning and help me find out what the hell is going on?" asked Dan. "With your experience in nursing and the help of Bishop Casey's brother Bill, it might work.

"Bill Casey has been a friend for a long, long time. He took care of me when I first moved to New York, arranging a part-time job, a basketball coaching assignment and seeing to it that my credits from studying in Rome applied toward a journalism degree at Fordham.

"Bill and I have shared good and bad times together. I helped him out of a difficult situation at the St. Vincent's Home For Boys in Brooklyn where he was the director for many years. His rough and tumble contact with the boys was misinterpreted and his low opinion of the new breed of social worker didn't help. Returning a favor when he needed it cemented our relationship.

"With Bill's knowledge of the hospital layout and his fluency in Italian, we might have something that will work.

"My plan would be to introduce you as the new personal nurse for Father O'Neill, a priest from Baltimore, who is in the same hospital as Cardinal Baracini. Once inside perhaps you can find the Cardinal's room and let us know what is going on.

"Father O'Neill is a priest from Baltimore studying in Rome. You will have a letter from Bishop Casey directing you to take over the care of his friend. This is not an unusual request from the US when a priest studying in Rome is hospitalized. O'Neill fell and broke a hip and he needs help in rehabilitation more than anything else. More than all these details, I want you with me. What do you think?"

"Dan, I am confused. I want to try to find a way for both of us. From what you are telling me, I could not turn down a chance to make sure you are alright," she replied. "If I can help you look after your old friend, I will come to Rome. When should I leave?"

221

"I have booked you and Bill Casey on the early morning fight to London," responded Dan, "with a transfer to Rome that should put you in here late in the day. Bill Casey has my hotel location and will bring you there. I will leave a key at the desk. If I am not in when you arrive, wait for me. We should discuss the latest details as soon as we can so you could be at the hospital by 8 AM. Bill will have papers signed by Bishop Casey assigning you to the case. Let's hope it can develop from there."

"How will I know Bill Casey when I meet him?" asked Meggie.

"That won't be too difficult," answered Dan. "Bill is a person who stands out in a room. He is about six foot and around 240 pounds with short red hair and a booming voice. He always looks like he is running for office the way he introduces himself. His humor is infectious. The noise in his conversation should get your attention if you are nearby.

"I have you both booked business class. Once checked in, just go to the business class lounge and he'll find you."

"I'll be on the morning flight," said Meggie, "and be in Rome to help you any way I can.

"I'm looking forward to being with you," said Meggie with the voice Dan had been thinking about since he last saw her.

"We have much to think about," said Dan. "I hope we have time together to sort out the rocks on our path. I know my pursuing you is making a mess of our lives but give me time and I will find a way forward," concluded Dan.

"I want to be with you," Meggie responded. "Let's leave it there for a while."

His calls finished and not feeling much like sleeping, Dan decided to go out for a walk. Images from the past kept thrusting up from recesses of his mind.

He remembered the way to the "five church walk" he was led on as a seminarian as an introduction to the Church's view of the history of Rome. Those times had been replaced by a world utterly beyond understanding.

Where was that restaurant where he was saved by Lou's quick thinking? The spray of bullets found their mark at the front table but the ricochets brought their waiter down on top of them in the process.

Where was the park where they left the body of that young girl? *How could he have been so stupid to walk into that situation,* he asked himself. That girl's body, along with the body of Tom Feely's stepfather, had the potential of bringing a life sentence behind bars. Instead, here he was in the Eternal City trying to save a friend for a second time

He realized that the past is simply that, the past. It doesn't exist anymore. The ghosts had their time but this was a new time. New choices, new dangers! It was sunrise by the time he returned to his room and collapsed for a nap.

They are on their way to Rome by now, he thought, as he made his way to the Vatican Press Office for the daily briefing. It was generally boring, giving a schedule of the activity of the Cardinals as they pondered their coming days inside the Sistine Chapel. The carefully worded press release described the prescribed services for the recently departed Pope, no change in the position of the Vatican on the sanctuary given to Teekah and no mention of Cardinal Baracini.

Dan decided to call Victoria. Perhaps he could still use her without asking background questions and see if she had any success in finding Vatican credentials.

Twenty-seven
Report to the Vice President

"Thanks for the quick response, Rich," said Ed Anderson, turning in his deputy director's chair and glancing out the window of his office at the Langley guard post. "Your report sheds a different light on the situation in Rome. I'll talk to you about the next steps later in the day. Nice work. Thanks again," he said, signaling to the analyst that their meeting was completed.

As soon as the door to his office clicked shut, Ed picked up the grey phone at the edge of his credenza. He waited momentarily for an answer.

"Yes, Ed, what is on your mind?" came the voice from the other end.

"Sorry to bother you, Mr. Vice President, but according to our arrangement, I'm to call for a meeting when I think the situation urgent. Going by the developments of this morning, we've reached such a point."

"Ed, I'll be free in thirty minutes. Come to my office."

Although his was a face well known to the White House security detail, Anderson was checked several times before gaining access to the offices in the West Wing. Within a few impatient minutes the Deputy Director of the CIA was shown in to the Vice President.

"I appreciate the confidentiality of these meetings," Anderson began. "These topics are always as sensitive as any subject can get."

"You and I have been around this City long enough to know the value of relationships," replied the Vice President. "What do you have for me today?"

"My purpose in calling you," said Anderson, "is our continuous tracking in the Vatican sanctuary of Ali Teekah, the reliability of our plan to capture him and the leaks that are the basis of articles in the *Tribune*."

"We've discussed these plans before," interrupted the Vice President. "You know I have been reluctant from the beginning. We were fortunate to have kept our involvement with the Israelis secret when the Russians failed but that may be the last time we get away with it. The current plan is even more open to our direct involvement. I personally don't see the value of the reward justifying the risk. We are proceeding at the urging of the President and his concerns about the upcoming campaign. You didn't hear that from me, right?"

"Right, Sir."

"However, I am interested in what you have found out about leaks to the *Tribune*. If we don't crack down on these goddamn journalists, confidentiality will become a permanent joke with people like me a prominent part of the tomfoolery!"

Anderson moved his chair to the edge of the large paper filled desk, opened a plain manila envelope and took a deep breath.

"What I am gong to share with you now has not been in the official reports on the subject before, mainly because they involve personal issues affecting General Feely. The General was able to retrieve very important documents from crime families in Palermo. We have been aware of the importance of the Palermo network for sometime but our tracking of Teekah activities and his transfer to the Vatican opened up new sources of information. The general negotiated an unusual agreement with one of our operatives and we obtained truly significant confidential documents. He sent them back to the US following standard protocols. We believe his wife gave access to the documents to a reporter from the *Washington Tribune*."

"No shit," exclaimed the Vice President. "Just what we need in the midst of an election campaign. I hope you have some good news for me in that envelope as well!"

"I'm afraid not," answered Anderson. "Under our routine tracking of investigative reporters, we found the General's wife's having an affair with Dan Gerard, a new reporter with the *Washington Tribune*. The first of the articles in the *Tribune* about the poisoning of the previous Pope some years ago came within a few days of the documents arriving at the General's house while he was away. The articles provided the details on how the poisoning was done through the papal household staff. This is a fact we had only just confirmed ourselves. Nobody has blown open a rats' nest of comparable horror in this century! Nobody!

"The follow up articles on CIA payments going through the Vatican Bank might have come from the same documents that fell into Gerard's hands. He is in Rome now and we have confirmed he found a source on the bank's operations. If we don't create pressure through legal action against him and his publisher our problems are going to get worse, very much worse."

"Have you confronted the General with this?" asked the Vice President.

"Just the part about his wife having an affair, not my suspicion about the leaks. I became concerned about the reply. He gave no instructions about watching her specifically. When I suggested we do a full background check on Gerard, he said not to. I thought it was counter to his usual behavior so I authorized a full check anyway. We found some interesting information about Gerard and the General.

"It seems the General, his wife and Dan Gerard come from Albany, New York. The General's stepfather was found floating in the Hudson River with a kitchen knife in his chest, about two weeks after his mother moved out of Albany and Feely reported to West Point. At the time, the police concluded that the stepfather, a known street character, died in a brawl.

"However, the knife created suspicion that it didn't happen that way. Gerard went off to the seminary around the same time and later was selected to continue his studies in Rome before he returned to the US and began a career in journalism.

"Now comes an interesting connection," offered Anderson as he removed pictures from the envelope.

"In our facial scan of the pictures we found in the Palermo Documents, we had a match with Gerard from a current picture. One of the women in the old picture file with Gerard also came up in a scan of Italian newspaper files. She made the papers when she fell in front of a train in Rome.

"Falling in front of trains is a problem faced by friends of the Bellardinos' in Rome. The incident happened around the time Gerard left Rome for good. We could create questions about her being pregnant at the time and that it was her condition that was the reason for Gerard being ejected from the seminary. We need to create doubt about Gerard's background at the same time we initiate actions against the paper. I have additional thoughts along these lines," added Anderson.

"If we obtain a court order directing the paper to identify its sources while calling for a special prosecutor, we will see if Gerard and the publisher want to risk jail time to protect her and the General. With our threat to expose, Gerard would have to think twice before ignoring us. I recommend we begin this process immediately," Anderson urged.

"Alright, alright," came the reply. "Have Justice initiate papers. I will sign off on the issue of National Security."

"In addition to the action by the Justice Department, I would propose another step.

"This one is sensitive," Anderson continued. "I propose to put the General's wife under close surveillance, including listening devices. We have begun a similar program on Gerard himself but in view of my suspicions about the source of the leak we should add her immediately. To have this done to a family member of the White House staff is not unheard of but certainly unusual. It better not be done by the CIA."

"I agree again, Ed," came the reply. "Report the results of the surveillance on Gerard and the General's wife to me personally. And see if you can leak the personal details on Gerard to our usual press sources tied in to the usual unnamed officials.

"I remain concerned about our ability to complete the capture plan without a major backlash. If we have any sense that the plan is compromised, it has to be stopped. Making the grab just before the start of the Conclave seems to be very bad timing to me but it's not my call.

"I expect you to get to me immediately with any indication the plan may fail so I can tell the President. The people at State are as jittery as I am," added the Vice President, "but Feely has the President's ear for the moment. Solid information that raises a question about confidence in Feely, or negative information about his wife, would be most important."

Anderson offered a personal comment.

"I believe General Feely intends to move away from the approved Option One plan to capture Teekah after he is taken by others. He would prefer to have US forces combine with the mercenaries to make the seizure.

"Although he is concerned with the task of taking Teekah from others. His preference is to make the move himself for what it may mean personally, in the next administration. The information given directly to the President will be slanted to support more direct US involvement."

"I agree with your assessment," responded the Vice President. "This has already been the subject of more than one meeting with the President. Thank you for your concern."

The Vice President rose and walked Ed Anderson to the door of his office. "I appreciate your coming to me directly," he said. "Proceed on the same basis as before. I'll wait to hear your reports."

By the time Anderson had driven off the White House grounds, the Vice President was sitting before the Commander in Chief briefing him about General Feely, the leak and the implications of the plan to capture Teekah. Being the first with confidential information always confirms the value of a relationship, as he well knew.

The President was aware of the risks with General Feely's involvement but expressed confidence that the general would make a credible White House sacrificial offering to Congress if the plan backfired. He was content to let the situation in Rome play out under Feely's direction with additional steps to assure that Presidential involvement was clouded.

An agreement was reached on insisting that the CIA have more input on the Teekah situation with General Feely and make that role difficult to track if the worst happened. Agreement was also reached on initiating actions by the Justice Department against the *Washington Tribune* and against Gerard personally. Gerard's questionable background would be released to the *Tribune*'s competitor news organizations for their consideration.

The Vice President agreed to twice a day briefings with General Feely in the Milan Consulate, as time for the capture grew near.

Twenty-eight
Casey at the Bat

Meggie found her way to the business class lounge at JFK airport and nervously awaited the arrival of her traveling companion, Father Bill Casey. Although emotions moved her to accept Dan's invitation, could emotion convince her that there was a way out of this triangle?

The echo of laughter off the walls of the lounge announced the arrival of a special passenger. His broad and open smile could be seen through the hugs and handshakes he was distributing around the front desk. The six foot frame was topped off by short cropped red hair and a smooth protruding jaw constantly in motion. Meggie had found her contact and without a Roman collar.

Without interrupting his greetings, the new arrival glanced in her direction and walked directly to where she was seated.

"I am sorry to disturb you," he began, "but I am looking for a friend of Dan Gerard's and I was wondering if you might be that person?"

"You must be Bill Casey," she responded.

"And you must be the Albany Meggie I have heard so much about."

The two engaged in friendly conversation punctuated by the laughter that was part of the Casey style. He helped her get seated on the upper deck of the 747. Within a few minutes their conversation was directed at the hospital situation they were traveling to resolve. She reviewed her nursing career and Casey recalled his six-month stint as a hospital chaplain. Neither would have responded to the call except for the person asking.

Bill included a discussion of the baseball career he gave up to join the priesthood, his need to leave Albany when his younger brother returned from his studies in Rome and the success he found running the Boys Home in Brooklyn. He was pleased with his long relationship with Dan which included helping him out of the mess he had created with the new social workers of the Brooklyn Diocese.

Bill Casey relished the conversation over the Atlantic and as the dinner trays were being removed, turned the talk to the situation in Rome.

"The Church is in a bureaucratic mess," began Casey. "There are hundreds and hundreds of people living in Vatican City without a clue about their real function. With such an entrenched top heavy culture, it is easy for slippery insiders to do whatever they please.

"I remember the CBS interview with Pope John XXIII after he was elected. He was asked by Walter Cronkite, 'How many people work in the Vatican?' After thinking about the question for a moment, he responded, 'About half.' That revealed the insight of a man who understood the problems and was determined to change the culture. It probably put all the wrong people on notice that a sword of Damocles was being hoisted over Rome.

"From the details Dan gave me over the phone," continued Casey, "it certainly sounds like an attempt to keep the doors and windows closed at a critical moment. However, I repeated to Dan my favorite saying about large institutions, 'Don't attribute to a conspiracy that which can be explained by incompetence.' The global institution I am a part of has more than its share of incompetence."

Bill removed a packet of papers from his coat pocket and gave them to Meggie. "These are the instructions to the hospital in Rome authorizing you to take personal care of Father O'Neill. They have the seal of my brother's office as Bishop of Baltimore.

"I can read some Italian," said Meggie, "so I should be able to explain their intent to the hospital staff. I hope you speak the language enough to get us through the barriers that hospitals like to throw at you."

"I've been to Rome so many times I actually understand the local culture. The hospital will be willing to listen but whether they let us in is another story," said Bill. "Having all the right papers and speaking the language might not make a difference. Once someone gives you the first no it can take days to change their mind. The first attempt is the important one."

Casey's ease with Italian expedited airport clearances. They arrived at Dan's hotel under bright sunshine. The request for Dan's room key was more difficult but if Bill could do at the hospital what he accomplished at the front desk, Meggie was sure the day would be a good one.

When the door to the small room opened and the lights switched on, the calm of the day exploded. A blur of a man pushed past Meggie and ran into the arms of a waiting Bill Casey. Bill pushed the intruder back into the room and a furious struggle began.

After bouncing off the bed, the night table and onto the floor, the two men came to their feet moving ever so slowly around each other looking for an advantage. Meggie watched in shocked silence at what was unfolding.

The intruder came to a crouch, in a martial arts position. Casey had his hands raised as he did so often on the streets of Brooklyn. The two circled for a moment and then, with a few quick strokes Casey was down from a combination of rapidly thrown hand and foot movements. As the thinner, younger man raced for the door, he was brought down by a grab from his fallen opponent.

The two were back on their feet once again facing each other. This time a Brooklyn feint distracted the intruder long enough for Casey's right to land squarely in the intruder's face with all the force 240 pounds could deliver. The blow surprised and stunned the younger man. Casey threw him to the floor with a body hold he used many times with the wrestling team at St. Vincent's.

"Call security, Meggie; this guy's not going anywhere," Casey shouted.

When Dan arrived at the room moments later, he was startled to find hotel, police and EMS personnel around his old friend with a concerned Meggie treating a badly damaged Casey hand.

"What happened?" he asked as he put his arm around Meggie to relieve the anguish that twisted across her face.

"A thief was in the room when they opened the door," explained the hotel manager. "We have not had an incident like this for quite some time and the hotel sincerely apologizes."

"It looks like the other guy took the brunt of the battle," said the police official, who seemed absorbed with his report writing. "The man's jaw appeared broken and several teeth were missing. Your friend here has a damaged hand that needs attention. We know the intruder. He has a long record. We are glad to have him in custody. One of our police cars will take you to the hospital," the official offered.

"Which one?" asked Dan.

DaVinci, of course," came the answer.

While Dan and Meggie waited for Bill to emerge from the treatment room, they used the opportunity to wander the halls and examine the security procedures. It was this facility that held Cardinal Baracini. They compared notes on the morning's strategy.

It was hours later before the three friends could share a glass of wine at the hotel restaurant. The conversation was focused on what had to be done the next day to gain entrance to Lou's room. The exchange of glances between Meggie and Dan was all that was needed to quiet their internal debate.

Dan was awake early the next morning completing his briefing for Tim and the staff. Tim already knew about the hotel incident from one of the New York tabloids. Their headline read "Brooklyn Priest Nabs Intruder" with a picture of Bill emerging from the hospital showing his right hand in a cast. It was more of a story than the boredom of Conclave preliminaries. Tim was relieved there was no mention of Dan.

A short time later, Casey received a call from the US delegation attending the Conclave, inviting him to join them for lunch with his brother. It was an invitation he gladly accepted for later in the day. The three went back to the hospital to present the credentials of the private nurse for the ailing priest from Baltimore, Father F.X. O'Neill.

The administrator's office was crammed with complaining people unable to receive emergency care due to the flood of tourist injuries in the city. Casey presented the papers introducing Meggie as private nurse with his usual flair and lighthearted good humor over his treatment the night before. She was escorted upstairs to her patient while Dan and Bill drifted around the employee cafeteria looking for a loose employee ID card.

232

Meggie returned within the hour and gave him a single ID card she had picked up at the nurses station on her floor. It was going to take her a full shift to learn the routines. She suggested Dan come back to pick her up in later in the day. She would leave a message at the hotel if she needed him sooner.

Bill left to go off to his lunch. Dan decided to call Victoria. to finish their last conversation about access into Vatican City. Maybe she could help in making a hospital ID for him using the card Meggie gave him as an example.

Victoria sounded glad to hear from him and suggested that he meet with Rosa on the credential issue. They agreed to have Rosa meet him in an hour at the Spanish Steps and take him to a friend who could produce a hospital ID.

Twenty-nine
The Bus Stop

Dan sat on the Spanish Steps, his back against a small pillar. He watched Rosa emerge from the afternoon crowd wearing form fitting clothes barely hiding the figure beneath. Her gracious smile was a greeting in its own right. "Nice to see you again," she exclaimed.

"Victoria explained our meeting," Rosa said, as she grasped Dan's hand and gave him a warm kiss on the cheek. "After we finish our business, maybe you and I can finally spend some time together. We won't be far from my apartment if you would like to freshen up a little."

"First," she added in a smooth Italian accent, "we have to take a short bus ride across town to the friend who can create the ID you are looking for. We will be free after that."

"Good," came Dan's response, "I need several ID's."

They walked away from the Steps moving down crowded streets mixing with the tourists sharing gossip Conclave.

The bus stop was filled with people hoping to squeeze their way onto the next vehicle. Dan was aware of Rosa's sudden attention and felt her hand slip from the edge of his neck, onto his shoulder and begin massaging his back with her moving fingers. He was aware of her personal attention.

As the bus pulled up to the curb, Dan suddenly felt another hand on his shoulder, at the same moment Rosa lurched under the huge wheels. The crowd screamed in horror at the sight exploding before their eyes. Dan stood frozen by the suddenness of what had just happened. The hand that had been on his shoulder now had him by the arm, guiding him away from the crowd, the barrel of a gun pressed against his ribs.

"Don't do anything stupid" were the only words he heard from the short man moving them both away from the crowd pushing toward the accident scene.

Several blocks of silent walking made Dan all the more aware of the pounding heartbeat in his neck. Dan followed the push to a small outdoors café and the chairs under an awning. It was then he could look into the eyes of a killer.

"I urge you to hear me out before you decide to make a move that you might regret," the stranger said. "I must have your promise to give me that chance?"

Having no idea of what he would do in any case, he nodded assurance.

"What you just witnessed was what Rosa had in store for you. She has completed similar tasks before and quite successfully." The man had Dan's full attention.

"I have been paid, not only to follow you, but to see that you don't have any mysterious accidents during your stay in Rome. Rosa and her friends are well known to me and my associates. We compete for similar business opportunities. Clever Italians make easy money herding unaware Americans. If you had fallen under that bus, I would have lost a considerable sum from my final payment."

Dan's thoughts turned to Meggie. How could he have been so foolish not to think he would become a target the same way as Lou? She was alone in the hospital! Why was the intruder in his room? He had no time to listen. He needed to get back to the hospital.

"I don't know who you are or who hired you," said Dan. "I owe you my thanks if what just happened is as you describe. I need to get on with business. To get out of here quickly and to save us both a lot of time, let's agree to be companions for a while. Join me in a cab to my next stop."

A smile came over the man's face. "I never followed someone by sharing a cab before but it makes sense."

"Good," said Dan. "Let's go back to my hotel. If I don't make my next appointment, I will be missed."

The two men sat in the rear of a small cab. They were quiet as it moved through the streets of Rome.

Just as a light changed and the cab turned a sharp corner, Dan opened the door and rolled out onto the street. Before the cab could stop, he was on his feet and running into the crowd. He sat down at the first sidewalk table and through the folds of a newspaper saw his guide rush by him. After a few moments, he walked slowly back to a cabstand and returned to the hotel.

Entering his room Dan was surprised to find Bill Casey already back on the phone. He signaled him to remain quiet, hang up the phone and not to make a sound. Dan told Bill to be prepared for a visitor and to remain in the shower with the water running until someone opened the door.

Bill handed him a package of Vatican credentials given to him at lunch. They identified the holder as a member of the official US delegation. The Cardinals thought it would be wise if Bill spent most of his time inside the Vatican and not with members of the press. Dan kept the Vatican credentials with him as he went out the window. "Turn the shower on, Bill, and make as much noise as you can in the bathroom. My newfound friend will be arriving soon.

"We need to meet in two hours in the student cafeteria of the North American College, provided you can get there without being followed. I had a narrow escape this morning and when I add that to your recent encounter, we are in more hot water than we know. Don't make any more calls from this room, keep your eyes open and watch your step.

"I am getting close to what is making some people extremely uncomfortable. We should know more by the end of the day" were the final words Dan uttered as he climbed onto the fire escape of the old building.

It was a good ten minutes before Bill heard the door of the room open slowly. He remained behind the door of the bathroom with the water running. A few seconds later the door to the shower room opened far enough for him to hear the words "Oh shit" as the door slammed shut and the intruder ran into the hallway.

Thirty

Friendship Counts

The alley behind the hotel was awash with debris that made moving to the street time-consuming. Dan's thoughts were about Meggie alone at the hospital and now badly in need of company. It was time for a gamble. It was worth a try. After ten minutes on a pay phone struggling with his Italian, Dan was connected to Dominic Bagilio in New York.

"Look, Dominic," began Dan, "I didn't exactly follow your advice in my looking around Rome for answers. I have annoyed some of the wrong people and they are trying to rearrange my life for me. I avoided a staged accident this morning but I am not sure my luck will hold up. I wanted to tip you off to the trouble and for any backlash that might be coming your way for having referred me."

"I told you, Dan," said Dominic, "they don't follow rules over there. They don't care about anybody or anything. If they tried once and failed, they will keep trying until they get it right. My advice is to get out of Rome as fast as you can."

"I know I should leave, but my friend Cardinal Baracini is in the hospital under very strange circumstances. He can't be left on his own. Just calling you and telling you my plans could be the wrong thing but I have always felt we were friends. I need help for the next few days from someone who understands how the locals work but isn't one of them. Can you help me? If you say no, I'll understand. If you say yes, it could mean a great deal to a lot of people."

"Dan," replied Dominic, "you know how it works with me. Once you are in with me, you are in forever. You have proven yourself to me on more than one occasion. I don't leave my friends when they get in trouble. Besides, you just called me to warn me about a backlash. That says it all to me.

"I know who can help in the jam you are in. I want you to call Nick Testa at the following number. He is a free agent but loyal to me for any number of reasons. He understands how the game is played. He has kept himself alive for a long time doing just that. Wait about an hour before you call so I can get a message to him. Once you contact him, you can trust him with your life. Good luck buddy." With that, Dominic was gone!

Meggie came down as soon as she got the call from Dan in the lobby of the hospital. He alerted her to the growing danger but did not go into the details of Rosa's accident.

Meggie had located the Cardinal's room. He was on the same floor as Father O'Neill so she had reason to float around. She was confident she would have a chance to read his charts when the change of shift took place in an hour.

"Can you get me up to see him?" asked Dan.

"Not until you have an ID card. There are no visitors allowed on the floor so you wouldn't be able to make it off the elevator without one," she answered.

"I am about to take care of the ID problem and make us all a set of Vatican credentials in the process," said Dan. "I'm going over to join Bill now. We will be meeting a new contact who will help us with arrangements and the credentials. I'll be back here after that to hear the details on our patient. Don't leave the hospital for any reason. Remain in sight of the other staff. If you feel threatened go to the first floor security office and be there for me. Just don't leave the hospital alone. Carelessness now means something I don't want to say! OK?"

The back entrance to the college cafeteria was as Dan remembered it. He found Bill waiting for him at a corner table. He gave Bill the details of his morning to make sure he understood what was at stake. "I can't ask you to stay on any longer, Bill," Dan whispered. "It is getting out of hand. I can't ask you to remain involved. I might want you to take Meggie back to the States tonight."

"I'm staying for the Conclave," replied Bill. "I'll put Meggie on a plane for you if you want but I intend to be here anyway. Helping you is not an issue."

"If my phone call to a friend of a friend from New York doesn't work, I am not sure where that leaves us," answered Dan. "Stay with me while I meet this new contact and help me

decide if I can trust him more than the last Dominic introduction."

It was almost three hours later when Meggie received the
call from the lobby that Dan had returned. When she met him
in the lobby, Dan introduced her to Nick Testa, a friend of a
friend, who resolved the ID problem and would be helping them
the rest of the evening.

Meggie's first impression of Nick was that he had the appearance of a model and not someone who could help with the
hospital situation. Her opinion changed with the first words out
of his mouth and with the look in his eye. When she examined
the hospital IDs Nick had produced, she realized Dan had found
the right kind of help.

She took Dan aside and told him she had learned much
about Lou's condition. After the change of shift, she was able to
read the records. They didn't make sense. Few tests had been
done that a heart problem would have demanded. He was heavily sedated and not responsive. If they could stop the medication
for a while and give him something to counter the sedatives, he
might be able to talk to them.

"When is the next shift change?" asked Dan.

"Around midnight," responded Meggie.

"Here's what we will do," said Dan. "At the shift change, we
will switch Father O'Neill with Lou, moving them to each other's
room. If we can get Lou into a room where we can work on him
without interruption, we might be able to get him to tell us what
happened. Give O'Neill an extra sleeping pill for the night so he
doesn't wake up in a strange room and make a commotion. Perhaps in four hours we can get Lou to speak to us and return him
to his room by the time the morning shift comes on duty.

"We have enough ID cards to get us on the floor. With Bill
Casey, we will make the switch. What do you think?" asked Dan.

"I don't like any of this so far," said Meggie. "One more thing
I don't like doesn't make a difference."

Dan explained the plan to Bill and Nick. They agreed it was
worth a try. Bill and Nick would create a disturbance down at
the other end of the hall. When the floor staff goes to see what
was all about, Dan would wheel up a stretcher for the switch.

Meggie had to make sure that she changed wrist identifiers quickly and then changed them back later in the morning.

At exactly the change of shift, Meggie heard a crash at the far end of the floor. She looked out into the hallway just as Dan turned the corner with the wheeled stretcher. Father O'Neill was sleeping quietly after the extra pill and did not wake as he was placed on the stretcher. Meggie checked the nurse's station outside Lou's room. Between the disturbance down the hall and the shift change, the area was momentarily empty. The transfer was completed in less than five minutes. She and Dan huddled in the far room with the sleeping Cardinal and tried their best to wake him.

Meggie pointed out the range of medical information contained in Lou's charts. It was contradictory at best. Dan could not get Lou to wake no matter how hard he tried. As the hours ticked away, Lou was no closer to waking up than he was when they made the switch.

With less than an hour to go before the next shift, there was a commotion down the hall. Meggie could see nurses and doctors running frantically from station to station and many new faces among them. When she inquired about the cause of the commotion, she was told that Cardinal Baracini had suffered another heart attack. He was dead.

Thirty-one
Teekah's Resolve

It was a strange sight for a Swiss Guard to see inside the Vatican. Three young children chasing a soccer ball down the hallway leading to the Vatican Library with a nun trying to keep up. The library door swung open and the group was ushered inside. At the far end of the library, a floor to ceiling tapestry had been pushed aside to allow passage into a private room. The Teekah family were all present, along with the security people led by Ali's deputy, Anwar Saeed.

"The next phase of our plan is about to take place," Ali Teekah quietly announced to the nervous group before him. "The payment we promised has been made and the first transfer is assured.

"You, my dear," said Ali, looking into the eyes of his wife, "will be taken with the children to the Papal summer residence north of the city with a group of nuns from Jerusalem. They are friends and they have the necessary papers and protection to assure your safety. At the right time, you will be taken by tour bus to a seaport for a trip to Messina. I will come to meet you. Our friends in Palermo have planned the trip to our own home and place of peace for our family. We have found the time we needed to assure our safety. Now we must move again.

"Anwar," continued Ali, "divide the security force between our two groups. When we separate, we need to relocate to the new hiding place within the Vatican City network of tunnels. When they think we are in their library we will be somewhere else. It is comforting to know that our drawings from home provide more information on the tunnel systems than local maps. It seems that each Pope created his own personal escape route not trusting the path selected by his predecessors. With the number of underground networks it is a wonder the buildings remain standing."

"I have taken care of everything, Ali," came Saeed's quiet reply. "My people will be equally divided between the family movement and our task here to secure hostages for the escape. The group from Jerusalem is large enough and friendly enough to offer more than the required cover for the family. Your precious cargo will remain safe, I assure you.

"However, to assure the family is not detected," continued Saeed, "we should maintain the appearance that we remain in the library. If an attempt is made for our capture, it would be made in this room. In this way, we can prepare the same surprise that greeted those who tried to seize you on the West Bank. All unannounced guests will be treated with the same welcome! Our friends have provided the means to defend ourselves.

"The French attempt to capture us is likely to come before the start of the Conclave. If that is the case, the diversion we have planned should allow us to take the hostages we discussed and then choose between the two escape routes prepared.

"I am confident our plan is proceeding as we hoped. Our escape will be in the midst of complete chaos. The details have been discussed in Palermo. The reward for success is too great to permit failure."

With the family and the security members assembled as a single group, they gave thanks to Allah within a short distance of the tomb of Peter.

Thirty-two
The Farm House

It was several hours later, when Bill Casey arrived with the fax from Baltimore ordering the transfer of Father F.X. O'Neill from the DaVinci hospital to a nursing home. The hospital corridors were filled with newsmen seeking details on the final moments of the young Cardinal. Casey presented the transfer notice at the admissions office along with the identification of the two ambulance attendants who were pushing the stretcher to the elevator. Once on the floor, the private nurse attending to Father O'Neill directed the attendants into the room and assisted them with the patient, who remained asleep during the move.

When the elevator doors opened onto the lobby, the nurse and attendants found it crawling with more reporters demanding a statement from hospital officials. The security men were happy to have an excuse to force the crowd aside so the stretcher could pass.

The ambulance attendants closed the doors and drove away in the midst of the outdoor confusion that mirrored the chaos inside. Within blocks of the hospital, Nick informed Dan they were being followed. He told him to make a few turns at the next intersection and to pay close attention to his instructions, doing exactly what he said when he said it.

After some tense moments with demanding Roman drivers, the ambulance broke free of traffic and lost the pursuers. Once outside the city, Nick gave Dan directions to a safe haven he had used in the past. It was in a fairly remote rural area where a relative maintained a farm.

The ambulance rumbled down a dirt road and slipped into the barn of a farmhouse the doors closing behind it immediately. The patient was still not awake as he was carried to an upstairs room overlooking an open field.

"It could be a while," said Meggie. "He is really out of it."

The elderly woman in the kitchen began preparing breakfast for her newly arrived guests. The weary friends found themselves at a large wooden table in an ancient kitchen, dominated by a floor to ceiling open fireplace and a polished wood floor. Utensils and dishes had been placed around the table in anticipation of their arrival.

"What now, Dan?" asked Bill Casey, as he dropped his weary body into one of the wooden chairs.

"We have to wait for our friend upstairs to regain consciousness and see if he is willing to talk," said Dan. "We'll need a copy of a paper to show him, so he can see for himself that he died in the hospital. That may encourage him to give us the whole story. For now, we have to do all we can to wake him. Any ideas, Meggie?" asked Dan.

"A few," she said. "Let's get his clothes off and get him into the tub upstairs and pour some of this coffee into him at the same time. With luck, he should come around in a few hours. Let's hope that all he has in him are sedatives."

Dan turned to Nick with the next question.

"Do you think we were followed?"

"No," was Nick's quick answer. "It's my business to know the answer to that kind of question. I have come here before. No one has ever followed me. Why should this be different"

"Without your help, Nick," smiled Dan, "we would all be in jail by now, or worse. I don't know how you arranged for us to be here or how to express our appreciation for what you have done but thank you."

"A call from Dominic is enough for me," replied Nick. "I can't begin to tell you how he helped me and my family on more than one occasion, with no repayment except friendship. If you have helped him, my helping you repays my debt. Just let me know what has to be done," ended Nick as he moved to a large freezer at the end of the kitchen and began removing the ingredients for the next meal.

At the Vatican

The second report to Cardinal Delgado clarified the situation at the hospital. "Your Eminence," the anxious young priest began, "the body in the morgue was a Father F.X. O'Neill, a priest from Baltimore who was on the same floor as Cardinal Baracini. The patient in O'Neill's room was to be transferred by ambulance this morning to Holy Family Nursing Home outside the city. In our call to the home, we learned they had no record of any planned transfer and no one has shown up yet with any new admission.

"In checking the details further, we learned that a hospital staff member recalled that the person with the transfer papers had his right hand in a cast. There was a report in the paper yesterday of a priest from Brooklyn who broke his hand in a fight with an intruder in his hotel room. If it is the same person, he was in a room in the hotel registered to a Daniel Gerard, a reporter for the *Washington Tribune*."

"Thank you," responded the Cardinal. "I would ask all of you to leave me for a while."

After the room emptied, the Cardinal began his telephone conversation. "I have always left these matters entirely up to you with no questions asked. I expected a better result than the one we have. I don't know how you can contain this thing for the next few days but you better see that it's done. I never wanted to be involved in these matters and now I find myself in the middle of a mess of your doing. You need to resolve this situation immediately and let me concentrate on what only I can do. Failure to correct this error now will have tragic consequences for us all.

"In addition, immediately double the security on our guest. We have learned of at least one more capture plan that is currently underway. I hope your management of this task is more efficient than your last."

That said, the phone came down on its receiver with a force that sent it to the floor!

The Cardinal buzzed his aide in from the outer office. "Assemble the Group of Twelve a soon as possible," he said. "The meeting will be here in my office. Put it on my schedule as the usual Opus Dei weekly conference. Ask Mr. Collins, of Security, to join us and be prepared to give us a full report on the new security measures underway."

"Do you want Monsignor Flores to attend as he did last time?" came a question from the aide.

245

"Yes, of course, he was a major help at the last meeting. His services will be needed again. Advise him to be present."

Alone, the Cardinal rose and walked to the window overlooking St. Peter's Square. He stared at the thousands gathering below him. *So close and yet so far,* he thought. *After all these years of careful planning, I pray we can make it just a few more days and rescue our Church from destruction.* He could almost hear himself announcing to the world at the end of the Hall of Blessings, "Habemus Papem!"

Thirty-three
Unveiling

Meggie burst into the kitchen as Dan came in from outside, fresh eggs in his hand.

"He is coming around, he is waking up," she shouted. "Come upstairs with me!"

Dan and Bill raced up the stairs and into the middle bedroom just as Lou raised his head from the pillow and looked around the room in bewilderment.

"Where am I?" Lou murmured, as he tried to focus his bloodshot eyes on the strange surroundings.

Meggie put a cold cloth across his head as Dan pulled a wooden stool next to the bedside.

"Where are you?" Dan repeated. "I will tell you where you are. You are back from the dead but narrowly."

"What are you talking about? Who are these people and where am I?" Lou stuttered as he began to emerge from his fog.

"Not too fast with the questions," Meggie said to Dan. "Let's get some food and water into him and give him time to focus."

It was almost a full hour later when Lou slowly walked into the kitchen and tried to understand the group before him. The introductions were difficult and confused Lou even more. Dan's presence and the strength of their relationship provided a sense of comfort and a willingness to talk.

"The newspaper reports of my death are the strangest words I have ever read," Lou stammered. "When I consider what is about to happen in Rome, I feel I have an obligation like no man before me. I am just not sure what to do next.

Dan spoke, "Lou, remembering all that you and I been through why not finally let the truth dictate what is said. We can take it from there. You have the pieces of a puzzle we haven't been able to figure out. You need to tell us what you know."

"I'll do my best," started Lou, "but my mind is truly in a fog."

Lou pulled his chair closer to the old table, gripped a faded coffee mug for strength and looked into eyes he could see were waiting to hear the details of the treachery that had nearly cost him his life.

"Lou," Dan continued, "I know this is confusing but we don't have the luxury of taking time to go over everything. Try to get some basics out where we can understand them.

"When the Vatican decided to provide sanctuary to a known terrorist, that decision brought us back together. Start there. What was the issue that was so important it forced Church leadership to do something it didn't want to do?"

"If you want me to start there, I will," said Lou. "The real story, however, starts years before. I must go there to answer your question.

"I can't summarize two thousand years of Church history in the next few minutes but I can provide points that will help you understand what has happened to me and my church.

"First, some background. It will help to explain why the Ali Teekah demand for sanctuary was successful. In any blackmail attempt, there must be something that needs to be hidden and an understanding of the impact of disclosure. Both of these elements were present."

The farmhouse kitchen slowly became a classroom with Lou as instructor.

"The main point I ask you to keep in mind," began Lou as he pulled the padded stool closer to the table, "is the importance of Chartres. Not just the cathedral but the entire Chartres area outside Paris and its history. It holds the key to understanding the difficulty of hundreds of years.

"The first step taken in trying to understand the puzzle that has baffled men for centuries was taken by Pope John XXIII. Once elected, he was not willing to be a pawn of the Curia and he walked his own path of openness and truth. When he learned of long held Church secrets inside the Vatican he summoned a group of scholars. He personally gave them the task of unraveling the misinformation that existed within the Vatican Archives concerning long held secrets. That group produced a preliminary report that prompted John to call the Second Vatican Council.

248

Their work confirmed his desire to open the windows of the Church and bring in fresh air.

"The preliminary findings brought together hundreds of years of history surrounding the Chartres area and gave it more significance than at any time before. After this revelation, it is true that Pope John had the collected works on Chartres as bedside reading. His favorite reading was *Clairvaux, The Valley of Light*.

"Chartres Cathedral is located on an the site of a Druid mystery centered on an earth line linking it to sites in Stonehenge and the Pyramids. It was the center of devotion to the Devine Feminine under the title of the Black Madonna, as far back as Celtic times. This was a very important issue raised by the study group.

"Is it possible that the concept of a virgin being impregnated by the gods to deliver a Divine son goes back well before the Christian gospels? In a variety of anthropological investigations the virgin birth concept is prevalent in cultures as far away as the South Pacific and well removed from Western Europe. Could it be part of the Divine plan revealed to man as well as foretold in the Old Testament and fulfilled in Jesus? Could the Divine be talking to men of all kinds? This debate stirred up a storm of emotional opposition and contributed to keeping it hidden.

Lou paused to massage his face and ask for more coffee. He thought quietly for a moment and continued.

"Another troubling concept of the group's focus was the influence of the heavens on man's activities. Was the Divine communicating a plan through the stars? With the signs of the Zodiac on the veil in the Temple of Solomon and the wise men following the star at the Nativity, what after all is the message? In addition, all around Chartres evidence was found that the area was covered with the signs of the Zodiac and structures aligned to capture the rays of the sun during the changes of the seasons. You can imagine Vatican scholars trying to handle this topic.

"The first records of a Christian Mystery School at Chartres go back to 1006 when a connection was made to the so-called earth energies in the area. The first school encouraged the study of Egyptian and Greek art.

"The area takes on greater significance when the leading families of Europe decided to consolidate over 600 years of their own spiritual collections at Chartres around 1100. In order to protect their merged collection, they directed a son of one of their own families, Bernard of Clairvaux, to take charge of a new Mystery School along with thirty other members of these same families. These men established a basis to promote and protect the family secrets and relationships. The society was called the Troyes. Fraternity. It was the Church Council of Troyes that eventually launched the Second Crusade and established the Order of the Knights Templar following the plan of the closed society.

"Having the ability to centralize religious study beyond the eyes of the official church had a very positive effect beyond what anyone realized. Disparate groups came together at the Mystery School to share their spiritual understandings. It included the Sufi School of Spanish Mystics, a group of Jewish and Islamic scholars, the Rabbi Rashi Kabbalistic Academy from Troyes, a band of astrologers working under Arab rule in Toledo, texts from the Temple of Solomon and manuscripts from the Orleans Spirit School. Chartres became the most important center of religious thought and study at the time.

"Added to this knowledge came contributions from the Crusades and the Templar exploits in Jerusalem. The Knights were a creation of the same families that established the center at the Chartres Abbey. They gave them the task of exploring not only Jerusalem but the mysteries of the Mid East. Bernard of Clairvaux, as appointed leader of the abbey, was one of the principal supporters of the Templars and the voice that encouraged Europe to launch the second Crusade.

"The study group found considerable evidence that the Templars sent back findings from under the temple Mount to Bernard for interpretation. About this same time, remarkable changes occur in geometric designs, alchemy and astrological relationships that are the basis for building the great cathedrals of Europe. The alchemical transformations that produced the famous blue and red stained glass at Chartres baffles experts to this day. No one has been able to duplicate the effect. In addition, the cathedral abounds with clues about Templar activities and legitimizes the signs of the Zodiac by including them in the church's stained glass windows.

"The Templars met their demise in 1307 when they refused to give up their findings from the Crusades. They were smart enough to hide their treasure when they understood the fate that awaited men who opposed king and pope.

"The Abbey at Clairvaux, with its vast spiritual knowledge, remained in the background until many years later. In the fifteenth century the Vatican became intrigued with a spiritual work from the fourteenth century Mid East called *The Cloud of the Unknowing*. They turned to Clairvaux to decipher the text. It gave them more than they expected.

"The response by the monks revealed the ability of the Abbey to truly reach into the spirit world for guidance. *The Cloud of the Unknowing* was a collection of near death experiences. After hundreds of years of study, the monks had similar accounts that confirmed the authenticity of returning from near death and provided examples from many other sources. Encouraged by this, the Vatican developed a close relationship with the Chartres School. As a result, they found the clues that led to the Templar hiding place for the Holy Grail and its documents.

"The Grail was removed from a strange island in the Baltic. The Island of Bornholm, a place later found to have astrological links to the Pyramids and Stonehenge. The island had an unusual array of Churches, hundreds of stone altars from years earlier and a history of strange happenings. The Knights must have been pleased with its selection.

"Once the Grail was secured and relocated, the abbey was abandoned and the monks scattered across Europe to protect the secrets. Not having the very people who understood the mystical meaning of the Grail and the Templar documents, the discovery did not have the impact it might have had. Mysticism within the Church was declared evil. Those who spoke about it were declared heretical and threatened with death if they persisted in their beliefs. The Inquisition followed shortly thereafter

"Here, the first great deception of the Church begins. Desiring to keep Christians bound to an organized clergy that shared power with the nobility, a veil of lies was created to discourage further searching for the Cup of Christ. A so-called bloodline theory of the Grail was created to camouflage the truth and at the same time to flatter the nobility.

"More than two hundred years later," said Lou, "an event occurred that forced the Vatican to examine what had been hidden away.

"As with all secrets, people come to know something was being hidden. The 'Secrets of Fatima' developed as a different concern. The Church had decided to continue the Grail deception. It found a new hiding place away from Portugal rather than coming to grips with the truth.

"Finally," said Lou, "came the study commissioned by John XXIII. He ordered a complete examination of all the documents in the Vatican Library, an investigation of the material concerning the Holy Grail, the Chartres Mystery School and all its reported mystic experiences.

"The work was divided into four areas to prevent any single group from grasping the significance of one area as it related to others. The findings were brought together and summarized in a preliminary report. It was called, *The History of Mysticism and the Holy Grail*. The first report was given to Pope John. It influenced him in calling for the Vatican Council.

"The Pope's study team related the history of mysticism to man's struggle to understand messages from the Creator. It offered the proposition that God has been speaking to man for centuries but until men could share the information in peace with each other, the message was never comprehensible. When worked on together, the path would open and the message would become clear.

"The final evidence supporting the study's assumptions surfaced when the elderly leader of John's study group, Father Villieu, was given a copy of *The Tibetan Book of the Dead*. It was a compilation of the years of recording Tibetan monks' near death experiences in mountain retreats long closed to the rest of the world. The details from Tibet coincided exactly with the descriptions of the same near death experiences Villieu understood the monks at Chartres had uncovered centuries earlier. The explanation of the path of enlightenment by the monks in Tibet matched the path of illumination established by the Templars.

"The history of the Chartres Black Madonna was particularly troubling to the Opus Dei type of Curia theologian. They wanted the gospel story of the Virgin birth to stand alone and not to admit discussions of similar pagan thoughts. They failed to recognize the earlier worship could well be an announcement of the Divine Plan for salvation from the beginning and should be considered.

"When Pope John died before the conclusion of the Council," Lou continued, "it enabled the Curia and the conservative forces of Opus Dei to prevent further discussion of the study and to make their move to return the Church to the absolute central control it had before that Council. They held firm to their belief that the only path to God was through their Church. There was no reason to honor the practices of others.

"By this time the Opus Dei faction in the Church had centralized their influence in a select Group of Twelve within the Curia. I was invited to be part of the group by its leader, Cardinal Delgado. You remember him, Dan," remarked Lou, "as one of the leaders of Opus Dei at the time of the Conclave called after the death of John XXIII.

"With the death of the Vatican scholar, Father Villieu and the disclosure of his private papers, the Group of Twelve was forced by other Church factions to agree to a new review of the study.

"The latest review offered ideas that were considered even more threatening than before," continued Lou. "Some of the issues presented had significance well beyond Christianity, including the findings about astrological relationships between the sky above and the earth below. Unfortunately, one of the review leaders chosen to clarify the significance of the findings initiated discussions with experts outside the Vatican. This outside contact with subject matter experts resulted in new questions coming from around the world. The Opus Dei leadership decided it was too dangerous to continue. The outside discussions included contacts in Jerusalem. This was the contact that opened the door to Teekah and his associates.

"The Group of Twelve concluded that the Church should not depart from the path it had followed for two thousand years. The Mystic Study report was tabled once again.

253

"However, like all secrets, there were some who just couldn't keep it to themselves. As hard as the Curia tried to keep the findings of the study buried, the more it was talked about. I was given responsibility for the safekeeping of the reports and for quieting further discussion, without much success, I may add.

"When the findings in the Mystic Study Report and the hiding of the Grail were presented as the basis of the blackmail by Ali Teekah, Opus Dei had no choice but to provide sanctuary. If they didn't, the result would have been the loss of the Grail and the release of the Vatican secrets right at the moment they knew the Pope was dying. The timing on the part of Teekah was perfect," emphasized Lou.

"The granting of sanctuary was justified by the Group of Twelve as a plan to keep Teekah inside the Vatican, have the Grail and documents returned and after the election of the new Pope, turn Teekah over to world authorities as a gesture of global peace.

"In the final analysis, the contents of the Mystic Study Report were seen as even more problematic than the hiding of the Grail.

"I think I have covered the blackmail issue and the decision to grant sanctuary to Ali Teekah," concluded Lou.

The walls of the farmhouse kitchen had never absorbed such things before. Those around the table sat in silence as they tried to grasp what had just been said.

Dan broke the spell. "I don't know what to say. If we had a group of scholars with us, it would take days to divide the story into manageable pieces. Here's my sense of what can be done as events are unfolding in the Vatican.

"The power brokers are about to make their final moves in selecting a new Church leader. What you have told us, if known, would sink their plan. If they contain Teekah, as they think they can, that problem can be dealt with in its turn. Let's focus on disrupting the Opus Dei power play and the dynamics of the Conclave and see where that takes us."

After the group at the table had expressed their reactions to Lou's explanation and Dan's suggestion, Dan attempted to redirect the discussion.

"I'm sorry to add another issue," he offered, "but experience compels me to ask one more question.

"Lou," Dan began, "the trouble I have with your history is that while it covers a great deal of theology and grabbing for power, you've left out the other half of the struggle. Who has controlled the money?"

Having drained another cup of coffee, Lou continued.

"The Vatican lost control of its money long ago. The leaders were convinced that they should not be concerned about such worldly matters as money. They were determined to focus energy and resources on theology not wealth. The Church's past position on charging interest is used as an example of why it should leave money management to experts. This argument presented at the time simply called for money matters being turned over to 'others,' whoever they might be," added Lou.

"The Vatican Bank today is controlled by so-called professionals. This has been the case for as long as I can remember. The Bellardino family is the point of contact for the Vatican in the bank operation. They are connected to Rossello interests in Palermo. What happens beyond that, is anybody's guess.

"Whatever money the Vatican requires it simply asked for and it is delivered. I have little understanding of its operations. One of the vice-chairmen of the bank board, Darci DiNome, is the only Bellardino family representative known to me. He also sits on the Opus Dei group of twelve but not as a voting member. He attends our meetings but rarely offers an opinion about anything," said Lou with some embarrassment.

"DiNome and Delgado have a unique relationship," he continued. "From what I see, Delgado just wants things taken care of and doesn't want to hear any details. DiNome nods his head and that is usually the end of it."

"I'm not sure I buy your answer about the banking relationship," said Dan, "not that you haven't told us what you believe is the case but from my experience, anyone sitting at the head of an appointed power structure usually has a hand in the till. Knowing the little I do about Delgado, I would be surprised if his hands weren't as dirty as others who have found themselves with his power.

255

"There is a great deal of wealth that no one seems to know about," said Dan. "The old saying, power corrupts and absolute power corrupts absolutely seems to apply. The bank's money must be spread around to a great many people to make things happen."

"You may be right, Dan," replied Lou, "I just haven't seen anything about DiNome that frightened me, until today."

"We are on the right path," Dan added, "but who figured you for death and why was I so close to joining you?" This question caught Meggie by surprise. Her face showed it.

After looking at Dan and Meggie for a moment, Lou continued.

"The pictures, Dan. They brought down the house of cards. What I thought had been an individual's poor choice, turned out to be a plan to compel my cooperation and guarantee my loyalty. The pictures of others apparently caught in the same web, forced me to see the situation for what it really was. I confronted Delgado.

"I called him for an immediate appointment and demanded that it include the full Group of Twelve. When I arrived in his office, only DiNome and Delgado were there. When I let them examine the file you gave me, they claimed the pictures were forgeries, a plot to disgrace the Church.

"I told them that if that was indeed the case, then the plot had been going on for some time. I had been shown the pictures by members of the Bellardino family years ago. I was comforted by the thought that they had destroyed the negatives and promised to keep my secret. Only now did I see pictures of others and had to assume that they existed for as long as mine.

"Delgado looked at DiNome. The anguish in their faces told me I had undone the deception. They both knew the truth. Delgado's voice was choked with bitterness and disgust.

"I told Delgado," Lou went on, "that the Bellardinos were not as careful as they should have been with our secret. A reporter for the *Washington Tribune* had confronted me, not only my picture, but pictures of others I knew who were regulars at the Bellardino Villa.

"I guess I crossed a line," said Lou, "when I told Delgado it was time for me to stop living a lie and let the truth be known.

256

If I admitted my failings, perhaps others would do the same. It was high time to sweep the board clean.

"I demanded again to meet with the group of the Opus Dei twelve, as I had requested earlier. Delgado said they were on the way and that the meeting would convene in about twenty minutes. He asked that I go to my office and wait for his call to return when the others arrived.

"I received a call from Delgado's office about half an hour later. As I walked from my office to his, I was assaulted in the hallway. I felt a sharp pain in my neck and then passed out. The next thing I remember is waking up in the bedroom upstairs."

With that explanation, Lou moved from the table to the open kitchen door and looked out into the yard where chickens were roaming in the afternoon sun. He held his head with the one hand resting on the half open door and pushed the hair from his face with the other. He pursed his lips in an attempt to control his feelings.

Nick rose from the table and opened the refrigerator door to find a cold drink. He turned to his seated companions and offered a comment.

"If the people inside the Vatican think they can double cross Teekah and hand him over to somebody they are in for a surprise," he said letting the cold beer run down his throat.

"One crisis at a time," said Dan. "Let's think this through step by step. The Opus Dei plan that Lou described, is to work the Conclave to reach their goal and turn to the terrorist situation later. Let's go with the idea I proposed earlier and try to disrupt their plan. Does anyone have any other ideas?" There was silence.

Dan walked over to Lou at the kitchen door and turned him around to face the group. "Are you ready to run again to get the truth out?" he asked.

Lou lifted Dan's hand from his shoulder, and looking him in the eye, asked, "At this point what else is left?"

Nick and Dan left the kitchen and walked into the olive trees. They returned ten minutes later.

"OK," said Dan, "this is the proposal. To meet our first objective, we present Lou's information to those who will enter the Sistine Chapel to vote. The fact that you are back from the dead,

257

Lou, should make it enough for you to be allowed to address them as a Cardinal. You belong in the Conclave anyway."

Lou interrupted. "The Mystic Study Report is critical," he began. "If we could get a copy of the report it would be extremely important for all to see. I have the only two copies I know of in my office. One is in my safe and one is hidden in my other files. If we can get those documents it would decide the outcome."

"Alright, we will go back to your office and try to collect the report," said Dan. "It seems to me that with that report and copies of the picture file I gave you, you would have a great presentation to offer to the next General Congregation meeting."

"If you can get into the safe in my office," interrupted Lou, "you could retrieve my Conclave security credentials as well. They would be a great help in moving through the checkpoints."

"How does everyone feel about the idea?" Dan asked.

With the group's murmured assent, Dan and Nick would leave the farmhouse and drive to Lou's residence at nightfall.

Thirty-four
Back to the Residence

Nick brought the motorcycle to a stop several blocks from Lou's residence. Dan let out a long held sigh of relief. The trip as back seat rider had left the scenery a blur and his fingers frozen to the seat grips. He was more at ease meandering past the house searching for signs of life. The back door opened quietly. Total darkness greeted the two visitors.

Dan recalled the downstairs layout of the residence from his earlier visits and followed Nick's slow and deliberate moves through the first floor. With Lou's sketch of the upstairs etched in his mind, Dan was confident he could find the safe. Climbing the stairs, Dan found the room of the housekeeper, who had greeted him at the door during his earlier visits. The bed was occupied but silent.

The safe was behind a tiled wall panel beneath the wash basin in Lou's office, as he had described it. Nick had it opened quickly. Dan started through the files while Nick continued searching the upstairs. The Mystic Study Report was in the safe. Dan moved to a large file cabinet at the other end of the room for the second copy hidden in a folder marked Personnel Transfers.

Dan's nervous efforts to stuff the needed documents in his back pack were interrupted by a soft voice at the doorway to the office. "Thank you for finding the second copy," said the observer, "I never could locate it." Lou's housekeeper stood in the doorway, a gun pointed at Dan. "I am sorry I cannot greet you as I did in the past but this is a very special occasion. I would like to thank you for the substantial sum of money your body will bring me when I give it to those who are looking for you."

The gunman's eyes suddenly opened wide, very wide. His jaw dropped open and a look of disbelief came across his face. Blood spread over his shirt and ran down to his waist. His hand went limp. The gun slipped from his fingers. His head moved slowly to one side with an arm moving across his mouth. As he slumped to the floor, Nick's face emerged from behind his back. Nick withdrew the knife that had so abruptly ended the conversation.

"If you have what you want, let's be on our way," whispered Nick. "I don't think he is the only one watching this place."

Dan stuffed the report documents and the set of Vatican credentials into his backpack. They moved down the stairs.

"Not the back door," Nick motioned. "Let's try a basement window."

Looking through one of the basement windows they saw a pair of shoes move past the glass.

"Back upstairs," Nick said. "Wait for me by the back door."

Within minutes, Dan heard a window open and a thump in the bushes, followed by muffled gunshots. No sooner than he heard the shots than Nick appeared at the back door, grabbed Dan by the arm and the men dashed into the darkness. They were on the motorcycle in a moment speeding away. Shots were fired at them as they sped into the darkness.

Nick moved briskly in and out of traffic to make sure no one was following before slowing to a steady pace back to the farmhouse. The dirt driveway was a welcome sight. With the roar of the engine finally leaving his ears, Dan asked Nick what had occurred when he went back upstairs at the residence.

"We needed a diversion," replied Nick. "I threw the servant's body out a side window to attract the attention of whoever was waiting for us to emerge. They were so busy reacting to the noise they did not see us leave the house until it was too late. We can tell Lou his friend helped us escape."

Thirty-five
The Plan Unfolds

Dan opened his bag on the kitchen table in front of Lou and Bill Casey.

"I think we have what we need," said Dan. "Take a look, Lou," he added as he placed the files in Lou's hands.

"It's all here," said Lou, "both copies of the Mystic Study Report and the complete set of credentials. The credentials are crucial to moving around inside the Papal apartments. The Mystic Report and a copy of your pictures, Dan, are really the keys to influencing the Conclave. I can't believe you found this and got out without a problem."

"Let's just say we got out," offered Dan.

They were discussing the details of moving through checkpoints when Meggie entered the kitchen. After a few minutes of listening to the details of the plan, she asked a question.

"Who will I be with inside the Vatican?"

"You aren't going," Dan said, "it's too dangerous. Nick and I just learned how dangerous it will be."

Meggie stood up from her chair, walked across the room to the open kitchen door and then turned back and faced the three men at the table.

"You call me from the comfort of home in Washington, you use me to gain access to the hospital, I help you switch bodies and legitimize the transfer to the so-called nursing home. I nurse Lou back to his senses and now you tell me I'm staying here for the finale? I don't think so," she ended as she returned to the table and repeated her earlier question. "Who will I be going with?"

"Let's you and I work together," said Bill Casey. "We did a good enough job getting out of the hospital, no?"

"Well, now that the teams are settled," she said, "let's review the assignments once we are inside."

After showing a frustrated look for an appropriate amount of time, Dan began a summary of what they had been discussing. "The objective is to get Lou inside to the final meeting place with the Cardinals before they go into the Sistine Chapel," started Dan. That meeting will be held in the Pauline Chapel. We need Lou hidden near there. Tomorrow is the last day of preparation and the only chance to get Lou in front of the Cardinals before deliberation begins. When Lou is recognized, it must be in front of a very large group to reduce the chance of something else happening to him."

The group moved to one side of the table as Dan spread open a set of drawings. "Nick has provided these sketches of the buildings inside Vatican City," said Dan as he rolled open the detailed papers. "He has marked off a series of corridors linking each building and traced the location of escape tunnels throughout the area. The idea is to use the tunnel closest to the Pauline chapel as the hiding place. At the given time, Lou can enter the meeting, assuming we can distract outside security while he identifies himself. I'll leave that up to you, Nick. The trick is to get Lou to this location without being discovered and bring him out at the right moment."

"Not shown on these drawings," commented Lou, "are the servant corridors around the Papal apartments that provide direct access to and from the kitchens in the basement to the offices on the main level. I am aware of their existence. I have never been in them."

"Bill," said Dan, "you and Meggie, dressed as members of the household staff can find your way into the kitchen and locate the private corridors the servants use to move inside the buildings. Nick and I will move Lou to the tunnel entrance circled on this map. If for some reason this first location doesn't work, there are two more locations noted as backup sites you should remember if you can't find us. Nick and I will locate the most direct route between the tunnels and let you know where we are."

At this point Lou interrupted. "I have a pair of Vatican City security radios in my office. If there is any way you can get in there, the radios would be helpful to keep us in touch and let us know what the security people are doing."

"Communications are always difficult," responded Nick, "I like the idea of searching for the radios but I would be surprised if they are still there and if your office isn't under surveillance."

"Let's add that part to the plan," said Dan. "As soon as we are able to get Lou into hiding we'll search for the radios. After our first assignments," he added, "we will meet back at the marked tunnel entrance about one hour after we hide Lou and separate for our independent searches.

"Lou," asked Dan, "are you sure you can find the main tunnel entrances?"

"I think so," he replied. "I've been in them a number of times in moving around the offices. I don't know where they all lead but I have used portions of them often enough to feel certain I can find them. These credentials taken from my residence," Lou remarked, "are for the Cardinals and their direct staff only. Don't show them until we are well inside the Vatican. The other two sets of identification must be shown together, only at exterior checkpoints or they will be confiscated."

Turning to Nick, Lou offered a compliment. "I have never seen drawings like these of the Vatican and the escape routes. They are quite accurate. Your identification cards with the pictures and the fingerprints look as good as any I have ever seen. I don't know how you did it in such a short time but from what I know, they will work if presented properly. The outfits you provided appear authentic and would reflect a religious group coming to the Conclave."

Nick broke his silence.

"I know you are all focused on your first objective of getting the information to the Cardinals but you have not given enough attention to Ali Teekah and what he plans to be doing during all this. The Vatican plan to keep him until after the new Pope is elected and deal with him later, is doomed from the start. He realizes how important this election is. My guess is that he will make his own move at the same time. He is not in the habit of waiting for others to act."

Nick turned to Lou and asked, "Tell us what you know about Ali, where he is and who is handling his security."

"I'm sorry I haven't given you the details before," Lou apologized. "I have been thinking about my speech.

"Once the agreement was made with Ali," began Lou, "the Bellardino family was brought in to arrange the details of the transfer and provide security in the Vatican. Ali's family and eight men accompanied him on the trip. His second in command, Anwar Saeed, was the one who made the contact with Cardinal Delgado and negotiated the terms of the agreement.

"Saeed is part of the group with Ali now. He seems to be the point of contact and handles all the communications. The entire group is housed in a room built years ago at the far end of the Vatican Library. It was another of those hiding places prepared for the Pope if the city came under siege. It does not appear on drawings of the Vatican and it has its own exit to the tunnel system."

"How close is the library room to the Pauline Chapel?" asked Nick.

"If you look at your drawings," answered Lou, "it's about fifty yards from the Chapel down two side corridors, just past Delgado's office. The library entrance can be gated off and secured so no one in the library can get out through the regular entrance. I heard the discussion of how to keep Ali from interfering with the Conclave once it began. The entire security force around Ali is from the Bellardino family. They plan to lock Ali's group in the room when the Cardinals go into the Sistine Chapel."

"Good," said Nick, "at least I know what they are thinking, if anything happens. We should watch the gates to the library entrance as a signal for when you can move into the meeting, Lou."

Dan rose from his chair and filled his cup one more time. He turned to Lou and said, "We are all with you, whatever happens."

Dan addressed the rest. "I think we should all try to get some rest for the next few hours and be ready to move at four A.M. At sunrise, a school bus will arrive with our traveling group of priests and nuns arranged by Nick. We will ride to St. Peter's Square and see if we can make this work."

The quiet of the kitchen was broken by sounds of the chairs moving across the floor as the meeting came to a close. Articles of clothing were selected by each of the party as they prepared for the morning ride.

After the kitchen emptied, Dan and Meggie were alone. She left the house and walked across the yard to the well. Dan joined her, and pulled up a bucket of water and offered her a drink. It was a warm summer evening with the trees barely moving in the breeze.

"I am sorry we haven't had time together," Dan began. "I wish it could be different."

"At least I'm with you," she answered.

"I don't want that to end," he said.

Rather than answer him, she walked toward the stable.

Dan caught up with her at an open stall where she was stroking the head of a large black horse they had commented on earlier in the day. They had watched it, with its colt, feed on the grass in the open meadow behind the house.

"The last time we were together at a stable," remembered Dan, "was at my uncle's house on Western Avenue and we went riding around his corral. I hope we have the time to enjoy simple moments again."

"I am trying not to think too far in advance," she said, stroking the forehead of the big animal coming between the two lovers. "The excitement has been good for me," she said. "It keeps me from thinking about the problems I have with the rest of my life. I don't want to focus on how I suddenly preferred to respond to my emotions, without the slightest thought about my obligations."

Meggie left the stall and slowly walked out behind the barn.

Dan followed and grabbed her hand. "I don't know where this is going," he said. "I want to be part of history. I want to do what is right and I want to be with you."

"That's fine for you to say," Meggie responded, "but what about us? What is the right thing for us? What is the right thing for me?

"I want to be part of history too," she said. "But, after this is over, will there be any history for you and me?"

Dan pulled her to him and kissed her gently. "All I know," he said, is that I will never let you slip away again."

They walked back into the house hand in hand, meeting Bill Casey on the porch.

"I never imagined I would ever be as involved as I have been these past days," said Bill. "After I annoyed all those geniuses in the Bishop's office in Brooklyn and they banished me to a parish in New Jersey, I thought life was bound to be very dull. I was wrong again. My record remains intact.

"Here I am in Rome," he continued, "invited as an official part of the US delegation to the Conclave. Not only that, but I am about to disrupt an official party, which has always been my pleasure in the past. I guess that is why my brother is a Bishop and I am off in the fields doing God's work alone. Thank you, Dan! I'm having the time of my life!

"More than that, I want to thank you for all we shared in the past and most importantly, for thinking of me when you really did need help. There is something special about being asked to help. It says everything about friendship; for me anyway."

Bill rose from his chair on the creaky porch, and with the first rays of the morning sun peeking over his shoulder, put Dan in one of his bear hugs, squeezing him as he had done many times in the past.

"Let's pray everything works out for us," Bill said, as he reached out to include Meggie in the hug.

266

Thirty-six
Preparing to Act

Leaving the Library

"They are well out of the city and headed for the boat to Messina," said Anwar Saeed to a nervous Ali Teekah huddling in their new catacomb hiding place beneath St. Peter's Square.

"Thank you," said Ali, "you know they are more important to me than my life. Now that I know they are safely on their way, we can bargain our way into the next half of the plan. Did you finish with the wiring of the library room?"

"It is complete, just as we discussed," replied Anwar. "The materials delivered by our friends were as we requested. They are all in place. Any attempt to break into the room or lock the outside gates will detonate the explosives and create large amounts of smoke to hide our move. We will be able to hear and feel the impact from where we will be hiding. When that occurs, our group will move through the tunnels to Delgado's office to look for him and other captives. With the Conclave about to begin, he will agree to our demands or all will be lost."

"Are you comfortable with using the same escape plan we used for the family?" asked Ali.

"As comfortable as I can be under the circumstances," came the reply. "Our friends in Palermo have proven themselves trustworthy so far. Their advice has been reliable. We in turn have delivered the sum of money promised with more to come. It seems to be working well. I expect them to continue to cooperate. If there are signals that we are in danger, our backup plan is quite acceptable to me. We used it once to move out into St. Peter's Square and we were not detected. Whatever plan we use, the streets of Rome are so congested that we will have no problem losing ourselves in the crowd."

"Thank you my friend," said Ali, "you have never failed me before. I am sure this time will be no different. Let's try to rest for a while. The day will be a busy one!"

Washington, DC

While the catacomb meeting was taking place beneath St. Peter's, Ed Anderson was at the home of the Vice President for another briefing.

"I am sorry to ask to see you at this time of night," he began, "but there are developments in Rome that you should know about. You told me to let you know if our plan was in danger of failing. I think it is," he said with an air of disappointment.

The Vice President, in nightclothes and bathrobe, sat down at the desk in his den and reached for the "special phone."

"Can you give me the whereabouts of the President at this time please? I'll wait," he said while looking at Ed and signaling him to go on with his report.

The Deputy CIA Director continued his briefing. "We detected a group leaving Vatican City through one of the escape tunnels under the complex. By the time we located them they were at the coast. It appears to be Ali's family making the escape we thought they would attempt. By the make up of the party, we don't think Ali is with them. It appears that Ali has found a secure way out of Vatican City and can make his own move out before our plan to grab him is executed. The element of surprise seems gone and the chance of failure greatly increased."

"Does General Feely know about the move of the family out of the Vatican?" asked the Vice President.

"No. According to your instructions, we have not been sharing intelligence with the Feely group in Italy. They might know through their own surveillance but I doubt that. There are indications that he may be going ahead with the Option Two: U.S. force-led assault attack plan thinking the entire group is still inside waiting for the outcome of the Conclave. Our strike forces were moved into position near the Vatican. The feedback from the Jordanian mercenaries indicates Feely's desire to move on his own.

"In addition, Feely's wife is in Rome along with the reporter Gerard. One of our people kept Gerard from having a neatly arranged Rossello "traffic accident." His involvement might distract our Palermo friends from supporting us the way they promised. There are too many wild cards in this hand now to let it play out. Do you want to put the brakes on while we still can?"

The special phone was returned to its receiver before the requested information was delivered to the Vice President.

"You know, Ed, I think we will let the good General handle this one on his own. Let's see how well he is prepared for surprises. Thank you for coming over here so late. Continue to monitor the situation and let me know as soon as anything happens, so I can brief the President before anyone else.

"What has been the response of the *Washington Tribune* to the actions initiated by Justice?" inquired the Vice President.

"The *Tribune* has stonewalled us as we expected," replied Ed. "They continue with their line of reporting. We have issued a second subpoena to the editor of the *Tribune* for Gerard's failure to respond to the original subpoena. If he shows his face in Rome there is reason to take him into custody. His continuing story on the poisoning of the last Pope and CIA involvement with the Vatican Bank are enough for court action. The media is working itself up to one of its Beltway feeding frenzies. I hope we can throw cold water on the fire soon."

"I have given Justice blank check on this one," said the Vice President, "including a special prosecutor, which they love. We will make this a test case and keep confidential sources cover from being used this way by others in the future."

"I'll initiate new investigative actions in the morning," added Anderson, "and as usual, describe it as my independent decision."

The same old thoughts plagued Anderson while driving from the Vice Presidential residence. His actions had always been meant to protect the best interests of his country. He has been skeptical about the capture plan from the outset but felt it necessary to go along with the administration. When the plan changed to include violence inside the Vatican, he looked for ways to slow it down. One terrorist was simply not worth the political gain or the uproar his capture would cause. Now the worst of all cases might occur. An embarrassment to the administration requiring a search for a scapegoat with the CIA the first place to look! There should be a difference between power politics and diplomacy but he was never the one asked to make that distinction.

Thirty-seven
Milan, US Consulate

It was shortly after midnight when the briefing began in the basement of the US Consulate in Milan. General Feely's team had been at work most of the day examining the discovered plan by a French led team to seize Ali Teekah inside the Vatican. It was time to decide on a course of action.

Colonel Garvey led the briefing on French plan for the benefit of leaders of the American commando force poised to seize the terrorist.

"The first alert came to us about twelve hours ago," Garvey began. "One of our people on the Papal household staff informed us that Vatican security forces discovered a member of a Croatian TV team coming out of one of the restricted tunnel entrances near the Library room where the Teekah group was hiding. They checked the status of the entire Portugal delegation. The TV crew had obtained permission to film a documentary about the Conclave with the approval of one of the French bishops.

"Checking the Bishop's staff they found that several members of the French delegation had questionable credentials. With this information, the Vatican security chief searched the rooms of both the TV crew and the entire French delegation. Automatic weapons and plastic explosives were found along with other items that indicated an assault was planned. As a result, several members of the French delegation were arrested. The Cardinals were moved to another building.

"Here are the pictures taken of those arrested," said Garvey, as the screen behind him displayed the faces of those planning for the capture of the terrorist. "This episode removes the last remaining effort we are aware of to seize Ali. Vatican security should feel confident the Conclave is safe."

Turning to a screen displaying a picture of Messina and its suburbs, Garvey continued. "Ali's wife and family have been located just outside of Messina. We do not know how they left Vatican City but they had to have had inside assistance. It appears they are awaiting transport to a location outside of Italy. With this change, we have alerted the Jordanian team to be prepared to make our own joint assault sometime this morning before Ali makes a move to join his family. We have been assured that Ali will be sealed inside the Library room later today to prevent him from interfering with the start of the Conclave.

"The next slide," said Garvey, "gives the location where our forces will meet the combined team outside Rome and proceed to implement our plan. The details of the various escape scenarios planned by Ali remain as confirmed this morning.

"We have implemented the variation in the plan you requested, General, following your conversation with the President. Our main force will be positioned just outside the Vatican tunnel complex on the edge of the City and take Teekah when the attack teams emerge from the tunnel. This reduces the U.S. exposure considerably but as we know, the effort will be U.S. directed.

"This slide," said Garvey, "gives the identities of the group who moved Cardinal Baracini from the hospital after the confusion about his second heart attack. The CIA has been tracking Dan Gerard, the reporter from the *Washington Tribune*, since his arrival in Rome. One of our operatives saved him from the bus treatment so often used by the Rossello family for people who ask too many questions about the Vatican Bank.

"One of Gerard's accomplices is a Brooklyn priest seen here, who outfought one of the Rossello security men searching Gerard's hotel room when they thought he was otherwise occupied with one of their ladies. Father Brooklyn did quite a job. His picture appeared in the papers the next day. We confirmed he was one of the group at the hospital who moved the Cardinal to an unknown location.

"There are at least two other members of the rescue group who we have not identified, a woman and a local man. The CIA is searching for their identities.

"This next slide," continued Garvey, "is the residence of Cardinal Baracini. Someone broke into his office and removed documents a night ago. The security man inside the residence was killed. The intruders escaped on a motorcycle. The episode tells us there is an experienced group at work with the Cardinal. We do not fully understand why he was targeted for elimination but it is clear the Cardinal represents a major embarrassment. The Bellardino family has been unable to determine what exactly was taken from the residence but a safe in the bedroom office was opened during the break in.

"We have concluded," said Garvey as he turned off the projector, "that both the Russian and French teams have been excluded from any attempt at seizing Ali. No one else is poised to enter the Vatican if we don't. The group working with Cardinal Baracini does not appear to be concerned about Ali. They are almost certainly trying to produce the Cardinal for some public statement. We don't believe this will interfere with our plans, but nevertheless, we have taken steps to prevent any move by the Cardinal back into Vatican City.

"The final move of our assault team," added Garvey, "was completed several hours ago with the acceptance of the credentials of the Brazilian delegation to be seated in the next General Congregation meeting. If we don't move now, we will be forced to wait until after the Conclave has concluded and that could be a number of days or even weeks. The order to move is awaiting your approval. Your reaction, General?"

Tom Feely moved from his chair at the end of the table and refilled his coffee cup. He walked around the room, without saying a word.

"I don't like it, Pat," he said to Garvey. "If Teekah was able to move his family out of the Vatican why didn't he go with them? Why is it our friends, who know everything, didn't know that? What else aren't they sharing?

"We have been told that the Teekah party was searched very thoroughly," continued Feely, moving to the back of the room. "When sanctuary was provided they were all clean and they have been monitored closely ever since. I am uncomfortable with the trap that might be out there for us, perhaps in the same way he took out the Russians some weeks ago. If we must go in directly, how can you respond to my uneasiness, Pat?" ended Feely.

"First and most important," Garvey replied. "Ali Teekah and his party were searched and double searched before entering Vatican City. They do not have access to weapons and explosives as they did on the West Bank. That is why this environment is one of the best for us to take a gamble.

"Sir, we can't be 100 percent sure of anything but a Church enclosure limits the extent of the response.

"We can only operate based upon the information we have. Our plan has a very low risk profile, not that a surprise couldn't happen, but we think it is a low risk. With time now of the essence, it is either go or wait until after the Conclave is finished. We think the activity taking place inside the Vatican is so unusual and so intense, that it adds a dimension that works to our benefit. The decision is yours, however."

"Why haven't we had an update on CIA intelligence?" asked Feely.

"You know, sir," Garvey answered, "it all has to come through the Vice President and he has yet to clear the latest update after your conversation with the President."

"As of now," asked Feely, "our sources of intelligence at Langley have not informed us of the Teekah escape?"

"No sir," came Garvey's reply. "We were informed by one of the contacts we made during our last visit to Palermo and he has been reliable. The problem we are having is lack of confirmation from Langley. Our communications with them have slowed down considerably in the past few hours. The CIA support seems to follow a pattern of helping when they judge it politic. But what can you expect from an Air Force, General—once they leave their planes, you never are sure what they will do."

"It won't be the first time Central Intelligence failed to keep the troops in the field fully briefed. For that very reason we are often forced to collect our own intelligence and develop our own plans for back up," observed the General, a look of disgust crossing his face.

"What is the latest on the location of the Grail and the documents moved by Teekah and returned to the Vatican?" continued the General.

274

Colonel Garvey responded quickly. "We are close on the heels of the move but have yet to find the new hiding place. We know the Grail package was scheduled to arrive in Seville as part of a group of touring religious leaders from Jerusalem. These arrangements were confirmed in telephone conversations between Cardinal Delgado and his office in Madrid.

"However, when the group arrived in Seville, the Grail items were missing and so were several members of the escort group from Jerusalem. Our contacts in Jerusalem are working through the Maronites, who seem to have had some unusual contacts these past few weeks from Cardinal Delgado's office but we don't understand why. Indications are that the Grail is headed away from Seville, perhaps to Jerusalem.

"The Vice President assured us that Israeli forces will be at our disposal if needed for an intercept. I am confident that if it moves toward Jerusalem, we will have the Grail in our possession shortly."

"If we fail in our attempt to catch Ali but take possession of the Grail, the President will be equally as happy," observed Feely. "Assuming that we remain one step removed in the process."

"There is one other item that may help us in the next day to control Dan Gerard and his companions," added Garvey.

"The Justice Department has been successful in initiating an investigation about the stories in the *Washington Tribune* by Dan Gerard and forcing him to reveal his sources or go to jail. Subpoenas have been served on the editor of the *Tribune* and direct him to have Gerard appear to testify. His failure to appear gives us reason to take him into custody if he is seen. The Italian authorities have been alerted to this possibility."

General Feely returned to his seat at the head of the table. "Good briefing, Pat, as usual. However, this is the second time we have been poised to capture a terrorist and meet the needs of our President. I don't want to fail a second time. Let's go with our plan as it stands. We have to move on our own and lead the assault with the Jordanians or Teekah will be gone again! We can't wait for CIA support or nothing will happen!

"Alert all team members that they should commence their portion of the plan immediately. I want to speak personally with

275

the team leader who will take the combined assault team into the tunnel network. Thank you all for your efforts," said Feely as he looked into the eyes of his team. I will remain here at the Consulate but stay in contact with you for minute-by-minute briefings on what is taking place. Pat, take command of the communications center and don't leave it until Ali is in our hands."

"Yes sir," came the reply. "We are going to get him this time," answered Garvey.

Thirty-eight
The Chapel

Sunrise crept across the dirt road leading to the farmhouse as the old tour bus emerged from a dust cloud. Meggie, sitting alone on the front porch, was the first to sight it and alerted the others.

Nick quickly moved everyone out of the kitchen and to the rear of the house. Meggie noticed him pass a small handgun to Dan. It was the first time she had seen a weapon. It made her consider outcomes previously unthought of.

The bus came to a noisy halt thirty feet from the porch. A short suntanned woman, in black clothes with long black hair, came toward the house. There were several men and women looking out the half open windows of the bus. One of the men left the vehicle and adjusted three large duffel bags tied to the roof rack.

Nick greeted the woman on the roadway. After an embrace, they turned and boarded the bus. Within a few minutes all of the occupants were seated in the kitchen. Nick introduced Eva, a woman in her early thirties with a big smile and warm friendly voice. She was one of the leaders of the new companions who would help them gain entrance to the Vatican.

Nick also introduced Angelo, a longtime friend who had been in similar forays in the past. The embraces exchanged among Nick, Angelo and Eva made the rest of the company feel at ease with the new members. Eva began the briefing with new information gathered describing the variety of Vatican security checkpoints around the City. She responded quickly to Nick's questions and was obviously prepared for what lay ahead.

Nick opened a new set of Vatican drawings brought by Eva and compared them with those studied earlier. Lou confirmed the key checkpoints, tunnel entrances and the location of his office.

Eva's examination of the Conclave pre-approval list published by the Italian police, indicated a large contingent of nuns and priests coming from the religious centers around Compost-ella to attend the ceremonies of the Conclave. Nick decided it would be best to attempt to enter Vatican City as part of this group. The three men and four women from the bus, along with his own gorup of five, would create a group of six men and six women coming to the Vatican.

Eva's credentials would identify her as Mother Superior of the Convent of the Good Shepheard in Compostella and the leader of the nuns. Angelo would pose as leader of the priests from the Cathedral of St James.

Eva would do all the communicating with checkpoint personnel since the rest of the party would presumably speak only Spanish. All IDs had to be crosschecked to show Spanish clearance at the checkpoints and Italian pre-approval for the Vatican.

After the traditional travel clothes for nuns and priests, the paler-skinned Americans were offered makeup to present a darker Spanish look.

The question of weapons was debated before they left the farmhouse. Nick would not enter the Vatican without one. The others wanted no part of weapons. A compromise plan was agreed upon.

The weapons were hidden behind the vehicle's front and rear lights. Lou had outlined where the metal detectors would be placed at checkpoints and where weapons would have the best chance of making it inside. In addition, a cabinet inside his office was stocked with handguns for the Vatican police. Nick liked the idea of a backup if needed. Lou and Bill Casey both declined to carry weapons; Dan kept the one Nick had passed to him earlier.

Meggie was the only other person who could speak Spanish. It was agreed she would become Eva's assistant at the checkpoints if needed. They forged a quick friendship as they coordinated details of possible security question responses.

The change of clothes, the packing of bags and the slow movement toward the bus brought a moment of reality to Dan's mind. He found Meggie's hand and with a squeeze caught her attention. "I love you," he whispered. She nodded and smiled.

Five men sat on one side of the bus and six women sat on the other side. Angelo had the task as bus driver and the first to show the vehicle's papers. Nick and Eva had two front seats behind the driver and reminded everyone to either speak Spanish or just grunt if anyone came into the vehicle. Nick repeated once again that they were from the Church of St. James and the convent of the Good Shepherd in Compostella. Demeanor was critical. Everyone should look engrossed in prayer to anyone looking in.

Dan and Meggie sat across from each other in the middle of the bus as it rumbled down the long driveway. Dan reached out for her hand again, hoping to see a smile replace the frozen look that dominated her soft features. She returned his touch but kept staring at the front of the bus as it made its way toward the city.

Roman traffic kept the dust covered vehicle moving at a snail's pace right up to the first police checkpoint. When the blue uniformed Italian police officer entered the bus and began checking the driver's papers, Dan could not help but think of World War II movies with Gestapo men checking papers at boarder crossings. *What are we getting ourselves into*? he thought.

Angelo had to remove several of the bags from the roof rack for inspection, as another officer checked the photo IDs with each passenger while performing a physical search of everyone on the bus. He hesitated to perform the usual inspection pat down when he saw the nuns stand before him. Eva began a running conversation with the security men, answering their questions in Italian. There was a sigh of relief and some laughter as the bus moved to its next stop.

The security force at the second stop presented a more serious investigation than the first. Each passenger was asked to leave the bus and all packages in the roof rack were opened and all baggage in the bus was removed and opened on the pavement. Mirrors were used to check under the vehicle. A heated exchange began between Angelo and one of the security officers. The officer refused to allow the vehicle to continue and told Angelo to turn around. Eva joined the discussion with two of the other guards. Finally, after everyone, except Eva and Angelo, were back on the bus, two men came on board and began checking again each picture ID with the individual.

All seemed to go well with the security force until the official came to Meggie. No matter how hard she tried, or how much makeup she applied, her features and skin were out of place beneath the nun's clothes. She answered the officer's Italian questions in Spanish and turned to Eva for translations from Italian to Spanish. The two women spoke to each other in Spanish and Eva then in Italian to the official. The two men then exited the bus and made several phone calls. After several minutes of heated conversation with Eva and with her uncontrolled sobbing, the security men became exasperated and allowed the bus to proceed to its restricted parking area. They were inside Vatican City.

Once out of the bus, the group divided into the three designated teams; the first with Nick, Dan and Lou was to locate the tunnel entrances outside the papal apartments as Lou's primary hiding place. The second team, led by Eva with Meggie and Bill Casey at her side were to mix with the household serving staff and locate the various servant corridors in the building hoping to move to and from the kitchen area. The third team, led by Angelo, was assigned the task of determining the exact location of Ali Teekah and his security force.

Having passed through all the metal detectors, the group removed the weapons from the headlights and taillights and hid them on their person. Team one would be the first to present their special Vatican credentials for entry inside the Papal apartment complex. If the first group didn't make it inside, there would be no reason for the others to attempt entry.

Nick carefully presented the double credentials according to Lou's instructions. Within a few minutes and without questions, team one passed through the final checkpoint. A commotion behind them caught their attention. Eva's papers were creating a problem. Several officials were called over to join in the examination and one seemed to be engaged on the phone. All of team two was asked to step aside and wait for further instructions.

What would happen if only half of the team made it inside? Dan asked himself. Eva continued her conversations with the officers. The rest of the team sat on the floor in silence. With the seated group blocking access through the gate and the waiting line growing longer, the guards relented and allowed everyone to pass. The third team approached the checkpoint after their friends were allowed inside. Without questions they were given clearance. All were now inside the hallways of the Papal Palace.

Those hallways were crowed with household staff, visiting delegations and those anxious to test their ability to mix with the Curia during important events. The new visitors mixed easily with the crowd.

Within minutes, they assembled at the junction of the two corridors described by Lou and shown on Nick's map. After a short wait for the hallway traffic to clear, Lou moved them into a tunnel entrance behind a statue of St. James, which led to a small alcove a short distance off the hallway. They seemed to have found their hiding place.

Bill Casey, Meggie and Eva changed into the clothes of household staff. Nick and Dan began their first task of leaving the tunnel and finding Lou's office to retrieve the set of Vatican radios. Everyone was asked to remain in the tunnel until they returned.

Lou's directions led them without delay to his office. A nun in a chair reading a prayer book blocked the door. She stood up as the two men dressed as priests approached her. In a quiet voice and with her head slightly bowed, she asked if she could be of assistance. They showed Lou's special pass and presented the key to the tall oak door behind her. She took their key and managed to open the door allowing them to enter the office.

Before Dan could cross the room, Nick had grabbed the nun, dragged her inside and shut the door behind them. Nick gave her a sharp blow to the head with the butt of his pistol. She went limp.

"What the hell are you doing?" cried Dan.

"She has a holster on her hip. We can't take chances with a fake nun this early in the day," he responded. Nick pulled up the nun's long black skirt and revealed a revolver with silencer strapped to her leg. Nick tied her to a chair, stuffed a cloth into her mouth and shoved her into a closet.

"Find the radios, check for the handguns and let's get out of here," said Nick.

The radios and handguns were in the locked cabinet as Lou had described. Dan moved the radios onto Lou's cluttered desk amid the pictures and plaques that decorated his work space. *Office environments tell tales about the tenant,* thought Dan, as he passed by a wall of pictures with a variety of smiling faces greeting the Pope.

When they returned to the tunnel, their companions were still there and anxious to get on with their plans. Once the radios were distributed and the special voice signals repeated, the groups moved out.

Bill Casey, Meggie, Eva and the women headed for the kitchen facilities that served the complex, looking for the concealed servant corridors described by Lou.

Nick and Dan were to locate the next hiding place for Lou, close to the Pauline Chapel where the College of Cardinals would meet for their final pre-Conclave assembly. Angelo's team began their search for the possible locations of Ali Teekah and his security force around the Vatican Library.

Nick and Dan were mingling in the halls without difficulty when Nick made a change in plans. "I am going to join Angelo at the Vatican Library," he said. "I want to locate Ali before we make another other move with Lou. Try to find the second tunnel entrance. I'll meet you back in this area in a few minutes." Before Dan could reply, Nick had slipped down a side hall.

Dan found the tunnel entrance Lou had described. There in the crowd in front of him was the familiar face of Monsignor Roberto Flores. He was older and heavier but there was no doubt about who it was. Dan moved to the side and watched Flores go into an office with two security men stationed outside the door. Dan returned to the meeting point just as Nick turned the corner.

"How was the Library?" asked Dan.

"Not good," came the reply. "If I feel uneasy about the set up I saw, Ali must have the same feeling," said Nick. "Let's get Lou and make the move to the entrance you just found."

When they returned to make the move, Lou had gone. Nick and Dan waited for almost ten minutes before trying their first radio signal to the other team members for a status report.

No one had any idea of the whereabouts of Lou. He was in the tunnel when they last saw him. Eva and Meggie had been successful in mixing with the kitchen staff and had delivered trays of food to various groups meeting throughout the building. Their journeys with food carts enabled them to learn a great deal about the service corridor network but they had seen no sign of Lou.

Bill Casey was on his own but they were not sure where. Angelo and the members of his group were seen by Eva when she delivered coffee to the workforce stacking chairs in meeting rooms but he did not check in. "All continue," was the coded signal.

After an hour searching for Lou, frustration was taking a toll. "Without Lou, the plan is a bust," Dan said to Nick. "We need to make something happen. Let's split up, Nick, and see what we can find out on our own. I'll go back to an office down the hall and see if an old friend of mine shows up. He led me to Lou once before. Maybe he can do it again."

"I'm going into the tunnel complex," said Nick. "Maybe Lou drifted down this tunnel or someone came upon him from the other end, without him hearing them. I'll meet you back here, or signal you on the radio in thirty minutes," concluded Nick, as he stepped into the darkness of the tunnel.

Dan moved back down the empty hallway to the office that Flores had entered. The security men still stood by the door.

While Dan waited outside the office, there was an explosion somewhere inside Vatican City. It shook the building and almost knocked him off his feet. The sight and smell of acrid smoke was immediate, indicating the blast had not been too far away.

The door Dan was watching opened and Flores ran out, followed by a group of staff and security guards racing toward the sound of the explosion. With the office left unguarded and the halls filling with smoke, Dan decided to look inside. He was in for only a moment when he heard the sound of returning voices. He was forced to hide in long window drapes blocking the midday sun.

Flores reentered the office and moved directly to the phone on the edge of the big desk sitting in the center of the room. "We understand it was in the Library," he said, in a voice unable to speak fast enough into the receiver. "We were on the call from Saeed demanding the meeting with the Opus Dei leadership, when the explosion occurred. We think we know where he is calling from but we have been unable to confirm the exact location. It is within Vatican City. Since he escaped the explosion, he must be out of the library. We must assume Ali and his people are with him. Our task now is to find them and bring them into our offices where they can be controlled.

"What," shouted Flores, "how could he have Baracini here in the complex? It must be a ploy to force our hand. I don't believe it. Get proof first, before we do anything else." The room was filling with smoke and the noise of the fire brigade in the hallway was making conversation difficult.

"I understand," Flores said, as he hung up the phone while attempting to cover his mouth with a cloth. The group then left the room and went back into the crowded hallway.

Just as Dan emerged from behind the window drapes, a security man entered the room.

"What are you doing here?" the guard said.

"I returned to find some papers I left here at the earlier meeting with Monsignor Flores," he sputtered out.

"Don't move," the guard said, drawing a gun from its holster and pointing it at Dan, "and I mean, don't move a muscle."

The guard made several calls over his radio and was joined by his associates. They quickly searched Dan, removed his gun and threw him into one of the chairs. Within minutes, an unexpected reunion took place between two men who had followed very different paths from when they first met during an earlier Conclave.

"What have we here?" said Monsignor Flores, as he paced around Dan. "A dressed up priest who looks very much like an American seminarian I once knew. He always thought he knew everything, a typical American attitude. Some things never change regardless of how foolish they are."

With that statement a figure entered the room. Dan knew at a glance he was not going to be helpful.

"These matters are best handled by me," the new arrival said. "Why don't you join Cardinal Delgado and help him manage the concerns created by the unfortunate boiler explosion," he said to Flores.

Flores answered with sarcasm, "Darci, this is one case I really don't want to know about what happens."

284

"Don't worry," came the reply. "As usual, you won't."

With that exchange, Flores left the room.

Darci DiNome directed all the security guards to leave the room but one. He told him to tie Dan to the chair, which he did. "Dispose of him in the same manner as others," Darci said.

A quick nod came from the guard. He remained with Dan until three plainclothesmen entered the room. They tied Dan's hands in front of him holding a prayer book and they all left together walking down the smoke filled hallways next to the Papal apartments, mixing with the fire brigades working throughout the building.

With the four of them walking slowly down a long corridor, no one gave any attention to the nun pushing a food cart toward them except Dan. The good nun, her head bowed was Eva.

Within several yards of passing Eva, the security men shoved Dan into a side office away from the confusion of the crowded corridors and closed the door. He was tied to a small chair in a corner of the room and two of the men left. The silence that dominated the room for what seemed a very long time, was broken by a knock at the door. One of the two remaining security men opened the door just enough to see two sisters holding food trays. After some exchange of words at the door, the guard returned his gun to his belt and directed the food trays to a small table at the far end of the room. Once the door was closed, the sisters stood in front of the two guards and fired a single shot from the guns taped to the bottom of each of their trays. The guards collapsed to the floor.

In the hallway, chaos seemed to be increasing with the billowing smoke creating a need for more shouting. Eva untied Dan and took him into a side corridor she had discovered as part of the service pathway. She used her radio to contact Nick. He was still in the tunnel complex trying to locate Lou. Dan gave him the details of the Library explosion and the information that Lou could be in the hands of Teekah and his people now loose somewhere inside Vatican City.

Nick gave the pre-arranged radio signal for all the groups to return to the original tunnel meeting point as quickly as possible. Of the original twelve in the bus, only six were able to return; Meggie and Bill Casey were not among them.

Nick's assessment of the explosion and heavy smoke convinced him it was part of a plan to create a diversion to allow Ali to escape. The fact that they now had a valuable hostage might well change the plan and create some kind of negotiating session. "Where might that take place, Dan?" Nick asked.

"My guess is back at the office complex I just left," replied Dan, "but everyone seems to be leaving the building except the fire brigade. When I was in his office, Flores was on the phone with someone else who informed him about the capture of Lou. We need to find that office and locate the center of operations."

Nick barked instructions. "Eva, you and Dan look for the office. I'll go back into the tunnel complex with the rest of the group. It is the only path to safety for Ali and we need to locate which tunnel is his choice for escape. Keep the radios on and hope that the rest of our group can contact us."

Thirty-nine
The Confrontation

Meggie's assignment as part of the kitchen detail was not of her choosing. She was pushed into the mess created by an over-turned soup kettle when the explosion occurred. Many of the kitchen help left the area; she was asked to stay and help clean up. She was still on her hands and knees when she glanced through the chaos and saw Lou being led by two men out the rear exit to a delivery truck.

One of the men returned, disappearing into the hallway. She had no idea what had happened. She knew she had to get to the group. She picked up a pail and moved to the sink to refill. Once out of the work area, Meggie was on her way to find her companions.

No one was at the contact tunnel. She was about to leave when Bill Casey grabbed her hand. He had the Vatican radio but couldn't make it work. Meggie told him what she had seen and was sure Lou was in the delivery truck. Bill saw that it was urgent to get to him. They raced back to the kitchen.

Finally making radio contact with Nick, Bill sent the signal that they had seen their lost companion taken out the service entrance near the kitchen corridor. They entered the kitchen as he spoke.

Moving through crowded work stations, Bill weaved his way to the service exit, Meggie at his heels. The lone guard at the doorway was startled by the sudden face-to-face encounter with the big Brooklyn man. Bill launched a flurry of questions at the guard, as Meggie tried to walk around the two men.

A second guard entered the hallway, shutting the door behind him, and pushing Meggie into Bill in the process.

Sensing an encounter, Bill used his remaining good hand to throw a first punch into the face of the guard closest to him. The force of the blow sent the man into the doorway, crumpling to the floor. Before Bill could turn to the other guard, a single shot flew past Meggie's head bringing Bill to his knees. With eyes wide open and hands clutching his chest, Casey fell to his side and over on his back. A third uniformed man opened the door of the service truck to see the reason for the gunshot.

Meggie looked past the standing guard into the truck and yelled, "Lou," as she saw the familiar face. She was grabbed from behind and pushed into the truck next to Lou, while the men struggled to push Bill's body into the truck with the other captives.

"We better take her with him to the tunnel to join Saeed," one guard said to another.

"She seems to know him. She might be of value."

The three uniformed guards, one hostage Cardinal and one very unusual kitchen nun left the side of the truck, descended a narrow flight of stairs to a basement corridor and moved into a dark passageway inside a boiler room. Once inside the boiler room, they radioed Anwar Saeed to join them. They reported their captive to be in the designated hiding place but with a woman disguised as a nun, an apparent friend of the hostage. They were told to remain in place. Saeed was on his way to join them.

Meanwhile, Dan and Eva continued their search for Delgado's office amid the smoke and confusion in the hallways. Dan observed dignitaries enter an office along with a number of plainclothes security men from his earlier confrontation.

The importance of this office was confirmed when an enraged Cardinal Delgado opened the door to yell at a departing servant through the smoke.

Inside the office, the Opus Dei group assembled, minus one of their voting members now reported to be in the hands of Ali Teekah. Once seated, they listened to a briefing by Darci DiNome. He was detailing the plan to close in on Ali Teekah and retake him before the start of the Conclave.

"The calls to Cardinal Delgado by Ali Teekah were a fabrication," began DiNome, "since Baracini could not be in the Vatican. The hostage claim was merely trying to buy time for Ali's escape. We must continue to talk to Ali, so his exact location can be determined and he can be found. Once he is back in our hands, we can bring order to this building."

It was Delgado's turn. "My friends," he said, with a calmness that hid the turmoil inside, "we must not allow ourselves to be distracted by the disorder around us. We are very close to achieving our objectives and regaining control of our embattled Church. Now is not the time for an uncertainty that allows the more determined to deny us our right."

Delgado's speech was interrupted by the door to the office swinging open and with the announcement, "A caller claims that he is Teekah and that you must speak to him. The call is on line three."

The Cardinal returned to the large swivel chair behind his desk, held the telephone in his right hand and quietly said, "This is Cardinal Delgado."

"My good Cardinal," came the reply. "This is your house guest Ali Teekah. We have business to complete which will allow you to focus your attention on personal objectives. That business involves my departure from the comforts of Vatican City to a secure location. I find it necessary to meet with you and your associate Darci DiNome to complete the arrangements. To insure the safety of myself, and my friends, we have detained Cardinal Baracini who is not nearly as dead as most people think.

"Once we are on our way, we will see that reports of his death are not disputed. If I am not given my safety, the Cardinal will make an appearance at your Conclave and undoubtedly disrupt your plans by his appearance. It seems like a simple arrangement to me. Where can you and I and DiNome meet?"

"I need time to consider your demands and how we can do what you ask," came Delgado's reply.

"There is no time," snarled Ali. "Decide now!"

His outward calm completely gone, Delgado shouted into the phone, "Alright," he said, "we will meet you in my assistant's office in the corridor on the second floor. It is room twenty-one. The name Monsignor Roberto Flores is on the side panel. How long will it take you to be there?"

"I will be there in twenty minutes," said Ali, "and I caution you, it is to be with just the two of you and no more or Baracini will make his surprise appearance."

"Agreed," concluded Delgado as he returned the phone to his desk. He turned to Darci DiNome and said, "You and I have a meeting to attend. The rest of the group should remain here until we return."

Nick emerged from the tunnel exit and met Dan and Eva outside Delgado's office. He had heard the signal from Bill Casey and was headed for the kitchen area, He wanted to learn if they had made contact on their own. Nick's group split in two and headed for the kitchen from different directions. Dan and Eva remained to watch the office areas.

Making their way through the crowds in the hallways, Nick entered the kitchen but did not find his companions. The area was filled with people moving in all directions, some cooking, some cleaning and some loading food carts. Just as he was leaving, he noticed the rear service door.

Nick walked slowly toward the door moving his hand inside his shirt to locate the handle of his gun. He opened the door slowly and found the hallway empty. The outside door was partially blocked by a delivery truck. No one was in the cab. Nick moved to the rear and carefully opened the door. As light filled the back of the truck, he saw Bill Casey on his back in a pool of blood.

Nick jumped into the truck and held Bill's head in his hands."They never used guns in Brooklyn," Bill said, "just knives and clubs." After a few more gasps for air, he added, "Lou was here and so was Meggie." He drifted off into unconsciousness.

Nick leaped from the truck, directing his companions to search all exit and entrance locations around the service entrance. He headed for the basement stairs and utility rooms. The basement hallway was dark and quiet with several doors off the long corridor. The first door led to a storage area. The next was to the heating and air conditioning systems. Entering the boiler room, he noticed drops of blood on the edge of the molding. He left the hallway and returned to his companions to consider their options.

Dan and Eva watched Delgado and DiNome leave the office and walk down the hall. The security men outside did not follow them as they mixed with the hallway crowd. While talking on the radio, DiNome motioned Delgado to enter Flores's office. The door closed quickly behind them.

Eva was the first to notice a uniformed security contingent escorting a strange man down the hallway and stop in front of Flores's office. One guard remained outside and one escorted the man into the room and closed the door.

"We meet again," said Ali as he offered a hand to Cardinal Delgado. "I hope you followed my instructions," he said, as he moved across the room.

"Exactly," the Cardinal replied.

"Good," said Ali, as he fired a single shot into the forehead of Darci DiNome.

DiNome fell backwards, eyes open wide, his mouth gasping for a last breath as his body slipped down a blood-spattered wall to the floor.

"Our negotiations are now over," said Ali. "You will now be joining me as I leave Vatican City. Within a few hours, you can return having escaped from the hands of the terrorist and complete your business. With your associate no longer able to direct an effort to stop me, the chances of my plan succeeding have just increased substantially."

Dan and Eva saw the door to the Flores office open; Cardinal Delgado was now part of the guarded escort moving down the hallway toward his office.

Dan gave Eva her directions, "We have to break up this group somehow. The expression on Delgado's face says it all. He realizes he is powerless and scared to death. I might be wrong, but the guy in the center looks familiar. What do you think?"

"I heard a gun with a silencer on it from inside the room," Eva said. "I have heard them often enough to know that sound."

With a uniformed guard contingent leading Ali and Cardinal Delgado toward them, Eva dropped a food tray in their path, fell to her knees and began cleaning up the debris.

When the group marched past her, she reached out and brought down one of the uniformed men at the same time Dan reached for Ali. The remaining guard produced a gun from under his shirt and fired once at Eva. Although hit, she returned fire with the pistol pulled from her waist bringing him down with a single shot. Ali made a well-placed chop across Dan's neck. Dan

291

went motionless. The commotion brought security men from the corners of the smoke-filled corridor.

Ali and his remaining security man grabbed the horrified Cardinal and moved him down the hall to his own office. Ali came into the room holding a gun to Delgado's head much to the horror of the Opus Dei group remaining there. They were herded across the room by Ali's lone companion and told to remain quiet.

The intercom buzzed on the big desk in the center of the room.

"Answer it," Ali directed.

"This is Cardinal Delgado," said the voice into the phone. "Yes, we are alright. The door will remain locked and I'll let you know when I need your assistance. Thank you."

Ali then turned to the group. "You will select one of your group to accompany me and Cardinal Delgado to the kitchen where I will begin my escape. You will remain here with my assistant, waiting for my signal that we have reached safety. If you fail to follow our instructions there will be severe consequences for all of you and these ancient walls."

Ali threw open his jacket, as did his companion, revealing bomber belts fully loaded with high explosives. "When all is lost for us, all will be lost for you.

"Now that we understand the situation," Ali said, let's get on with the selection. Who will accompany us?"

The desk telephone had been ringing constantly and Ali directed that it be answered.

"This is Cardinal Delgado," the nervous voice declared into the receiver.

"This is Colonel Kenneth Collins, the commander of the Vatican City Security," the voice on the other end of the line said.

"We are aware that you are a prisoner in your own office. There is little chance of negotiating any way out of the situation. We plan on breaking down the door to your office within three minutes from the end of this conversation. We urge everyone to fall on the floor at that time and allow us to fill the room with automatic gun fire and perhaps take them by surprise. You have three minutes." The phone then offered the standard dial tone.

Cardinal Delgado announced to Ali that the security forces would like to begin some kind of negotiations on the terms of their safe passage and would he consider the offer?

292

Ali turned to his accomplice, told him to move behind the group and keep his gun pointed at the door.

"We always enjoy negotiations," said Ali, "but they need to be done with caution. Tell them I will discuss the terms."

Cardinal Delgado then turned to his companions and said, "Before we begin negotiations, let us begin with a prayer."

Speaking in Latin he announced, "When I fall to my knees, you do likewise."

He began his prayer two minutes and forty-five seconds after the phone call. He suddenly fell to his knees. The other followed his lead. The door to the office flew open and several men burst into the room, guns blazing!

The explosion that followed blew the outside walls of the office into St. Peter's square. The office itself disappeared in a fireball and a portion of the third floor of the Papal apartments fell into the second. Billows of smoke raced down each corridor engulfing the surviving inhabitants who were sure the end had come.

Several minutes of eerie silence gripped the area until those still alive were able to stand and speak amidst the cries for help from the injured..

The sound of the explosion brought two of the three guards out from the boiler room beneath the kitchen. When they exited the doorway, Nick shot both of them from his perch above the staircase. A short time later, three shots rang out from inside the basement.

Nick slowly descended the stairs into the basement corridor where he could hear a woman's soft cries coming from inside the passage. The door to the boiler room swung open. His eyes first fell on Meggie and Lou huddled together in the far corner of the room. Angelo was slumped over against a pipe, a single wound in the center of his chest. There, across the room next to Lou, was Anwar Saeed, the deputy to Ali Teekah, with a single wound between both eyes. The remaining guard was dead at his feet.

Meggie's face was buried in Lou's chest and could not look up. "Are you alright?" Nick said.

Lou answered for both of them. "We have to get out of here."

Dan and Eva dug themselves from the debris created by the destruction in the hallway outside Delgado's office. The corridors filled with smoke and demented human beings.

Forty
Aftermath

Several days passed before the chaos within the Vatican was brought under control, the dead accounted for and preparations made to resume the Conclave.

Lou lost no time in distributing copies of the Mystic Study Report along with the pictures Dan supplied from the *Washington Tribune,* to the remaining delegates to the Conclave. The first scheduled meeting of the General Congregation agreed to hear Cardinal Baracini's explanation of his reported death, sudden reappearance at the height of the turmoil and take questions on the documents he had distributed.

The newly appointed Dean of the College of Cardinals, Anthony Cardinal Romano, called the meeting to order with a moment of prayer for Cardinal Delgado and those lost in the explosions. He then called Kenneth Collins, Chief of Vatican City Security, to the podium to brief the assembly on the events of the past few days.

Collin's tall slender frame towered over the podium as he placed papers before him. His black uniform, white shirt and gold insignia were in sharp contrast to the scarlet capes that peered up at him from those assembled in the audience. Gripping the sides of the podium firmly, he drew a deep breath and began the briefing he had been dreading.

"I am ashamed to stand before you and attempt to explain such a major failure in a security program we thought was perfectly designed," Collins began. "We had assured Cardinal Delgado that our program was capable of preventing any intrusion on the workings of the Conclave.

"Although we examined Ali Teekah and his party thoroughly upon their accepting our offer of sanctuary, we failed to prevent their obtaining explosive devices once they were inside the Vatican. This could not have been accomplished without inside assistance. I am sorry to report that we have evidence such assistance was in fact delivered from a very high level. Furthermore, similar assistance was provided to allow Ali's family to leave Vatican City and make their way to the coast to leave for a new hiding place.

"It was disloyalty from within," said Collins, as he hammered the podium, "that led to death and destruction of these past few days. After two thousand years, we still have to reckon with the consequences of a Judas treachery!"

With that display of frustration, Collins relaxed as he reviewed the details of the events that had brought carnage to the ancient city.

"We are on the way to a full understanding of this betrayal and identification of the culprits," continued Collins. "We will not rest until we have knowledge of the full extent of the conspiracy and can present hard, cold facts to the world.

"The wiring of the Library hiding room with explosives was not just a precaution taken to protect his family, but an essential part of Ali's plan to create a diversion to engage our security forces at a crucial moment in his escape. The plan included taking a number of hostages to assure his protection while he made his flight from the City. He was aware of outside attempts to capture him and he used that knowledge to stage the events that occurred at the Library.

"We have obtained some of this information from a member of a foreign assault group who survived the library explosion and who is now in the custody of Italian authorities. In addition, we found considerable evidence on the bodies of those who perished in the assault to permit identification of the responsible parties. We intend to release this information to the press when the preliminary investigation is finished.

"The investigation has been developed in cooperation with the Italian authorities and more will be presented to you at the appropriate time.

"The explosion in Cardinal Delgado's office requires its own explanation," continued Collins. "I offered to participate in the negotiating session arranged by Cardinal Delgado with Ali Teekah and recommended against his proceeding on his own. For whatever reason, the Cardinal disregarded my advice and met with Ali. It was during this negotiation session that the situation became critical. First, we had the shooting of our associate Darci DiNome by Ali Teekah himself, followed by the seizure of Cardinal Delgado as their first hostage. When Ali attempted to take additional hostages and move to join the other members of his party, an unusual confrontation took place in the hallway, changing the nature of the crisis.

"A member of Ali's security force was shot by associates of Cardinal Baracini, who were attempting to deliver him to his rightful place at the Conclave. I will address this in a few moments.

"The actions of the Baracini supporters prevented him from becoming a casualty. Their initiative alerted us to Ali's whereabouts and brought the situation to its conclusion.

"Ali's move into Cardinal Delgado's office offered us the best opportunity to rescue the hostages before they were taken from the Vatican.

"At this point, I did not consider Ali's willingness to utilize a suicide bomber's belt as part of his plan. We were confident of our ability to deny Ali and his party access to weapons and explosives. It was not only a fatal assumption but it was a failure of imagination on my part and doomed our rescue attempt.

"We attempted to coordinate our assault of the office area with those inside. I felt the element of surprise would give us the advantage. I was wrong in this assumption and wrong in other judgments as well.

"At the very moment the second explosion rocked the Vatican, Cardinal Baracini's associates engaged the remaining members of Ali's group. They shot three men in the boiler room beneath the kitchen, including Anwar Saeed, Ali's deputy. They rescued Cardinal Baracini who had become part of the hostage plan.

"The Teekah escape had several options, one being the use of a delivery truck at the kitchen of the Papal apartments as a way out of Vatican City in the midst of the confusion. With staff response centered on the damage in the Library, the delivery truck scheme became their first choice. Their escape was underway when the Baracini group brought it to a halt. They deserve our thanks for what was skillfully done at a critical moment.

"In reviewing the events leading up to the agreement on sanctuary, you should know the issues were managed by Cardinal Delgado and his Group of Twelve. From the documents distributed by Cardinal Baracini, we understand the presence of the Grail, its exchange and the need to relocate. Vatican security was not aware of the transfer of the Grail from the terrorists but were briefed after it occurred. We had no part in the relocation, nor in the selection of its present hiding place, wherever that may be.

"The new location for the Grail was selected by members of the Opus Dei Group of Twelve. They perished in the office explosion. We do, however have clues on the whereabouts of the Grail. We are cooperating with international agencies in tracking its movement. However, as we speak we have located neither the Grail nor its documents."

Collins had arrived at the most sensitive part of his presentation. With anguish on his face, he addressed the assault on Cardinal Baracini and his hospital confinement.

"The reports in the *Washington Tribune* about the sudden illness of Cardinal Baracini appear to be correct. The relationships of certain Vatican officials have been clouded for some time. My requests to clarify these relationships in the past were never answered to my satisfaction. My failure to understand relationships at the highest level and the failure to understand the need to negotiate at the time of crisis, leave me no alternative but to leave a position I have devoted my life to.

"To avoid further embarrassment, I have submitted my resignation as security chief effective immediately. Questions on these details will be handled by my deputy."

His statement ended, Collins collected his papers, turned and walked briskly from the stage making no eye contact with anyone. Cardinal Romano's expression reflected his surprise at the announcement. He walked back to the podium slowly and waited for the noise in the room to subside. With one hand resting on the gold chain draped across his chest and with the other on the edge of the podium, Cardinal Romano began his introduction of Cardinal Baracini.

"Before allowing our colleague to provide us with the explanations he promised when he distributed his documents," he

298

began, "I caution all of you to remember those who have perished. Keep in mind their inability to defend themselves or to explain their actions.

"We have been provided with a summary report covering hundreds of years of Church history, covering events that occurred in a different time and with different values. Taken on its face, this information has the potential of shattering the faith of people around the world. We are compelled to approach our understanding of these facts with caution."

Romano drew a large breath before discussing the next issue. "The photographs that accompanied the other documents are, by themselves, disturbing. As we know, pictures can be made to show events that never occurred. I urge you to listen, but more importantly, I urge you to reflect on the validity of the written and spoken word and the limited experience of one observer before coming to conclusions."

The Cardinal turned to the lone figure sitting near him and indicated it was time to speak. When Baracini rose from his chair the murmur of voices began again. The room fell silent as the six-foot frame of Louis Baracini, clothed in Cardinal's scarlet, removed the microphone from the podium and walked to the edge of the chapel railing.

"My brothers," said Lou, as he glanced at those sitting before him, "I agree with the cautions given you by our fellow Cardinal. I am only one man commenting on what he has seen and heard. You need to evaluate for yourselves, if anything I have given you, or may say to you this day, requires change in the direction of our Church. If change is needed, you should ask yourself if it should begin with the leadership you will be voting upon shortly.

"I agree with the need for caution as expressed by our colleague Cardinal Romano. However, I ask you to keep in mind the words from Dante's *Inferno,* 'The hottest place in hell is reserved for those who remain neutral in times of crisis!' I am not reluctant to tell you that even if God forgives the neutral among you, I will despise those who now choose to straddle. I have paid in body and spirit for my part in all that has brought us to this point. The least you can do is stand for that which is good and just."

299

Walking slowly across the front of the assembly, Baracini searched for words that would lead him into his painful explanation. He was looking for the friendly eyes he knew were mingled in the crowd before him.

"If there was any doubt in your minds that our Church is in the most perilous of times in its history and that the world is truly watching, the events of the past week must have removed that doubt.

"The last few days cry out for explanation. I want to tell you all that I know. Give me the chance to present the details and I will answer your questions.

"The decision to grant sanctuary to a terrorist was forced upon us to prevent disclosure of information Church leaders had concealed from the faithful for many years. Yes, I want to talk about the secrets of the Vatican, secrets that some of us have heard whispers about but never understood. Let the truth be told and the Holy Spirit guide the outcome.

"Much of that undisclosed information from the Vatican Archives is described in the summary report you now have in your possession. It lacks the supporting evidence studied by the original group but it should be considered on the credibility of those who prepared it. For the first time, there is a written discussion of issues that in the past were only talked about in the smallest of circles.

"Based upon the documents, the importance of the Chartres Cathedral as link to the spiritual plan of the Creator cannot be minimized. We have much to learn from the history of mankind's efforts to reach the Divine in the area around Chartres. St. Bernard of Clairvaux established his abbey in the area. He described it as the entrance to Heavenly Jerusalem and a Fortress of God.

"An important decision was made in the Middle Ages to conceal truth. It was made with the best of intentions but nevertheless it must be called a deception. It continued as a deception as men chose to hide truth rather than open themselves to its power.

"When the existence of hidden knowledge became known to Pope John XXIII, he took action to investigate the treasure of

300

library documents and consider how to deal with the implications of disclosure. He established the Mystic Study Group. He directed it to investigate the history of mysticism, as well as the circumstances surrounding the finding of the Holy Grail on the Island of Bornholm.

"The preliminary report was startling in its findings. It directly influenced the Pope in the calling of the Second Vatican Council," said Baracini to startled faces now turning to each other in his audience.

"The Mystic Study Report in your hands explains how the Church discovered the path to finding the Grail in the fifteenth century. It began in Rome with a study of a fourteenth century guide to contemplative meditation and near death experiences entitled *The Cloud of the Unknowing*. The study of this document by Vatican scholars in the fifteenth century and the collaboration with the Abbey of St. Bernard in Clairvaux led to a joint effort to find the hiding place of the Grail.

"The Abbey had been the center of spiritual studies for longer than anyone realized. Its founder, St. Bernard, was a supporter of the order of the Knights Templar. We now understand the Island of Bornholm, with its own spiritual significance, was a logical place for the Templars to transfer their secrets when they lost favor with the King of France and the Pope. The Templar connection to the Abbey has long been known but we have come closer to understanding its significance through these efforts.

"What no one understood, until the Mystic Study Group studied the documents, was the extent of the Abbey's collection and the importance of its location near Chartres. The material covered man's contact with the spirit world in a variety of civilizations and cultures throughout the ages, many of the experiences having astrological linkages with each other.

"When the Grail was hidden again, the Church closed the Abbey. The monks were dispersed throughout Europe to prevent any future disclosure. Those who understood the importance of what they had, were prevented from explaining it."

Baracini was now at ease with his audience, sensing their full attention. His words were entering minds willing to hear the truth. He continued in a stronger and more determined tone.

301

"As you weigh the efforts of the Study Group, I ask you to consider the significance of the Chartres Mystery School location, its connection to Santiago de Compostella, Stonehenge and other age old sites of worship. When the scholars examined the relationships of these locations the results astonished them! They all are found along similar astrological lines, giving justification to the Knights Templar Path to Enlightenment through Compostella.

"Should we begin to consider the possibility that the heavens can guide us in our search for the Divine? How many men have gone to the stake for giving voice to that conclusion? One of the conclusions of all this work strikes me as worthy of serious reflection.

"Other religious experiences demand our respect and cooperation for without them we will never find a clear path to our Creator.

"I refer to the references in the documents to the reaching out of St. Francis of Assisi to Islamic leaders during the Fifth Crusade. He sailed to the Egyptian court of Al-Malik al Kamil, nephew of the Great Saladin. Saladin had defeated the Christian forces of the Third Crusade. Francis could have been executed for acting as he did but he was well received. He stayed for a week and exchanged religious thoughts with Al-Malik.

"Francis was searching for a dialogue to replace years of conflict. This was a time when the most visible signs of Christianity were war and the atrocities of red crossed crusaders. The Papal indulgences granted to all who joined the crusades was no more than a Christian imitation of Muslim jihad. A voice was crying to be heard.

"John XXIII attempted to open such a dialogue when he served as Ambassodor to Turkey and later when he became Pope. He knew the two societies had been bad neighbors for fourteen centuries often eager to misunderstand each other.

"Medieval Spain created an environment where Christian, Islamic and Jewish scholars lived and worked together, so it has actually been done before by flesh and blood human beings. We stand in desperate need of a contemporary figure like St. Francis or Pope John to create such an environment. All religions create a spectrum of voices that range from pacifist to terrorist. The

302

voices can be heard from Belfast to Baghdad. Someone must reach out to the voices of moderation."

Barracini moved back to the podium to gather his thoughts before beginning the most difficult portion of his address.

"The first terrorist explosion rocked the Vatican Library and brought a sad ending to some of the documents assembled by the original study group. The balance are with the Grail, wherever that might be at this moment. You have the benefit of the summary report I distributed to all of you. I hope it will be considered in your Conclave discussions.

"If all of this is not painful enough," sighed Baracini, "I must now comment on a failure in leadership, of which I was a part.

"In my search for personal importance, I was willing to accept a structure of authority that I knew was not properly focused. The leaders of our Church were content to surrender the details of finance and administration to others so they could devote their energies to doctrinal purity and liturgical correctness.

"I now view this long ago choice as a well intended but misguided decision. I thought I would be able to change the lack of attention to the needs of the poor. I was wrong. I was committed to the redistribution of wealth for the poor without regard to where it came from. However, once forces of immorality, indeed criminality, controlled the economic resources of the Vatican, there was no way the system could be changed.

"Control of the finances of the Vatican was managed by outsiders, through the Vatican Bank, while past Church leaders were content on fashioning the appropriate responses of the faithful at church services.

"We lost a fine Pope some years ago, when he tried to suggest changes to the influence of these outsiders. We knew he was in danger at the time but completely underestimated the arrogance and the boldness of those who opposed him. We are today sadly aware of the consequences.

"When the pictures you received a few days ago were given to me by a close friend, they pushed me over a wall I had been trying to climb for many years. I had been controlling a frustration that grew from constant discussion of theological trivia, while the Vatican Bank became a pit of clandestine corruption.

I suddenly realized that the pictures were just one of many indirect pressures brought upon those who question the actions of men in power. I never grasped that my indiscretion was planned and was not the result of personal weaknesses. How did the godless come to lord it over the God seekers?

"When I saw the pictures I realized that others had been compromised the way I was. It was the most devastating experience of my life. I was manipulated by a power structure utterly indifferent to clarity.

"Over time, as the group in power became comfortable with the lack of an accountability, a policy emerged that accepted the age old human weakness of allowing ends to justify means. When I expressed my intention last week of permitting truth to speak for itself, I became a victim of that policy.

"Let me add," concluded Lou, "that all the stories in the *Washington Tribune* about the attempt on my life and the transfer from the hospital are true. If it was not for the interest of a true friend, the outcome of all this would have been wholly different. I would not be standing before you and these revelations would have been pushed off for God knows how long.

"The task before the Conclave is difficult. I ask that you consider the harm that has been done by the failure to trust in the truth. Fail in this effort and those who scorn the Church will be handed a historic triumph. We cannot live in fear of the truth."

With this Baracini ended his presentation and began to answer the questions hanging on the lips of those seated in the room. It was more than an hour later that Cardinal Romano stepped forward and ended the session to allow other business of the Congregation to take place. Following the thanks for his efforts, Lou made a final statement.

"The end of this session is the end of my time in the Vatican," he said with a sigh of relief. "When I leave this platform before you, I leave Rome to return to my home in Chicago. I will not participate in the Conclave. I have resigned my official position. I need to reflect on how to find a new path for my priestly vocation."

Lou placed the microphone back onto the podium, shook hands with Romano and began to walk from the chapel. The silence was interrupted first by a single sound of applause. The single applause grew until the room echoed with the sounds of a hundred hands. As Lou found his way down the center aisle those applauding stood and continued their salute until he was well into the hallway. In the corridor, Dan greeted him with a warm embrace. He could not help but notice the tears on Lou's face.

"Thank you, my friend," whispered Lou. "We have been on quite a trip since we first met on that cramped old steamship on our way to Rome. Where we go from here is the big question."

Dan and Lou walked down the Hallway of Blessings past the great window that would reveal a new Pope to the world in the coming weeks. When they reached St. Peter's Square, they were swallowed by the crowds.

Forty-one
Habemus Papem

The next morning, the long procession moved into the Sistine Chapel and the world began its wait.

Dan and Meggie watched the events from Bill Casey's hospital room. He was having difficulty drinking with a straw while balancing his cup with his hands in plaster casts from his battles across Rome. He was trying to ignore the pain from bullet wounds but not doing a good job at all.

Nick was asking about Brooklyn. After these past few days, he was interested in going there and meeting people who were lucky enough to have Bill Casey for a friend.

Eva, with one arm in a sling, said she had to been to Brooklyn one time but that she preferred Italy. She thought the drivers in Brooklyn were too dangerous to be on the road and she didn't feel safe in the taxis.

The room was filled with laughs and regrets by these few who played a part in history. With the news becoming boring and night approaching, the group said their good-byes in the lobby of the hospital where a few days before they had spirited Lou to safety.

Dan and Meggie found themselves walking down a small side street from the hospital and into a sidewalk café. There was a period of silence as they sipped their wine and gazed into the few rays left from the setting summer sun.

"I still feel as I did yesterday," said Meggie, reaching across the table and touching the back of Dan's hand. "I wish I didn't but I do. You know what I've been saying. I can't ignore my feelings, especially when they involve so many people.

"I know it takes time to sort out conflicting emotions. I have taken the time but am still conflicted. I was happy during the days we had together," she continued, "but at the same time, as you know, I was troubled.

"We are trying to change the past. It can't be done. I need to go back to the life that was built on promises I gave, even though I understand the mistakes I made back then. We can't ignore the obligations of the present."

Dan remained quiet while Meggie shared her feelings. He resisted the urge to go to her and take her in his arms and keep the tears from flowing. Before he could do anything, Meggie rose to her feet and came around to his chair to kiss his cheek. She took his chin in her hands and while looking into his eyes said, "I hope you will let me do what has to be done. It will not be easy. I ask you to let it happen."

She draped a sweater around her shoulders, gave Dan one of her good-bye looks and walked down the crowed street into the darkness.

The night swallowed her shadow, robbing him of his breath. Dan was aware of a familiar but distant feeling. It took him to that night on the bank of the Hudson when he truly plunged into an abyss. *Why do we ignore the past when we try to understand the present?* he thought. *Is that an American thing or have men done it since the Garden of Eden?*

The next morning Dan watched the TV images of white smoke coming from the small pipe on top of the Sistine Chapel as he handled his morning coffee. Church bells throughout Rome began to ring with anticipation of the grand announcement. An hour later, the doors overlooking St. Peter's square opened wide and the age old proclamation was made to the crowd. "Habemus Papem." We have a Pope!

Okay, Okay, Dan said to himself, *just give us his Italian name.*

"Eduardo Cardinale Castillo," came the answer from the balcony.

"Lord God Almighty!" exclaimed Dan, "Mexico has a Pope!"

And the name chosen? Dan wondered.

Pope Juan Diego the first, came the proclamation, in honor of the peasant visionary of Guadalupe. North America had arrived after half a millenium.

Dan knew this choice was a clear break with the past. Whether real change could be made was left for the test of time. *After the revelations of the past week there isn't much left I'm*

307

afraid, he thought. The Church has been shown to be just another creation of men, frail men burdened by the same problems of other human institutions. Change must come. Surely it would not require something even more compelling than what had been seen in the days just past? Or would it?

"No, goddamn it, that's not possible!" he exclaimed.

"What's not possible, Signore?" asked the puzzled waiter clearing the table.

Forty-two
Washington, DC

The mid-week lunch for President and Vice President was more formal than usual. Their conversation concerned the growing campaign dialogue about the possible involvement of the US in the failed attempt to capture Ali Teekah.

"After weeks of reports and counter reports, I am certainly not pleased with the outcome of the Ali Teekah matter," said the President. "With more professional planning, we would have the polls showing the election to be within our grasp. Now it appears we will be drawn into an international mess. General Feely has complained to me bitterly about the lack of cooperation between the intelligence agencies; he described it as the same old bureaucratic problem of service rivalry. He feels he could have succeeded if he knew more about the planned French assault on the library and the details we had from our inside people. He doesn't appear to be wrong in his assertions," added the President to his Vice President sitting across the table.

"It appears my worst fears will come true," added the President. "We will be connected to the incident by the General's presence in Italy along with the confessions of the survivor of the assault on the Library. I want to hear your plan for damage control during the campaign and what we can do with the General in the meantime," ended the President, as he returned his cup to its saucer looking with barely concealed annoyance at his lunch companion.

"Once you understand the precautions I put in place and the plan I have for the General," replied the Vice President, "you will be able to manage the anxiety I know is eating at you."

Pushing his chair back from the table and crossing his legs, the Vice President lit up one of his baby cigars and began his explanation.

"My recommendations on the Teekah capture plan were always conditional," began the Vice President. "It required us to allow one of the other known groups to make the primary assault. If they were successful, we would take Teekah from them sometime after they were away from the assault area. Our involvement was to be secondary.

"Our inside information worked very well as evidenced by the circumstances of the failed Russian and Syrian attempt on the West Bank. We were well positioned and well informed to intercept the retreating units on the coast at that time. Our double agent, Colonel Kashani, was killed in the assault so there was no record of our involvement. Rome was different.

"The agent we recruited to keep us informed on the French attempt to capture Ali was captured by Italian authorities. He will claim the French were the primary attack force in the assault even though the French team was discovered before they could make their move. If we develop this point, the French can be blamed for the entire mess. The Jordanian mercenary held by the authorities is not enough to drag us into it.

"We have since released sufficient information to the authorities," continued the Vice President, "through a third party, to implicate the French in both attempts. We expect the news organizations to pick up on this in the next few days. It should sufficiently cloud the situation to keep it beneath the surface during the campaign.

"If the State Department can put pressure on the Italians to follow their normally slow pace on investigations, the election will be over before the issue is ever settled. Asking the Italians to go slow doesn't seem to be a very big favor. I would urge you to direct the Secretary to speak to the Italian government," said the Vice President, a smile of assurance on his face.

"For the protection of the White House," he continued, "it would be to our benefit to find another assignment for General Feely to keep him removed from questions about his presence in Italy. I propose he be made Deputy Commander of our forces in Korea as a signal that you understand the growing tension in that part of the world and want an experienced officer on the team there. By the time questions about the Teekah incident become known, the General will be out of Washington for months and beyond the reach of the local media.

"Another reason for the assignment to Korea is to relocate the General's wife out of Washington as well. We have now confirmed she was part of the group responsible for the rescue of Cardinal Baracini and was having an affair with Dan Gerard, the *Washington Tribune* reporter. It seems obvious she was one of his sources for the articles on the Vatican crisis. I have given instructions to Justice to delay the investigation of the leaks on the CIA's use of the Vatican Bank to let her get out of town first."

"The results are still a problem," replied the President. "Although your analysis and recommendations seem sound, I am not convinced about your assumptions on when the Teekah incident will become headline news."

"I will talk to State about pressure on the Italian government. When they are aware of our plan to implicate the French they should be happy to assist."

"Make the arrangements to move General Feely to the Korean assignment as soon as possible," added the President. "I will be unavailable to him for a while. I don't want to be involved until after the election. I know I don't need to remind you but make sure your suggestions to Justice on the investigation of the *Washington Tribune* are done verbally."

The two men finished lunch and took their usual stroll in the Rose Garden.

Forty-three
The *Washington Tribune*

Dan was not looking forward to his meeting with Jack Roman. The paper was feeling the pressure about the story of the CIA and its Vatican connections. Questions about sources and the ability to keep them confidential were being carried in great detail by competitor news organizations. Roman never received negative competitor news very well, even with the good mood brought on by the worldwide exclusive the *Tribune* had delivered on the Vatican crisis. The morning meeting was Jack's idea for Dan to outline his plan for a possible grand jury appearance and his schedule for follow up stories on the CIA.

The corner office was as cluttered and noisy as ever, as Dan appeared at the open door of the private domain of his managing editor.

"These people are just leaving," announced Roman as he saw Dan in the hallway. "Don't go anywhere until we have time to talk."

When Dan entered the office, Jack moved from behind his desk to a couch by the window, indicating this was to be a friendly meeting. He had the latest draft front page in his hands with page one, column one, dedicated to the Pope's announcements. Jack started with the usual rapid fire questions for a page one story.

"This sounds to me like the Pope is turning the place upside down all at once," began Jack. "Give me the short version of what is going on."

"You are right on target," answered Dan. "Look at the four big moves just announced.

"First, the Roman Curia as we know it is abolished. The high ranking bureaucrats filling those offices are being sent to the missions to fulfill their first obligation to save souls.

"Second, the Curia is being replaced with leaders elected by a Council of Bishops from all the countries of the world. Each

312

one chosen will have a term limit on his assignment and return to his country when it's finished. No more lifetime bureaucratic posts in the Vatican.

"Third, the Vatican Bank is abolished. All financial affairs are being transferred to the World Bank. The plan is for financial administration to be taken over by leading money managers throughout the world with full transparency.

"The new Council on Religious Dialogue is an outreach effort to all the world's religions. Maybe, after centuries of misunderstandings, religious strife might come to an end."

"Dan," interrupted Roman, "it's been a great job so far but we have an obligation to follow up with a strong line of reporting on the actions taken by all those with agendas during the terrorist hunt. We are hearing that the attempt to capture Teekah that destroyed the Vatican Library was CIA directed and led by US forces assisted by foreign mercenaries.

"It seems General Feely was in Italy at the time of the incident doing his usual behind the scenes routine and working with the Vatican Bank insiders as well. I want to know what your plan is to follow up on these stories so we don't lose our momentum."

"Well, Jack," said Dan with an apologetic tone in his voice, "it's the issue on follow up that I want to talk to you about. This event from start to finish and the extent of my personal involvement forced me to reconsider my career and my family. I have pretty much ignored my family since my move here. The nature of the work requires travel and late nights. My children have been looking to relatives to help them cope with life's problems. That is not how I want it to be.

"I have tried to comfort them and help manage their lives but I can't do that from a distance. I want to be able to share in their lives up close not through a telephone.

"I have accepted the position of Assistant Managing Editor of the *Albany Times Union*. It will be my first attempt as an editor rather than a reporter. It will keep me home most nights. More importantly, it will give two children a family environment they need at this time in their lives. It's the old battle between career and family. It's time for family to have a share of the pie," said Dan as he glanced out the editor's corner office window and once more took in the sight of the Capitol dome.

"More importantly for me personally," continued Dan, "I feel the need to return 'up home', back to Albany where I began. If home is where the heart is, it's Albany for me. It is an existence centered on the simpler things in life.

"What I am saying is, my decision and my mind are made up. I thank you for the opportunity you gave me to play. I will always prize the difference we made together."

Jack Roman slowly removed his glasses and dropped the draft pages on the conference table cluttered with half filled cups of coffee. He stood up and rubbing an aching back, looked out on the Washington landscape. He turned to Dan and gave a surprising response.

"What you are doing is something I thought about throughout my career," he said, "but never had the nerve to do. It was always going to be after the next big story or some other milestone. The time never seemed right. Many times I regretted the delay and the price my family paid for my staying so involved with work. I sacrificed too much. So did my wife and children."

Sitting down again, the boss looked at Dan and with a grimace and a sigh in his voice, he said, "I admire your choice to take back control of your life. You gave much more than you took from us while you were here. We will miss your contributions. The *Times Union* will benefit from your presence.

"You'll need to keep in touch with our lawyers as we walk through this grand jury investigation. It will be some time before they decide if they want to push the investigation to the limit and threaten you with jail. Those kind of conflicts usually are delayed to occur outside an election year. You should have time in Albany to get settled but be prepared to come back to Washington if we call you," concluded Roman as the men walked together down the long hallway to Dan's office.

The good-byes to Tim Scanlon and the rest of the staff who worked on the Vatican crisis were harder than Dan had anticipated. They had been on the phone daily throughout the events in Rome and enjoyed the success together. There were genuinely warm good-byes and sad farewells.

314

When Dan taped over the last packing box in his office he couldn't help but look out his window as he had months before trying to understand the crisis he was about to face. The same red lights made their way onto his office wall and the same trees blocked the same buildings. Although the view had not changed, he thought he saw many things more clearly now.

After loading the car and the final embrace with Tim, Dan invited him to join him in a final drink at the Willard Hotel. Tim declined but said he would have one for Dan that night at home with his family.

The hotel lounge seemed as comforting as ever and the familiar piano player was at his best. The corner bar stool against the wall was vacant and the bartender gave Dan a friendly hello. As the feeling of the first drink hit his tired body, his senses were awakened by the opening tones of "A Theme From A Summer Place."

A smile came over Dan's face while he swiveled his chair to watch the piano player finish his song. There, next to the piano, stood Meggie.

Their eyes met for a few short moments. The familiar soft smile graced her face as she walked toward him. Dan sat patiently watching her step around the many tables in the lounge to reach the corner where he was perched.

"Tim said you might be here," she said as she sat on the stool next to him. "I heard you were leaving the paper. I was hoping you might buy me a drink before you left."

"You can't imagine how many times I picked up the phone to call you," Dan said, "but kept remembering your request to me in Rome, to 'let you do what had to be done.' I didn't want to do anything that might cause more grief. I hoped it all worked out for you the way you wanted," he said as he raised his glass to her in a toast.

"Give me some time and I'll let you know what has happened since Rome."

"It is worth a drink to know where you are going," replied Dan, "for those nights when our times together come rushing back and I want to picture you in new surroundings."

Meggie began her account of her confrontation with Tom and her mixed emotions. She began with her determination to repair any damage that had been done to her marriage, to do whatever Tom wanted to keep their relationship together.

"I was not surprised to learn that Tom knew about us," she sighed, glancing into the glass of wine held in her trembling hands. "But rather than go into those details, Tom went all the way back to our days in Albany. He admitted for the first time, he may well have taken advantage of my emotional state after my mother's death to get what he felt was out of his reach, our marriage.

"He thought he could handle emotional problems created by a decision made in haste. He did a good job of giving me a full life, with experiences around the world. He realized it came with negatives as well.

"The agent orange damage done in Vietnam prevented us from having a family and he felt bad about that. I handled the problem well with the distractions of my own activities. All in all, he felt comfortable with our relationship, that is, until we met in Paris.

"Tom remarked how my emotions and behavior seemed to change after that meeting. He was concerned about the time required for me to return to my old self, if ever. When my brother had the accident in Albany, he thought it was an opportunity to test me to see if feelings from the past had any grip on me.

"He said he called to involve you, understanding very well the situation but did it anyway. It was part of a plan to test us both," she said as she sipped her first taste of wine.

"He wanted to see if you would go to Albany at all. If you did, he wanted to see how I would react to the meeting. He thought you might not go and then, I might not react to your being there.

"As it turned out, he was wrong in both cases. What he was worrying about proved to be a real worry.

"Tom's first thoughts were similar to mine. He wanted to work things out but then changed his mind after he received his new assignment. He is being sent to be the Deputy Commander in Korea, a hardship assignment that would keep us apart for most of the next eighteen months. The separation would delay any relationship repair.

"More than having time to make repairs, Tom felt it was time to admit mistakes and get on with the future. He told me he had filed for a divorce. It would be the best for both of us," Meggie concluded as she looked away from Dan and back toward the piano player.

After a few moments of silence, she continued.

"I could have insisted that we remain together. Wait for the time to come for us to work out the difficulties.

"Tom never asked me what I wanted. He made the decision for both of us, as he so often did. This time I said nothing and let him walk away. In the end, he was married to the Army and will always be happy with her. She was his first love from the start. Whatever time was left over, was mine. I am not disappointed with a chance to find a life of my own.

"I've thought about new directions for days," Meggie continued, "and even considered going back to him if he asked. I realized it is over. I've decided on a new path for myself as you have. I've accepted a nursing position at Tampa Medical center where I plan to start next week. So let's drink to new lives we are starting," she said as she raised her glass in the air.

Dan sat in silence, watching her lower her glass to her lap.

"I thought about not telling you and letting you start your new life too but I wanted to at least say good-bye, considering what we have been through. I called Tim and he said he thought you might be here. So, here's to us both, as we start our new lives."

Looking into Meggie's eyes, Dan asked, "Are you all done? Is that the end of your story and your good-bye speech?"

She said nothing in reply, but nodded gently over the rim of the wine glass.

After a few moments, Dan reached across and took her hand as it was fumbling in her purse to find something to catch the tears she knew were coming.

"Here is my farewell speech to you," Dan began. "I want you to listen closely because you know how poor I am at speeches.

"I didn't call you out of respect for the message you gave me our last night in Rome. I wanted to honor your request. I thought it would help in repairing your relationship with Tom. I owed you both that.

"Now you tell me you tried to make it work with Tom. It is his decision to leave. You are prepared to go off on your own as I go off on my own. Let's share good-byes.

"If you are not going to be with Tom, there is no way I could let you go off on your own. Not when I am looking for a new life myself.

"It's a rare occasion when life offers a chance to correct a mistake. We have that chance. Let's not make the same mistake again.

"Meggie," said Dan, reaching out and taking both her hands in his. "I want you anyway I can have you. You can come tomorrow or next week. You can move in with me or live on your own. You can agree to marry me now or wait until your powers of reasoning overcome your emotions. Any decision that keeps us together is what I want. I don't care which of the choices you select just as long as you come with me!"

"That is my going away speech," said Dan as he let go of both her hands. "I'd like to hear your answer. I badly want to hear it now."

Meggie pulled her hands back into her lap and turned the bar stool away from Dan so she could see the piano and the many people sitting in the lounge. She turned back to Dan just as the "Memories" theme from *Cats* drifted across the room.

"How much time do I have to think about it?" asked Meggie.

"Thirty seconds, and I am not much for handling disappointment," he concluded.

"The answer," she said, "is that you can have all of me for as long as you want, starting whenever you want!"

Two people sitting in silence let go of the baggage that had piled up around them, creating walls that imprisoned, concealed and separated. They had finished one journey. The next would bring them home. No baggage was needed for that one.

Ecclesiastical establishments tend to great ignorance and corruption, of which facilitate the execution of mischievous projects.

—James Madison